Kira Shay

FSF Publications

Cover art and design by TJ Geisen

e-Book ISBN 978-0-9961485-7-3
Print ISBN 978-0-9961485-6-6

Manufactured in the United States of America.

First US Printing: 2017

www.fivesmilingfish.com

Also by Five Smiling Fish:

Angel's Prophecy
by Kira Shay
http://www.fivesmilingfish.com/kira-shay/

Emerald Door
by Megan E. Vaughn
http://www.fivesmilingfish.com/megan-e-vaughn/

From the Darkest Corner
An Anthology
http://www.fivesmilingfish.com/collab/

From Hellbat Publications:

The Devil's Codex
by Sidney Reetz
https://www.sidneyreetz.com/book-list

Dedicated to my brother, Matt
To Hell and back. Always.

Endless Thanks and Appreciation to:

Will Minor, for not only supporting my writing
habit, but for maniacally encouraging it.

Sidney Reetz and Megan Vaughn, my sister authors
without whom my life would be much poorer.

TJ Geison for the breathtaking cover art.

Amanda Griffis for your willingness to read and for
being fan enough to keep me going.

Beth Lake for having the patience to deal with my
addiction to commas and exclamation points!

Tom Dushku for not laughing because I still need
technical assistance.

And thanks to YOU for reading!

Chapter One

My body moved, but I wasn't the one in control. While the presence inside my mind was alien, I could still recognize the intense sensations of hate and anger for what they were. Though I fought against the movement, my lips twisted into a contorted grimace that made my face hurt. Of their own accord, my legs propelled me toward the young man who had his back to me.

"Orion." It was my voice that called his name; though the quality and tenor was different. It was strong as steel and commanding. The young man turned with a confused expression. My voice continued to speak, "You should have given him the mirror."

As soon as I heard those words, I knew what had taken over me. I fought to break free, but I was powerless; it had complete control of my body.

Under the direction of this alien force, my hands reached up to his shoulders. The contact sent a strange prickling sensation through my limbs. The presence recoiled at the feel of Ryan's arm though my hands did not remove themselves. I did my best to soften my expression to let him know it wasn't me doing this.

Instead, my body leaned closer to him, almost as if the creature controlling me were drinking in his fear. My lips grazed his ear and my voice explained to him silkily, "It would have been so much easier if you had just given me the mirror."

The confusion on Ryan's face morphed into terror. He stumbled back. "No. Stella, not you," he half whispered, sounding defeated.

"Yes, Orion," the presence said through me. I sensed the creature's triumph and fought harder. It was no use.

The next words that came out of my mouth chilled me to the bone. "And if you don't do what I ask, then your girlfriend will suffer. I promise you."

I knew, without a shadow of a doubt, that it meant what it said.

At once, I found myself at the top of a mound of boulders just off-shore. The ocean crashed onto the rocks below. The wind, in its icy fury, carried the sound of Ryan screaming my name. Twisting, I looked down at the beach. When I spotted Ryan, so small from my vantage point, I realized what I had done; I was able to move again!

The relief was short-lived. Just as I was about to start climbing down, my muscles locked up, preventing me from going any further.

"I don't think so," the presence inside me said. "If Orion doesn't want to deal, then I will give you a chance to save your life. Where is the mirror, witch?" The presence started mucking around in my head, searching for the information it wanted. Immediately, my mental barriers went up, locking it out of my thoughts.

Still, the presence pried.

Adding to my defense, I latched onto the first thing outside of the mirror that I could think of; my brother. I pictured him before he went into the military: his narrow face, his warm, brown eyes, and his curly mop of light brown hair. I envisioned him in such acute detail that I could almost hear him call my name.

The presence cursed and I felt a flash of satisfaction. He wasn't going to get the information out of me, no matter how hard he tried.

"You had your chance, witch. I will get the mirror, one way or another."

Again, my body moved without my consent. The force within drove my feet over the rocks and launched my body into the salty air.

Terror gripped me as I plummeted. The presence within didn't allow my arms or legs to move; locked tight in death's grip, I braced for the final, icy plunge.

I jolted awake just as I hit the water in the nightmare. The emotions from the dream shuddered through me and I brought the thick sheet up around my shoulders to ward off the sudden chill. A ragged sigh escaped my lips allowing the remnants of my fear to permeate the otherwise sterilized hospital air. In the darkness of the room, the soft beeps of the monitors next to my bed reminded me that I was safe and that it had only been a dream . . . hadn't it?

I fumbled for the bed control which had gotten tangled in the sheets. Once it was free and in my hand, I pressed a button causing a blinding light to shine above me. It took a full minute for my eyes to adjust. The curtain that divided the room pulled back to reveal an empty bed and a closed window. Small streams of sunlight peeked through the window shades, setting the whole thing aglow.

The table next to me overflowed flowers and balloons and cards. It was amazing how fast word traveled about my accident. In the three days since waking up in the ICU of St. John's Hospital, everyone had written or sent flowers. I'd heard from the family back in Italy, my new teachers, everyone. Well, everyone except Ryan.

For the millionth time, I wondered where he was and if he was alright. I needed to hear from him. Maybe he could fill in the blank spots in my memory. The nightmares seemed so real, so vivid. It couldn't just be my imagination.

Settling back against the pillows, I struggled to piece together what happened. Ryan and I made an agreement: I'd help him end the war between Heaven and Hell and in return, he'd help me bring about the Age of the Daughter. The two events didn't seem completely separate, but we weren't exactly sure how they were related.

My family has a legend about a messiah, kind of a witch's version of Jesus or Mohammed or Buddha. According to the stories, the Daughter will begin a new era. Peace and prosperity would grace the earth. Knowledge would illuminate the darkest corners of the human world. The Daughter would rid the world of war, famine, disease, and suffering and replace them with health, peace, compassion, and abundance.

Nona calls me the catalyst to the Age of the Daughter. Ever since I was young, she told me I was destined to do great things. She promised one day I would meet a creature who was both of this world and another. He would guide me on the path to becoming the legend she spoke so much about. Thinking something was nice to believe in and actually believing in it were two different things. I never took Nona seriously about the legend until the day I met Ryan.

The first time I saw him, I knew he was the one Nona had told me about. There had been an immediate deep-seated recognition as if I'd always known him.

Ryan's an angel, or at least his parents were. They were both Grigori—part of the last choir of angels that stayed on earth to keep the balance of power between the Heavenly Host and the Fallen Ones. Angels don't have the ability to procreate with each other, so how Ryan came about was somewhat of a mystery.

The first time we touched, I felt an electric tingle and I knew for certain together we would bring the legends I'd grown up with to life.

Now Ryan was missing and I was healing from a fight that I couldn't remember.

All I could recall was Ryan and I going to the beach find his Uncle Azra when someone attacked us. My memory held only hazy images of imposing inhuman figures. Muted arguments between Ryan and a wicked looking person on a cliff replayed in my mind. Then there was just darkness.

My cell phone rested next to the get well cards on the bedside table. The display proclaimed it was three o'clock in the afternoon and that there were no waiting texts or missed calls. I pulled up Ryan's number and hesitated for only a moment before pushing the call button.

It rang until it went to voicemail. I hung up without leaving a message and tossed the phone back onto the table. My frustration and anger made me want to scream. Where the hell was he? Why would he stay away for so long without even a text?

Three days of sitting in this room were more than enough. I hated hospitals. They smelled like death except with the sickly sweet aroma of hand sanitizer. I needed to get out of here as much as I needed my memory back. Soon I would be out of here and if Ryan wasn't going to come to me, then I would just have to find him and demand to know what happened.

Just as I had decided to take action, my grandmother strode into the room.

"Good, you are awake. I was wondering if you would be before I went home for supper. How are you feeling, my dear? Did you have a nice nap?" Nona smiled warmly as she settled herself on the stiff-backed chair next to the bed. Though it didn't look comfortable, she hadn't made any complaints.

Her attire was casual for her; a pale blue button down dress with quarter-length sleeves and a skirt that brushed her thin calves. At her throat was a delicate golden chain from which dangled an oval locket. Her long silver hair coiled around her head in a braid.

I always admired Nona. More than just the matriarch and high priestess of the family, she was the stability in my life after a dead mother and an absentee father. I trusted Nona more than anyone else in the world, except for my brother. I doubted she would approve of me leaving the hospital just because I hadn't heard from one wayward angel.

"Have they said when I can go home?" I asked.

"Dr. Salinas said perhaps tomorrow." Nona must have seen the annoyance cross my face because she told me gently, "It's important that you are healing properly. You don't want to come back to the hospital because you over did things. Now, do you remember anything else from that night?" It was the same question she asked every time she saw me since I landed in the hospital.

"No. There are still a lot of black spots. Have you heard from Ryan?" I knew the answer before I asked, but I held my breath for it anyway.

Nona hesitated for a fraction of a second before admitting, "We haven't seen him since he brought you here."

"I wish I knew where he was," I sighed. "He could fill me in on what happened."

Nona reached up and patted my arm in sympathy. "I know, my dear. It's a difficult situation. We just have to trust that the Goddess will show us what we need to know."

I made a face as I wriggled into a more comfortable position, trying not to let my irritation show too much. This wasn't Nona's fault.

"You have to be patient," Nona admonished. When I didn't respond, she changed the subject. "If you don't come home tomorrow then the twins are going to set up your phone to do—what is it? A face chat? Video call? Whatever it is with Thomas. He's worried and he wants to hear from you."

I groaned and allowed my head to fall back onto the pillows. "You told my brother? Why would you worry him like that? I'm fine."

"You're in the hospital, Stella. It's right that he should know."

Thomas was my half-brother from my father's first

marriage. Though he was only five years older than me, he acted like the age difference was more like twenty years. He'd joined the Army a couple of years ago and now was stationed in the Middle East.

I was heartbroken when he left for the Army. He and I had always been close. Even before my father abandoned us, Thomas took on the male role model aspect for me.

It must have driven him nuts to know I was in the hospital and there was nothing he could do about it. I was in for a long lecture, depending on how much of the story Nona told him.

"The important thing is that you are safe and whoever it was on the beach didn't get what they were after. Ryan will turn up. I'm sure of it."

At her words, ice went through my veins and my dream came rushing back to me. Ascher had wanted the mirror. Was I so sure he hadn't gotten it?

"Nona, where's my bag?" The alarm in my voice made my grandmother frown.

"It's in the cabinet over there, why?"

"Will you get it for me, please? I need to check something."

Frowning, Nona did as I asked, passing me the small, patchwork messenger bag. Immediately I upended the contents onto the bed. I sifted through the odds and ends until my fingers closed around the velvet drawstring bag. As I crushed the familiar pouch in my fist, my worst fear wrapped itself around my heart.

Empty. No, there was something there . . .

"Stella?" Nona asked, "What's going on?"

Ignoring her, I yanked the strings to open the pouch for confirmation. Sure enough, there was a piece of folded paper crumpled by my grasp and nothing else. I unfolded the lined sheet and what I saw took my breath away.

It was a sketch of my favorite painting: *The Farewell*

of Eucharis and Telemachus by Jaques Louis David. The scene depicted a girl clinging to a boy with her head on his shoulder and her hands clasped about his neck in a sad embrace. The youth posed with his back more to the girl, gazing out to his audience with a grim and resolute face. His hand rested on the girl's knee and his other hand held a spear. A hunting dog stared at the boy.

From the girl's closed eyes and the slight frown upon her lips, showing the sorrow of one who knows this embrace will be the last one. Resignation and sadness emanated from her.

Besides the lack of color, the sketch differed from the real painting in that the faces of Eucharis and Telemachus were replaced with mine and Ryan's.

Below the sketch was a scrawled message: *"Doubt thou the stars are fire, doubt that the sun doth move, doubt truth to be a liar, bur never doubt I love. Ryan"*

What the hell did that mean?

I stared at the paper, my mind reaching for explanations I would never be able to confirm. The message didn't do any good; it only created more questions that I couldn't get any answers to. Furious, I crumpled the paper and tossed it onto the floor.

"You stupid idiot!" I yelled though I wasn't sure if I was referring to myself or to Ryan.

"Stella, what is going on?" Nona's tone held a stern warning.

Despair filled me to the brim and threatened to spill over. I'd lost the mirror. Keeping it safe was the one duty, the one expectation my grandmother had of me and I failed. Failed spectacularly. Now I had to explain that to the woman who had given me the responsibility.

It wasn't really a mirror. The mirror part was the disguise my family put on an object that a goddess gave to us generations ago. Legend had it that the object was some sort of tool that would help advance the Age of the Daughter. My family kept this heavenly object safe for hundreds of years. If it ever got into the wrong hands, it could mean the end of the world as we know it.

Nona gave the mirror to me after I told her about meeting Ryan for the first time. She believed I was the one who would finally use it and bring the family legends to life.

Instead, I'm the one who lost it.

My grandmother waited for my explanation.

With my voice hoarse, I confessed, "I think Ryan took the mirror."

"What?"

I couldn't even bring myself to look at her because of the shame I felt. Tears welled up in my eyes. I hated myself for crying, but I couldn't stop because I was beyond furious. "He must have stolen it while I was unconscious. It was in my bag. The mirror is what Ascher was after."

With my confession done, I chanced a look at my grandmother.

Her thin face was somehow sharper than before. Her eyes narrowed in fury and disappointment. "Do you have any idea what you have done?" The words were so harsh with anger that they cut the air between us. I winced at them.

"I'm sorry, Nona."

My apology only served to enrage her more. "Sorry? Stella Seraphina Evangeline, you have lost the most dangerous item on earth; an object that our family was sworn to guard. Your carelessness put the entire world in danger and all you can say for yourself is *sorry*?"

"I didn't do it on purpose!" I knew it was stupid to talk back to her right then; I'd never seen her so angry before. Still, I felt the need to explain myself. "I took the mirror to the Getty to see if Ryan knew how to use it. I forgot to take it out of my bag when we got back home. I'm sorry. It was a stupid move."

For a moment, my grandmother was too angry to

speak. With visible effort, she calmed enough to say, "Give me your phone, Stella. I am calling the twins to come pick me up. There's no time to waste."

"What are you going to do?" The question came out a whisper as I handed her my phone.

"I'm calling the Stregheria together for a meeting. They need to know the mirror was stolen."

I stared at the drawing as Nona called for a ride. As angry as she was with me, I was more upset with myself. How stupid had I been to trust Ryan with my family's secrets? How could I know he'd betray me though?

Truth be told, it made my determination to find the angel that much stronger. It was my fault the mirror was taken, so it was my responsibility to get it back. As soon as Nona left, I'd break out of the hospital and hunt Ryan down. He owed me more than an explanation now.

Nona hung up the phone and passed it back to me. "They twins will be here in a few minutes to pick me up." She paused and watched me carefully. Anger still marked her features though it was more controlled. At last, she spoke, "This is something you have to take responsibility for, Stella. You're the guardian of the mirror. You lost it. Now you will have a major part to play to bring it back. Do you understand?"

There was nothing to do except nod.

Seeing my stricken expression, Nona's tone softened. "I'll be back in the morning and we can talk about this more. For now, get some rest." She planted a kiss on my forehead and collected her bag. She left the room with one last glance back and a disappointed shake of her head.

Then I was alone.

I forced myself to wait until seven o'clock—well after supper had been delivered and cleaned up—before making my escape. Yes, I was tired and no, I wasn't sure how to get out of the hospital. Those minor details weren't going to get in my way.

I had to find Ryan and the mirror. Part of me held onto the hope that Ryan had taken the mirror to hide it. Maybe he'd kept it safe when I couldn't and was going to give it back to me. That didn't explain the sketch and the cryptic note.

My body ached and it hurt to move. Working against my protesting muscles, I eased out of bed. The linoleum was freezing and I wished that I had socks. Being in bed so long made me unsteady on my feet. Stumbling, I had to clutch onto the bed to steady myself. I only got a couple of steps in before the IV line tugged against my skin. Well that wasn't going to get me far.

Bracing for the sting, I yanked the line out of my hand. Immediately, alarms started beeping from the machine stand next to me.

A passing nurse poked her head into the room. "Everything alright in here?"

Smiling, I said, "Yeah. My IV came out when I stood up. I just needed to go to the bathroom."

The nurse nodded and went to the beeping machine next to the bed. She fiddled with some buttons and the noise stopped. "I'll be back in a few minutes to reattach your IV." She smiled as she left me to my own devices.

On my way to the bathroom, I grabbed my bag and the change of clothes that Nona had brought for when I'd get discharged. Laying on the floor next to them was the crumpled picture that Ryan had drawn. I picked it up and smoothed it out as best as I could. For reasons I wasn't quite clear about, I folded it and took it with me.

The bathroom was large enough to accommodate those who had to wrestle with walkers and wheelchairs. The door felt heavy, but it clicked silently closed. I wasn't sure how long before they would come in to check on me, so there was no time to waste. After slipping into a shirt and pulling on my jeans, I tried to tear the hospital bracelet from my wrist. It was impossible. I settled for painfully squeezing my hand out of the plastic wrapped paper and tossed it into the garbage.

On the way out of the bathroom, I caught a glimpse of my face in the mirror. I looked like shit. Angry red scrapes and cuts marred my bruised skin. Dark shadows around my nose and my brown eyes gave me a certain raccoon-like appearance.

There was no time to worry about how I looked. I pulled on my hoodie and sucked in a deep breath. Even after three days of resting in the hospital, the simple act of raising my arms over my head caused a sharp shooting pain in my side. Damn these injuries!

To get out of the hospital, I'd use an invisibility spell. Well, it's not exactly complete invisibility. It worked like a shield, refracting the surrounding light to disguise my movements. It was originally created for me to sneak out of the house; now it would be vital if I were going to get out of here.

I quieted my thoughts as I'd been taught. Focus was important; without it, the spell wouldn't work. The words of the incantation repeated in my head, the syllables coming out under my breath in a rhythm. The beat that fell in time with the cadence of my heart.

The power of a spell isn't something that's seen; it's something that's felt. Energy stirs around inside of you and it lets you know when it is ready. As soon as I was sure the incantation was working, I eased open the oversized door to the bathroom and crept out. I locked the door and allowed it to close again, hoping the nurse would just assume I was still in there.

With all the confidence I could muster, I strode out into the hallway. My pace was as normal as I could make it between my urge to rush away and the injuries which prevented me from going too fast. As long as I made it out of the hospital, that's what counted.

The nurses at the hub-like station didn't look up or stop their conversations as I passed. The spell was working! I continued to the elevator. As luck would have it, the doors opened on their own just as I approached. A man wheeling a gurney passed by without as much as a glance my way. I slipped into the elevator and pressed the button that would take me to the ground floor.

The energy flickered around me. Sweat popped up on my forehead from the effort of keeping the spell going. I wasn't sure if I could keep it up long enough to get completely out of the hospital.

After what seemed like forever, the elevator stopped. My focus renewed as the doors slid open with a ping. Directly ahead was the exit guarded by a uniformed cop. Now was not the time to chicken out or to doubt. Lifting my chin, I continued forward, watching him out of the corner of my eye.

He looked bored. As his gaze wandered in my direction, he blinked and shook his head. My control must have slipped, making me visible once again. There was no point in trying to recapture the spell. Let him think that he just hadn't noticed me before.

As confidently as I could, I gave him a single nod and walked through the front door.

Chapter Two

I stood underneath the awning and stared out at the cold, damp night. Now that I was out of the hospital and listening to the rain pattering on the parked cars, I realized there were a few flaws in my plan. First, it was freezing! My hoodie was definitely not enough to keep out the damp cold. Second, Ryan's apartment was in Camarillo—a good twenty minute drive on the freeway and who knew how long if I took the backroads.

Just as I was starting to rethink my grand escape, a taxi pulled up under the archway. A man in a suit stepped out of the back and headed for the doors of the hospital. Before the cab could leave, I hurried as fast as my aching limbs would allow and climbed into the backseat.

"Thank you," I gasped, allowing the warmth of the car to come over me.

"Where to?" the cabbie asked.

I gave him the cross streets as I pawed through my bag, hoping to have enough cash. Luckily, there were a couple of twenties in my wallet.

The drive to Camarillo took longer than I remembered. It wasn't helped by the cab driver's persistent silence or the old-time country-western music on the radio. I was more than relieved when we arrived. As I eased out of the car, I struggled to remember where I was going. Ryan's apartment was on the top floor of the five-story building. It was a wide, open space that met the sky unflinchingly. As the tallest building in the area, it was the perfect home for an angel; it was so close to the heavens, so open and free.

It wasn't raining anymore, but the thunder

rumbling overhead was threat enough that it would start again at any moment. My muscles screamed in agony as I forced myself to ascend the stairs. My legs gave out just as I reached the top. I clung to the stucco wall to keep upright. In hindsight, leaving the hospital so soon was probably a mistake.

As soon as I was in front of Ryan's door, a moment of doubt came over me. What if I was wrong? What if he didn't take the mirror? Or worse. What if I was right and he had played me from the moment I had met him? I shook off the what-if scenarios and straightened my back. I'd come this far, I wasn't going to give up now. My determination propelled me the rest of the way. I knocked boldly on the door.

Nothing happened.

I knocked again.

Still, no one answered.

Well, I didn't come all this way just to stand on the doorstep. I turned the handle and, to my surprise, the door creaked open. The apartment was dark and, for a moment, my resolve wavered. No. I was going to get my mirror back. Holding my head high, I forced myself over the threshold.

With my hands gripping the walls for stability, I shuffled my way to the living room. The curtains were drawn and everything was still and shadowed. My hand hit a light switch on the wall and the apartment was illuminated.

The whole place was trashed. Furniture was scattered and toppled in no discernable pattern. Clothing, dishes, and random magazines littered every surface. The kitchen was in shambles. Cabinets were left open and the sink overflowed with unwashed dishes.

Despite the mess, it looked like no one had been there for a while.

Well crap.

I'd assumed someone would be home, so it took a

minute to re-evaluate my plan. It was unclear if the apartment was still occupied. For all the clutter, there wasn't anything that indicated it was completely abandoned. If he wasn't going to come back then he would have taken more things, right?

What was I going to do, wait until Ryan decided to come back?

Or could I make him come to me? I was a witch after all. I could draw him in with a binding spell. To do that, I would need something of his, something that I could use as a link.

Casting my gaze around the destroyed apartment, I searched for something I could use. I grit my teeth against the increasing ache in my body. I'd have to do this swiftly. With a pronounced limp, I went to one of the bedrooms. It must have been Ryan's because boy clothes were strewn haphazardly among skateboards and random sketches. Like the rest of the apartment, dirty dishes covered most surfaces and there was a pervading funk in the air that proclaimed unwashed male.

I didn't want to take his dirty laundry—that was just gross—so I looked around for something that wasn't covered in dirt or growing mold.

The bathroom. Maybe he left some hairs in a comb or maybe a toothbrush. As a rule, DNA had a much better track record in spells than common everyday objects.

Keeping with the general theme of the apartment, the bathroom was a mess. Towels crumpled on the floor and the garbage was overflowing. The mirror looked like it hadn't been cleaned in a long while. Still, I was in luck. There, sitting in a heap on the porcelain sink was a blood caked washcloth. As gross as it was, blood is the best thing for spell work. I don't know what made me so sure, but I was positive that it was Ryan's. Bits of it flaked off of the terrycloth.

A sharp bang from the front room made me jump. An indistinct voice muttered through the thin walls.

Pocketing the cloth, I forced myself to stand up straight. I didn't have enough energy to even attempt the invisibility spell. My muscles protested and shook with pain. I wasn't about to confront whoever was out there by showing weakness. I also wasn't going to sit in here waiting to be found.

Mustering my strength, I walked into the front room. What greeted me was a goat chewing on a plastic bowl and a ragged looking angel in swim trunks with a bottle in his hand. Beneath the shaggy hair and sloppy appearance, I recognized Ryan's uncle, Azra. On the outside, he looked like your typical surfer; all tanned and muscled and blonde. Because of my magical powers, I could see the shadow of his wings, barely visible past his vibrant blue and green aura. While he didn't notice me, the goat, Beth, stopped chewing and looked up. She let out a bleat and plodded over.

"You can't tell me what to do," Azra mumbled belligerently. "You're not the boss of me." He stumbled around the kitchen, opening cabinets and examining what was inside. "Why isn't there any food in this house? I gave you the grocery money a week ago."

Not sure who he was talking to, I called out, "Azra?"

The sound of his name caused him swivel around with a bottle pressed to his lips. When he saw me, he sputtered, losing both his mouthful of liquid and the dark colored glass bottle which shattered at his feet. Faster than I could blink, he leapt up onto the counter and drew a pair of nun chucks from out of thin air. He waved them around in a manner that reminded me of a toddler playing with spaghetti. "What are you doing here, Strega?"

"I'm looking for Ryan," I said, sounding more confident and in control than I felt. Azra was a loose cannon and I wasn't sure what I could say that would calm him down.

The angel paused and waited for me to make a

move. When I didn't do anything, he jumped off the counter, his flip flop covered feet crunched on broken glass. Scowling at the ground, he went to the fridge and shouted over his shoulder, "He's not here. He hasn't been here for days."

Azra's words sent chills through me. "What?"

He pawed around the inside of the fridge, ignoring my question. When he emerged, he had another dark colored wine bottle. He twisted the screw top off and eyed me as he took a deep swig. After he swallowed, he observed, "You look like hell. At least you got rid of your infestation."

"My what?"

"You are the only one in that little head of yours, aren't you?"

My frustration got the better of me and I snapped at the Grigori. "Of course it's just me! Who else would it be?"

"You would say that if you had someone else controlling you," Azra reasoned. He took another drink. "The last time I saw you conscious, there was definitely a hitchhiker controlling your strings."

It took a long moment for his words to fully process in my mind. They brought forth hazy memories. Flashes of dark water and the ever so soft whispers of someone else in my head manifested. My lungs burned with the memory of being unable to draw breath. I shook with the remembrance. "Are you saying I was possessed?"

"If the shoe fits, honey. Prove that scumbag Ascher isn't still using you like a puppet, otherwise, don't let the door hit you in the ass on the way out."

My breath caught in my throat. Ascher took over my body? It was my nightmare all over again.

Beth rubbed her nose against my fingers.

"Beth!" Azra exclaimed, noticing the goat's behavior. "Stop that. She's dangerous! Besides, she doesn't have any food for you. Come back over here."

The goat ignored him and commenced nuzzling me. The physical contact broke me out of the embrace of the nightmare. Focusing on the goat and her coarse hair against my hand, I fought against the nightmare images.

Beth reminded me of a cat who wanted attention. She was a strange goat; not like any of the others back in Italy that my family kept. What possessed Azra to keep her in such an urban setting, I'll never know. Goats needed space and, I suspected, a healthier diet than whatever Azra was providing her. I wished I'd brought some carrots or something.

"Stupid goat stealing Strega Girl," the Grigori muttered under his breath.

Irritated at his childish attitude, I gave up on trying to make sense out of the sudden flashes of memory. "Look, I don't have time for this. Where's Ryan?"

Azra glowered at me. "What makes you think I know? He never came home."

My heart skipped a beat and I started to shake. That wasn't possible. Ryan had to be around. He was the only way I'd get any answers. My voice wavered as I tried to remain calm. "What do you mean he never came home?"

"Just that. I haven't seen him since that night."

It was getting harder and harder to control myself. When I was finally able to speak, my voice was low. "You are telling me that you have no idea where he is?"

Azra huffed and crossed his arms. "Oh, I have an idea. I think Ascher somehow won him over to the dark side. Ryan's been a little shit ever since Ascher came back into town. I'm sure he's brainwashed my nephew into doing his bidding."

Something snapped inside of me. Any pain I felt evaporated with the sudden surge of anger. The firm control I had over my power broke and energy poured out of me. The air pulsed and I dimly became aware of the change in the air pressure. Lights flickered, reacting somehow to the electrical charge surrounding us. I felt the crackle of power on my skin.

My initial despair churned into rage. My worst fear had been realized; Ryan probably planned this from the start. He knew I was the guardian of the mirror. He tricked me into trusting him so he could steal what my family had protected for generations. It disgusted me how willingly I'd fallen for his lies. If I was being honest, I hated how hard I had fallen for him.

Beth backed away, bleating questioningly. It didn't matter though; I focused solely on the downward spiral of rage inside me. The energy sparking from my fingertips drew Azra's attention.

"Whoa!" The Grigori jumped back, alarmed. "I didn't mean to call you stupid. Calm down, okay?"

"Take me to Ryan right now," I ordered.

"I can't! Ascher has him hidden away. Besides, I am not taking you anywhere. You're too weak and too easily controlled by the enemy."

"You will take me to Ryan!" I screamed. Using the built up energy, I lunged forward, catching Azra by surprise. He yelped as we tumbled onto the floor.

My body moved on its own accord, fueled by my power—a direct result of the emotions swirling chaotically inside me.

Azra didn't just sit idly by and let me attack; he shoved me backward hard enough to slam me into one of the end tables sitting next to the couch. It wasn't enough to stop me. With adrenaline pumping through my system to shut out the pain of my injuries, I scrambled to my feet.

"Stop hiding him! Tell me where he is!" I shouted.

"What? I'm not hiding anything, you crazy witch! Did that jump off the cliff scramble your brains or were insane before that?"

Trembling with fury, I couldn't even respond to him. I would make him take me to his wayward nephew whether he liked it or not.

Letting out a scream, I ran toward the angel, intending to take him down again. This time he was ready for me. In a single dexterous move, he twirled to the left. His hands made contact and he propelled me forward along my path, adding an extra shove along the way. I hit the edge of the kitchen counter with my stomach. It knocked the breath out of me and pissed me off even more.

"Are you sure you're the only one in that head of yours? This is crazy even for a witch."

Gasping for air, I centered my attention on a large glass bowl sitting on the kitchen counter. Dark, sludgy liquid sloshed in the bottom as the container shook under my power. That was it; I couldn't get it to levitate because it was so heavy.

That didn't mean I was helpless. I clutched the bowl and charged it with the energy coating my hands until there was enough power in it to stun whatever it struck. Whirling around to get the angel in my sight, I lobbed the bowl straight at his head. Foul-smelling liquid arched out of the bowl and into the air. The bowl itself spun off too far to the right. Azra's face was splashed with the liquid while the bowl grazed his arm.

"For the love of everything sacred, that's disgusting!"

While he wiped his face with his good arm, I took my chance and focused my energy. I couldn't make the bowl fly, but manifesting wind was much easier.

A strong breeze started swirling in the apartment. Papers got caught up in the currents and fluttered between us, making it difficult for him to see where I was coming from. He was way too big for me to take down, so I used my power. Tendrils of energy pinned his limbs to the floor. When I was sure he wasn't going to break free of my magical restraints, I grabbed a hunk of his hair and pulled.

"OW!" He struggled more to break free as I

retreated to a safe distance and sunk to the floor.

With my power expended, I was finally drained. It took several minutes lying on the apartment floor to catch my breath. The wind died down and the sheaves of papers and magazines rained down upon us. The magical pressure in the air dissipated almost as quickly as it had come.

Unfortunately, with everything else, my restraints on Azra also faded. There was a grunt and then he was above me, a glowing blade inches away from my face.

"Don't try anything else, Strega Girl. It is seven years of bad luck to kill one of your kind, but don't think I won't make the exception."

From my position on the floor, I held up the strands of sun bleached blonde hair in a trembling fist. "Do you know what I can do with this? I can curse you. I can make you wish you were never created."

The angel's eyes widened and his jaw opened. The terror in his expression was confirmation enough that he would listen to me.

"Now. Take. Me. To. Ryan." I forced myself into a sitting position.

He held his hands out. "Stop with the hocus pocus. I get that you're pissed at him. I'll find him, I'll bring him back and you two can have your lover's quarrel."

"I just want the mirror back," I hissed.

"Okay, okay." The Grigori had backed up all the way to the opposite wall and cowered behind Beth. "I can't bring you with me. I think that would constitute as kidnapping. If the authorities aren't hunting us down, I'll be able to track him easier. I'll bring your mirror back, I promise."

As much as I hated to admit it, he had a point. "Fine. You have five days. If you don't come back with it before then, I will use these." I raised the strands of his hair still clenched between my fingers.

"You don't have to threaten me, Strega Girl! I keep

my promises." Azra sounded indignant. Well, as indignant as possible when clutching a goat in front of him like a shield.

Beth seconded his protest with a persuasive bleat.

"Whatever," I said. I couldn't hold it back anymore, a couple of tears slid down my cheek. That show of weakness frustrated me and I scrubbed the tears roughly from my face.

Azra saw the dampness and panic made his blue eyes widen. "Hey, hey, it's okay. You don't have to do that. I'll find him."

His reaction to my tears just made me angrier. Glowering, I said in a hard voice, "I don't care about him. I just want my mirror."

He threw his hands up, showing he wasn't trying to argue with me. "Mirror got it. No problem. I'm going now." He started for the door.

I wanted to go home. It had been a mistake to come here. My legs wouldn't cooperate and my wobbling attempt to get to my feet had me sprawled back on the floor.

There was a steady clip-clop coming closer to me. Beth nuzzled my cheek.

"Bethesda!" Azra called from the door. "Come here this instant! We are leaving!"

The animal looked back at Azra and turned up her nose.

"You traitorous goat!" Azra started toward her. Beth whipped her head away from him in an obvious snub. It caused him to stop short and a choked sort of whimper escaped his lips. "Beth? Beth, I'm sorry. You know I didn't mean that."

The goat continued to ignore him.

With a sheepish and apologetic expression, he asked, "While I find your mirror, will you mind watching over Beth? She hates traveling."

I blinked to keep myself awake. "What am I going to

do with a goat?"

"Take care of her. She likes alfalfa and Chex Mix. If you can take her surfing every few days that would be great. She needs to keep practicing."

I didn't have a chance to protest. Everything was getting fuzzy around the edges of my vision and my breath came with more difficulty. I had over done things.

Careful not to touch me, Azra breezed past. He patted his goat affectionately on her flank. "I will be back for you."

Beth bleated softly in response and rubbed her face against his arm. It was a touching scene, except I was stuck on one thing. What on earth was I going to do with a goat?

Chapter Three

Azra called a cab to take me and Beth to my house. Being crammed in the back seat of a Prius with a large dairy goat didn't do much for my aching body or my temperament. I couldn't rest yet. I still had to figure out how to explain what happened to my grandmother.

All too soon the cab ride came to an end.

"Will you just drop me off here?" I asked as we turned the corner. My chances of sneaking into the house were better if I went through the backyard instead of the front door.

I handed the cabbie all the cash that Azra had given me. The guy deserved a good tip for the bites Beth took out of the back seat. When we were out of the car, I took Beth by the leash and crept across the neighbor's lawn to the gate on the side of my house. The latch was old and the gate creaked when I pulled it open.

Lights burned in the kitchen and I heard the voices of my cousins. My body ached with every move. I forced myself to double over and crouch under the window that sat over the sink. Based on how little light was cast into the back yard, I could tell that the curtains over the arcadia door were drawn shut. Good. That would make waiting easier.

I checked my phone; it was just after ten o'clock. Nona would be in bed by now. I wasn't sure about Donatella. Some nights she stayed up later than others. If I waited about an hour and a half, then for sure she would be asleep. So would Aurelia. The only ones left would be the twins and there was a good chance they would be going out to hang with friends soon.

All I had to do was wait them out and then sneak

into the house and climb into bed. The thought of my bed tortured me with longing. I imagined sliding into the cool sheets, pulling up the old quilt, and surrounding myself with pillows. That would be better than Heaven right about now.

Instead, I was stuck in the back yard, waiting in the cold night air. Our backyard was more or less an expanse of grass surrounded by a cinderblock wall. The twins had taken it upon themselves to build a fire pit in the middle of the yard. Beth wandered around, nibbling on the overgrown weeds. I settled down to wait in one of the four lawn chairs that surrounded a well-used homemade fire pit.

It was hard to get comfortable in the lawn chair, but I did my best. I just had to wait until all the lights went out. It shouldn't take that long.

What I failed to account for was how exhausted I was. Now that the adrenaline and rage weren't pumping through my system, I hurt more than I ever had in the hospital. There was no winning against the pain. For the millionth time that evening, I conceded that my escape from the hospital may have been too rash of a decision.

The bright patio light turned on. The grating, gravelly sound of the sliding arcadia door echoed against the cinder block walls covered in ivy.

There was no time to hide. I could only whip my head around to see my cousin, Justin, come of the house.

He was going to see me. There was no way around it, so I decided to say in the most cheerful voice I could muster, "Hey, Justin."

He jumped. If I'd been feeling better, I would have laughed. As it was, I settled for a weak smile.

"Stella? What are you doing here?"

"Well, I was in the neighborhood . . ."

My cousin didn't find my response at all amusing. "You're supposed to be in the hospital."

Painfully, I got to my feet. "Yeah, well, there was

something I had to take care of."

"What was so important? You know Nona is going to go ballistic when she finds out you checked yourself out." The grin on his face showed how much he looked forward to the fireworks between Nona and me. After all, it was a rare occasion when he wasn't the one getting yelled at.

Nathan poked his head out around the curtain. His jaw hit the floor when he saw me. Stunned, he emerged onto the back porch to stand next to his brother. "Stella?" he asked with as much alarm as his twin had.

"You're just in time, Nate. She was about to tell me why she checked herself out of the hospital." Justin leaned forward, his hands crammed in the front pockets of his zipped up black, patched hoodie. The hood covered his un-styled Mohawk. He was an inch shorter than Nathan, standing at about six foot four and had a narrower face. Other than that, they looked the same, even down to the different colored Mohawks they wore. The real differences were in their personalities.

Justin was the one who did the majority of the talking. He had an easy smile and a way with people that gave him the ability to talk himself out of fights just as much as he got into them.

Nathan was the silent one. He spoke only rarely, preferring to keep his thoughts to himself or at least to those that he trusted.

"Out with it," Justin demanded.

"Out with what?" Playing coy wasn't going to work and I knew it. I just wanted to go to bed.

"Don't be stupid. You wouldn't be here unless something major happened. Did Ryan show up after all? Or maybe his crazy uncle? Did they chase you out of the hospital? Did they follow you here?" He peered over my shoulder into the darkened yard.

"No, it wasn't anything like that."

"Hey!" Nathan pointed. "There's a goat in our

backyard!"

Glancing back, I saw Beth inspect one of the chairs.

Justin almost hopped with giddiness. "How did you get a goat? Is it one of those fainting ones? You know, you scare it and it falls over and plays dead? Mom is going to flip! She hates goats."

"No. That's, um—"

The house phone rang, cutting off my answer and making the three of us jump. One ring, two rings, three rings, and then silence.

"Come on," Nathan reached out a hand to help me. "Nona's going to kill you when she finds out you're here. I don't want her to kill us because we didn't make you come in out of the cold."

I accepted his hand while trying my best not to stumble. "Gee, thanks." My legs wobbled underneath me and I tightened my grip on Justin's hand, hoping I wouldn't fall. Soon enough, I was on the couch and off my feet.

Nona stalked into the living room just as Nathan draped an old quilt over me. When she saw me laying there, she cried out angrily, "Stella Seraphina Evangeline! Why are you not in the hospital where you belong?"

"She said Ryan and his nut-job uncle chased her out," Justin piped up.

Nona and I both scowled at him and he smiled sheepishly in the face of our annoyance. "I suppose you two want to talk in private. No problem. C'mon, Nathan." He grabbed his twin by the shirt as they backed out of the room.

Turning her irritation back to me, Nona demanded, "Well? What was so important that you had to sneak out of the hospital?"

"I didn't sneak out!" I protested, even though I knew it was a lie. By Nona's pursed lips she knew it too. "Okay, I did sneak out, but I had a good reason."

"A good reason? Do you know that those poor

nurses turned that hospital upside down looking for you? I just got off the phone with them! They've called the police to help find you! What possible reason could be good enough to cause so much trouble?"

The boys must have forgotten to close the glass door because at that precise moment, Beth sauntered into the house. She gave a loud *baa*, and proceeded toward the couch.

The sight of the goat rendered my grandmother speechless. The sound of hushed giggling issued from around the corner in the hall. The twins tried to hold back desperate laughter as they listened in.

Beth burrowed her nose under the quilt searching for my hand.

After a long moment of silence, my grandmother asked in a tight, controlled tone, "Stella, what is a goat doing in my living room?"

"That's part of what I want to explain," I said.

Donatella and Aurelia walked into the room, intent on seeing what all the ruckus was about.

"Whoa!" Donatella shouted when she noticed the goat. "What the hell is going on? Stella? I thought you were missing?"

"She isn't missing. She brought home a goat," Nona answered. Letting out a long sigh, she started issuing orders. "Auri, go put the kettle on. Make some sage and comfrey tea for Stella. Boys, I know you are in the hall, I can hear you snickering to each other. Come get the goat and tie it up in the back yard. Donatella, please call the hospital back and explain that we have found her and she is safe." When Nona issued orders in that tone of voice, you immediately did what she said. My cousins did exactly that.

Donatella was speechless in her annoyance. As she returned to her room to call the hospital, she shook her head.

The twins had emerged from around the corner to

grab ahold of the goat. Beth, not wanting to leave my side, didn't make it easy on them; Nathan ended up having to pick her up and carry her back outside. To her credit, Beth only kicked a little bit and didn't bite either of them.

Nona sat next to me, her lips forming a thin line of disappointment that was more punishing than anything else. I could feel Nona's gray eyes on me as she considered what to say. Finally, she drew in a heavy breath and said, "You're still weak, Stella. What if something happened to you? You have no defense at all. What on earth were you thinking?"

"I had to, Nona. You'd have done the same thing," I responded quietly.

"No, I would have known better than to pull such an idiotic stunt. Did you ever stop to think that you are too important to jeopardize in such a way? You haven't healed completely. You've probably done more damage to yourself with this escapade."

The twins came in from the back yard hesitantly. Taking note of the tense atmosphere around us, they gave each other a meaningful look and made a beeline for their room. This wasn't the time to make light of the situation. I envied their ability to leave.

Aurelia emerged from the kitchen, a mug of tea gingerly held between her hands. Setting it on the table beside the couch, she asked, "Is there anything else you need, Nona?"

Our grandmother gave a dismissive wave. "Thank you, Aurelia. Go on back to bed. I'm sorry we had to wake you. Tell your mother that I need to talk to Stella in private for a while. I know she needs to get up early for work. She and I can talk about this in the morning."

My cousin nodded, a mixture of curiosity and anger plain on her face. Giving me a sidelong glance, she left the room, presumably to go back to bed. In reality, it was far more likely that she, her brothers, and their mother would be listening from the hallway. Aurelia was a few months younger than me. She was usually quiet, almost meek. Despite her mother trying to make us compete for pretty much everything, Auri and I had a tentative friendship.

I picked up the mug and sipped the hot liquid, trying to put my thoughts in order.

"So?" Nona prompted me. The tone of her voice warned me that she would not ask again.

There was no other way to say it, so I blurted it out. "Ryan took the mirror to Ascher. He's the one that attacked us on the beach."

Within the space of those words, my grandmother's face became ashen. Horror widened her eyes. "Are you certain?"

"Yes. When I left the hospital, I went to confront Ryan about the mirror being missing."

"And?"

I hung my head. "He wasn't there. Instead, I ran into his uncle. Azra said he hadn't seen Ryan since the night of the fight. He said Ryan went with Ascher." As the words tumbled out of my mouth, the initial fury I felt rose up again. I'd expended most of my reserved power earlier, so there were no magical side effects to go along with my pumping blood like before.

My grandmother was a different story. She had enough control not to allow her power to spark from her finger tips, but the air in the room became dense making her anger and fear palpable.

"How could this have happened?" she hissed, as she rose to her feet and started pacing.

I didn't have an explanation. The same question had been running through my own mind on a loop.

"Did Azra know where Ascher is? Or Ryan? Is there a way for us to find them?"

I shook my head. "No, he doesn't know where Ascher is or even if Ryan is with him."

Nona cursed under her breath.

"He is out there looking for Ryan right now. That's why I have the goat with me. I'm watching her until Azra comes back."

My grandmother was skeptical. "Do you think that will work? Do you think that an angel as unstable as Azra will honor any sort of agreement with us? The last time he was here, he threatened to kill us all."

"He thought we were a threat." Still, when her words sunk in, I wasn't as sure as I had been. At last, I conceded, "If he doesn't follow through, then I guess I'll have to find Ryan myself."

"How are you going to track an angel? No, he's not even an angel—he's something else entirely. There's never been a creature like him before." Nona's words were sharp with frustration. "We don't know what he's capable of, especially now that he has the mirror."

"When I was at Ryan's apartment, I grabbed this." I fished the bloody washcloth out of my hoodie pocket and held it out to my grandmother. "This is his blood. With it, we can find Ryan and force him to tell us where the mirror is."

With a small appraising smile, she took the towel. "Very good, my little witchling." Nona tilted her head to the side and summoned, "Maxwell!"

Within moments the air next to her shimmered and a short man in a long brown trench coat appeared. His brown fedora slanted low on his brow, covering his dark hair. He looked tired and more translucent than usual.

"Yes, Sylvia?"

Max was the family ghost. He died long before I was born and had somehow attached himself to my grandmother. Growing up, I thought everyone had a family ghost. It wasn't until I was much older that I realized how rare a creature like Max was. Few spirits would stick around, especially in service to a family that wasn't even theirs.

Max had some unique powers for a ghost because of his relationship with my family. He was able to move certain things and pick them up if they weren't too heavy. He could appear to be as real as anyone until you tried to touch him. He had even learned how to cast a few spells. All in all, he was a tough creature.

That's why seeing Max so drained struck me. He'd been on the beach the night of the accident. This was the first time I'd seen him since then. If he still hadn't recovered, just how badly had he been hurt? How was it even possible for a ghost to be injured? Nona spoke before I could ask.

"Max, I need you to visit Bianca. Tell my sister that we will be arriving in the next day or so. We need to convene the Stregheria."

Donatella stepped out from the hall. "Nona you can't be serious! We can't just drop everything and go to Italy this week. I've got a job and the kids have school."

"This is a family emergency," Nona argued. "The mirror has been stolen. It is imperative that we get it back. This is our top priority."

Donatella's jaw dropped in momentary disbelief. She recovered and was ready with a declared 'I told you so'. "I knew we couldn't trust Ryan! You insisted on leaving him alone with Stella and now look what's happened! You said he was trustworthy."

"I am well aware of what I said," Nona snapped.

Donatella was persistent. "Fine. The mirror was stolen. Great. You and Stella should go to Italy. She's the reason why the mirror is missing. She should be the one to get it back."

"To track down the mirror, we need the power of the whole Stregheria. That includes you and Aurelia. Max, let Bianca know all of us will be there."

Max nodded and disappeared without even a glance in my direction.

A Stregheria was a family of Italian witches. While

everyone in the family was part of the Stregheria, not everyone in the family could do magic. In our case, Stregheria also referred to the core coven of thirteen magically inclined family members who undertook the magical workings for the family.

Nona was the high priestess of the coven and the head of the family. She had a fair amount of precognitive powers about certain things. She called it her intuition and she followed it religiously. Her intuition drove her to make a life in America when her grandchildren were born and it was what made us move to Oxnard which led me to find Ryan.

"Nona, I can't just—"

"You will find a way, Donatella. Even if you have to take a later flight, you will be there."

Angry and wanting to lash out, my cousin spat, "You know you're wrong about her. Stella isn't the one that will fulfill the family legend. This whole situation just proves it. She's managed to lose something our family has protected for ages in what? A week? How much longer are you going to delude yourself, Nona? Why won't you see what's in front of you?"

My temper flared at her attack "I was unconscious! How was I supposed to stop Ryan from taking it if I wasn't even awake?"

"Stop it both of you! This is no time to bicker amongst ourselves. Donatella, the current situation doesn't change my thoughts on that matter. No matter how much you want Aurelia to be the One of Legend, she just is not. Please, let's focus on the matter at hand instead of this old argument!"

Furious, my cousin stormed out of the room, muttering under her breath.

Nona turned back to me. "The Stregheria will help find the thief, however, you will be responsible for designing the spell to do it. It has to be ready by the time we arrive."

"What? What do you mean? I've never created a full ritual before. Don't you have something that will work? That's the whole reason why I grabbed the washcloth! I know your spells require something of the person."

"This is your responsibility. You were given the mirror and you allowed it to be stolen. This spell is for you to create."

"How? I don't know how to do something like this."

"Drink your tea," Nona told me as she went to where her purse hung. Reaching into her bag, she pulled out a well-worn book. It was only about half the size of a paperback and bound in age-discolored doeskin. The silver-plated edges needed a good polishing. Emblazoned on the front was the sign of the triple goddess: a circle and a crescent on either side representing the three phases of the moon.

I recognized it as the Book of Mysteries; a compilation of spells and charms passed down through generations of our family. She returned to the couch and handed me the well-worn book.

"My mother passed this down to me and her grandmother passed it onto her before that. This book contains lifetimes of accumulated knowledge. I was saving it for when you were old enough. While you certainly are not ready, this is an emergency. The knowledge of your ancestors will help prepare you. We honor the family by learning their lessons while adding our own to the book. In this way, the knowledge of the Old Ways will never be lost."

I accepted the book, feeling the weight of generations who had contributed to it. A mixture of excitement and dread flooded through me. I'd waited years to comb through this book, to learn the secrets that it held. Now that I needed to know specific things, the sheer amount of knowledge that I held intimidated me.

"Now, I have things to get done. I suggest you start researching." Nona went back to her bedroom, leaving me wrapped up on the couch.

Once she was out of the room, I closed my eyes. How in the hell was I going to come up with a full tracking spell for an angel? Sure I could do little charms, but a locating ceremony on someone that wasn't supposed to exist? One the entire coven would participate in? This was way out of my league.

Despite my exhaustion and my misgivings, I wasn't about to sleep. There was too much riding on me getting this spell just right. After taking a large gulp of the now tepid tea, I opened the Book of Mysteries. The pages were jam packed with hastily scratched notes. Though I spoke Italian fluently, reading it was a different matter. I could read enough to understand that they were notes on the lunar cycles, herbal lore, and observations of the natural world. Bits of recipes and spells were scattered through the notes. There were no dates; the change in handwriting was proof of the years it took to compile this information.

As I skimmed through the pages, one note scribbled in the margins grabbed my attention: *We keep the sacred object safe, for if it is lost, the end will soon follow.*

That's when the enormity of the situation hit me. Ryan meant to destroy the world with the mirror and, despite my broken heart, I had to stop him.

Chapter Four

"WHY IS THE GOAT IN THE HOUSE?" Donatella's earsplitting shriek jerked me awake, causing me to fall from the couch. My body twisted and the stack of loose-leaf notebook paper slid off of the couch and scattered on the living room floor. I landed in a heap on Beth, who had, until that point, been lying next to me. She stood and sniffed at my hair before baaing irritably at Donatella who loomed over us.

"Stella! Get the goat out of here! Are you crazy? Why would you even let it in?"

"Huh?" All I could do was blink at her demands. I thought it was a dream, but the stiffness in my limbs proved otherwise.

Frustrated that I wasn't moving faster, Donatella let out a shrill sound of rage as she grabbed hold of Beth's collar. In a couple of long, jerky steps, she yanked the goat toward the arcadia door. Beth balked at being dragged out of the house and put most of her weight against Donatella's grip

Nona appeared in the living room in her housecoat. "What on earth is going on out here?"

"Your golden granddaughter let the goat inside!" Donatella shouted as she struggled with the arcadia door and an uncooperative goat.

"I didn't," I protested, getting to my feet. My muscles trembled with the effort of trying to stand and I lost my balance, falling back onto the couch.

Beth tore out of Donatella's grip and jumped back to me. Leaping up onto the couch, she wiggled her head under my arm.

"Why you little—" Donatella's fists clenched

together. Her stance widened just enough to let me know she was about to do something stupid and magical.

As I expected, sparks of erratic energy shot from my cousin's fingers. In short, choppy motions, she wove that energy into what appeared to be a dimly shining net of pale blue light.

Nona must have seen it too because she gave a sharp wave of her hand, effortlessly erasing Donatella's energy netting. "Don't make this situation worse, Donatella."

"Worse?" The word dripped in furious indignation.

"I'm taking care of Beth until Azra comes back. He went to do something for me," I spoke up before Donatella could say anything more.

"Beth? The goat's name is Beth?" It was always the small details that she fixated upon.

Beth, for her part, stayed quiet.

"Stella," Nona said, sternly, "get Beth outside. She is to stay there while she is with us, do you understand? Everyone will need to pack; we leave for Italy tonight."

Donatella gave me a smug smile as I eased off the couch.

"Tonight? I can't go!" Aurelia protested, stepping out of the hall. I hadn't even known she was there. "I've got a date with Peter."

"Who is Peter?" I asked, surprised. I'd never known her to go out with anyone, ever.

"Peter's my boyfriend. Nona, please, he just got back from a family trip. I haven't seen him in days!"

"You're going to have to cancel it," Nona answered firmly. "We have a family emergency." My grandmother regarded me. "Have you come up with anything?"

I cast a look at the scattered pieces of scribbled on notebook paper with notes and half-baked ideas strewn about the room. "Not yet. I have some ideas, though."

"Oh, fantastic," Donatella snickered. "We have to drop everything to help get the mirror back and she doesn't even have a plan."

My patience evaporated in the wake of Donatella's muttering. "Look, I messed up. I freely admit it and I'm the one trying to fix my mistakes. No one asked you to butt in."

"Really? Why are we going to Italy? Why is the Stregheria gathering if not to find the mirror that *you* lost?"

"The mirror is the responsibility of the entire family. If it gets into the wrong hands, then the entire world is in danger," Nona interrupted. Her fingers pressed against her temple as though she were trying to extinguish a headache by pure pressure.

"You should have thought about that before you gave it to her," Donatella retorted.

"Enough! We need to work together on this and not cast blame. Now, we are leaving tonight."

"What about the goat?" My cousin asked, plainly not liking the message Nona was giving. "What do we do with it while we are out fixing Stella's mistake?"

I bristled. "You know what—"

Nona stopped me. "The boys will stay here and take care of Beth until Azra returns."

"That's not fair!" Aurelia cried. She stomped her foot in frustration. "Why do they get to stay?"

I blinked at her show of temper. This was unlike her. Usually, Aurelia was more patient and understanding than this.

"They will stay here to watch after the goat. Besides, you know as well as I that they don't do magic. Really, Aurelia. This tantrum is unbecoming."

The admonishment from our grandmother sent my cousin bursting into tears and running back to her room.

"What's her problem?" I asked.

"She had a date tonight. You know, not everything revolves around you like some people think." Donatella retorted. **"We have to put our entire lives on hold all** because you lost the mirror."

"I didn't lose it. It was stolen," I snarled.

Her words dripped with venom, "Yeah, by your angel boyfriend. Did you truly believe he was into you for your personality? Please! It's obvious he used you to get his hands on the mirror. You were just too stupid and self-absorbed to see it."

My fists clenched at my sides. A dozen different insults and come backs rushed along the tip of my tongue, but I held them back. The worst part of her attack was that she could be right. What if Ryan hadn't cared about me? What if all along he'd been after the mirror? The sudden ache in my chest brought forth tears that I fought against. Doubt broke my heart.

Seeing she'd hit her mark, Donatella left me on the brink of tears and went to comfort her daughter.

I looked at Nona helplessly, the angry and heartbroken tears welled in my eyes. "I didn't mean for the mirror to get stolen."

Nona sighed. "I know. The fact remains that it was. Now we have to find it. How are you feeling?"

"How do you think?" At her exasperated look, I amended, "I'm just tired."

"You're staying in bed today. You need to rest as much as possible if you are going to be any good to the Stregheria."

"Alright," I conceded, wiping away the tears on my cheek. I could do research from bed. Bed sounded amazing right then.

"Take Beth outside and go get changed. I will make you some breakfast. Here, give her these outside." Nona handed me a few carrots.

I let out a soft groan and got to my feet. Beth did the same and followed me to the backyard.

The morning was damp with the ocean in the air.

I gave Beth the carrots and got a bucket of water for her. The goat followed me eagerly; she was a social creature and didn't want to leave my side. I bet Azra hadn't left her alone since getting her.

"You have to stay out here for a bit. Donatella will make gyros out of you if you get in her way," I explained. There was no way to know if she understood me, but Beth explored the grassy area and set about munching. After watching her for a little while, I was about to go back inside when the arcadia door slid open and Justin came out.

He glanced at me with glee in his eyes. "Great job in bringing the goat home by the way. Mom is so pissed! I thought she was going to have a serious meltdown."

I couldn't help but return the smile. "I didn't do it to make your mom angry. Beth isn't going to stay forever. I'm just watching her for a friend." I supposed I could call Azra a friend at this point.

"Oh, sure." His grin was as wide as ever.

I went back in the house, looking forward to changing into some sweatpants and a t-shirt. Aurelia was waiting for me in our shared bedroom.

It was a small room, painted purple with a tiny closet. The sliding door was completely missing, creating an alcove for our clothes and shoes. Nothing in the room was divided into hers and mine; our things coexisted side by side. The bunk beds were a homemade creation of a queen bed on stilts, high enough off the ground that an entire dresser could fit underneath. A twin bed closer to the floor fit partially underneath the stilts.

Auri stood next to her bed with her backpack open in front of her. When she saw me, she crammed her notebook into the bag. "I can't go to Italy! I have things to do! You will just have to fix this on your own, Stella."

"I'm sorry," I said, standing near the dresser we shared. She was genuinely angry and I didn't want to provoke her any further.

"How long will we have to be there?" she demanded. "I have a boyfriend. You don't understand what it's like. I have to be with him. If I go across the world, there's a chance he'll lose interest in me. I don't want to give him up!"

I stepped forward and grabbed her hand. "Calm down! No one is asking you to give up your boyfriend. I doubt he will just forget about you because you are gone for a few days. If I get this right, then we won't be gone longer than a week. Look, I messed up big time. I can't do this on my own. I need your help to fix it. Please?"

She let go of my hand and mumbled, "Fine. If we're leaving tonight, then I need to tell Peter." She slammed the bedroom door in a huff, leaving me to puzzle out what had gotten into her.

***

When Nona came to check on me, I'd settled into my top bunk, paging through the Book of Mysteries and adding to my notes from the night before.

"Are you resting?" she asked.

I set the book down with a heavy sigh. "No, I'm reading."

"Well, take a break. Someone wants to talk to you."

Nathan followed my grandmother in to the room. Nona stood to one side while he set up the laptop he had been carrying. Once it was ready to go, Nathan and Nona left the room.

Before she closed the door, she advised, "He'll understand more than you think."

The computer made a pinging sound and I looked down as Nona shut the door behind her. Thomas' face appeared on the screen, his expression was solemn. Bracing myself, I hit a key on the laptop so that my own face popped up in a small box on the lower right-hand corner.

My brother looked nothing like me. While I had inherited my mother's straight, fair hair and dark eyes,

Thomas had our father's dark curls and had Nona's piercing gray gaze. He'd cut those curls when he'd gone into the military. I missed them. He looked thinner than the last time I'd spoken with him. Had it been only two weeks ago? Bags showed under his eyes despite his newly developed tan.

There was nothing distinguishing in his surroundings. The only thing that showed he was in the military was his set of dog tags shining against his white tank top.

"Hey little sister," he greeted me seriously. "I'm glad to see that you're still among the living."

"It was close for a minute." I watched the questions pile up behind Thomas' eyes. Before he could get the first one past his teeth, I asked, "How are you doing? You look like you've lost weight. Aren't they feeding you?"

He frowned. "Nice try little sister. Tell me what happened. Why were you in the hospital?"

This was what I dreaded explaining the most, so naturally, it would be the first thing he would demand. Instead of looking at my brother, my gaze cast down to my lap.

"Come on, Stella," Thomas demanded roughly, his voice deepening with frustration. "I don't have all day. How the hell did you land in the hospital?"

I winced at the harshness of his question. My brother had always been protective of me. How much could I tell him without making him crazy with worry?

"Remember the guy I told you about? The one in my English and Math classes?"

He looked confused. "Yeah, I remember. What does he have to do with you being in the hospital?" His eyes widened as a thought struck him. The flush of rage crept up his neck. "Do you mean to tell me that *he* did this to you?"

"No! No! He tried to protect me," I protested.

The red began to flood his face. He slammed his

hands down on the table, causing the camera to shake. "Protect you?" he all but spat. "From who? From what? What sort of protection puts you in the hospital?"

"I know," I sighed, trying to be patient. This was what I feared would happen; Thomas would get so wrapped up in his assumptions that he wouldn't listen to anything I said. "Listen to me, Thomas. Do you remember what I told you about Ryan?"

My brother shook his head.

"Nona thinks he's going to end of the Age of the Son. She thinks that he will pave the way for the Lady of the Legend." I waited for a moment, allowing my words to sink in. When Thomas stared at me in stony silence, I pressed on. "We got into a little trouble and we had to fight our way out. Ryan didn't do this to me. He wouldn't." The words came out confidently, but the doubt in my heart fluttered.

"Nona thinks he's the one and he couldn't prevent you from getting hurt?" Thomas repeated skeptically.

I shook my head. "Someone named Ascher did this to me."

Thomas' mouth settled into a grim line. "Go on," he said in a low voice.

I held my hands out. "That's all I know! We went to the beach to find Ryan's uncle because he knew what the next step would be. An army of demons and angels ambushed us. They wanted the mirror."

"Are you telling me a gang of monsters jumped you because they wanted an old hand-me-down mirror? Look, it is okay if you can't remember. You don't need to make up stories."

"I'm not making anything up! Why the hell would I make up something like that?" I shot back.

"I don't pretend to know why you do most of the things you do. All I know is that you were injured bad enough to stay in the hospital for four days. Now, the only explanation of how you got hurt is a tale of demons and angels!" He shook his head in disbelief.

"It's the truth! I can't help it if you don't like it!" I knew I was yelling, but I didn't care. This whole conversation was going all wrong. I wasn't sure how to stop it now that it was in mid-swing, so I just went with it and let my anger to carry me through. "There was a time not too long ago when you would have believed me. Has the Army changed you so much?"

"You know what, sure I've changed. That's not a bad thing. How can you expect me to accept that sort of a tale without questioning it?"

"How can you question it? Thomas, I've never lied to you, ever. Why would I start now? You grew up in Stregheria too. Even if you don't do the magic part, you know it is real!"

"Ugh!" He ran his hands over his shaved head in frustration. He didn't talk for a full minute as he closed his eyes and took a deep breath. I could see his lips moving silently as he counted to ten. It was something I saw him do many times when he was dealing with our father. That hurt more than him thinking I was lying.

At last, my brother spoke in a slow, deliberate tone, "All I'm trying to do is find out what happened. I want to know who hurt you. I want to know you are getting better. I'm trying to look out for you."

I bit back my sharp retort. Fighting wasn't going to make it any better. "I know. I know you're doing what you can and I know it's frustrating not knowing. Believe me."

"Then tell me what you remember," Thomas suggested. "Quit going on about that story Nona crammed down your throat and just tell me what happened."

"I did tell you. You wouldn't listen." I let the sentence hang in the air between us until he caved.

"Alright, I give up. I promise to listen and not make any more comments."

"It's like I told you. Ryan and I fought them off as best as we could. My power was used up protecting us. The last thing I remember is something controlling my body. Everything got blurry and then there was nothing. When I woke up, I was in the hospital and the mirror was gone."

Thomas pressed his lips together as he considered what question to ask next. I could tell he was trying to give me the benefit of the doubt. "No one knows what happened after you blacked out?"

"Ryan does, wherever he is," I muttered.

"What does that mean?"

"It means I haven't seen Ryan since that night. No one has. All we know is that he took the mirror."

Thomas scowled. "Why would he do that?"

"I don't know," I said, the words catching in my throat.

He must have heard the pain I was trying to hide because instantly, his expression softened. When he spoke, there was no trace of frustration. "I'm sorry Stella. I wish I could be there to make it better."

"You can't make it better, but thanks for wanting to." I gave him a watery smile.

Thomas sighed and said, "Listen, I have to go." He pointed his finger at me sternly. "I want you to get a lot of rest. Maybe once you heal a bit more your memory will come back."

"Yeah, well, be careful over there too. You need to come back in one piece."

He flashed me a winning smile. "I'm always careful, little sister. I'll be home soon."

I returned his smile. "You better. I love you."

"Love you too. I'll talk to you later."

"Bye." I waited for him to sign off first before I disconnected. With my mind buzzing, I shut down the laptop and picked up the Book of Mysteries again. Please, just let me come up with the right spell!

Chapter Five

By the time we boarded the plane that night, I had a better idea of how to complete the spell. My seat was next to Auri but I spent most of the trip with my headphones on and scribbling notes in my journal. It was just as well; she was still mad about having to cancel her date so she spent her time sulking.

Creating a way to track down an angel that didn't want to be found was difficult, especially when you weren't sure what powers they had. I mean, what if he could block my spell with some freakish power that only angel hybrids had? There was just no way to know.

I still had to try. The one spell that could hopefully do what I needed was a binding. There was a small incantation written in the margins of the book where one could bind one object with another. Because of the protection magic my ancestors had placed on the mirror, I couldn't bind anything to it. The theory did give me another idea.

If I could make this small incantation work with living things instead of objects, then I could bind myself to Ryan. I'd be drawn to where he was. The tricky part was nailing down a way for him not to feel his end of the binding. If I could do that, then I could sneak up on him.

With only a couple more hours to Perugia, I set to work creating a ritual to find someone that shouldn't exist.

***

Perugia was a large city and Sant'Egidio airport was a reflection of that. The terminals were packed with people when the plane landed. Because of the large crowds, Nona, Auri, and Donatella fell into a different customs line than I did. My line moved much slower than theirs and it wasn't long before I lost sight of them. It was no worry; we'd traveled enough as a family to know where we would meet if we got separated.

Confidently, if not slowly due to my injuries, I wove through the throngs of people toward the baggage claim.

"You should take it easy," a voice said. It came from the empty air right next to me.

The sound of that voice gave me a reason to smirk. "I thought you were avoiding me, Max. I haven't seen you in almost a week."

The ghost came into view. He was still too translucent, like a dim reflection in bright sunlight. "Yeah, well, someone has to keep an eye on you." The words sounded bitter.

"Listen, about what happened that night; it wasn't your fault. You know that, right?"

The specter gave a noncommittal shrug. "It is what it is. Tell me something, is there any way you will just forget this and let Ryan disappear like he wanted to?"

I gave a sharp laugh. "You must be joking, right?" When Max didn't respond, I continued harshly. "Not a chance in hell. He took something from me and I have to get it back."

Max snorted. "Is getting your mirror back the only reason you are looking for him?"

"What other reason would there be?" I did my best to keep my face neutral even as my hand went to my pocket where Ryan's crumpled drawing was. I felt the rough edges of the folded page and it caused a lump in my throat. There was no way I was letting Max know how brokenhearted I was. No one could know.

"Don't play dumb, Stella. It doesn't suit you. I just want to make sure you aren't doing this because of your feelings for him."

I didn't answer; there was nothing I could say. I wasn't sure my feelings weren't a factor in what I was about to do. The anger I felt about being lied to was good. Along with that came the dismayed hope that this was all just some dream. The emotions fueled me and I needed every bit of strength I could get for this spell. The problem lay in that it was almost impossible to sort out which emotions were driving me toward Ryan; the anger, the lovesickness, or the hope. I quickened my pace. The baggage area wasn't far.

A growl of frustration emanated from the ghost. "Dammit Stella, listen to me. If you have to get the mirror back, do it, but don't go carrying a torch for him. It'll just complicate things. Those feelings will prevent you from doing what has to be done."

I laughed at him to cover up my inner struggle. "Max, what does carrying a torch even mean? Come on, you've been around long enough, you don't have to talk like you're stuck in the twenties all the time."

Max scowled at my attempted light heartedness. Taking a breath, I said, "Look, Ryan stole from me. If there's any sort of emotion I have for him going into this, it is anger. Until I get to the bottom of what happened that's all there is to it."

I spotted Nona, Donatella, and Auri waiting for me near the baggage claim.

Before we got into earshot of the family, Max whispered in my ear. "You're a horrible liar. I know you still have feelings for him. These angels are dangerous, Stella. Promise you will be careful."

I gave a curt nod. "I promise."

He faded from view, but I knew he was still around.

"Stella, come on," Auri called as she waved me over.

"Sorry," I said when I was close enough. "Got stuck in customs. Did my bag make it?"

My cousin pointed at my duffel bag laying at her feet. "Already grabbed it for you."

I moved to pick it up, but my grandmother stopped me. "Stella, dear. You shouldn't be lifting that. Here. Let Luciano get that for you." She gestured to one of her nephews—a large man about fifty years old. Luciano was Bianca's eldest son. He had an easy smile and thick black hair that was just beginning to show signs of gray. He slung my heavy duffel over his shoulder and picked up the rest of the bags as well. He guided us to the car.

Auri, Donatella, and I crammed into the back while Nona accepted the passenger seat next to Luciano. They talked in swift Italian as Nona inquired about how he'd been faring since she had last seen him. I ignored the small talk and stared out of the window, watching the city give way to the suburbs and then to farmland.

The village where my family resided was just outside of San Gemini in Umbria. It was small, but near enough to one the larger towns that it wasn't completely isolated. My family lived there for centuries. In fact, I think our family was one of the first to farm there. While we sold some of the land to allow the town to grow, most of the farmlands that surrounded the recently paved streets were still in the family. The sprawling vineyards and olive groves interspersed with houses, occupied by various relatives. Beyond the fields was a forest where my cousins and I often searched for truffles when we visited during the winter months.

Luciano drove us to the main house. It was a tall, three-story brick building with small windows. Situated to the side of the house was a large garden partially obscured by the ivy-covered trellises. The ivy was for protection, Nona told me once. Traditionally, ivy grew around witches' homes as a barrier for unfriendly spirits. That's why any Strega worth her salt kept the ivy green and growing.

I hadn't realized how much I missed this place until we turned onto the gravel driveway and saw the house.

As soon as the car stopped, I was out, stretching in

the winter sunshine. I breathed in the cool air, filling my lungs with the smells of home. It felt good to be back.

"Sylvia!" came a joyful cry. Spinning around to where the shout came from, I saw my aunt throw open her arms and come bounding down the steps to embrace her oldest sister.

Aunt Bianca was a shapely woman with dark brown hair peppered with gray. She wore a modest dress, orthopedic white shoes, and a blue and white checkered apron with a pocket on the front.

"Bianca!" Compared to her sister, my grandmother looked ancient and small. Nona embraced Bianca with a fierce joy.

"How was your trip? You must be famished. Come in, come in." She caught sight of me and exclaimed in fast Italian, "Stella? Is that you? My how you have grown! Aurelia! Donatella, she becomes more and more like you every time I see her!" Bianca was a whirlwind of excitement. Her hands fluttered as she clucked over each of us. Soon enough, we were ushered into the large house, our bags taken by Luciano to our respective rooms upstairs.

Even though it had been almost a year since I had last been here, everything looked the same. Once we were past the doorway, the house opened up to a sitting room crammed with floral upholstered chairs and couches. Lace doilies dripped from the furniture. End tables and bookshelves dotted the room. They supported hundreds of pictures in a variety of frames ranging from the crudely shaped olive wood to the opulent gold gilt. Generations of the family were never so well represented as in this room.

Beyond the sitting room and to the left were the kitchen and a staircase down to the root cellar. In the kitchen sat the ancient stone hearth that was older than the house itself. The smells that came from that part of the house could drive someone crazy. There was always something cooking. Always. Even now, the scent of roasting meat and fresh baked bread teased me. Next to the kitchen, in an enclosed room, was an expansive table with several chairs.

A rickety staircase spiraled up to the second and third floors where the bedrooms were. The main house was usually reserved for the matriarch and her immediate family, but there was always room for guests. Beyond the staircase was a small room outfitted with an old mahogany desk reserved for the business of managing the farms, presses, vineyards, and winery.

A simple way of looking at the extent of influence my family has is to compare it to a country with the main house as the capital. The matriarch was the ruler, the decision maker, and the caretaker of the family in general. The family was large with many branches off shooting in different directions. Still, they all contributed in some way like tending the fields, operating the olive press, and managing the winery. In return, the family made sure each person was taken care of. It was a complicated system of dependency between family members, but it was what made us strong. We looked after our own.

Being the matriarch was an all-consuming task. Everyone in the family relied on her; she was the keeper of history, the wisdom of the ages, the glue that held everything together. Without a matriarch, the estate and indeed, the family, would flounder and fade away.

Which was why there was such an uproar when Nona decided to go to America. It was kind of akin to the pope deciding that he would live in Brazil and somehow still manage the Vatican. The family wasn't at all prepared for it. Nona decided to share her responsibilities with her sister, Bianca. Bianca would oversee the day-to-day issues that came up. Nona would return every summer, or as the need arose, to take care of the things that Bianca couldn't.

I didn't always go with her on these trips back home. Sometimes I'd stay with my brother or some other family member that lived in the states. It's surprising how many Stregheria there were outside of Italy. Family was always family, though, no matter where they were in the world.

"Stella," Nona called my name, snapping me out of my thoughts. "We have some things to discuss before tonight's events."

Donatella and Aurelia had already gone up to their rooms to get settled, both choosing to ignore me for the time being. At least being back in the family estate had cooled their anger somewhat.

Bianca smiled and gave me a conspiratorial wink. "Tonight we will open a bottle of your wine for supper. We missed your last birthday, so we will have to make up for it."

I smiled at the thought. Every time the family welcomed a new baby, our winery made a select few bottles with a special label with the child's name on it. Once the child reached sixteen, they would open a bottle to celebrate. Other bottles were reserved for special events such as weddings and new babies.

I settled into a comfortable wing backed armchair and waited for Nona to sit on the edge of a plush couch. It was only when Bianca had left the room that she spoke.

"Are you prepared for tonight?" she asked.

I cleared my throat, anxious that my spell wasn't going to be good enough. "I propose a binding. I have Ryan's blood. I can bind something to him. We will be able to tell where he is and then we can get the mirror back that way."

My grandmother smoothed out her dress. "Interesting. How do you intend on binding something to an angel?"

"It's the same principle as binding two objects

together. I found a similar spell in the Book of Mysteries. The only difference is that instead of objects, it will be two living things. I am going to bind myself to him."

Whatever she thought I was going to say, it wasn't that. Her stunned look was hard to read. "You? Stella, do you know what you are saying?"

"I know there are risks."

"I don't think you understand them. When you bind yourself to someone, you share their thoughts, their emotions. You see what they see and hear what they hear. No one has ever successfully bound themselves to another person, let alone an angel. It would drive you mad."

While her warnings scared me, they didn't shake my resolve. "Well? What would you have me do? I can't ask anyone else to do it for me. I was the one that trusted him. I was the one that lost the mirror. That means that I am the one responsible for getting it back."

"There has to be another way, Stella. What if we just use a tracker spell on him?" Nona suggested. Worry crept into her voice and I realized that my solution scared her.

I shook my head. I'd already thought about the other options. "No simple tracking spell will work on Ryan; he's the son of two Grigori. They spent centuries evading detection from anyone. He probably has powers we can't even guess at. What I am suggesting makes sense. Since he was born that means his body is of this world. I can use his blood to bind it to my own blood. It is the only thing strong enough to make the spell stick."

My grandmother gave a loud sigh. "What if I was the one to bind him instead?"

"No. You told me yourself; this is for me to do and you know it."

Nona was quiet for a long moment, her expression growing more and more pensive. Finally, she asked, "Do you know what we will need for this endeavor? Have you written the spell?" Resignation tinged her words.

"Not all the way," I answered. "I was hoping you could help me with some of the finer points?"

Nona glanced at the large grandfather clock ticking in the corner of the room. "The family will be here just after sundown. I suggest we get started."

It took four hours for us to finalize the spell that would bind me to Ryan. While I'd previously participated in group spell work, I'd never created a ceremony from scratch before. Nona was patient as she walked me through the process. Even Bianca gave suggestions when she popped in to check on us.

At last, it was complete. Nona was right; this spell was going to be risky. Even with all the power of the Stregheria behind me, there was no guarantee that I would come out of this unscathed.

"There's one more thing," Nona said as I wrote the final line of the spell.

"What's that?" I was exhausted and nervous. In a few hours, I was going to be my own guinea pig.

"We have to explain what happened to the Stregheria."

I licked my lips. "Why do we have to explain it?"

Nona gave a tsk of disappointment. "Really, Stella, it is only right that we tell them what this is about. We can't keep this a secret, especially if they are going to be participating in this ritual. The mirror is important to the whole Stregheria."

"You're right," I sighed. "I'll do it. It was my responsibility, so it makes sense that I have to tell the family. When do you think the best time would be?"

"Once everyone has gathered here, we will explain. I will welcome everyone and then you will have a chance to say what you need to say."

"Great," I said, feeling the anxiousness inside of me grow with the thought of confronting the whole coven.

"Just great."

Immediately, my grandmother admonished, "No need for that attitude, young lady. You need to show humility and remorse. You need to take responsibility."

My temper flared. "I am taking responsibility! I'm about to bind myself to the son of two angels to get the mirror. How is that *not* taking responsibility?"

Her eyes shut against my elevated voice as though she got a headache. "Enough. It has been an incredibly stressful couple of days. I didn't mean to imply that you aren't doing the responsible thing, but you do need to keep your attitude under control. You have every right to be angry. Remember, you must have your emotions under control to make this spell work properly. Do you understand?"

I did understand. Nona wanted me to be more of a leader instead of some emotional basket case. The problem was that things were so intense, I wasn't sure I could hide the feelings swirling inside me.

Aunt Bianca came in at that moment. "Oh, I'm sorry," she said taking in both mine and her sister's stances. "Am I interrupting?"

"Not at all," Nona said. "We've finished. Here is a list of the materials we need. Do we have them on hand?" She gave the list to Bianca who eyed it appraisingly.

"We have most of these things. There are a couple of items that we will need to go into town for. I'll send Maria to fetch them."

"I'll do it," I said, taking the list back from her. "I'd like to take a walk and get some air. It won't take me long." I purposefully got to my feet, feeling my muscles strain with use.

Bianca reached into her dress pocket and handed me some cash. "Take this. It should be more than enough to get a case of white candles and a spool of black ribbon."

"Thank you, Aunt Bianca," I said, pocketing the cash

and the list. My mind was heavy with the weight of the spell we were going to attempt as I left the house.

So wrapped up in my own thoughts, I wasn't paying attention to where I walked. My legs hit something large and furry. I stumbled gracelessly, falling onto the gravel with a loud crunch and a startled curse left my lips.

The goat I'd tripped over watched me drop and was courteous enough to nudge me with her head after I landed.

"Shouldn't you be in a pen somewhere?" I shouted as I brushed myself off. I had a couple of new scrapes to add to my already bruised body, but nothing too serious. Something nagged at the back of my mind. Something about the goat. She looked familiar. After regarding the animal, I took a look around, hoping to spot her owner. The goat tossed her head making something around her neck clink. That was when I caught sight of a collar. A pink, spiked collar with an identification tag typically made for dogs dangling from it.

No. It couldn't be.

Reaching up, I took the tag in my trembling hands. The name engraved on the thin piece of metal was *Bethesda*. The back of the tag was engraved *Return to Azra*.

I dropped the tag as though it burned and crawled backward away from the animal like my life depended on it.

"Beth?" I asked from my new vantage point. I studied the goat again, not believing the similarities. Yes, this goat had the exact same markings as Beth and there was the same weird intelligence in the creature's eyes.

"This isn't possible," I announced. "You can't be here. We left you in California. How on earth did you get here?"

Beth, of course, didn't answer. Instead, she wandered away to munch on some grass.

Disturbed beyond reason, I tried to understand how

she could be here with me in Italy when we specifically left her with the twins.

"Am I dreaming? Is this some sort of side effect from the pain meds at the hospital?" I sat there amid the gravel on the drive way trying to make sense of why Beth was here.

"Stella! Are you alright?" Nona called from the doorway of the house. She must have heard me shout when I fell.

"No, I don't think I am alright. Do you see Beth or am I dreaming?" I pointed at the goat.

"What?" The question held surprise and disbelief. I gestured to the animal to punctuate my point. After a moment of stunned silence, Nona said, "Stay where you are. I'll be right down."

I didn't take my eyes off of the animal who was calmly chewing as she stared right back at me.

There was a clatter as Bianca and Nona raced down the porch steps to where I sat. Nona gasped as she saw Beth.

"How—?" she started, but fell silent. "Is that . . .?"

I nodded. "She even has the collar."

My grandmother gaped. "I don't believe it."

"What? I don't understand. What's the big deal about a goat?" Bianca asked. She walked toward Beth intending on shooing her away.

"Wait!" Nona and I both cried out at the same time. Bianca froze in place.

"That goat belongs to an unstable angel. We don't want to startle her or drive her away," Nona explained to her sister.

I got to my feet and dusted off my jeans. "I'm supposed to watch her while he's searching for his nephew. We left her with the twins back in California."

"Maybe this Azra person dropped her off?" Bianca suggested. All three of us scanned our surroundings. There was no sign of Azra anywhere.

"You know," I said as I pondered the goat, "She does belong to an angel. He's taught her how to surf. Maybe he's taught her how to teleport too?"

My aunt and my grandmother both shrugged.

"Well, she's with us now. Perhaps we'd better get her into a pen to keep her safe," Nona said. "Stella, you'd better get to town if you are going to make it back in time to get ready for the ceremony."

Agreeing with her, I started down the drive. Beth, ignoring the attempts of my aunt and my grandmother to corral her, followed close behind.

Realization dawned on me. "Nona, I don't think she is going to stay in that pen. I think she is going to come with me whether I like it or not."

I stopped walking and Beth stopped as well, proving my point.

Bianca and Nona traded glances. "I suppose you will just have to take her with you for now," Nona replied. "I'll call the twins and make sure they know she is safe. When you come back, we will have a place ready to keep her contained."

I didn't have time for this. Frustrated, I addressed the goat, "Alright then. Come on, Beth. We've got to hurry."

As though she understood, Beth trotted forward to walk beside me. I lifted my head and set myself to ignore the inevitable stares of the people in town. I muttered under my breath, "Nothing to see here. Just a girl walking her goat."

Chapter Six

Beth and I wandered through the quiet town. Surrounded by farmland, it was no more than a few streets with slightly larger buildings. Everything about the place was small and had the old world feel about it. There wasn't even a traffic stop.

My muscles screamed from the activity and my bed was calling my name. Maybe if I got back quickly enough, I would have time for a nap before the rest of the Stregheria arrived.

Soon, Beth and I arrived at the shop where we could get the items on the list. I glanced around, unsure of what to do with her. "I don't suppose if I asked you to sit and stay here that you would listen to me, would you?"

The goat nuzzled my hand in an assuring way before she plopped her hindquarters to the ground. My jaw dropped. I'd never seen a goat 'sit' on command. I could just imagine what else Azra taught her.

Banking on the fact that she'd still be there when I got back, I went into the shop. It didn't take me long. When I finally emerged with my purchases contained in a small paper bag, Beth was still right where I left her. The wind kicked up causing my hair to fly into my face.

I swept the errant strands behind my ears. "C'mon Beth. It's time to head home."

"Stella? Is that you?"

I whirled around at the sound of my name only to come face to face with the one person I hoped I wouldn't run into on this trip—my ex.

"Matteo?" I asked, even though there was no doubt in my mind who it was. I hadn't seen him in over a year, but he'd hardly changed. His brown hair was just long enough to run fingers through. The sparkle in his brown eyes and the easy smile on his lips were the same that I remembered.

He opened his arms wide and drew me into a tight embrace while laughing. "It's so good to see you! When did you come back?"

I tried not to squirm at the tightness of his grip. To my still healing body, the hug was agony and it was a relief when he finally let me go. I had to remember to speak in Italian instead of English. "Our flight got in this morning. How have you been?"

"Fantastic! I started working with my father and my brother at the mill." He glanced down, apparently just noticing the brown and white goat at my side. "Is he yours?"

"No, she is not. I'm just taking care of her for a friend."

His easy smiled erased the confusion on his face. "Come, have supper with me. We need to catch up. I want to hear all about America."

To be quite honest, supper with Matteo sounded good. It sounded normal. Right then there wasn't anything I wanted more than normal. A flash of Ryan's smiling face came and went. Well, there was something that I wanted more than normalcy. The problem was that he had to go and ruin it so now that wasn't an option.

I was just about to say yes when Beth stomped her hooves against the cobblestone street. With her whole body, she pushed me away from Matteo. As irritating as it was, she reminded me that I was on a mission and that my thoughts should be on the coming ceremony.

"I'm sorry Matteo. I have to get these things home."

His hopeful face faltered a bit but he recovered it quickly. "It's alright. I'll walk you home."

"You don't have to—"

"I insist." He grabbed my hand and we started a

leisurely pace back toward my family's house.

Beth trailed behind us. I was both pleased and concerned that he hadn't let go of my hand. "How long will you be visiting?"

That completely depended on how tonight's spell worked and how fast the results happened. Having never done something like this, I hazarded a guess. "I think we are going to be here for a week or so. It's a short visit this time around."

"I see. How is life in America?"

"Busy. A lot busier than here. We moved out of L.A. We're living on the coast."

"And your brother?"

"Thomas went into the Army. He's somewhere in the Middle East right now."

He squeezed my hand consolingly. "I hope he comes back soon. I always liked Thomas."

I laughed, taking my hand out of his grip. "Even when he and the twins roped you into setting fire to Mrs. Frangellini's vegetable garden?"

"We didn't set fire to the garden," he chuckled.

I raised my eyebrows. "No? Why was she at my house complaining to Nona about arson?"

He licked his lips, a familiar gesture that meant he was getting ready to tell a story. The speed of his speech slowed. "It wasn't arson. It was an accident. Your brother got a hold of some bottle rockets. He wanted to see how fast my remote control cars could go with a rocket strapped to them. Of course, I was on board. I mean, rockets and cars? What self-respecting eleven-year-old wouldn't be? Anyway, we took the cars into my backyard and strapped the bottle rockets onto them. What we didn't account for was how fast and how hot those rockets burned. In seconds the plastic melted. The fire on wheels skidded through the fence and into Mrs. Frangellini's garden."

We laughed together over the memory. It felt good

to laugh, but, at the same time, I felt like I was betraying Ryan somehow. *Ridiculous*, I thought. *I shouldn't worry about him. What does it matter if I'm talking to Matteo? It's not like we are flirting or anything.* Still, my heart balked at the thought.

"We were able to put the fire out, but not before some of her plants were charred to a crisp."

"Your father must have been furious with you."

His mischievous grin held a hint of pride. "Yes, but he didn't like Mrs. Frangellini much anyway. It was my mother that made the most fuss. She forbade me to play with your brother or the twins ever again. All it took was a couple of days of me moping around the house for her mind to change. It was better for me to be out using that energy in play rather than pestering her the whole day."

"My brother was grounded for a week once Nona found out what happened. He was supposed to be old enough to know better. I can't remember what happened to the twins. They never mention it."

"How are the twins? You said you are living with them in America, yes? Did they come back with you on this trip?"

I made a face. "They aren't here, but Aurelia and her mom are. I hate living with Donatella. She's annoying and doesn't like to mind her own business."

He nodded, letting the information sink in and forming the inevitable question that was bound to come out. There was the space of a few heartbeats before he opened his mouth. "Are you seeing anyone in particular back in America?"

Ryan's face flashed in my mind. We walked in silence for a moment while I searched for what to say. "Yes, there was someone, but he left." The words sounded hollow to me and I hoped he couldn't read my face well enough to know how upset I was about it.

Matteo brightened at my answer, but then covered it up with a mask of concern, "Are you alright?"

I smiled a fake smile and lied to cover up the brokenness I felt, "Yeah. He wasn't important."

"I see . . ."

We stopped at the end of the drive outside of my family's main house. Beth remained positioned between us as Matteo gazed hopefully at me. "Are you sure you cannot have supper with me tonight?"

"Sorry, Matteo. I've got a family thing." The chest-fallen look on his face pulled at my heart-strings.

He went to give me another hug, but Beth prevented him by being in the way. We tried to maneuver around her, but she adjusted to remain in the middle. Finally, Matteo just hugged me over the goat.

"I missed you, Stella."

I fought against the feeling of his arms around me and the scent of his shampoo. I didn't relax into his embrace, but rather patted him awkwardly on the back.

"Listen, I'm pretty serious about the guy in America," I said when he let me go.

Matteo frowned. "You said he left you. It doesn't sound like he is too serious about you."

As much as I hated it that statement stung. Matteo had a point, but that didn't mean he could just come in here and try to get me back.

"It's too soon, Matteo," I said. "I just can't right now."

He grabbed hold of my hands. "Let me take you to lunch tomorrow. Just as friends. You can tell me more about America and what you've been doing for the last year."

Beth nuzzled the bag I was carrying and let out a pitiful noise. She moved to take a bite out of it and I swung my arm upwards to prevent her.

The goat stomped on Matteo's foot, intent on the paper bag. With a curse, he hopped backward, his left foot off the ground.

"Beth!" I admonished. "Why are you being so clumsy?"

The goat didn't even bother to look at me as she lowered her head in an obvious threat to the Italian boy.

"She is a protective goat," he said, forcing a laugh.

"I'm so sorry! Are you alright?"

"Yes, I'll be fine. You better get home or she will turn on you," he joked, limping more than a little.

"Are you sure you're okay?"

"I am, I promise. I'll pick you up tomorrow at one." He waved as he hobbled away, not giving me a chance to decline.

I stared after him, feeling at once grateful and also a bit sad.

There was a tug at my jeans. I looked down to find Beth staring at me with the fabric of my pants between her teeth.

"Stop that," I told her and swatted her nose.

She let go of my jeans and emitted an angry baa in my direction.

"I don't care. If you rip my jeans, I'll leave you here when I go back to America."

Beth backed up a pace or two.

"That's better."

"Stella!" Nona called my name from the front porch.

"Coming!" I shouted back and started trudging up the drive. It was time to focus on what I was here to do. Beth followed a couple of paces behind me.

"Was that Matteo I saw?" Nona asked as I climbed the porch steps.

"Yeah. He saw me in town and walked me home."

Nona frowned in disapproval. "You can't afford to be distracted right now, Stella."

"I know, I know. I just ran into him and he walked me home. That's it."

Her intense gaze studied me for a long moment. "Alright. Keep your focus on the task at hand."

"I am, believe me."

"Good. The others will be arriving shortly." She

regarded Beth with amazement. "I still don't know how you got here. The twins didn't even realize you were missing." Looking up at me, she took the bag and stepped forward to grab Beth's collar. "I will put Beth out into the pasture. If she winds up in your room, I expect you to get her out of the house."

I headed up the stairs just as Donatella came down.

"Where the hell have you been?" she demanded.

I grit my teeth as I pushed past her. "I had to go get some things for tonight." Without another word, I went to change for the ceremony.

My room was just like I had last seen it; the same posters and art projects hung on the walls and the bed still had the same quilt draped over it. The sameness was comforting.

My ritual clothing had been recently laundered and hung on the backside of my bedroom door. It was a simple white linen dress with a pale cord belt. A dark hooded cloak with deep inner pockets went over the ensemble. The rituals were usually performed barefoot. The pitcher of spring water next to the washbowl had sprigs of rosemary in it that leant a certain astringent aroma. Taking a cleansing breath and clearing my mind, I poured the water into the matching porcelain basin.

Stregheria spells were more ritualistic than my usual on the fly energy work. They had to be because it wasn't just one person putting power into the spell; it was thirteen. Rituals tended to focus group energy more efficiently. They also required even more focus than individual spells.

As I'd been taught how years ago, I blessed the water and the herbs, murmuring the familiar prayer under my breath.

Keeping my mind focused on the purpose before me, I washed with the blessed water, beginning with the top of my head and working down to the soles of my feet. I slipped into the linen dress, my mind alive with the spell work. As I tied the cord around my waist, a knock came at my bedroom door.

Aurelia's voice called out, "Stella, are you up?"

"Yes," I answered as I smoothed my skirt.

Aurelia came into the room. She was robed in the same white linen and a cord around her waist. The cloak draped over her arm and her golden hair fell loose over her shoulders.

"It's time to go downstairs. Everyone's waiting."

"Thanks, Auri. I'll be down in a second. I just need to get a couple more things together."

My cousin watched as I took a bundle out of my suitcase. "Do you even know what you are doing?"

"What?" I looked at her with surprise.

Her expression remained neutral, so it was difficult to tell if I'd heard the condescension or if I'd imagined it.

"I mean, do you know this will get the mirror back? Is this ritual a sure thing?"

I chose my words cautiously as I tied the bundle. "Nothing is ever a sure thing, Auri. But this is the best chance we have."

Glancing up, I saw her eyeing the roll.

"What is that?"

"This is the closest thing to a guarantee I can get."

Chapter Seven

By the time I made it downstairs, the three elders and nine others who represented the extended branches of the family had gathered in the family room. This coven did most of the magic for the Stregheria as a whole. Only a few family members showed magical abilities and even fewer were strong enough to even be considered for a coven position. I was lucky enough on my last birthday to be initiated as one of its most junior members.

Even after the cleansing that was supposed to calm me, I was more nervous than ever. So much was at stake and there was no other way to do this. Together, the Stregheria had protected the mirror for generations. They'd managed to hide the rarest, most powerful object in the world and to protect it for centuries. Maybe, just maybe, we could find it if we combined our strength.

I paused outside of the dining room to gather my thoughts. The sound of everyone talking all at once made each voice change into an indecipherable clamor. Words couldn't be distinguished, but overall tones of curiosity, worry, and impatience were felt. They were all waiting for me. With a deep cleansing breath, I entered the room.

The chattering voices paid me no heed. Nona sat at the head of the dining room table with Aunt Bianca to her right and Uncle Roderigo to her left. As soon as Nona caught sight of me hanging by the doorway, she held up a bony hand. With that simple gesture, it only took a matter of moments for everyone to fall silent.

If anyone questioned the level of authority my grandmother held, all they'd need to see was this show of deference.

When she was sure she had everyone's attention,

Nona lowered her hand. "Thank you all for coming on such short notice. As some of you may already be aware, we are here to retrieve something that was taken from us. Something that has been our family's responsibility to keep safe for many generations now."

"What is it, Sylvia? What has been taken?" inquired a hooded someone from around the table—by the voice I think it was my uncle Marcus.

Instead of answering him right away, Nona looked toward me. Several people followed her gaze as she spoke. "Stella, I think it is best that you explain."

Now everyone was looking at me and I felt a quiver of anxiousness.

Donatella snickered behind her hand with our cousins Lisbeth and Maria. Aurelia sat to the right of her mother, expressionless and waiting.

"The mirror," I started and then stopped, unsure of what to say. Wringing my hands together, I forced myself to begin again. "The sacred mirror was stolen a few days ago by an angel. I need your help to get it back."

Murmurs erupted as soon as my confession was uttered. My cheeks flushed with embarrassment and anger as I watched my family turn to my grandmother.

"Sylvia, how could you allow this to happen?"

"Why weren't we consulted about this?"

"Who decided this girl could be entrusted with something so important?"

"Why was the mirror allowed away from home in the first place? It would have been protected by the spells around the property."

Nona remained tall in her chair. Her eyes never left mine. As the questions grew louder and more insistent, Nona raised her hand once again in a gesture for silence.

The crowd quieted, though this time it took longer than before.

"Let her finish. There is more to tell."

Fifteen pairs of eyes retrained their attention and

waited for me to continue.

The urge to defend myself with excuses was strong, but I ignored it. Instead, I stuck with the facts of the matter. "I don't know why he took the mirror. I don't know where he is or what he's planning. What I do know is that we have to get it back. Protecting this object has been the duty of this family for centuries. I need your help, your power backing mine, to get it back to the safety of the family. Please."

It took a while for my plea to sink in. A lot of nervous shifting and a few coughs accompanied their consideration.

Finally, Marcus spoke. "I suppose you want us to help put a tracking spell on the mirror?"

Nona answered just as I was opening my mouth to do the same. "The mirror cannot be tracked. That was part of the spell that disguised it for so many years. My grandmother's inner circle enchanted the object into the appearance of a mirror and reinforced those protective spells around it. Unfortunately, that means not even we can find it. The spell they used was all inclusive. We have no choice but to track down the angel that stole the mirror."

"I know how to do it. I just need your help," I added.

The room exploded into a cacophony of noise. It was hard to pick out any one comment from the slew of exclamations and protests. Peppered through the loud arguing were demands for answers.

"Enough! Quiet down!" Aunt Bianca shouted as she got to her feet. She circled the room, eyeing the coven members fiercely. Once everyone was silent, she began to lecture us. "This is a fine way for family to treat one another. Stella is coming to us for help."

"She shouldn't have had the mirror in the first place! It should have stayed with one of the elders to keep safe," someone shouted. I couldn't see who it was, but it sounded like Lisbeth.

Donatella nodded in vehement agreement.

Aunt Bianca put her hands on her wide hips. "Does that change the fact that the mirror still needs to be found? No! Stop focusing on the past. We have the present to deal with right now. Anyone else have any reasons why we shouldn't help one of our own?"

No one said a word

Bianca turned to me. "Stella, we are with you. Tell us what you need us to do."

Relieved, I set the notes of the spell on the table. "This is my plan."

Within an hour, Nona and I led the Stregheria to the sacred space; a clearing just beyond the main house and surrounded by a ring of giant, ancient oaks. Inside the clearing was a circle made from old stones that defined the borders of the space.

Something was off. There was a nagging feeling at the back of my neck that we were being watched. I stood to the side and scanned the trees for any sign of movement.

"What's wrong, Stella?" Nona asked, noticing that my attention was elsewhere.

"Someone's watching. It doesn't feel safe."

Nona tsked, "There's nothing to worry about. No one will attack us. A long time ago, my grandmother's grandmother set up a spell around the property. If anyone crossed into our territory meaning us harm, their powers or their intent would be curbed. I assure you, we are quite safe."

Her reassurances filled me with confidence as we started filing into the sacred space. Before entering the circle, we each stopped and offered a small silent prayer. Nona entered the clearing first, followed by Roderigo and Bianca.

Many of the coven glared at me as they took their places in the circle, but they kept their silence. At least they were helping. I had to remain positive. At last, it was my turn to enter the circle. I stepped forward, my dress swishing against my legs, and paused at the boundary of the grove.

"Goddess, please let this work," I pleaded under my breath.

As I stepped over the threshold of the circle, there was a shift in the air. A subtle electricity that left my skin tingling and lifted my awareness. Usually, I would have taken my place along the edge with Aurelia, but tonight was different.

In the center of the clearing was a large, flat-topped boulder that served as the altar. As tall as my waist, the boulder was maybe two and a half feet in diameter. Its surface was pockmarked and edged in moss. The top already held the traditional items of ritual work: chalice, dagger, incense, candle, seashell, salt, and water. As the youngest members, the job of preparing the altar before ceremonies was left to me and Aurelia. She must have done it by herself when I was getting ready.

From within the folds of my cloak, I withdrew the rag I retrieved from Ryan's apartment along with the other specialized things I needed. After I placed the bundle on the altar, it was time to begin.

Like parts of a well-choreographed dance, the members of the coven began shifting clockwise. The chanting began in a whisper, but it grew louder and louder along with the pounding tattoo of bare feet on solid ground. I joined in the chanting, not leaving my spot at the altar. The words were old—older than I even knew. They rolled off of my lips, under my breath as though they were always there. I didn't have to think about them at all. The energy built between us flowed around our feet, solidifying our purpose. We sealed the circle, shouting in unison the final words of the chant.

As the echoes of our voice faded into the surrounding trees, we all turned to face the east. One of us spoke the incantation, calling forth the spirits of the east to serve as a guardian for the magic we were about to do. When they finished, there was a glimmer in the air above the eastern quarter of the circle; the guardian was there. Another member called forth the spirit of the south, then another the west, and the last the north. The crackle of energy, both ours and the guardians, was visible in the night air. It made the hairs on my arms stand on end. The power arched over us in a kaleidoscope of colors.

Finally, the opening of the ceremony was complete. Now it was time to get to work. I regarded the items on the altar: Ryan's bloody washcloth, my own blood on a square of fabric, the ball black ribbon, and a solitary white candle.

"By the Lord and Lady, by Diana and Apollon, I bless this ribbon. May it serve its purpose to bind and guide me to what I am searching for." I handed the ball of ribbon along with the ritual dagger to Nona. She murmured the same prayer and drew out a length of ribbon. She cut her portion and passed the ball along. Everyone followed suit, adding their energy and their will to each strand they cut.

While the ribbon and the dagger were passed around the circle, I focused my attention on the two pieces of bloody fabric in front of me.

In my mind, I drew the connection between the blood on Ryan's washcloth to the blood on mine. Bound and tied together, we could not run from each other long. As I twisted the two cloths together, I envisioned a cord, silver and shimmering, but strong as steel between us. When the image was in my head, I twisted two of the imaginary strands together in a thick rope around the two cloths and ended it in a knot.

The remaining ribbon made its way back to me. I said my prayer for strength and accuracy and cut my own length.

Nona approached the altar. "Is it ready?"

Wordlessly, I held the bundle of cloth by both ends and faced my grandmother. She took her length of ribbon and wrapped it around the bundle nine times. "Orion Gregory, son of angels, I bind thee to Stella Seraphina Evangeline, daughter of this Stregheria. Never will you go anywhere that she cannot find you. Never will you hide from her what is hers. I bind you to her in this realm and the next. As above, so below, by the Lord and Lady make it so."

She tied her ribbon and took the bundle from my hands. When she finished, she faced the person to her right, Roderigo, and held the bundle for him as he tied his length of ribbon around it, also nine times, and repeated the spell.

All around the circle the knot went, covered by lengths of black ribbon. Each knot was another layer to the binding, another layer of power over my own. As the energy collected, the charm started to glow; dim at first but growing stronger. Just as energy gathered in the object, clouds and lightning gathered in the sky above. Thunder cracked above us as if in response to the power we were raising.

Auri held the wrapped parcel out to me, now completely covered in shining black ribbon. I started the chant, infusing power into each syllable, into each word. The ribbon went around nine times and I tied it off, completing the shell of energy around the pieces of fabric.

The effect it had was almost instantaneous. A rush of images overcame me; dizzying pictures of blurry faces and strange buildings. A cacophony of voices, all screaming at the top of their lungs overtook my ears. It was all so fast and so loud that there was no way to make any sense of it. With the bound cloths still clenched in my hand, I tried to cover my ears and closed my eyes, but the sights and the sounds wouldn't go away. Hands caught hold of my arms and held me steady on my feet. The whole Stregheria surrounded me and kept me from falling to the ground.

"We must finish the spell," I heard Nona say through the noise. "Quickly now!"

She was right; there was just a little more to go. Blocking out the noise and the sights, I refocused my mind on the task at hand. Power seethed off of the bundle. There was so much energy that it made my hand go numb.

I grasped onto it and shouted the final words. "Orion Gregory, I bind you to me by the power of Diana and the Stregheria that follows her. I vow that I won't stop until I find you and what was stolen from me! As above, so below!"

Lighting flashed and thunder boomed above us. The energy stored in the binding shook its way through my limbs. The noise and the images faded. My senses were my own once again.

There was a crash and, at first, I thought it was another burst of thunder; the sky flared brightly. It wasn't lightning. Someone had broken through our circle. The kaleidoscope of colors that bubbled around the clearing flared before sputtering out altogether. Many of the Stregheria screamed in distress. Confusion and alarm swept through the group. Another crash sent several people scattering to the edges of the clearing.

The circle had broken. All of the power we'd harnessed released before it was time. It spiraled up and out of the protective boundary, sucking up the energy in the circle out into the universe. The result was that most of the Stregheria's energy was immediately drained.

We were defenseless.

Chaos ensued as a glowing figure hovered over us.

Squinting, I barely made out the form of a man with giant wings surrounded by a light that swirled around him in tendrils. A sword unlike any I had ever seen shimmered with an otherworldly glint. It seemed to be made of the brightest metal that was almost incandescent.

The members of the Stregheria screamed and tried to find cover. With our powers drained, there was nothing we could do to defend against a magical attack.

The figure didn't attack us. Instead, it flapped its giant wings and lowered itself down to the ground. The closer it got the more I could make out a blindingly bright breast plate, sandals, and luminous tunic. Bracers encased the wrists of what appeared to be a man. His hair was blonde and blown back from the wind revealing a stern but familiar face.

"Azra?" I asked, dumbfounded.

The figure's gaze rested on me and at once I felt small and insignificant at the feet of this majestic celestial being. His sword arm swung slowly from his side and he pointed the ethereal blade at my face.

"Strega Girl," his voice boomed louder than thunder and resonated within my chest. It took a lot for me not to bow my head away from the terrifying sound of my own name. "Where is my goat?"

Chapter Eight

"W-what?" I stammered.

"Beth. Where is Beth?" the echoing thunder-like voice repeated.

Confusion prevented me from doing anything but stare at the glowing blade with mounting horror. Before I could think to speak, Nona stepped between me and the angry Grigori. Armed with only the ceremonial dagger, she infused it with a small bit of the energy she had left. Within seconds it was glowing and she touched its tip to the angelic weapon. "I would thank you to not point that thing at my granddaughter."

He yelped as though he had been stung and dropped his sword, completely breaking his intimidating front. The sword itself disappeared.

Azra looked livid. His tanned skin reddened. He opened his mouth to say something, but before he could utter a single syllable, his power disappeared. All that remained was the Azra I recognized; a tall, lean surfer in blue board shorts and flip-flops.

Panic made his eyes widen as he realized his powers were gone. "Why you conniving little—"

A cloak was flung over his head by some of the Stregheria who had been waiting for the protection spell to take effect. Two of them latched onto the angel at his sides, pinning the cloak over him.

Azra struggled and kicked. He swung his arms violently, but the couple of hits he made were by accident. It took no less than four coven members to restrain him. Muffled shouts and barely intelligible curses issued from under the cloak.

I had to get this under control. "Aurelia, go get Beth. I don't think we will be able to talk to him until he knows she is safe."

My cousin set off toward the house at a dead run. The rest of the Stregheria encircled the still fighting angel, ready to help the four keeping Azra down at a moment's notice.

"You told me anyone who came with the intent to harm us wouldn't be able to," I said to Nona.

"It seems there was a delay. The spells may need refreshing. I will talk to Bianca about it later."

Uncle Marcus, who had been holding Azra's legs, lost his grip. The angel thrashed, kicking Marcus in the face and the chest. With his legs free, he used them to gain traction to propel the other two family members backward. Off balance with a flailing angel, it was only a matter of time before one of them let go. The rest of the Stregheria descended upon the Grigori, resolute on keeping him in place. In the struggle, the cloak slipped from over his head.

"Let me go this instant you wart covered goat-thieves! I will not be man-handled by some no good, cheating, goat stealing, half-rate magicians!"

"Silence!" Marcus yelled and punched Azra in the head. "You attacked us!"

It didn't stop the angel from slinging more insults and curses in both English and Italian.

Soon, Aurelia returned, leading Beth on a rope. Nona patted the goat affectionately as she took the makeshift leash. When she had the animal in hand, she signaled for Azra to be released. The ones holding onto him traded terrified glances as they did what Nona bid. They scrambled away from the irate angel as fast as they could.

Azra jumped to his feet, fists in the air, ready to take on the whole coven. I expected him to attack immediately, but the sight of Beth brought him up short.

Nona offered the leash to Azra. "I believe this is who you were looking for?"

"Beth!" Azra dropped his fists and grabbed ahold of the goat's neck. "Beth you are okay! I've been so worried!"

"I assure you that she has been well taken care of," I said, stepping forward. I wanted him to focus on me so the brunt of his anger didn't go onto anyone else in my family.

The angel glared at me from over the goat's neck. He finished looking her over and then stood up to face me. "Strega Girl, when I asked you to watch her, taking her out of the country was not in the bargain. How could you do that? Without leaving me a note or anything?"

"We didn't take her with us. We left her in California with the twins. I don't know how she got here. She just showed up this afternoon."

Azra scowled. "You expect me to believe that? She's a goat. She can't just appear places."

"Whatever," I replied. I didn't feel up to arguing with him.

"Is that the only reason why you are here? To get the goat?" Nona asked.

"That and to tell your curse happy granddaughter that her quest is hopeless. Ryan doesn't want to be found. She is out of luck." Azra removed the rope from Beth's collar, doing his best not to make eye contact with Nona. Every so often, he would swivel his head around, making sure we all stayed put and no one would ambush him again. Beads of sweat popped up on his brow. "Now, I have fulfilled my end of the bargain. We have no more business. I want the hair you took from me so I know you and your other Sanderson sister wannabes aren't going to do anything with them."

"No," I spoke up, realizing this was my opportunity. "No, I still need your help. We just got done with a spell that will lead us right to Ryan." I held up the bundle of black knots by the excess ribbon.

Azra laughed, but it was a nervous sort of chuckle. "Us? As in you and me? You don't honestly believe I'd come along on that fools journey, do you?"

"I have a little piece of hair and a curse that says you will," I countered.

A smug look crossed Azra's face. "Oh, I've thought of that." From the pocket of his board shorts, he pulled out a large, sparkly something on a cord. As he held it aloft, I saw a glitter-dipped Christmas ornament of a pink flamingo with one or two bright pink feathers glued to it.

"What is that?"

"This is my protection from your shenanigans. An old shaman in Florida said it would prevent any curse you could throw at me!"

"I'm game to try," I said, convinced that he was lying. A glittery flamingo ornament couldn't keep him safe. Especially in Stregheria territory.

"I did what you asked! Ryan is in hiding and he knows enough that if he doesn't want to be found, he won't be. I can't make him come out to play. Now, give me back my hair."

"Why? You just said your little flamingo would protect you from any curse. What does it matter if I keep the hair?"

"It's bad form to leave bits of yourself in the hands of the enemy. Give me what is mine and Beth and I will get out of here with all our pieces." He withdrew a pink leash studded with rhinestones from his board shorts pocket. After clipping it to Beth's matching collar, he put his hands on his hips. "Well? Hand over the angel DNA."

I crossed my arms, determined not to budge. "No. There's still something I need your help with."

When he realized I was serious, he made a face. "Fine. It's been real, Strega Girl. No offense, but I hope I never see you or your collection of Hogwarts rejects again." He closed his eyes and waited.

Nothing happened.

He screwed up his face and concentrated even more.

Still, nothing happened.

Squinting one eye open, he checked his surroundings. When he saw me, he opened both eyes and balled his fists at his side. His tanned face deepened to an ugly red flush. "What the hell did you do? Why can't we leave?"

I'd never seen him so angry and the prospect of it took me by surprise. Even without his armor and his weapons, he was a formidable enemy. A furious enemy that we were now stuck with.

"Because you threatened the Stregheria, a protection spell was activated. You aren't going anywhere. You are stuck in the circle until there isn't any more danger to my family"

The fury on Azra's face had my heart thumping with fear. I had to remind myself that he didn't have any power and we far outnumbered him. Then again, we didn't have any power either.

The other coven members shifted anxiously. It seemed they were itching to remove themselves from the circle and away from such a dangerous threat. I had to give them credit; they stayed with us.

Nona continued to talk in a low, calm voice. "I give you my word that it will wear off on its own. Until then, please, let's discuss the situation like civilized people."

Azra's face turned sour. "There's nothing to discuss! I'm not helping you. If Ryan played you, then too bad! I don't know what to tell you besides I raised him better than that!"

I interrupted whatever my grandmother's response was going to be by stepping closer to Azra. "Can you just pretend to understand the importance of what we are trying to do, please? If what he stole gets into the wrong hands the entire world is in danger."

"That is not my problem!" He started easing backward, small steps at a time. He kept as many of the Stregheria in sight as possible. "Holding me and Beth hostage isn't going to change the situation."

I opened my mouth to argue, but he found a way out. Quick as lightning, Azra picked up Beth, dodged both Marcus and Bianca and made a mad dash to the edge of the circle.

He ran head first into the border of energy at the edge of the clearing. The spell my great-great grandmother placed was still strong; there was a sharp crackle as though a power line had fallen. A bright flash of light accompanied the sudden sizzle that permeated the air. When the light faded, and I was able to see again, Azra was on the ground.

For one horrifying moment, I thought he was dead. Then his arm twitched and I breathed again. Azra got to his feet. Beth, unscathed, nibbled on the grass on the other side of the circle.

The Stregheria gathered around Nona and me, ready to protect us if necessary. Though what exactly they could do without any powers, I didn't know.

Nona stepped beyond the protection of the family to face Azra. "You are stuck here until the spell wears off. So let's talk. The least you can do is hear us out."

The angel cast a wary look at the other members of the coven. "If I agree to listen, then when this hocus pocus is done, none of you will stop me from leaving?"

"As the matriarch and the high priestess of the Stregheria, I give you my word."

Azra's mouth twitched as he considered his options. There weren't any and he knew it. At last, he caved. "Fine. Start talking."

Nona and I glanced at each other for the barest of moments before I began speaking. "I know where Ryan will be, but I need you to take me to him. I can't travel as fast as he can. If I could just talk to him I could get the mirror back."

Azra scoffed. "Even if you could catch up to him, what makes you think Ryan will listen to you? He's made his choice."

"Do you know what that mirror can do?" My frustration laced my tone. I couldn't help it. "That is a sacred object from a goddess. It has the power to obliterate life as we know it. My family has protected it for centuries. We have to get it back."

He offered no response, no argument; he just sat back with a contemplative expression.

"Prove it," he said finally, "prove you can track him."

Unsure, I glanced at my grandmother. She gave me a single nod. It was time to find out if my spell worked.

Breathing deeply, I centered my thoughts on Ryan and clasped the knotted bundle in front of me. In a sudden burst, random images flashed through my mind. They overtook my senses until I couldn't discern the grove or my family around me.

The sun was setting wherever Ryan was and it was warm—warmer than it should be for February. Moisture-sucking wind pressed against him. He travelled in a convertible. The noise from the wind and the road overtook all other sound. The scenery was sparse. Prickly looking shrubs and a brown landscape blurred together in a drab kaleidoscope of desert. The smell of dust and exhaust assaulted my nose. A sign appeared along the side of the road. Tucson 21 miles, it stated.

A giddy feeling erupted in my chest. The spell worked!

With effort, I brought myself back to the grove. The desert faded, replaced by the sight of my family and the stars in the night sky above me. I was on my back with Nona and Bianca hovering over me.

"Tucson, Arizona. That is where he is," I said, still trying to get my bearings.

My aunt and my grandmother helped me up. Nona

looked both proud and concerned all at once.

Azra stood a few feet away with his arms across his chest. "Why on earth would he be in Tucson? There's nothing there except for a couple of piss poor fraternities."

I shrugged, still adjusting to the odd sensation of being in two places at once. Now that the channel was open, I wasn't sure how to close the link down, or if I should. "I don't know, but that's where he is."

"How do you know this?" Disbelief was written all over his face.

"I told you, it is a spell. This is where I need your help. By the time I got a flight to Arizona, they could be in Cairo. I'd never catch up to them."

Azra crossed his arms and pursed his lips. "You think if you get to him, you can make him give you back that thing he took?"

"Yes. That is the general idea."

"What about Ascher? How are you going to handle him? Last time you two squared off he ended up possessing you."

Nona raised her eyebrow at this new information.

I kept my mouth shut and lowered my head, not sure how else to respond. I didn't know what I would do if I came face to face with Ascher again.

"That's what I thought." Azra stood up and brushed the dirt from his board shorts. "As lovely as this meeting has been, I'm not going to help you."

My head snapped up and I rose to my feet. "You have to! I can't do this alone!"

"No, I don't have to. Just because you say he is in Arizona doesn't mean he's really there. I'm not convinced that you can find him. Even if you somehow, miraculously *do* manage to stumble on him, you have no way to make him do anything. It sounds like a colossal waste of time; time that Beth and I could spend training for the upcoming surf competition in Maui."

"If Ascher has the mirror, he can use it to take out most of the world's population. Consider the mirror a weapon of mass destruction. You can't just say 'oh well' and move on."

"Like hell I can't!" Azra roared.

"Enough of this," Nona interjected. "I don't like this any more than you do, but if we are going to get the mirror back, then risks need to be taken. If we are going to keep this world safe, then we have to overcome our own reservations and work together. You are the only way that Stella can get to Ryan quickly enough. What's more, you can offer her some protection against Ascher and even Ryan himself."

The glare Azra gave us was enough to make my resolve waver. His arm fell to his side and he summoned his blade from thin air. How he was able to get it after the protection spell had been activated, I'll never know.

"You know, I'm not supposed to hurt humans, even if they are witches. That doesn't mean I won't. I've already given you my answer. Now, I'm giving you one more chance to let me go. If you don't, then I will be forced to hurt you." He raised his weapon, ready fight his way out of the circle if need be.

My grandmother's usually calm and serene face grew hard. She took precisely measured steps toward Azra. There was no trace of fear in her eyes as she got within striking distance. The Stregheria drew closer as well, ready to defend their leader.

Azra looked panicked, but he stood his ground.

Nona touched the glowing blade aimed at her chest. The angel gasped, but other than that, there was no sound. With her hand in contact with the weapon, its glow dimmed until there was nothing but a tarnished metal blade. The power of the weapon balled in my grandmother's hand; a crackling, pulsing sphere of electricity sparking in the night.

My own mouth fell open. I didn't know Nona could

do something like that.

She held the ball of power and, with her other hand, she peeled bits of energy off of it as though it were an orange. All eyes were on her as she began talking. "While I don't like the idea of Stella going off to do this, it is something she must do. You will go with her because if you don't, then this entire coven will curse you for all eternity." She flicked the piece of the energy at Azra. He jumped back out of reflex and it sizzled in the grass at his feet. There was an expression of abject horror on the angel's face.

None of this made my grandmother pause. She continued, her eyes fixed on Azra as she kept playing with the energy she stole from his weapon. "Our grandchildren's grandchildren will continue the curse long after we are gone. I guarantee that everything you hold dear, your goat, your surfing, will be impacted. The results will not be pleasant." She flicked another bit of energy at him, which he tried to dodge but failed. He cried out in pain when the celestial energy touched his skin. "You know I can deliver on my promise. You know how powerful I am; I can see it in your eyes. Do you want to put your faith in a cheap plastic flamingo ornament to protect you against me and my family?" By the time she finished speaking, she was inches away from Azra. The ball of energy sizzled and she held it up to him, waiting for his answer.

A mixture of anger and fear crossed the angel's face. He was in a corner and he didn't like it one bit. If I were in his shoes, I don't think I would have liked it either. Ultimately, he dipped his head in a brisk acquiescing nod, never taking his eyes off of my grandmother. "Fine. But I want it known that I am doing this under duress."

Nona gave a grim smile. "So noted." She held the ball of energy to the metal blade. It absorbed back in as though she had never taken it. "Stella, you best get ready. Azra wants to leave soon."

Chapter Nine

I wanted to leave immediately, but practicality called for at least a change of clothes. The Stregheria, along with an angry Azra, trooped up to the main house to wait.

Leaving Azra in the parlor with my family, I raced upstairs to my room. I could only carry my messenger bag, so I had to be selective about what I took. I traded my ceremonial clothes for a pair of jeans, good hiking boots, layered shirts, and my hoodie. The first thing that went into my bag was Nona's Book of Mysteries. If I was going up against angels and demons and who knew what else, then I'd definitely need the knowledge contained in that book. I crammed a flashlight, a lighter, some of my magical tools, as well as a spare change of clothes. The knotted bundle of ribbon went into my pocket. There was no telling how long I would be gone or how far this journey would take me. I just hoped I had everything I'd need.

With my bag slung over my shoulder, I clomped down the stairs.

Nona met me at the bottom of the stairwell.

Seeing her alone caused a slight bit of panic. "Where's Azra? The rest of the family?"

"Azra is outside with Beth, waiting. Marcus and Bianca are there with him to make sure he doesn't leave without you."

"Good," I moved as if to pass her, but she held up her arm, stopping me. "Are you sure you want to do this? It's not too late to change your mind."

Her question was out of place with the forceful woman who threatened an angel ten minutes ago.

"Of course I'm ready. It's the only way we are going to get the mirror back."

Her eyes searched mine for more than a few heartbeats before she said, "Very well then." Slipping a ring off of her finger, she pressed it into my palm. "Wear this. It is a protection charm that my grandmother gave to me. It will help keep you safe."

I eyed the opal and silver ring with sadness. It took the simple act of Nona giving me a protection ring for it to hit home that there was a chance I might not come back.

"Thank you." I put the ring on my finger and flung my arms around my grandmother.

"Just promise me that you will be careful out there, Stella." She sounded close to tears and she hugged me a bit tighter.

"I promise," I whispered.

At last, she pulled away. "Best not to keep him waiting. Max will check in on you from time to time. If you need help, all you have to do is summon him. Do you have everything?"

"I think so."

Together, we walked out the front door.

Just as Nona said, Azra and Beth were waiting for me in the front drive. It seemed they were in the middle of an argument. Well, Azra was arguing. Beth chewed on some grass. Aunt Bianca and Uncle Marcus stood to the side, watching the angel and the goat. When they saw Nona and I come out, they started walking toward us.

"I don't think this angel is completely right in the head," Bianca whispered. "He's been arguing with that animal for the last ten minutes."

As if to punctuate Bianca's statement, Azra growled, "All I'm saying is that you don't always have to agree with her. Would it hurt you to back me up once in a while?" When he caught sight of us and he stood up straight, stiffening his spine as though bracing for a particularly nasty impact.

"Ready?" I asked him.

He made a face at me.

Nona gave me another quick embrace. "Be careful. Remember what I told you. If you need anything, let Max know."

"Thank you. I'll be back with the mirror." I cast her, Marcus, and Bianca one more smile before I went to meet up with the waiting angel and goat. I asked him, "Do I close my eyes and click my heels or something?"

Ignoring my question, he gestured to my messenger bag. "You pack light for a girl. That's good at least." He jumped up and down, waving his arms above his head. It looked like he was getting ready to run a marathon or something.

When he finished stretching, he said, "Rule number one. Do not distract me. You can look around and ogle all you want, but don't talk to me. I have to keep focused to get us there in one piece."

"One piece? What do you mean 'one piece'?" I couldn't keep the alarm out of my voice. It was the first time I even considered that Azra couldn't travel with me safely.

"Rule number two," Azra went on, "keep your legs and arms still. Any flailing on your part will throw off my trajectory. We don't want to end up in Tulsa when we are aiming for Tokyo. Rule number three, no magic shenanigans while in flight. I have no idea what it will do, so don't even try it. And finally, rule number four, in case of an emergency water landing, hold your breath. Any questions?"

Reflexively I held up my hand to get his attention. "Yeah. What do you mean by one piece?"

A grin spread across his tan face and I swear that his blue eyes lit up with mischievous glee. He didn't respond. Instead, he scooped me up into his arms, making me squeak in surprise.

"Rule number one," he reminded me. Before I could open my mouth again, I buried my face into his shoulder. A hum emitted from the back of his throat that was surprisingly loud from behind closed lips. It was a deep, melodious sound that made me both sleepy and alert all at once.

My body slipped into stillness as easily as though I was meditating; my mind was as sharp and observant as ever.

Air rushed around us and while I could hear it, I couldn't feel it. Logically, I knew we had to be moving, but it felt like he was just holding me. After a while, I chanced a look around. It was all just a smear of colors. My eyes strained to pick out individual objects, but my brain wasn't cooperating. Dizziness overcame curiosity and I pressed my face against Azra's shoulder once again.

The humming continued, making me relax. For the first time, I understood the phrase 'voice of an angel'. It was strangely comfortable nestled in his arms. My breath evened out and my limbs grew heavier. I sunk into the dream.

Memories whirled around me just out of reach. I chased after them. They were like butterflies following a breeze and they rose higher than I could reach. The feel of grass was thick and soft against my skin. I found myself laying under a large elm tree, my hands clasped around something on my stomach. Curious, I looked down at the heavy object. It was the Book of Mysteries, except it was different. This one was oversized and the binding was much coarser than mine or Nona's.

"Little witch, little witch," a voice jeered on the back of the breeze. Alarmed, I got up, allowing the book to fall onto the grass. There was no one near. I scanned the branches of the tree, but only saw the rustling of leaves.

Something was off about this place. The tree wasn't

normal. It was dark and sinister; its leaves muted shades of black and gray. Picking up the book, I held it close against my chest, my fear building . . .

"Wake up!" Someone shook me roughly. "We're here."

Groggily, I opened my eyes to a dry, sparse landscape of dirt. I was laying on the ground with Beth not too far away. Nothing looked familiar. There was just a pervading sense of dry. A sudden craving for water nestled itself in the back of my mind. "Where are we?"

"A few miles outside Tucson. You said you could find Ryan. So? Where is he?"

I raised myself up to a sitting position and looked around. No buildings were in sight. As far as the eyes could see there was just brush and rocks. In the distance a mountain stood out against the flat land like a beacon. "I don't know where he is."

The angel rounded on me, looming over my sitting form. "What do mean you don't know? I kept my end of the bargain and I fully expect you to keep yours."

"It's not an exact science!" I shouted back. "I can tell the general area where he is, not his precise location." Frustrated, I got to my feet. What was I supposed to do now?

Azra ran his fingers through his hair. "You conniving little witch. You tricked me. I should just leave you here and let your family come and get you."

I got to my feet. "Don't you dare! Let's just think a minute. You know Ryan best. Is there anywhere he would go in town? Or even where Ascher would go?"

Though I was sure he was angry enough to disappear, he paused. I could see the wheels turning in his mind, working out where they would have gone. That pause to think proved that he really did want to find Ryan, even if it was just to ask why. "I don't think they would stay anywhere near my safe house and I don't know where Ascher's are."

I sighed and looked at the horizon. A city, even one as small as Tucson, Arizona was a lot of ground to cover.

Azra continued, "There is a way to find out if they've been around."

"How?"

"Ascher is working with Fallen Ones. It just so happens that we Grigori can find Fallen Ones like a valley girl can find a mall."

"What? Is that a good thing?"

He groaned. "I forget how damn young you are. Yes, that is a good thing. We Grigori have an internal radar for demons. It means I can find a Fallen One and strong-arm it into telling us where Ascher has been. Maybe we can even confirm Ryan is with him."

I dusted off my jeans and picked up my bag. "Let's go then. Where do we start?"

"We start with lunch. Can't hunt Fallen Ones on an empty stomach," Azra replied, tugging on Beth's leash. He started walking and I had no choice but to follow.

Two hours later, we sat on the patio of an upscale vegan restaurant outside of the University. It was then that I decided Azra was full of shit. Beth, tied to the fence next to us, was the topic of many passersby. We had already eaten. Well, Azra had already eaten; I was too anxious to eat anything. The waitress had even delivered the check, but he still wasn't ready to go.

"Come on, Azra. We need to find Ryan." It had to have been the twentieth reminder in the last thirty minutes. Azra was too busy smiling at the college girls who stopped to pay attention to Beth to listen to me. The goat couldn't care less about the simpering, high-pitched squeals the girls affected when confronted with an animal on the street. Azra was eating it up.

"Yeah, she is a fierce surfer. Really tears up the waves."

I slammed my foot into his shin under the table.

Azra winced and told the three sorority girls, "Excuse me for a moment." He got up from the table and grabbed my arm, jerking me to my feet. He led me over to an empty corner of the patio and hissed, "What is your problem?"

I wrenched my arm out of his grip. "My problem is that we are sitting here wasting time when we should be out looking for Ryan. You said you can find the Fallen Ones and they would lead us to Ascher. Why aren't we doing that now?"

"That is exactly what I am doing, you ignorant little snot!" The words passed his lips so forcefully that spittle flew out and into my face. "I have to get the lay of the land first. Then I can figure out the most likely place to find the bastards."

"How are you doing that by flirting with anything in a skirt that walks past?"

The angel closed his eyes as though he were counting to ten. "Trust me. I've been hunting these things far longer than your family has been terrifying small children. I know what I am doing." He walked back to the table before I could raise my argument again. Affecting an easy-go-lucky smile, he announced, "Sorry, ladies. Where were we?"

It was my turn to close my eyes and center myself. He did have a point; he had been hunting Fallen Ones for millennia. Who was I to question his methods? At the same time, it felt like we were standing still and I couldn't afford that. It was time to take this to the next level and maybe get something out of this place before Ryan was completely gone.

I walked back to the table and sat down. By then, the college girls had moved on, still giggling over the goat and the friendly surfer that was so out of place.

"How much longer do you need to figure out where they are?" I asked, picking up my drink. There was mostly ice left, so I jabbed my straw at the frozen clumps, breaking them apart.

"Not long. We have to wait until nightfall. They won't come out during the day usually; it's too bright for them."

"So they're like vampires?"

He rolled his eyes. "You know, what is it with you people? Vampires aren't the only supernatural creatures that come out at night. Besides, they are rare. The likelihood of you coming across a vampire in this day in age is slim to none."

"Okay, okay, sorry," I put my cup of ice down. "They come out at night, gotcha. What do they look like, exactly? What do I need to be on the lookout for?"

He sipped his beer and looked around the street. College kids roamed all over the place with their bikes, backpacks, and skateboards. Even with school in session, the street teemed with life.

"What do you know about Fallen Ones?"

"They are fallen angels, specifically the ones who sided with Lucifer."

He looked moderately impressed. "Good. What else?"

That's when I drew a blank. "They are . . . bad?"

He couldn't keep the smirk off of his face if he tried. "Well done, Strega Girl. I can see you don't need my help at all."

I stuck my tongue out at him. "Just tell me."

"Only since you asked so politely. Waitress? Another round of that wonderful hummus, please. Can I also have another beer? Oh, and another Shirley Temple for my friend here? Thanks."

"Water, please," I corrected the waitress. She gave me a sympathetic nod and went off to the kitchen, scooping up the untouched bill on the way. "Azra, how can you still be hungry? You've done nothing but eat since we arrived."

"If I'm going up against an army of Fallen Ones, I'm gonna need the energy. Besides, everyone has room for more hummus."

"Whatever. Just tell me what I need to know about the Fallen Ones."

"You've already got the basics. Used to be angels, did the ultimate skydive. They come up to earth whenever they can and make life a living Hell, if you pardon the expression, for some hapless mortal."

"How? Like possession?"

Azra nodded, "That's one way. Let's just say that they are super nasty things without much sense of hygiene or common decency. Now, the important thing for you to know is how to dodge them and how to defend . . ." He trailed off in the middle of his sentence. His eyes widened and he flattened his palms on the table.

"What?" I turned to look over my shoulder to see what he was gaping at.

"No!" he hissed and reached out to jerk my chin back toward him. His eyes never wavered from the spot behind me. "Don't look! He'll see you."

"Who?" I whispered back. "Is it Ryan? Ascher?" I was terrified, but I was also desperate to see who Azra was talking about.

"Shhh!" he admonished.

I struggled to keep my eyes on the angel, waiting for some sort of sign on what to do next.

Instead of saying anything, he stood up, his chair scraping against the concrete. The sound was almost deafening.

Just as I was about to ask again what was happening, he broke out into a run. He dodged tables, waiters, and hungry people with moderate success. Among the startled cries and the crash of dishes hitting the floor, Azra bellowed after whichever poor soul he was gunning for. "Stop, Hellion! Creature of Sin! Satan's Spawn! I say stop right where you are!"

A Fallen One? In the middle of the afternoon? Hadn't he just told me that they only come out at night?

I wasted no time in untying Beth's leash and pulling her after me as I followed Azra's wake of wreckage.

Beth and I burst out of the restaurant to the open street. The crowd wasn't so thick that I couldn't see the two figures dashing toward the red brick of the University gate.

I took off after them, the goat keeping pace with my run. When we reached the University, I was breathing a lot harder than I should have been. The driveway to a house with a sign proclaiming "Old Main" was on an incline. By the time I reached the ivy-covered avenue of red buildings beyond Old Main, my legs were burning. Dammit! I needed to get into shape.

Azra and his quarry ducked behind the Sciences building. There was a suspicious lack of traffic along the bike path between that and the adjacent structure. That was where Azra had finally caught who he was chasing.

He had the person pinned against the wall and was shouting in a language I couldn't understand. The words sounded old and, knowing Azra, they were probably offensive.

"What's going on?" I gasped.

He moved and I caught sight of the perpetrator. It was the palest human being I'd ever seen. No, not human. There was something not right about the thing's eyes. There was no other way to put it than they were just wrong. I remembered seeing eyes like that before. The night on the beach when Ryan and I fought for our lives came to mind.

An overwhelming anger surged through me when I realized that Azra had a Fallen One in his grasp. It was the first one I had seen since the night of the attack. Blood rushed to my face and all I could hear was the echoes of that night. My hands balled into fists.

"Hey!" A male voice called out from behind me.

"Leave that demon alone!"

I turned, only to be roughly shoved aside by a man shorter than me. He flew at Azra, grabbing him by the arms and pulling him off the Fallen One.

The creature wasted no time in running away, leaving Azra thrashing against the human who struggled to hold him back.

I dropped Beth's leash and ran to help Azra. The man kept himself behind the angel, never giving him an opportunity to get a firm grip. I snatched at the man's jacket, pulling it back as hard as I could.

"Get off of him!" I screamed. It didn't do any good. I had to do something else.

Reaching deep into myself, I brought my power up, infusing my words and braiding those around my intentions. The power filled my hands until they glowed with it. Still muttering the words under my breath, I placed my hands around the man's neck.

My intention was to render him unconscious, kind of like a forced sleep, just to get him off of Azra. But that wasn't what happened.

He slammed his head backward, knocking me squarely in the forehead. The blow sent me off balance and before I knew it, I landed hard on the decorative gravel and rocks.

He spun around and when he saw me, he shrieked so loudly that I covered my ears. "Stay away, you blasphemer! You will not enchant me away from the service of the Son!"

Azra didn't let the confusing declarations get in the way of punching the screaming man in the face. It shut him up. Another shove from the angel had the man on the ground next to me. He sat there stunned for a second, blinking.

"Help me hold him!" I shouted as I grabbed the man's sleeve. He thrashed against my touch. Azra tried to hold him down.

Somehow, despite both of our efforts, the man squirmed free of us. As he got to his feet, he shouted, "The Son will punish you for your insolence. His enemies will be defeated even as his followers exulted!" He bolted.

Azra and I looked at each other, both at a loss for words.

Finally, Azra muttered, "Well that was weird."

Chapter Ten

"What do you think he meant? About the Son?" I struggled to keep up with Azra's pace as we searched the University. "Do you think he knew the Fallen One?" Adrenaline pumped through me as what the man said turned over in my mind.

"Stop asking me questions! Look, you have a job to do. Hurry up and find Ryan already."

"I told you, it doesn't work like that. I just get visions of where he is and what he's doing. It's not like GPS."

Azra's lip curled. "So have another vision already and let's get this done with. What happened just now is incredibly strange. No human has ever interrupted the hunt before. It's not a good omen." Anger mingled with worry made his words clipped. He kept glancing around as though he expected an ambush from either a Fallen One or another human.

"You're right. Come in here. Let's see if I can narrow down the search." I motioned to an empty classroom. When the door closed behind him and Beth, I pulled the ribbon charm out of my pocket and squeezed it in my hands. My eyes closed and I focused my thoughts on Ryan. Soon all sense of the room around me faded.

I was outside. The sun beat down on the large, rusting metal structures surrounding me. It took a while to understand that they were planes. Or at least they were once planes. Most were scrapped; whole sections were missing—noses, wings, even landing gear.

Standing next to these giants that once glided through the sky caused a twinge of sadness to lance through my heart. Was this what would happen to me once I'd outlived my usefulness? Would I end up buried in some forgotten field and only able to look up at the sky I'd never fly again?

The sudden emotion caught me off guard. These strange bits of aching desolation weren't coming from me. Gravel crunched under my feet as I made my way around the skeleton of an old war plane.

There were four people standing in a circle. I recognized Ryan immediately, but the three others I didn't know. They were all well-dressed, certainly over attired for the dusty plane graveyard. The two men and the woman looked more like they belonged in an office building somewhere.

As I crept closer, I noticed someone bound and gagged on the ground between them. It was a woman who had to be somewhere in her late fifties. She'd been stripped naked. Dirt and bruises decorated her sagging skin. Her gray hair, peppered with dark brown, was jagged as if cut by a dull knife. The woman sobbed. Tears and snot dripped down her gaunt face. It was a terrible sight.

"What did she do?" Ryan asked. I could barely hear him over the woman's crying. Still, his tone was bored and disinterested.

The tall, dark, lanky one next to Ryan answered. "It doesn't matter. All you need to know is that she is the enemy. You must prove you truly are on our side."

"This is unnecessary, Ascher," Ryan told him. There was an edge of frustration in his tone. "I am here. I haven't been in contact with my uncle. How many times do I have to prove my loyalty?"

Ascher placed his hands on his shoulders. "It is interesting that you bring up the subject of your loyalty. You understand, of course, if I am a little skeptical of your intentions."

"You have no reason to doubt me or my intentions."

"What about that little stand on the beach? You

managed to put a decent dent in my personal guard, you and that little Strega."

Ryan's face darkened and his violet eyes narrowed. "I was playing a part, Ash. I've explained this over and over again. I had her trust. It was only a matter of time before I got the mirror from her. You had to kill her in that pointless display of power."

Ascher inclined his head to the side. "Nevertheless, you will forgive my caution. If you want me to believe that your loyalty is with us, then you must follow orders."

"What orders?"

"Kill the woman."

Ryan blinked. "Kill her? Why?"

The two Fallen Ones smirked at Ryan's questions.

Ascher glared at them and the amusement drained from their faces. He then took a couple of steps forward so that he was standing over the crying woman. His boots were inches away from her tear-soaked face. He stared at her before kneeling down and brushing a tear from her smudged cheek.

"This woman is a witch. Quite a dangerous one, in fact. She and others of her kind stand against everything we are trying to accomplish." He faced the young angel. There was a maniacal light in his eyes. "Well? You now know why she has to die. It's time for you to prove yourself."

Ryan didn't move. His expression was blank.

A few minutes passed and Ascher chided, "Don't tell me you are going to be as much of a disappointment as Azra."

The unreadable expression Ryan hid behind morphed into one of disgust. He drew his Celestial Blade from the holder at his side. Two strides and one definitive swing of his blade separated the woman's head from her body.

The vision ended, sending me back to the classroom at the University. Azra stood over me, his hands on his hips.

"Well? Where is he?"

Words refused to come as I reeled in what I'd just seen. Ryan had cut off that woman's head! He did it without even blinking!

Breathing became difficult. My skin felt hot and ice cold all at once. What had I just seen?

The urge to throw up became overwhelming. I launched myself off of the floor and sought out the garbage can, just in case.

The weight of what I'd seen and heard centered in my chest like a ton of bricks. A secret part of me hoped none of this nightmare was true that it was all some sort of sick joke. I privately held onto the faith that Ryan wasn't the bad guy he was acting like. I wanted him to still be on my side. I wanted the hope that once we found him, everything would be sorted.

Everything I'd just witnessed dashed that hope, that last bit of faith I had in him. It left me heartbroken and terrified at what Ryan had become. Or maybe he'd always been like that. Maybe the person I thought I knew was the lie. Perhaps this was the first true glimpse of the real Ryan.

There was no way to hold back the tears this time. All the emotions I'd successfully kept at bay since waking up in the hospital crashed over me like a tidal wave. Everything: the anger, the fear, the hurt swirled inside my mind in faster and faster circles. Throughout was a pervasive sorrow that latched onto my soul and would never let go. Overwhelmed and heartbroken, I sat on the thin, gray carpet of the classroom and cried.

"Whoa! What in the blazes is going on?" Azra stepped backward as though the tears sliding down my cheeks were some sort of deadly acid.

I shook my head and did my best not to hyperventilate. If I could just concentrate on breathing evenly, this panic attack building in my chest wouldn't get any worse.

"Why are you crying?" Azra panicked. "I swear, you fell over on your own. I did not push you!"

The shouting angel only made me cry harder and the explanation of what was happening still wouldn't get past by teeth. My reactions were beyond my control. I finally purged the built up emotions since this whole nightmare began and there was no way to stop it, no matter how much Azra yelled.

I curled into a ball, clutching my bag and sobbing dejectedly into it. Time stood still as I rehashed all of the hurt and betrayal and the heart-rending realization that I had really fallen for Ryan and there was nothing I could do about it. I couldn't reconcile the two versions of him in my mind.

Azra stood uncomfortably to the side, clutching his elbows with a distressed expression. He sat down next to me and offered a tentative pat on the back.

At last, I couldn't cry anymore. My face was damp with tears and snot by the time my breathing became even and measured. The pressure in my chest was still there; I wasn't sure it would ever go away.

"What was all that about?" the angel asked. "Is this some sort of medical condition? I knew I should have had you sign a waiver."

"No," I sniffled. "I saw Ryan."

"Yeah, that's what you're supposed to do." He waited for a few heartbeats. When I didn't say anything more, he asked cautiously, "What's with the waterworks?"

"Ryan," I hiccupped. "They were in a junkyard with airplanes. He—he cut off a woman's head." The words were hollow and somehow surreal as the image replayed itself in my head. The weight over my heart imploded into an endless aching pit. "I thought he was trying to protect me somehow. Now . . . Now it's all horrible and I don't know who he is anymore."

Azra was quiet for a long time. When he did speak, it was slow and halting. "Listen, I'm not going to pretend I have any idea what you're talking about. I get that you're upset, but I'm not going to sit here and hold your hand because you're all," he waved his hand in front of my face, "emotional and whatever. It seems to me you've got a choice here. Now that you know what we are up against, do you want to keep chasing after him, or do you want to give up and go home?"

I wiped my face on my arm as I contemplated his question. There was a sense of finality to it; as though this was the only time he would give me this option. What I decided here and now was what I would have to live with for the rest of my life.

"There isn't a choice," I replied. "No matter what, I have to get the mirror back."

He nodded. "Alright then. We will catch up with Orion. But for the love of Pete's dragon, no more crying! Do you know how much uglier you are when you cry? It's unnerving."

I couldn't help but laugh.

Azra stood and gave me a hand up. "You said there were a lot of scrapped planes in your vision?"

"Yeah. The place was full of them."

He smiled. "I know where they are."

We were too late; there was no sign of Ryan or Ascher when we arrived at the plane graveyard in Tucson.

Well, that's not quite true. What we did find was the headless body of the woman I saw in the vision.

Finding a dead body was nothing at all like they show in the movies. I was completely taken off guard by not only the sight of the corpse but the smell of it. The coppery tang of blood and a strange, foul odor I couldn't identify permeated the air. Nausea overtook me.

Azra let out a curse under his breath as he inspected

the area. "Ryan couldn't have done this. There's no way."

If I hadn't seen him kill her, I would have said the same thing.

My hand covered my mouth as I surveyed the scene. The body had been moved so that she was on her back with her arms and legs splayed out. Strange drawings in black paint encircled the body.

I asked from behind my hand, "What are all those drawings?"

"I should be asking you. Those are witch runes."

If it wasn't such a serious situation, I would have laughed in his face. "Witch runes? What are you talking about?"

He gestured at the etchings around the body. "Those sigils. They are how your kind gets in contact with whatever unholy spirits you've tricked into doing your bidding. Don't act like you don't know what they are."

I frowned at the dark lines in the dirt. "I've never heard of any such thing." Walking around the circle of scribbles, I paid close attention to the setup. Candles stood at the four cardinal points. The barest traces of energy thrummed along the border of the circle.

"What kind of a witch are you? Obviously, this woman was a sacrifice of some sort."

I shook my head and kept my eyes on the corpse. "She wasn't sacrificed, she was executed. I saw Ryan chop her head off. I think they wanted this to look like some sort of ritual though. They staged the body like this and they took her head."

"Well, Ryan and Ascher aren't here anymore. Come on. We need to get out of here before the police show up."

I didn't understand his logic. "Why would the police show up? No one has been here except us and them. There's no reason they'd come here."

"Stop and think. If you're right and they did stage this to look like something a witch did, then they wanted it to be found, yes? Anonymous tips to the local police aren't exactly difficult to make. Now come on. We need to reconsider our plan anyway."

I took the angel's hand, giving a final look over the gruesome scene. If I hadn't watched her murder in my vision, I wouldn't have thought Ryan capable of such a thing. How could I have misjudged him so much?

***

Azra and I spent the next six weeks chasing after Ryan. Every time we thought we'd finally caught up to him, we were too late. As time pressed on, the visions grew stronger and stronger. There was no telling when they would show up. Soon, I wasn't just witnessing the horrible things that Ryan did; I was living and feeling it.

The acts he committed were too terrible to mention. More often than not, I'd jerk out of the visions screaming. Sleep was elusive and, when it did find me, so did the vivid nightmares rehashing the reality of how monstrous Ryan had become. Over those six weeks, more screams of pain and fear assaulted my ears than I ever wanted to hear in my lifetime. The smell of burning flesh mingling with wood smoke made me gag on more than one occasion.

Once, with me tagging along in his mind, Ryan decimated an entire village high in the mountains. Only a handful of humans survived and they were grotesquely disfigured by not only Ryan but a small group of Ascher's defected angels and demons. They laughed as they cut into the human flesh.

Another place, another group of people, but the screams and the smells were the same. He wasn't slinging a sword around this time. Instead, he focused on one human; a man who was intent on binding a girl who was no older than me to a stake in the ground. He broke her bones in the process. When she was secured, he began his gruesome work. With a stone knife, the man flayed the skin off the girl who shrieked against the dull, wet scraping noises. The man was glassy-eyed and vacant. Ryan controlled his actions, forcing him to do those sickening things.

I think I could have handled it if all I saw were those horrible moments; those hours of torture and pain he inflicted on other people. There would have been a clear line in my mind that he was not at all the person I thought I knew. No. It could never be that simple. Ryan wasn't always a monster.

When he was sure no one was looking, he made sure the survivors had enough food or that another village would take them in. After the remains of the dead had been burnt, he left flowers in the ashes and cried at their passing. He acted out small penances for the devastation he brought. It was enough to make me wonder why. What sort of game was he playing? There was no way to reconcile the two versions of Ryan I witnessed. I wasn't sure how much more I could take of these conflicting visions.

Sometimes there wasn't any destruction. I'd find him sitting in the quiet of an afternoon, sketching in a book. He always drew my face. These images were even more confusing because I felt the longing and the sorrow the thought of me brought him.

I grew to hate the visions, to resent the link I had with Ryan. Even though I couldn't read his mind, I still sensed his emotions. When he did those atrocious things, there was a certain grit, a sort of resignation to his actions. What's more, he didn't feel complete; a dark hole grew inside of him and he locked it up tight. I didn't want to know what he was holding back.

As time pressed on, I came to realize this entire venture was so much more than just getting the mirror back. He and Ascher waged a war on witches of all kinds across the globe via targeted attacks and torture. The more I stood witness to, the more enraged I became. Finding Ryan was no longer my only goal. Now, I wanted vengeance for my magical brothers and sisters.

Another sparse room faded into view. Ryan sat at a card table with a pad of paper and a pencil in his hand. He sketched his lines with confidence. His companions—the same group he usually went raiding with—sat in the other room conversing amicably enough. It was a rare, relaxed moment.

Ascher opened the front door accompanied by a brisk wind of snow flurries and ruined the calm. In his hands were two garment bags and a large black suitcase on wheels which he pulled using the extendable handle. Ryan's companions glanced up, but didn't move from their seats.

"It's all ready," Ascher announced, flashing a toothy smile. "We put our plan into action tonight."

Ryan didn't even look up from his sketch as he responded in a monotone voice, "You mean your plan. I have nothing to do with it."

Ascher chuckled. "You will. After all, you're the star. Here, I brought you some clothes. Go get changed. You need to look your best tonight."

Ryan got up from his seat and took one of the garment bags from the other Grigori. His movements indicated nothing but indifference. "Where are we going?"

"We are meeting with some of the great world leaders this side of the globe to put forward our human pawn to serve as the political focal point. Once he is in position, our armies can infiltrate the humans that follow him. It will be easier to have the majority of the humans working for us, rather than against us. That will be Mr. Xiao Ming's job.

"Your job will be to learn everything you can from this event. I want you to learn how these humans think, how they work, how they interact with each other. Who

they talk to, and what we can use against them if need be. Tomorrow, we will start preparing you for your next upcoming task."

With a sneer on his face, Ryan took the garment bag into the bathroom.

Once the door closed, Ascher sat at the table. He picked up the pad of paper that Ryan had been drawing on and eyed it speculatively. "Has he made any attempt to contact his uncle or this girl?" he asked the room in general.

The two Fallen Ones on the couch shifted and glanced at each other. The one with the long stringy black hair and round face answered, "Not at all."

Ascher continued gazing at the piece of paper. "I assume any escape attempt would have been reported. How about the human? Does he know that she is alive?"

The Fallen One shook his head. "No sir."

Ryan emerged moments later dressed in a stunning tux, complete with a jacket with tails and a top hat. "Is this necessary? I hate dressing up."

"You look good," Ascher assured him with a smile. He picked up the pad of paper that Ryan had been drawing on. "Are you still hung up on this trollop?" The question was joking, but the intent was piercing.

Ryan shrugged, unmoved by the matter. "It's something to draw." His heart beat a little faster.

Ascher considered the young Grigori. "I'll make sure you have better inspiration tonight. It's not at all fitting that you should be so preoccupied with a dead witch."

Ryan kept his face neutral though a chasm of pain lanced through his mind. "If you insist."

Ascher took his own garment bag and went to the bathroom.

Ryan crossed over to the table and gazed at his drawing. "Stella," he whispered. There was the merest hint of regret in his voice. Abruptly, he folded the drawing and stuffed it into his pocket.

Chapter Eleven

"Why is it so cold?" I shuddered in my hoodie, wishing for the umpteenth time that I'd packed more clothes. Who knew there were so many places in the world that snowed?

Azra stuck his tongue out to catch the snowflakes falling from the sky. He only had on his typical board shorts and flip-flops. "Because it's Russia. Everything is colder in Russia. I warned you it would be cold when we dropped off Beth in New Zealand to graze."

The last vision of Ryan and Ascher getting ready for some sort of event had brought us to St. Petersburg. It felt like it was late at night, but I couldn't be sure. We'd bounced at least five different time zones in the last hour. It could have been six in the morning for all I knew.

I was exhausted and in desperate need of rest. "You said you have a place here, right?" I asked, rubbing my arms to warm up.

Azra put his tongue back into his mouth and gave a quick glance around the snow-filled street. "Yeah, it's not far from here. You aimed us pretty good this time, Strega Girl. Much better than when we went to Dubai."

"That wasn't my fault!" I objected. "You're the one who landed us in the middle of that business meeting. It also wasn't my idea to start screaming the second we appeared in the conference room."

"They could have been a threat. I was trying to protect us. You humans are often scared off by the sudden appearance of a shouting madman. Besides, that building wasn't there the last time."

I scoffed. "Look, let's just get somewhere warm. I'm going to freeze over any second now."

Azra took my hand and the now familiar sensation of teleportation washed over me. When the wind died and I could focus, we stood inside the kitchen of a dark, cold, rundown house.

I looked at the drab rooms with interest. Of all the "safe-houses" Azra had, this one seemed to be the oldest and with much less care given to it. The furniture was clean but worn to the point of being threadbare. It was in complete contrast to the other upscale residences he had all over the world.

Before I could ask, he told me gruffly, "Upstairs there's a fireplace in the bedroom that's still in working order. I think I left enough wood in there to get it started. Go light the fire."

"Where will you be while I'm heating up the house?" I inquired.

The angel shrugged. "I'm just going to set a perimeter. Maybe there will be some sign of Ryan. I'll be back soon in any case."

Usually, I would argue and insist on going with him, but I was tired and it was too cold to fight. A fire sounded more than amazing.

"Fine. Come get me if you find anything, deal?"

"Sure." He eased the door closed behind him.

The stairs creaked as I went up. A few times I was sure they would fall out from under my feet, but they held steady. Old wallpaper peeled from the walls, exposing the crumbling drywall and the wood boards underneath. The bedroom looked comfortable; a large bed occupied the center of the room. To the left was a large and ornate fireplace. In front of the hearth were plush beige couches angled against each other. Dark throw pillows piled on top of the cushions. Between the couches was a wrought iron coffee table that supported a small metal statue of abstract art.

It was high time to check in. Nona would be wondering what was happening. The last time I contacted Max was right before the incident in Belize. That was when I had him take a message to my brother so he knew I was alright. There just hadn't been any time to call home since then. As I started a fire in the grate with the stack of wood next to the fireplace, I summoned Max. I felt his presence in the room just as the fire caught and started to grow.

"What a dump," Max scoffed.

"Hello to you too." I got to my feet and faced the apparition. He looked solid, almost like a real person. He wore his usual fedora and the tails of his trench coat swished around his legs as he strolled around inspecting the room.

"How goes the mission?" he asked. His hands tucked into his pockets and he looked anywhere but me. "It's been two weeks since we heard anything from you."

"We think he is here with Ascher. There have been rumors of a big party happening out here. A lot of Ascher's recruits were heading this way, so we thought we would check it out."

Max nodded, keeping his lips shut as though he were swallowing something bitter.

"What's wrong?" I asked. Usually Max had an opinion about everything Azra and I had done over the last six weeks. This sudden distance put me on edge.

Max answered almost casually, "Your grandmother wants you to come home."

"What?" I blinked, waiting for him to explain.

"It's been too long. You haven't gotten anywhere. Nona thinks it's time other measures are taken, measures that don't put you in harm's way."

I couldn't believe what I was hearing. "When I left, Nona understood how dangerous it was going to be and how long it might take. There is no other way. This is it; this is the only option we have to even have a chance at finding the mirror."

"And Sylvia thinks she made a mistake," Max

countered. "Consider the information you've asked me to bring back to her, for one second. All the horror stories of the torture Ryan's committed and the vivid descriptions of the carnage you and that oaf Azra have stumbled across. Did you think she'd just accept you getting in way over your head with every step you take toward this angelic idiot?"

"That angelic idiot is the only way we are going to get what's ours! Max, I am not giving up now. I can't. We are so close."

Even though I protested, the point Max and Nona wanted to make already hit home. Ryan had become more dangerous, almost too dangerous to keep tracking. Based on the visions and the first-hand accounts of the survivors Azra and I found, Ascher had himself a perfect little protégé who was every bit as sadistic and brutal as he was. It scared me more than I wanted to admit but it also pushed me to find him. Someone had to hold them accountable for all of the unspeakable acts they had committed.

I squashed down my apprehension and told Max, "Look, I appreciate the concern, but I'm fine. Go back to Nona and tell her I'm safe and that I'm not coming back without the mirror."

Though Max looked like he wanted to argue, he didn't. Instead, he asked, "Do you want me to at least stick around until that moron Azra gets back?"

"No. He's not going to be gone long. I'll call you again if we find Ryan." I turned my back on Max and started feeding more sticks into the growing fire. Eventually he left and I was alone once again.

I was staring into the flames, gripping the charm in my palms when the vision came over me.

Ryan sat in the back of the limo, gazing out the window and looking bored. On his left arm, was a woman, a Fallen One. She had a sinister sort of beauty with sleek black hair and sharp features. Dressed as if she was going to a Hollywood premier, she watched the passing streets from the opposite window.

Ascher was on Ryan's right, speaking in depth with a middle-aged Chinese man who sat across from them. Both wore tuxedos, like Ryan. There was another female Fallen One in the car. She had red hair and dressed similarly to her counterpart. She toyed with her diamond bracelet.

The car came to a stop in front of a plain, nondescript building. Ascher led the party up the steps murmuring something to the guard. The door opened and they were all admitted.

The interior was classier than the run down outside façade advertised. It was aglow with soft lights and candles. A band played in the background and many elegant people mingled with champagne flutes in their hands.

Ascher and the red-head integrated into the crowd followed closely by the Chinese man. They laughed and greeted people warmly. The other woman had hooked herself onto Ryan's arm. Together, they wandered through the throngs of people. Two goons followed Ryan at a respectful distance, obviously watching him.

They passed the dance floor and the woman leaned closer to Ryan and whispered something into his ear. He shrugged and together they whisked themselves onto the dance floor, moving with the grace of professionals. They made it through one song before a horrible pounding echoed through the room.

The band fell silent at the ominous sound and the room's chatter came to a halt as everyone turned to stare at the front entrance. The banging was strangely patterned, a staccato of varying intensity.

The door burst, barely hanging on its hinges. A man strode confidently into the club. His shaggy blonde hair in disarray and his tuxedo jacket askew. Besides the jacket, he wore a pair of bright blue swim trunks, a pair of flip-

flops, and a black bow tie around his neck. Coughing, he adjusted his jacket and smoothed back his hair. "Hi," he addressed the room, giving a small wave. "How's it going?"

People began talking again, whispering about the intrusion and speculations on whom it was.

Ryan rubbed his temple, looking to the point of fury at the appearance of his uncle. Turning, he strode off the dance floor.

Azra must have spotted him because he followed in a hurry. "Orion!"

Ryan pushed through the crowd with the woman still in tow. She slowed him down enough that Azra was able to catch up to him.

"Where are you going? Do you know how difficult it is to find you lately?"

His shoulder's tensed as he faced his uncle. "What are you doing here?" He kept his face blank and his back stiff.

"I've been looking for you!" he approached Ryan and gave him a huge hug. After pulling back, he straightened Ryan's jacket, smoothing out the lapel. "Where've you been? Why did you leave like that?"

Ryan remained stiff. "You wouldn't understand."

Azra's eyes flashed and his demeanor changed from relaxed to tense. "What exactly wouldn't I understand?"

Ryan met his uncle's glare head on and said as simply as possible, "Anything. You kept me sheltered and naive. You kept me from realizing my true potential."

"I protected you."

Ryan let out a rough, biting chuckle. "Protected? Smothered is more like it."

Azra narrowed his eyes and folded his arms across his chest. "So what? You decided that you had enough of me and then to leave without so much as a goodbye?"

By this time, a small crowd had gathered around them, listening to the odd exchange. Ascher spotted the disturbance and went toward them. "Azra, my friend, it is nice to see you. Still have your quirky sense of style, I see."

Azra clenched his fist and started forward. At his movement, the oversized guards adjusted so they were between him and a smug Ascher. Azra halted, realizing he was outnumbered. Taking a final chance, he pleaded with his nephew, "Come back. Stella's been worried about you. She wants you to come home."

Ryan's features darkened at the mention of the girl. When he spoke, his voice pitched low and dangerous. "Stella is dead." He turned his back to his uncle.

Azra wasn't about to allow him to go like that. "Orion, you're being a coward."

The words tipped Ryan over the edge. In a violent jerk, he whirled around and shoved Azra. There was a loud collective gasp and immediately the guards who had been standing on the side lines grabbed hold of Azra. Ryan lunged forward as he wrapped his arms around his uncle's midsection. There was so much force it propelled both of them and the guards into the crowd.

The sheer volume of people made the scuffle more confusing. Punches were thrown, elbows violently crashed against faces. All in all, the fight lasted no more than a minute before more guards came in to break it up.

Once Azra and Ryan separated, Ascher spoke above the hushed conversations of the gawking crowd. "That was spectacular. Azra you never fail to amuse. You understand we do have a strict invitation-only policy. I am going to have to ask you to leave. John, Laramy, please escort my friend here out. Make sure he doesn't come back."

The two Fallen Ones who held the intruding Grigori by both arms began shuffling to the door. Azra shook them off and straightened his jacket with dignity. "I will see you again Ash," he warned.

Ascher grinned in a sort of delighted anticipation. "I don't think so, Azra."

As his uncle was forced out of the room, Ryan turned his back and disappeared into the crowd.

The hotel suite was richly decorated. There was a couch in front of the fireplace and to the left of that was a large table. Ryan burst through the door, flinging his coat onto the floor. The woman who had accompanied him to the party followed more sedately and closed the door behind her.

"What the hell was he thinking coming here like that?" Ryan fumed. He stalked back and forth between the couches and the table.

The door to the suite opened and Ascher sauntered in with the red-head on his arm.

Ryan came around the corner to confront the older Grigori. "You promised he wouldn't be able to find me."

Ascher, having hung his coat and removed his gloves, went to stand across from Ryan. "I made no guarantees. What he had to say was interesting, don't you think? Your little witch alive and well?"

"He's lying. She was dead when I left."

Ascher eyed the young Grigori. "Are you certain? There's no way that your little witch could still be in the land of the living?"

Ryan turned his back to Ascher, obviously upset. "Azra is lying."

"I wonder why he would stoop so low as to lie about something like that," Ascher mused. "It doesn't seem like him at all." The Grigori pondered the situation, watching Ryan's reactions carefully.

The door to the room burst open and one of the guards stepped in. After a hasty bow of his head, he stammered, "Ascher, sir, something happened."

"Yes?" The Grigori tore his attention away from Ryan to focus on the nervous Fallen One.

"He escaped. The one you wanted us to kill."

Ascher drew in a sharp breath. "How?"

"I- I don't know, sir. He k-killed John and Laramy."

Ascher gave a swift, dismissive wave and the trembling Fallen One backed out of the room with sheer relief etched on his face.

Ryan asked, "You trusted Fallen Ones to kill Azra? That was stupid of you."

The older Grigori didn't respond. Instead, he closed his eyes as though he were praying for patience. Finally, he said, "Ladies, I thank you for your companionship this evening, however, I believe it has come to an end."

The two women didn't say anything; they simply gathered their purses and rose gracefully from their seats. Ascher took both of their arms and gave Ryan a polite nod before leaving. Ryan watched them go keeping his face a neutral mask.

When the door closed and he was alone, he rubbed his eyes with his palms. When his hand fell from his face, he placed it in his trouser pocket, and withdrew the note that Azra had slipped him during the fight. He read through it quickly, the information burning itself into his memory. When he was sure he knew every word, he tore it to pieces and scattered them out the window.

Picking up his sketchbook, he flipped it open. A rough drawing of the girl he thought he left behind stared at him from the page. To the sketch, he whispered, "Why did you have to come looking for me?"

Azra shook me out of the trance. "Strega Girl, wake up." He sounded weary.

Blinking my surroundings into focus, a rush of emotion flooded through me. I jumped to my feet and shoved the angel hard. "You left me here alone so you could get to him first. How could you do that? I thought we were in this together."

Azra stumbled backward. "Whoa, watch it! You had a vision, I take it? Look, I went after him alone for your own good."

"Yes, I did have a vision. What do you mean this was for my own good?"

"Then you saw what happened. He doesn't want to

come back."

I shouted at the top of my lungs, I was so furious. "Go back to the part where confronting Ryan without me was for my own good."

Azra heaved a sigh and sat on the couch. I stayed standing, my hands on my hips and waited.

"Let me ask you this. What you would have done if I took you to that party?"

Before I could open my mouth to answer, he said, "You'd have made a giant spectacle of yourself."

"What do you think you did?"

He inclined his head in a solemn nod. "Yes, but Ascher never thought I was dead. If you showed up slinging spells, they would have taken you out immediately, no questions asked. I doubt you would have even spoken two words to Ryan."

Begrudgingly, I had to agree. "Alright fine. Now what? You saw him; he's not going to give up and come back home. What do we do now?"

Azra ran his fingers through his hair. "This is the hard part. We wait. When Ryan and I fought, I slipped him a note. I told him you were with me and that you had to talk to him. I asked for him to come alone."

Alarm and a strange thrill ran through my body simultaneously. "Will he come?"

The angel shrugged. "There's no way to know."

***

My nerves kept me up late into the night. Azra had gone to keep watch after urging me to get some rest. There was no way I could sleep; I was on the verge of confronting Ryan myself. There were so many things I wanted to ask him, so many explanations I wanted to hear. On the other hand, I wasn't sure if I would be able to sit by and let him speak. I'd seen him do so many terrible things, I didn't think I could hold myself back from simply attacking.

There was another part to this inner conflict though. A secret part of me that I was ashamed of because I was excited to see him. I couldn't get rid of the butterflies in my stomach just like I couldn't unsee those quiet moments where he sketched my face over and over again. Were they real, those feelings I saw in him? Would it change anything if they were?

All of these questions and plans were worth nothing if he didn't show up.

I fed the fire and waited, anger and longing warring inside of me. It was two forty in the morning when I felt someone else in the room.

Assuming it was Azra coming to check on me, I called out, "I promise, I'll go to sleep. I just want to make sure the fire won't go out."

"Stella?" The voice didn't belong to Azra. Surprised, I whirled around to see a tall, shadowy figure next to the door. The outline was familiar. A thrill coursed through my veins and my heart beat wildly.

"Ryan?" I called out, daring to peek at the darkness outside of my circle of light.

Chapter Twelve

"What the hell are you doing here?" Ryan demanded as he strode forward into the light. His face contorted with anger or frustration, I couldn't tell which.

I didn't truly expect him to show up because when I finally confronted him, I choked. All I could do was stand there, stunned as he came toward me.

Even angry, the sight of his violet eyes made my breath catch in my throat. He looked the same as he always did; strong nose, thin, gangly frame, brown hair just long enough to shift every time he moved his head. There were so many things I wanted to do, so many things I'd plotted out in my mind and I couldn't recall a single one right then.

"You need to leave now!" His face was only inches away from mine and he seized my arm as though he intended to throw me out himself.

It was his sudden tingling grip on my arm that broke me out of my motionless state.

"Don't fucking touch me!" I yelled. Immediately, I jerked out of his grasp and sent out a current of energy between us. It zapped him as it went up and it was satisfying to see him jump back because of it. Remembering the visions about Ascher's protégé, the fear came on a wave of nausea. I had to stuff it deep inside and hope it didn't show.

Ryan, for his part, looked just as surprised as I had been. He recovered quickly and repeated in low, urgent tones, "You need to get out of here. It's not safe."

Him telling me what to do just pissed me off even more. I lobbed a ball of energy. "I'm not going anywhere until you give me answers."

He narrowly dodged the missile and headed straight for me. Before I could react, he had both of my wrists in his hands to prevent me from doing it again.

In return, I drew my arms back to bring Ryan closer and raised my knee to his groin as hard as I could. Wrenching my wrists out of his hold, I danced away, putting the coffee table between us.

Still doubled over, he gasped, "I'm serious. If they know you're alive, this will end badly."

I couldn't tell if that statement was a threat or not. Boldly, I stood my ground. "I'm not leaving."

"Dammit, Stella, just listen to me!" This time I caught the desperation in his voice.

Steeling my heart against his plea, I kept in mind the acts of terror he'd committed against my fellow witches. Heat coursed through my veins as a fresh wave of anger washed over me.

"Why should I listen to you? I've seen what you've done. You're a monster!"

Ryan winced at the words. Still, he didn't back down; he inched closer, with his arms outstretched as though to calm a wild animal.

"Don't come any closer!" I demanded. To punctuate my point, I drew a line of power between us. Green static filled the air.

That finally stopped him in his tracks. Each of us eyed the other, calculating the next move.

At last, Ryan broke the silence between us. "You don't understand."

"Oh, and I suppose you are going to tell me that what I saw wasn't what it looked like? That I am taking things out of context? You killed witches, Ryan! You inflicted so much pain and horror on innocent people!" With every word, more emotion poured out of me. The barrier between us flared brightly, fueled by my rage.

"How do you know what I've done?" The question sounded hollow. He wasn't even trying to deny any of it.

For a brief moment, I wondered how much to tell him. "A spell. I've had visions of you doing unspeakable things. By the time Azra and I get there, it's too late to stop you; we just see the carnage you leave behind."

Ryan didn't look at me; he kept his eyes on the ground and his arms hung at his sides. When he spoke, it was quiet and low. "Did you see what I did to help the survivors? Or the tears I've shed for the ones who died? How about the whole reason why I've had to do those things? Did your visions show you any of that?"

I crossed my arms over my chest, not wanting to be swayed. "What was the reason? What could possibly make you do such horrible things?"

He raised his head and made eye contact as he said, "You."

With that single syllable, he made everything I thought I knew disappear. My breath caught in my throat. Covering up my discomfort, I raised my chin and replied, "In case you've forgotten, you're the one who abandoned me after stealing my mirror. How exactly have I made you do a damn thing?"

Ryan sighed and gestured to the barrier of energy. "Can we please talk?"

"We are talking."

"Please, Stella. Sit down and I'll explain everything."

I considered the angel standing before me. His demeanor pleaded with me to give him a chance. Did I trust him though?

The whole reason why I'd been chasing after him for the last six weeks was to get my mirror back. When I'd seen the devastation he'd caused, my reasons for finding him increased to include finding out why. This was my one chance to get the answers I needed. I couldn't afford to let my anger get the best of the situation.

After weighing my options, I reluctantly dropped the energy shield. He breathed a sigh of relief before gesturing to the couch. "Please, sit."

Taking the farthest seat from him on the beige couch, I crossed my arms and waited. Ryan had enough sense not come any closer than he had to and sat at the opposite end, maintaining his distance.

I didn't say anything as he gathered his thoughts. When he began, it was halting and unsure, as though he was scared of the words that were about to come out.

"I didn't think you would be—"

"Alive?" I interjected.

"Here," he corrected. "I hoped Az had enough sense to get you away from here."

I pursed my lips to prevent from interrupting. The silence built up around us, cementing the tension in the air.

"I suppose I should start at the beginning." Ryan leaned forward to place his elbows on his knees. His hands clasped in front of him and he kept his face to the crackling fire. "The decision to go wasn't easy. You were unconscious and in the hospital. The doctors said you would live, but no one could say when you'd wake up.

"Ascher hurt you so badly . . . I knew if I didn't leave, if I didn't lead him away from you, Ascher would kill you just to get his hands on the mirror. So I took it and I went to Ascher. I had to convince him you were dead. " His violet eyes met mine as he said this and, for a brief, flickering moment, I saw the pain hidden in their depths. He was telling the truth.

Trembling with barely restrained anger, I asked, "Did you give him the mirror?"

Ryan let out a bitter laugh. "I've done some stupid things, but giving Ascher the mirror would have been the ultimate. If he had it, the whole world as we know it would be gone by now."

"What do you mean?"

"Ascher's on a mission. He's supposed to bring the mirror to his 'Lord and Master'," he raised his hands in quotation marks. "I doubt he actually intends on delivering it. Despite all the promises he makes his employer, he wants to be the one that ends all three realms—Heaven, the underworld, and earth. If he does, then he will take everyone down with him in this suicidal spiral. He will stop at nothing to get his hands on it."

I shifted uncomfortably, digesting everything he'd told me thus far. "Ascher's working for someone else? Who is it?"

"I don't know. He has meetings with whomever it is all the time. I've never gone with him." He leaned back against the cushions. "You don't know what it's like."

"Tell me." Though the demand came from my mouth, I wasn't sure I wanted to know.

His eyes lost their focus and he seemed to be looking inward. The firelight danced across his features. "There's so much senseless death. It took a while for Ascher to trust me. I had to prove I'd play by his rules, which meant participating in raids all over the world. There were three reasons behind the raids; two were directives from Ascher's 'Lord and master'. One was to track down any sign of the mirror. The second was to start a new wave of witch hunts. It was my job to torture, maim, and kill dozens of innocent people. The others I was with would stage the scenes to make it appear that witches had done those heinous things."

I swallowed thickly, flashes of my visions playing through my mind like a silent slideshow of terror. I could almost smell the blood in the air. My stomach rolled as I realized what Ryan 'willing participation' meant.

"What was the third reason?" My question came out in a whisper.

He rubbed his face and set his mouth in a grim line. "It was my training. You see, there's a part of me that loses control sometimes. It's like a darkness inside that waits. Once the darkness takes over, I destroy everything around me. I couldn't control it, I couldn't tell when it would happen. I'd just snap." He shook himself and looked at me, his eyes pleading for me to understand. "That's another reason why I had to leave; I couldn't trust myself to not hurt you if I lost control."

"Like at the Getty," I whispered, more to myself than to him.

My thoughts drifted back to the man who attacked me to get to the mirror the day before the battle on the beach. I remembered how Ryan shifted; how he turned into someone else and how he violently beat the man before I pulled him away.

He looked both pained and relieved that I understood. "Yes, but I did have some control then. When I completely lose it, I black out. Under Ascher's guidance, I've learned how to harness the anger and how to manage the destruction. I'm can fully control it now."

My anger surfaced again at this last admission. "You're saying that all of these acts were to protect me? That keeping me safe meant stealing my mirror and killing a lot of witches in the name of training?" I launched off the couch and stood over him, shouting. "You expect me to believe this shit?"

My explosive reaction had him on his feet as well. He yelled back at me, "It was the only way I knew how to keep you safe!"

I stood my ground, my face inches away from his as I stared him down.

He relented first, allowing his shoulders to sag. "It was stupid. I wish on all the stars that I never did it."

I hadn't anticipated the amount of remorse he showed. His sorrow-filled, regret ridden stance threatened to weaken my anger. I wasn't ready to not be angry. Not yet.

Latching onto my rage, I told him, "Ryan, I've had to deal with the repercussions of you leaving every day. I've been searching for what you stole, all the while believing you had betrayed me. I've seen the things you've done and they horrify me. Now, you are telling me that you did it all to protect me. What am I supposed to think? Why should I trust anything you say?"

He fell back onto the couch, his hands covering his head. The frustration and sadness coming off of him were almost palpable.

"Fine," I said when he didn't respond, "you want me out of here? Give me the mirror and I will go away. I'll leave you alone forever."

From behind his hands, Ryan mumbled, "I don't have it."

"What do you mean you don't have it? Where is it?"

Removing his hands from his face, he promised, "It's safe. I swear to you, it is safe."

"Explain," I demanded.

"It's hidden. I made sure no one would be able to find it before I went to Ascher."

My teeth grit at his evasion. "You didn't answer my question. Where is it? I want it back."

"I'll return it later when I am sure you'll be safe. I promise."

Lunging forward, I grabbed hold of the front of his shirt and pulled him close. Snarling into his face, I ordered, "Give it back now!"

His piercing eyes pinned me in place. He said in a soft, tender voice, "I can't. If Ascher knows you are alive and that you have the mirror, he will kill you without a second thought. I can't risk your life like that. I love you, Stella. I'd do anything to keep you safe, even if it means making you hate me."

I didn't know what to think. Releasing his shirt, I turned my back on him and went to stand next to the fire. I tossed another log into the flames as Ryan came up behind me. With the utmost care, he wrapped his arms around me, placing his body against my back. I stiffened at his touch, holding my spine rigid against his embrace. He stooped so his chin rested on my shoulder.

"I can't tell you how many times I've regretted my decision to leave. I've had waking dreams of you searching for me. Every one of those dreams was another hole in my heart. All I've done is hurt you. I wish I could take it all back and start over again."

I moved out of his grasp to regard him, an idea hatching in the back of my mind. "Why don't you just come back with me?"

He blinked. "You'd want me to come back? After everything I've done?"

I hesitated. Now that it was said out loud I couldn't take it back. Lifting my chin, I said, "It's better than you going back to be Ascher's lackey."

Ryan stepped forward. "No, that's not what I asked. I asked if *you* want me to come back."

Here it was; the moment of truth. Could I take him back knowing the things he had done? Could I trust him again?

The answer came out in a whisper as though I was afraid to admit it out loud. "Yes, I want you to come back."

There was a flush of relief across his face and his lips pressed against mine. I froze against the kiss, unsure of how to react. When our lips disengaged from his, he murmured, "I love you, Stella."

Feeling completely exposed and a little overwhelmed, I replied, "I love you too."

He kissed me again as he wrapped his arms around me. I clung to him, feeling all the anger and bitterness of the last six weeks fall away. Things were not perfect; there was a lot we still needed to work through, but this was the starting point.

Our kisses intensified. A long buried desire pulled him onto the couch. The room became unbearably warm. Ryan and I separated only long enough to remove our shirts. His skin was smooth and soft. I undid my bra and let it slide to the ground. He grabbed the back of my head and pressed his lips against mine once again. The kisses, the touches were the culmination of finally reconnecting and beginning again.

Everything disappeared except him. All I felt was Ryan's hands on my skin, his lips showering my body with kisses. I tasted him in my mouth and smelled his scent. The two of us were all that existed. What happened next was instinctual, almost automatic. We couldn't have stopped, even if we wanted. The decision was made and I surrendered myself to it willingly.

***

The fire had subsided enough that instead of dancing firelight, the room held a steady warm glow. I stared at the fire from the bed. Ryan's arms wrapped around me and his body pressed against my back. He nuzzled his face into my hair and kissed my neck.

I asked, still staring at the embers. "Should we tell Azra now or later that you're coming home?"

"Later. I don't want to leave this bed yet. Besides, you need to get some sleep," Ryan answered, a quirk of a smile on the corner of his mouth.

Exhaustion caught up with me and I hated myself for it. Stifling a yawn, I fought off the sleepiness. My eyelids weighed heavy. "Promise me that on the way home, we can stop and get the mirror out of hiding. I need to return it to my family."

Ryan planted a soft kiss on my forehead. "I promise. Go to sleep."

As my eyes closed, I felt the giddiness his promise created a fluttering sensation in my stomach like so many butterflies. I'd succeeded in my mission. Not only would I get the mirror back, Ryan would return with me. We could start again and do things right this time around. It was destiny at work.

Chapter Thirteen

"Stella!" Azra's scream woke me out of a deep sleep. On instinct, I leapt out of bed, ready to fight. The crashes and the bangs coming from downstairs meant either Azra was cooking breakfast or we were under attack. Since I didn't smell anything burning, it was safe to assume we were under attack.

"Ryan! Get up!" I hissed, keeping my eye on the door to the bedroom. When he didn't answer, I turned to shake him awake.

The bed was empty.

My heart skipped a beat as I took in my surroundings. The fire was on the verge of dying with only a few coals glowing in the bottom of the ashes. The air was frigid and made my bare skin break out in gooseflesh. There was no sign of Ryan anywhere in the room.

I was momentarily lost when I realized he was gone. How could he have left? He promised he'd be here, that he'd come back with me . . .

The door to the bedroom splintered open thanks to the ax that burst through the wood. Fallen Ones struggled to squeeze through the small opening. The sight of them catapulted me into action. I scrambled to find my scattered clothes and put them on. There was just enough time to slip on a shirt and a pair of jeans when the Fallen Ones broke through the door. I slung my bag over my shoulder and faced my enemy. There was no more time to wonder about Ryan. He'd lied and left me all over again. He probably led these Fallen Ones right to us. Anger blossomed and calcified in my chest.

"Stella! We've gotta go! Now!" Azra's urgent

warning seemed so far away. At least four demons inched closer to me. Instinctively, I put my back against the wall, not allowing any of them to slip behind me. I picked up the fire poker as a weapon.

"Kinda busy up here!" I yelled back. The Fallen Ones in front of me were big; much too big for me to handle on my own.

The horde surged forward, sensing I was off guard. Immediately, my energy burst forth to form a shimmering green protective force field around me. Something was wrong though. The energy crackled like lightning and it drained me more than it should have. It felt different; too wild and too much of it had come out.

Not knowing how long your defenses would last was a great motivator to move. I constricted the shield closer around me to conserve energy. Positioned just a few inches from my skin, the proximity of it zapped at me like static electricity. There was no time to make adjustments. I screamed as loud as I could—a distraction technique Azra had taught me—and dragged the poker through the smoldering coals. I flung what embers I could at the collection of demons. The embers blinded them and it was easy to make a run for it.

Just as I reached the splintered pieces of the wooden door, something grabbed me from behind. My shield was still intact; I felt my assailant electrocuted by it. An overwhelming stench of burning flesh filled the air and the heat of the energy pressed against my back. The Fallen One screamed as his arm was completely obliterated. Taking advantage of his pain, I twisted around to stab him with the poker. When he released me, I turned to the remaining demons, my fury driving me to attack. It wasn't enough to simply get away. These assholes were proof that Ryan betrayed me yet again. I wasn't about to let that go.

With my protective shield in place, I charged into the middle of the three Fallen Ones, brandishing the fire poker. Having just witnessed their friend get mutilated by my magic, they did more to avoid me than anything else. Rage drove me to target one of them. He was the biggest one there, standing over seven feet. His aura was sooty gray and his angular face was set in a scowl.

I was ready to fight. Siphoning some of the energy through the wrought iron in my hands, I sprang forward. As hard as I could I slammed the fire poker into his right kneecap. He tried to back away, but he moved too slowly. The energy sizzled and the fire poker reverberated with the impact. A whimper made it out of his mouth before he staggered backward. Immediately, he swung his blade and it knocked the poker out of my hands. That didn't deter me. Forming missiles of raw energy, I aimed for the damaged knee. They hit their target, causing the giant Fallen One to collapse to the ground in a roar of pain and anger. For good measure, I leapt over to him and kicked savagely at his groin and stomach; the energy encasing my feet added more oomph to the blows.

I thought of Ryan as I kicked him. The energy around me flared, jumping out to a two-foot radius instead of the original few inches. When it hit the Fallen One's skin, he burst into flames even as he shrieked and begged for it to stop.

The others watched, horrified and frozen in place. When the Fallen One's cries faded, I whirled around to face the other two, picking up the poker once again. Without giving them a chance to react, I charged, screaming as loud as I could.

One ran out of the room, plowing through several more who had found their way to where the action was. The other met me head on, his own blade clanging against the poker. An expert twist of his wrist sent my poker flying out of my hands. I braced myself to take him on with just my bare hands and sheer power.

The green shield fizzled and paled. I tried to pump more power into it, but there wasn't enough.

The Fallen One saw the shield fade and seized his chance by scooping me into his arms. There was no sizzle, no electrocution; my protection was gone. His arm encircled my stomach with my back to him.

"You're coming with me," the demon growled in my ear. His voice was low and rasping. "Our Lord wants a word with you."

Without my power, all I could do was kick, jab, and squirm as much as I could. I hit a soft spot and he released me with a harsh curse. In the same movement, he grabbed a hold of my other wrist, determined not to let me escape. Because his hand was so big, his grip was almost unbreakable.

Unable to get free, I desperately tried to summon the words to the spell that would activate the protective ring Nona gave to me. The words weren't coming. A sense of helplessness took hold, breaking through the rage that had fueled me thus far.

"Time to go, witchling." The familiar sensation of teleporting wasn't what I expected. Panicking, I struggled as much as I could.

Just as we were about to disappear, Azra crashed through what was left of the bedroom door and landed directly into my would-be kidnapper. That fall broke both his concentration and his grip. Wrenching my arm away, I bolted out of reach.

Along with his grand entrance, Azra had managed to lead a whole swarm of Fallen Ones into the room as well. They all shouted and did their best to overrun us; it was working. To give me time to think, I put the bed between me and them. Along the way, I snatched up my fire poker. There was no way to keep watch on all of them at once; they were a blur of faces that I couldn't even count.

Azra righted himself and drew his Celestial Blade. "Enough of this!" he shouted. "Line up! Single file. It will make killing you go a lot quicker."

Dark chuckling could be heard scattered among the

crowd. Some of them had a sense of humor, at least. They inched forward, forcing Azra backwards onto the bed.

"Stella," he said with utmost seriousness, "it's time to go out in a blaze of glory."

"What?"

"Turn up the heat in this joint, Charlie McGee!" He waved frantically while keeping his eyes and sword pointed at the closing in horde.

"I don't understand what you are trying to tell me!"

"Burn the house down!" he replied, gesturing to the dying fire in the hearth.

"Are you crazy? I can't do that!"

He twisted around for a second to look at me. For the first time I saw true fear in his eyes. "It's the only chance we have." He returned his attention back to the crowd of demons.

He was insane. What he was asking me to do was impossible. I wasn't a pyro.

The bed lurched, pushing me up against the wall. I had to do something.

It took longer than I liked to clear my mind. Eventually, the clashes of swords against other weapons and flesh faded like the sounds of distant bells. My breathing slowed and I heard my heartbeat pounding in my chest. When I was focused, I opened my eyes and stared at the remains of last night's fire, pouring every scrap of energy I could into my hands. Flinging my hands up, I directed the energy to the embers. They sparked encouragingly. I intensified my focus, willing more and more energy into the fireplace. The embers ignited into sharp, green flames.

Sweat dripped from my brow from the sheer effort. Finally, the fire was roaring in the hearth. Several Fallen Ones had to back away from the heat.

Now for the hard part. I gave a silent prayer that this would work. Maintaining a link of my power to the fireplace, I cupped my end of the energy in my palm.

Tongues of ghost fire licked my arm. When I couldn't hold it anymore, I flung the gathered energy fire toward the pressing mob of pale creatures before me. The fire in the hearth mirrored my movement, jumping out of the grate and burning the unlucky ones who were at the edge of the crowd.

Some managed to get out of the way, but others weren't so lucky. The threadbare carpets and the couches burst into flame. Several demons shrieked and ran as chaos ensued. Azra took that time to bounce up onto the bed and pull me with him. We clasped hands and I made a grab for my bag just as he teleported us and the bed.

We landed with an abrupt thump in a new, freezing cold, dark room.

"Where are we?" My teeth chattered as I asked the question.

Azra's answer was a string of curses. "The basement. They warded the house. We're trapped."

"What?" My chest tightened in panic. "How do we get out then?"

Azra jumped off the bed. "We have to get to an exit and fight our way out. We should be able to teleport beyond the walls."

A bloodcurdling scream heralded several people crashing through the basement door. Four of them pounded down the steps and more were sure to come.

Azra gave me a single, solemn nod which I returned. With a war cry of his own, he led the charge and I followed suit. Azra clashed with a black haired, pale wraith of a demon, his Celestial Blade flaring against the darkness of the room. I scrambled after him, my fire poker in hand.

I swung hard, aiming straight for the nearest black haired enemy. The surprise blow took him off guard and he stumbled backward into a pile of boxes. Without hesitation, I made a run for the stairs. Two others caught me, one by the hair and one by the arm. Their touch was so cold that I wondered if they were really flesh and blood.

I jabbed the poker at the face of the closest one. He twisted sideways so that the metal scraped across his freckled face. Dark, thick blood started welling in the jagged cut. Maniacal laughter erupted from his mouth. Distractedly, I noticed he was missing his front tooth.

I forced more energy into my hand. This time when I swung, the slap sizzled the flesh of the one tooth wonder. His unearthly scream was high-pitched. The sheer volume of it made my head ring, but it worked; he let me go and the one gripping my hair was next to get a blast of my power right in the face. This one kept holding on. The more power I used, the tighter he pulled, keeping his pain to himself.

"I'm coming, Strega Girl!" Azra bellowed from somewhere behind me.

There was an electric hum and a soft, metallic *ching* before the pressure on my head released. I fell forward from pure momentum, scraping my hands and knees on the rough cement floor.

Grunting, Azra hefted me up and propelled me forward. "Sorry about the hair. Come on. We have to get moving."

My mouth dropped open and I stopped to bring a hesitant hand up to my head. My hair. Had he cut my hair? Sure enough, there was an uneven piece missing from the back of my head. I could only imagine what it looked like.

"You can worry about it later," Azra hissed. "We've got to get out of here now!"

He was right. Adjusting my grip on the fire poker, I followed him up the creaking wooden steps.

The door was open, but it didn't look like anyone was around. The smell of fire was overwhelming. Ash and dust rained down from the ceiling and the sound of crackling flames was deafening. Azra gestured for me to keep close to him as he thrust his head out of the door.

Nothing happened. He eased himself out into the open. "Ok," he said, still scanning the room. "It looks like it is clear. Come—" He let out a grunt and doubled over, falling to his knees.

Panicked, I could only watch in horror as Azra pulled out what looked like a serrated boomerang from his stomach. His blood was bright against the glinting metal. Immediately I was at his side, trying to assess the extent of the damage.

Before I could get a good look, the sound of heavy footsteps came, echoing above the din of the burning building. I dodged back into the relative safety of the basement. I kept an eye on Azra, regretting that I couldn't move him.

A tall figure came into view. It paused in front of the Grigori, knelt down, and picked up the boomerang. It wasn't one of the Fallen Ones. No, this was an angel; I could tell by the radiance emanating from him. He wore something similar to an ancient Greek death mask over his face. Eyes, bluer than the bluest sky peered out from the eye holes in disgust at the fallen Watcher.

I had to protect Azra. Crouching low, I crept out of the basement with the fire poker, keeping the angel's back to me.

A section of the ceiling crashed behind me in a fiery heap. It was so loud and unexpected that I didn't have time to aim. I raised the poker above my head to strike. Before I could bring the weapon down, the angel pivoted around and snatched it out from mid-air. He lifted it up and me along with it. My courage faltered as those blue eyes froze me in place.

The building shuddered around us. Heat from the ever-growing fire became more and more intense. I expected to die right then and there. Mentally, I cursed the day I met Ryan. This was all his fault. Never in a million years would I have been in this position if it hadn't been for him.

There was a sickening wet crunch and the angel's blue eyes widened and then closed in pain. Time slowed down to a crawl. The angel's solid grip loosened and I fell, narrowly dodging hot, smoldering heaps of wood.

The angel collapsed backward, his legs severed at the knees. He didn't bleed. I remember wondering about that in my shock. There should have been blood. Azra got to his feet with one hand held the bloody wound on his stomach while the other gripped his glowing Celestial Blade. The expression on his face was cold and terrifying.

Azra stood over the angel, wrathful and stony. He used both hands to lift his blade and to bring it down with all his might, severing the angel's head. When it was finished, he sagged a bit, covered his wound and allowed the point of his blade to scrape along the ground. Within moments the angel's body started to shimmer and dissolve into pinpoints of light. They scattered on a ghost wind, spiraling upwards toward the heavens.

"Come on," Azra rasped, his voice hoarse. "We have to get out of here now."

An irrational fear of Azra swept over me. The Watcher I was gazing at was no longer Ryan's uncle. He wasn't the quirky almost slapstick character I had grown so fond of over these last few weeks. This was a dangerous being. A killer.

He reached for me, grimacing with pain. "Stella, we don't have time. This place is going to collapse. We need to get out of here now."

I couldn't bring myself to take his hand, but I did follow him out the front door.

A few darkly clad figures had gathered outside of the burning building, just beyond a translucent shield. That must have been the ward Azra was talking about. It shone in the light cast from the fire. When they saw us emerge from the building, they each lowered their hoods. Humans. I searched for Ryan's face among them, intent on killing him myself if he had been stupid enough to stick around. There was no sign of him.

As the humans chanted in unison, I strained to understand the Latin words, even with their odd accent. Then it dawned on me. "Are they praying?" I asked out loud.

"We've got bigger problems, Strega Girl," Azra warned. I turned to see Fallen Ones and a few Heavenly Host come out of the burning building, ready to fight.

"Surrender, Azra. You were always so stubborn. Join us," a human called out. He was young, with pale blonde hair and a crooked nose that must have been broken at one point and healed incorrectly. He stepped forward, away from the still chanting group.

"Ash, you coward," Azra spat, his arm folded against the wound on his stomach. "You couldn't come here yourself? You had to hide inside a human?"

The boy's mouth twisted into a contorted grin. "It's not cowardice, Az. It's intelligence. My mission is far too important to risk myself running after you. I don't think I needed to be here anyway. It appears my colleagues have you surrounded. It's time to give up. Surrender and my Lord will bless you with forgiveness. No more blood needs to be spilled tonight."

Azra scoffed, but I could see his trembling. "I'd rather use a cactus as a loofa than surrender." He stumbled a little and his face had gone ashen white from the pain. He didn't have much longer.

The boy serving as Ascher's host looked disappointed. "What a shame. You could have been so useful." He waved his hand, signaling his minions forward. "Kill them."

Ascher's army responded to the order, advancing enough to press us against the ward. I positioned myself next to Azra, pulling what little power I had left into my hands. Behind me the electric crackle of the ward snapped, reminding me that we were trapped.

"Can you teleport us out of here?" I whispered to Azra.

"Not with that ward up. Even if I could, we wouldn't get far."

"Far enough to get us out of this mess?" I pressed.

He thought about it before giving a brief nod.

"Alright. I'm going try something stupid. Get ready to teleport." I didn't allow myself to think as I thrust the hand that held my power into the ward.

The pain was indescribable. Fire never burned so hot and ice never felt so cold all at once. It was an eternity before the pressure around my fist subsided. I clung to consciousness with all of my might. Everything faded except the pain. When that left, it was replaced by the sensation of Azra's arms holding me up and the familiar butterflies in my stomach that signaled we were about to teleport. I opened my eyes in time to see the human that Ascher controlled scream in rage. The army rushed forward to stop us. They were too late; in a blink of an eye, we disappeared.

Chapter Fourteen

We landed on a snowbank and the thudding impact was hard enough to make me cry out in pain. Azra didn't utter a sound. He'd been right when he said he wouldn't be able to get us far. The smoke from the burning house tinged the air. If I squinted, I could see the glow of the blaze on the horizon.

"Azra, we gotta go," I said, picking myself off of the cold ground.

He didn't move. Bending over, I shoved him, but he remained still and lifeless.

"Azra?" I flipped him over. The wound in his stomach oozed blood. I bent my ear just over Azra's mouth to see if he was alive. He was breathing, but just barely. Immediately, I pressed one hand against the gaping hole, hoping it would be enough pressure to stop the bleeding a bit. So much blood gave a coppery tang to the air. I had to bind the wound. My bag was still faithfully on my shoulder. With my free hand, I rummaged around inside it, hoping there was something I could use to make a bandage.

I was in luck—a t-shirt was crumpled in the bottom. Using my teeth, I tore strips from the fabric. Binding a stomach wound on an unconscious angel was more difficult than it sounded, but I managed. When I was sure the bandage would hold, I turned my attention to where we were. Smoke from the burning house hung in the air. We were way too close to the mass of Ascher's followers for comfort. So far the street was quiet, but I couldn't count on that for long. We had to get out of here and quick.

"Max" I called into the night. "Max, I need you now!"

A few dogs barked at the sound of my voice. To keep my panic at bay, I focused on Azra.

"What?" Came the irritated reply. Max appeared at my side. "What's the big—oh shit!"

"He's hurt really bad. We have to get out of here," I explained in a rush.

Max gaped at Azra's body. "Did you kill him?"

If I could have smacked him, I would have. "No! Ascher's goons did this. Please, Max, help me. We have to get out of here fast."

This snapped Max out of his shock. "Alright, stay here. I'll see if there's anything around that can help." He disappeared. Azra and I were alone in the middle of what looked like a suburb of St. Petersburg. The houses on one side of the street were spread far enough apart to allow for deep shadows between them. A darkened cluster of buildings camped on the other side of the road.

Just as the cold started to settle in, Max appeared with a grocery cart and a few blankets. "This is all I could find."

I grimaced at the thought of stuffing the wounded angel into a cart, but what else could I do? "Help me get him into it."

Between the two of us, we hoisted Azra into the cart. I cringed at how painful it looked as we folded his limbs into the small space. We covered him with the blankets to keep out the cold.

I told Max, "We need to get out of here. Tell Nona where I am. I need help getting a train ticket to Italy. I don't know how long Azra is going to last. We have to get him medical attention."

Max grimaced. "Alright. Use your disguise spell to stay hidden. I'll be back soon."

"I can't. I don't have any power left."

The ghost's mouth formed into a thin, disapproving line. "Hold still." He closed his eyes and murmured words of power. A thin spider web of energy surrounded me and the shopping cart that held Azra. Though the spell was fragile, it was better than I could have done at that moment. "This won't make you invisible, but it is better than nothing. I'll get something more powerful from Sylvia. Be careful. I'll be back as soon as I can." He disappeared again, leaving me shivering in the cold.

I wheeled Azra away from the paved road and into the darkness between the two nearest houses. Every noise made me jump. Phantom footsteps echoed in the dark. I forced myself to stay still. It was hard to keep my nagging thoughts at bay in the solitude of the night. I locked those thoughts away; there wasn't any time to deal with them right now. My focus had to be on keeping both Azra and me safe until Max could get back with that disguise spell.

I peeked under the makeshift covering to check on Azra. The bandage was holding up. Only a little blood stained the pale blue fabric encircling his waist. That meant the bleeding had slowed. Whether it was because he was healing or that he didn't have any more to blood in him I wasn't sure.

"Check down there!" A distant voice cried out from the street. A few Fallen Ones from Ascher's army approached the shadows we huddled in. Tensing, I slouched back down to make myself as small as possible.

Azra groaned from inside the cart and my heart almost stopped.

"Did you hear that? I think it came from over here." The scraping of boots against the asphalt came closer. Azra moaned again, a little louder.

I couldn't reach the unconscious Grigori to cover his mouth. If I moved, it would give away our position. There was nothing else to do but hold my breath and hope they didn't notice us. They came close enough that I could smell them; ash mixed with sulfur. The stink almost made me gag.

Just as they were about to trip over me, a loud crash

sounded from the opposite end of the street. The footsteps receded and the noxious stench left. Chancing a look around the cart, all I could see were their backs. A few heartbeats later they were out of sight. Still, I waited, sure that any second they would come back around the corner.

"You can get up now," Max's voice said from my left. "Those idiots are long gone."

The sound of his voice made me breathe a deep sigh of relief and uncoil from the uncomfortable hunched position. It felt good to stretch out my legs. "Thank goodness."

Max materialized with a bag in his hands. "Sylvia had a feeling something was wrong. Here. There's a disguise charm, an invisibility charm, and enough money to get you and Captain Unconscious on a train back to Italy."

Max handed over the small cloth bag and I took it gratefully. "Can she help Azra? Did she say?"

The ghost shook his head. "There's no way to know until she sees him. She said it sounded like the whole coven would need to help from what I told her."

I bit my lip and nodded, fear clutching at my heart. If Azra died . . . no. I wouldn't think about it. Resolutely, I opened the bag and took out the disguise charm. It was a large clay disc inscribed with spells in a language far older than memory. A slender white ribbon looped through a hole at the top. I wrapped the charm around my neck and pressed the disc. As I did, Nona's magic circled around me, filling in for my own. A warmth flushed through my body like a fever as the illusion supplanted my own features. There was no way to see what I looked like or to check if it was enough of a disguise; I just had to hope everything was in place.

Reaching under the pile of tattered blankets, I slipped the invisibility charm around Azra. It took a moment for the charm to work. Soon, it appeared that only a few blankets were crumpled in an empty cart. "How far is the train station?"

Max pointed. "A mile or so that way. You are very lucky. It won't take long to get there."

"You'll come with me?" I asked. I didn't want to admit how terrified I was.

"Yes of course. I'm to escort you home." He gave a small bow.

The worry eased a bit in my chest. "Thank you, Max."

"Don't thank me yet. Wait until we get you safe."

We made our way through the streets of St. Petersburg, keeping a sharp eye out for Ascher's followers. The cold felt as though it had replaced my bones. My teeth chattered against my will. I began to think I'd never be warm again when we came upon the train station.

Max waited with Azra and the cart as I went to inspect the train schedule. As luck would have it, there was a train heading for Warsaw within the next thirty minutes. From there, I could get another train straight to Italy.

As I started back toward Max and Azra, I noticed three tall, black-clad figures scanning the crowd. I recognized the Fallen One with the missing tooth from the attack at the house. The other two were human; one was the boy Ascher had been using as a mouthpiece and the other was a heavyset woman with a long, brown braid trailing down her back.

The sight made my chest tighten. Getting on that train just got a million times harder.

Willing confidence into my disguise charm, I pretended to inspect the posted train schedule while I subtly watched Ascher's cohorts. At one point, they looked right at me. My heart raced and I had to remind myself that I didn't look like myself. Their attention didn't last long. When I was convinced they weren't watching me anymore, I forced my legs into a controlled stroll and I made my way back to Max.

"We have to get on that train. It is the only one heading south tonight," I whispered to my ghostly companion. "And, we have company." I motioned to the troublesome trio.

"Are they looking for us?" Max asked, his voice as soft as mine had been.

"Yeah. Any suggestions on bypassing them completely?"

"Act natural. You don't look anything like yourself. Ignore them and act like every other person in this place and you will be fine. As for getting on the train, this is where it gets a bit tricky," Max replied. "Sylvia couldn't get your passport. Even so, it wouldn't have shown you coming into this country anyway. We are going to have to sneak onto a train."

"Sneak on? How am I supposed to do that with an unconscious angel?"

Max shrugged. "I don't know. I'm just traveling with you, I don't make the plans."

My fingers combed through my knotted hair in frustrated thought. Then it came to me.

"Listen, we can steal another passenger's passport. You will have to get Azra onboard while he is wearing the invisibility charm. Ascher's goons would recognize him in a heartbeat and then we'd be in real trouble. Think you can you get him on the train yourself?"

Max looked doubtful. "I don't know . . ."

"Come on. I am counting on you. We have to get him on the train or he could die."

"Fine, but if things go wrong with this plan of yours, you get to tell Sylvia this was your idea."

I milled about the small crowd. Knowing Ascher's goons were watching made finding someone to steal a passport from even more dangerous. It was still possible they had the ability to disrupt a spell if they knew one was being cast. I couldn't underestimate these people. A couple of times, they came close enough to brush my hand. I was almost positive they recognized me. I held my breath until they walked away without a second glance.

Finally, I saw them: two American travelers who paid more attention to a worn map than their surroundings. The woman's bag was open and I could see the blue book resting just inside of it. As nonchalantly as I could, I got close enough to pluck the woman's passport out of her purse. They didn't notice a thing.

With a renewed sense of confidence, I bought a two berth compartment on the train bound for Warsaw. Once we were on the train, I'd have Max return the passport before the couple even knew it was missing.

With the ticket in my possession, I took a moment to watch the boy Ascher had possessed scan the crowd. Was the Grigori controlling him even now? Did the boy give that monster permission to use him that way? Disgust filled me at the memory of that foreign entity inside my mind, controlling my body.

The boy caught me staring at him. Hastily, I averted my gaze and took a meandering route around the station. When I was sure he wasn't watching, I returned to where Max and Azra waited.

"Well," Max asked.

"I got a two berth compartment. There's an American couple I stole a passport from. When we are safely on the train, I need you to return it to her. Can you bring Azra in on your own?"

"Yeah. I can do it. What about Ascher's people?"

"They're still there. We have to be careful."

An announcement boomed over the station's intercom. Though I couldn't speak Russian, I recognized the word Warsaw. They were calling for boarding. Max motioned for me to get going. Taking a deep breath, I went first, putting my faith in my grandmother's charm.

The woman with the braid eyed the queue of people getting onto the cars while the blond boy and the toothless demon talked in low tones. Her eyes skimmed right over me and I felt a small sense of victory.

The compartment was small, but more importantly, the door that separated it from the rest of the train was windowless and it locked from the inside.

I waited for Max and Azra, praying that they would make it. Soon enough, there was a knock at the compartment door.

"Max," I breathed and flung the door open only to meet thin air. "Max?"

"Get out of the way," Max hissed back. "Hurry, before someone runs into us."

Hastily, I backed out of the way. There was the soft grunt and a squeak as something was placed on the berth to the right.

"All right. You can close the door now," Max advised. I did as he asked and when I turned around, he was visible. He pointed, "He's on the bench here."

"What about Ascher's people? Did they get on the train? Did they see you?"

"No. They're still in the station."

Relieved, I poked the area around the bench, trying to locate the charm around Azra's neck. I found it and removed the disc. His body shimmered into sight. He looked horrible; paler than normal with hideous bruises. His eyes were sunken into his head and his lips were a disconcerting shade of blue.

"Hang on, Az. I'm gonna get us to a safety."

The angel was practically folded in half on the bench.

Moving to get him stretched out and into a semi-comfortable position, I said out loud, "I need to see if he is getting any worse. Will you return this to the woman? They should be in the station." I handed the passport to the ghost before turning my attention to Azra. Without a word, Max left the compartment.

Cautiously, I removed the bandage. Azra's wounds were large and gaping. Blood still seeped around the edges. During our six weeks together, Azra mentioned that he had some healing powers. They didn't appear to be doing him any good right now. I wondered if it was simply too much damage for his body to fix on its own. If that was the case, what chance did I have at helping him?

Max popped back into the compartment opposite of where Azra was spread out.

"Did Nona say there was anything I could do to help him before we get to Italy?" I asked the ghost.

A knock sounded at the door to the compartment and a gruff voice demanded something in Russian.

Panicked, I looked at Max and hissed, "What do I do?"

Another pounding on the door and the voice spoke louder and with more force.

"Alright!" I said loud enough for the person to hear. I replaced the invisibility charm around Azra and motioned for Max to hide. He faded from view. Smoothing my hair back, I took a breath before opening the door.

It was the train attendant. He gestured and spoke Russian to which I shook my head in confusion.

"I don't understand," I replied in Italian.

The attendant reached into his pocket and pulled out a ticket before pointing at me.

"Oh, yes." Comprehension of what he wanted dawned on me and I reached into my pocket and gave him the ticket I had purchased.

The Russian tore the ticket in half and handed part of them back to me. He gave a curt nod and closed the compartment door.

As soon as he was gone, my hands started to shake. A nervous laugh escaped my lips.

"Don't get too excited yet," Max cautioned from the corner. He gradually regained visibility. "We've still got a ways to go before we reach Italy."

A soft groan from Azra killed my enthusiasm more than Max's warning did. After removing the invisibility charm again, I sat on the bench and cradled Azra's head in my lap. A sheen of sweat glistened across his face.

"There has to be something we can do for him until we get there. Did Nona say?"

"No, but I can find out."

"Wait until we are on our way. Before you leave, check to make sure the three that were in the station didn't come aboard. We can't afford any more surprises."

"Of course."

As if on cue, the train started rolling forward. Max faded from view. Azra and I waited in the locked compartment with nothing but heavy silence.

Max returned within moments. "I didn't see them, so I checked the station. All three of them are still there."

"Good." I allowed myself to relax. "Let Nona know we are on our way."

"Will do," Max replied and once again disappeared.

There was time to think now. Catching up with Ryan had been a complete disaster. Not only had Azra gotten seriously wounded, but I didn't have the mirror. Ascher found out I was alive and now I was being hunted.

Then there was Ryan. Had everything he told me been a lie? From where I was sitting, I didn't know how it could be anything but. Stupidly, I'd bought the excuses. I believed his explanations. I even slept with him! Shame and fury burned in my veins as the memory of Ryan's lips against my skin surfaced in my mind. What had it gotten me?

Something nagged at the corners of my mind. If Ryan wanted me dead, then why didn't he kill me when I slept? Why make me believe he was coming back with me and that he'd forsake Ascher? There wasn't any point to that sort of mind game that I could see.

The visions and the horrifying scenes Azra and I came across on our search for Ryan warred with the tenderness of his touch and the love I swore I had seen in his eyes. Inner turmoil consumed me. I didn't know what to think anymore. Things had gotten too confusing too fast.

The weight of Azra's head in my lap and the soft, almost imperceptible rise and fall of his chest served as a reminder that I wasn't the only one Ryan lied to.

So consumed in my emotions, I almost didn't hear the knock on the compartment door.

Chapter Fifteen

"Who is it?" I called out in Italian. The only response was another knock.

I eased Azra's head off of my lap There was nothing in the compartment that would serve as a weapon; I'd lost the fire poker somewhere in the mess of getting on the train. Reaching deep inside, I gathered the minuscule amount of power I had left. There wasn't much so I had to be smart.

Polite knocking intensified into urgent pounding. The door shook on its hinges, straining against the small latch.

Finally, the door burst open and I came face to face with the toothless Fallen One. The cut across his face from the fire poker was raw and red against his pale skin.

Toothless wasn't the only one there; the young man Ascher had used as a host stepped in front of the demon.

"Stella Evangeline?" He asked in a thick accent.

I put myself between Azra and the intruders, preparing to fight. "What do you want?"

I studied my attacker. He looked young, maybe a year or two younger than me. Way too young to be mixed up with Ascher's crowd. I couldn't tell if Ascher was controlling him right then. The boy was too confident, as though he regularly threatened people on trains in the middle of the night.

There were no nervous ticks, no chinks in the armor of almost blatant indifference. Not to mention the evilly grinning Fallen One just behind him.

"What do you want?" I repeated more forcefully.

"I want the mirror. Tell me where it is."

"I don't have it." I focused on the tiny wavering spark of magic still inside me, readying it.

The man stepped closer. Now was my chance.

If there was one thing I learned during my time with Azra, it was to do the unexpected. I edged backwards, my hand groping for my bag. As I moved, Toothless and the blonde pressed forward.

Once I had the strap of my bag in hand, I swung my arm. My aim wasn't half bad; the bag slammed against the side of the human's face. He staggered off balance. I swung again to get Toothless, but missed my target. He was hit in the stomach, though it hardly affected him. He grabbed a hold of the straps and pulled me toward him with strong arms. Straining backward, I used the energy to charge the bag, whispering the incantation under my breath. The energy coursing through the fabric was enough to make Toothless curse and let go of the thing. That caused me to slam against the wall of the compartment, my head hitting the small windowsill. My bag landed on my stomach.

I must have knocked the bench that Azra was laying on because he emitted a soft groan and his arm fell over the side. Something clattered to the floor next to me. It was Azra's sword! Where had that come from?

Glancing at the Grigori on the bench, I caught the barest blink of his eye before Toothless stepped forward to tower over me.

There was no time to think. I grabbed Azra's sword; it was so heavy I couldn't lift it. A thrum of energy vibrated from the sword into me.

With all the strength I had, I thrust the blade up and into the Fallen One. He didn't scream so much as gasp in shock. The weight of him falling on the sword was too much to handle. The hilt pressed viciously into my stomach. Pain spurred me to kick Toothless to get him off.

Just like that, his body disintegrated into a cloud of

black ash that covered everything in the compartment. Seconds later, the particles melted through the floor of the train, presumably back into the earth.

The boy gaped as I got to my feet. Azra's sword started to burn. It dropped from my hands. I took two long strides toward him, my power flowing into my fingers and crackling sharply in the air.

With eyes wide, he turned and ran out of the compartment, making a hasty left to get further into the train car. He ran past the other passengers, throwing people out of his way.

I followed in his wake, stepping over the people he shoved aside. He couldn't escape.

Realizing I was gaining on him, he dodged into another compartment. By the time I reached him, he perched on the ledge, the window was thrown open. He cast one glance back at me, grinned wickedly, and jumped out of the train.

"No!" I shouted. I peered out into the darkness, unable to see where he had landed. I waited a minute or two, too stunned to move. What snapped me out of my shock was the thought that the jumper and Toothless weren't the only enemies on the train. I ran back to the compartment. Max waited next to an unconscious Azra. The Grigori's sword was in his hand instead of on the ground where I had dropped it.

"Where were you?" Max asked.

"Ascher's people attacked us. I had to chase them off." I said it like it wasn't a big deal, but my body still trembled from the fight. "What did Nona say about Azra's condition? Is there anything I can do to help him now?"

Max shook his head. "No. The only thing we can do is make sure he gets to the Stregheria."

The fact that Nona didn't have any helpful advice added a new element of fear. What if Azra died? What if I couldn't get him to Nona in time? What if more of

Ascher's followers caught up to us? The worry-generated questions circled my mind.

I returned to the bench with Azra and took his head back into my lap. Max stayed with us, keeping quiet company as I stared out the window.

The rest of the ride went smoothly, including the transfer of trains in Warsaw. No other Fallen Ones or possessed humans made any appearances and for that I was thankful. I doubted I could handle another fight right then.

Azra grew paler as time wore on. Occasionally he tossed and turned as though he were having bad dreams. The periods of complete and utter stillness between nightmares grew longer. More than once I had to check if he had died just because he was so motionless. I coaxed trickles of water down his throat and swabbed his lips with a damp rag. I changed out his bandages with proper gauze and cotton that Max had stolen from the infirmary on the train. Thinking it couldn't hurt, I added a good dose of antibiotic ointment to wound as I changed them.

After two and a half days of travel and two more train transfers, we arrived at the San Gemini train station. I hadn't slept the entire time. If it hadn't been for Max urging me to eat, I don't think I would have done that either.

Getting off the train was much easier than getting on it; one of the attendants gave me a wheelchair for Azra. When we disembarked, I scanned the crowd for any sign of Ascher or his religious nutjob goons. None were obvious, but that didn't mean they weren't there. I kept my eyes open.

It wasn't long before an oh-so familiar voice called out, "Stella?"

My head turned toward the sound of my name. The sight of my grandmother standing in the lobby of the station made me realize exactly how much I missed her.

"Nona!" I cried. In that instant, I became five years

old again and ran into her waiting arms. She seemed so tiny, it was hard to believe she was real. The smell of her—the lavender and rosemary—was unmistakable.

Nona squeezed me just as hard. Finally, she let go, and her strong, soft hands cupped my face as her sharp gray eyes searched mine. "My darling girl. Are you all right?"

I was so overcome I didn't trust myself to speak. That simple question brought everything roaring to the surface. I couldn't lie. Not to Nona, not after everything. I shook my head and did my best to hold back the tears. A couple fell from the corners of my eye anyway. It just made Nona hug me harder.

"Azra," I said, pulling away and wiped the wetness from my face. There would be time to tell her everything later, but first thing was first. "Can you help him?"

She let go and regarded Azra, taking stock of his slumped over body. "Our friend hasn't had an easy trip. Healing him is going to be more difficult than I anticipated. We need to get him to the house."

With worry in my heart, we wheeled Azra to the waiting car. He couldn't die. Not like this. Not after everything we had been through together.

Aunt Bianca waited for us at the car. Before we got in, she came around to give me a big hug.

"I'm so glad you are home safe," she whispered in my ear.

I hugged her back. "Me too."

The ride home was short and was made shorter by Bianca speeding through the streets. She was determined not to let and angel die in her car. "Bad luck," she insisted.

Nona and Bianca spoke of different remedies and spells they could attempt in swift Italian. I listened as I peered out of the window, on the lookout for anyone following us.

"You remember what Aunt Lydia taught us about

honey?" Bianca asked her sister.

"How it heals even the worst wounds? I suppose we could try it. We will have to call in some of the more experienced healers in the Stregheria. Perhaps they will have some ideas."

As soon as we parked, Bianca was out of the car and rushing to get an old high-backed wicker wheelchair from the porch. It took myself, Max, and Bianca several minutes to ease Azra out of the car and into the house. By the time we crossed the threshold, Nona had already spread linens over the parlor couch and had gathered the most basic wound care supplies.

Once Azra was situated on the couch, Nona and Bianca removed his dirty clothes and the now soiled bandage I'd put around his stomach. I watched from the edge of the room as they removed the blood-soaked gauze.

The wound had not improved. Old blood crusted along the edges while the middle was bright red and still oozing. Azra didn't move as they examined and cleaned the gaping hole with soft, damp cloths. I winced as they scrubbed hard at the dried blood caked onto his skin.

"How is he?" I asked.

Nona gently set about checking over Azra. She was quiet in her assessment. I found myself hoping she'd say something. Anything.

Looking at her sister, Nona said, "Let's try the honey."

Bianca immediately disappeared into the kitchen and returned with a jar full of thick amber liquid with a comb sitting in the middle.

Nona opened the jar and drizzled the thick amber hued syrup onto the edges of Azra's wound. There was a sizzle and a hiss as steam wafted up from the honey.

Azra's eyes flew open and he let out a guttural scream that put the hairs on the back of my neck on end. His muscles tensed and bunched under his skin. It appeared as though he were electrocuted.

Nona didn't seem at all surprised by his reaction. In fact, she wasted no time in pouring even more honey onto the wound. Azra's voice became hoarse from screaming.

Disturbed, I demanded, "What are you doing? Why is he yelling so much?"

"My guess would be that honey affects angels differently than it does humans," Nona said. She finished administering the syrup and dabbed at Azra's face with a damp cloth. His screams subsided into pitiful whimpers.

"How do you know it is helping him then? What if you're hurting him more?" I couldn't keep the panic out of my voice.

Nona replied, "He has a physical body, Stella, no matter what else he may be. See? His wounds aren't as bad as they were before. The honey does hurt, but it heals more. He's looking better already."

While it was true that Azra didn't look as pale as he had, I still wasn't convinced the honey was a good idea.

"Help me get a bandage around his waist."

Together, Bianca and Nona got a fresh bandage over his midsection. Then they tended to the angel's other wounds. By the time they finished, some color had returned to his face and he looked more peaceful.

"He should rest better now," Bianca said as she closed off the parlor door. "We will leave him to sleep until the rest of the Stregheria get here." She scooted us all out and turned off the lights.

Nona suggested, "Come, Stella. Let's get you cleaned up too."

I followed her upstairs to her bedroom. She sat me on her bed and turned on a light so she could inspect me closer.

I sat as still as I could while trying not to make eye contact.

She tsked at what she saw and for one terrifying

moment I thought she knew what I'd done with Ryan.

"You are too thin," she said. "That angel hasn't been feeding you. Oh, your beautiful hair!" She continued to poke and prod at me until she'd seen enough. "You should not be this bad off," Nona admonished. "What have I told you about using too much of the power at once?"

"I didn't have a choice," I replied in a strained whisper.

This made my grandmother pause. Forcing her hands into her lap, she contemplated me as though she were reading everything that had transpired right on my face. I couldn't bear to look at her so my gaze fell to the patterned rug beneath our feet. "Tell me what happened, Stella."

As I struggled to find the words, Nona opened one of her cabinets and pulled out a couple of glass stoppered bottles filled with dark liquid.

"We were in St. Petersburg. Azra found Ryan at a party earlier in the evening. He got a message to him that I was alive and wanted to talk."

"Did you talk to him?"

Talk, kiss, and other things, I thought. I didn't trust myself to speak so instead I gave a single nod.

Mixing ingredients into a new bottle, she didn't look at me as she asked the most crucial and the most difficult question of all, "And the mirror?"

"I don't know. He doesn't have it." I wanted to say more, but the taste of defeat and betrayal wouldn't allow the explanation past my lips. The words hung unsaid in the air between us.

My grandmother kept her disappointment pinned inside of her as she asked, "So you and Ryan talked. Then what happened?"

This was the bitter part. I swallowed thickly. "Ryan led Ascher's army right to us. We got trapped in the house and they attacked. We fought our way out.

Ascher's got human followers now; a bunch of religious freaks that let him possess them. Azra . . . an angel from Heaven got him in the stomach with a boomerang. I didn't think he would make it.

"It was only sheer luck that I had enough power to break their containment spell. As soon as we were through, Azra teleported us away. He was so bad off that we didn't make it more than eight blocks away from where we were. That's when I called Max."

Nona pursed her lips as she absorbed what I told her. We sat in silence for a long moment before she said, "I should never have let you go. This whole venture was a foolish gamble. We should have found a different way."

"There was no other way," I argued. "I had to do this."

"There is always another way, my sweet girl. We were just in too much of a rush to find it. If I had thought this through more instead of just reacting, you wouldn't have been in so much danger. Perhaps we would have gotten the mirror back already had we pursued a different option."

"If we had gone a different way, then we wouldn't know what we are up against," I pointed out.

Annoyance at my contradiction filled Nona's tone. "And what are we up against? Some rogue angels and a group of religious-minded humans?"

"It's more than that. Nona, Azra and I have seen horrible things all around the world. Terrible attacks on witches everywhere. I've seen him torture people—women and children that have magic. They are done on the orders from whomever Ascher is working for. This fight isn't over. If anything it is just beginning and it involves all the witches in the world."

Nona considered what I told her. She admitted, "There have been disturbing news stories lately about an increase of ritualistic homicides. No one has mentioned witches yet, but it wouldn't surprise me if a connection was made."

"They will. That's what Ascher and Ryan have been doing; they are generating hysteria to begin a new wave of witch hunts. I've seen it with my own eyes."

The pent-up emotions I'd been keeping at bay began to leak out. "Please, believe me. It is all going to get so much worse."

She stroked my cheek, her eyes kind and understanding, though now troubled with the news I'd given. How understanding would she be if she knew exactly what happened between Ryan and me? If she knew I'd almost killed our family by letting him come back with me?

Sensing how upset I was, Nona wrapped her shawl around my shoulders intending to comfort me. "Things may indeed get worse, but know that the Stregheria has seen its fair share of witch hunts and inquisitions. We have always survived them. We will survive this one too. Right now, let's focus on making sure you and Azra are healed. We can discuss our next steps later."

Soon enough, my scrapes and cuts had been attended to. If only she had a cure for the emotional wounds as well. Ryan's betrayal replayed over and over again in my mind. All I could think about was how stupid I'd been. How I'd fallen into Ryan's arms and how eagerly I'd believed his lies!

I felt dirty, used, and most of all ashamed. The shame was the worst. Under the weight of my self-loathing, I burst into tears. It was a purging sob that let loose the pent-up emotions since seeing Ryan.

Nona cradled me in her arms and murmured words of comfort as she allowed me to mourn.

Chapter Sixteen

The hot water of the shower felt divine to my sore body. It took a long time to wash away the dirt and ash from my skin because my arms kept shaking. When I washed my hair, I felt the extent of Azra's impromptu cut. It brought back vivid memories of the fight. Refusing to think about it any more than I had to, I rinsed in the cooling water.

Urging my aching muscles to move, I slipped into the most comfortable dress I had; a simple, cotton nightgown. On my way out of the room, I glanced at the mirror. My reflection stopped me in my tracks.

I looked like hell. Dark circles under my eyes gave my face a hollowed out appearance. Bruises darkened my usually pale skin. My hair, once even to my shoulders, now looked as though Edward Scissorhands had been on an acid trip and cut it while I was sleeping.

"Azra," I reminded my reflection and tore my gaze away from the mess I was. He was much more important than my vanity. I hobbled down the stairs.

The house was already teeming with people. That was the wonderful part about having a big, close-knit family; if you needed help, they would be there for you. At the same time, the problem with big, close-knit families was that everyone wanted to stop and ask me how I was. I kept my answers short and sweet, all the while moving toward the kitchen.

When I reached the kitchen door, Nona was there.

"Healing Azra is going to be quite an undertaking," she warned me, her voice pitched low and serious. "Are you sure you have enough strength to help?"

"It's my fault that he's in this position. I have to do

what I can," I responded.

Nona didn't argue. "I've explained a little of what happened, but the family wants more details before they decide to help. Come into the dining room and we will answer their questions before we head out to the grove."

My worries and regrets settled into the back of my mind as I followed my grandmother. There were only a few coven members waiting for us in the dining room: Uncle Roderigo, and my cousins Marcus and Lisbeth. They were the most adept healers in the Stregheria.

Aunt Bianca joined us just as Marcus began to speak. "We've never had to heal an angel before. I'm not even sure it is possible."

"He's the same one that threatened to kill us over a goat," Lisbeth added. "Even if it were possible, why should we heal him?"

Nona looked at me, expecting me to answer. I cleared my throat. "Azra's done more to help me locate the mirror in the last six weeks than anyone else. We've faced many enemies and he got hurt defending me against other angels. It would be wrong not to help him."

Lisbeth rolled her eyes even as Marcus repeated, "We don't even know if we can help him. We could just end up making everything worse."

"We still need to try," I pressed. "Azra saved my life. I owe him the same."

"What even happened?" Lisbeth asked.

Nona interjected. "We will get into that later. Right now, we need to know if you are going to help us or not."

The three of them glanced at each other, deciding. At last, Uncle Roderigo answered, "Of course we will help. Stella, can you tell us how your friend got hurt?"

"A serrated boomerang hit him in the stomach. It wasn't just a plain old boomerang either. I think it was a celestial one."

Roderigo frowned. "What do you mean, a celestial one?"

"They are special energy-based weapons angels have. From what Azra told me, an angel or a Fallen One can only truly die by a celestial weapon."

"It may be that the damage was to his spirit as well as his body," Marcus mused. "Perhaps if we looked at his aura, it could help us determine what the best method of healing would be."

Nona clapped her hands once at Marcus' pronouncement. "Excellent idea. Come on then. Everything has been set up in the grove. We haven't much time."

Together, the six of us trooped out to the sacred space.

Azra was laid out on a table in the center of the circle, just in front of the altar stone. They'd stripped him bare and done their best to wash the soot, ash, and grime from his skin. Someone must have washed his hair as well because though it was wet, it was clean. Without the dirt, his injuries didn't look as severe. The honey must have done some good after all because though the gash in his stomach appeared red and angry, it wasn't bleeding.

An additional table was set up to the right of where Azra was splayed. Several tools were arranged. A Strega's tools could be anything around them for spell work, but these were truly sacred. There was an obsidian dagger, a crystal disc, many non-shaped stones, cords of all colors, a marble mortar and pestle, and large mixing bowls made of metal. There were also bandages, unguents, salves, and several herbs, both fresh and dried. It looked like everyone took anything they thought would work and brought it to the clearing.

"Are we going to use all this?" I asked.

Bianca gave a glance over at the table and shrugged. "We might."

Nona stood next to Bianca and me as Marcus, Lisbeth, and Roderigo took their places around our patient.

"You aren't leading this?" I asked my grandmother in surprise.

She shook her head. "No, this work is for the healers. We will lend our magic to theirs. Remember, a high priestess knows the strengths of her Stregheria and understands when other talents are suited for the work before her."

I considered what she said as Roderigo gave a single nod and set the whole ritual into motion. Everything became silent and still as he called in the directions in his clear, ringing voice and stated our intent to heal Azra. The air became thick as Nona, Bianca, and I began moving clockwise. There were no chants; only a deep sort of hum that emanates from the back of your throat. In this instance words were meaningless; it was the sounds that carried the power.

Roderigo, Lisbeth, and Marcus focused their attention on the angel. As the energy in the circle built up, Azra's own aura—shreds of bright oceanic blue speckled with gold—amplified. The more it became visible, the more I could see what was wrong with him. His aura wasn't right; there were large black spots with curling tendrils attaching to the good, healthy looking parts. The dark spots pulsed with an energy of their own. I'd never seen anything like it before.

Azra had taken some serious damage, and not just the physical kind.

"Lisbeth, give me the obsidian dagger," Roderigo murmured. "We need to cut the infected parts of his aura out before it spreads more."

My cousin did as he asked as Marcus took his place across the table from Roderigo, ready to hold the angel's feet down. Lisbeth stood next to her father, placing her hands on Azra's shoulders. Roderigo moved above the angel, the dagger raised high.

It was at that precise moment that Azra's eyes flew

open.

The confusion on his face morphed into horror. I'm sure being held down along with the sight of my uncle standing over him with a knife is what fueled the terrified scream that came out of his mouth.

"What in the name of all that is sacred is happening?" Azra screeched. He scrambled off the table, kicking Marcus in the stomach and punching Lisbeth in the face in the process. The knife in Roderigo's hand was swept by Azra's forearm and the man was pushed to the side. I ran to Azra, meaning to calm him down. He jumped up on the table, one hand clutching at the wound in his stomach and the other outstretched as though to push anyone back who tried to approach him.

"Back off you wicked warlocks! Don't you dare come any closer! I will not be frog fodder!"

Marcus and Lisbeth recovered from Azra's attack. Before I could warn them to stay still, Marcus rushed to the Grigori and it was the worst thing he could have done right then.

"No! Don't!" I yelled, still too far away to stop him.

It was no use. Azra was disoriented and, in his mind, the enemy was rushing to attack. I can't blame him for trying to defending himself. There was no way he had the energy to physically take them on, but that didn't stop him from trying. Jumping off the table, he grabbed the nearest thing he could use to defend himself with: a handful of stones from the table of supplies. Rapidly, he aimed and threw them at Marcus. Each of them hit their target in the head with enough force to make Marcus stumble. The sphere of amethyst struck him between the eyes with a resonating thud and caused him to collapse in the grass.

"Azra, stop it!" I yelled.

He swiveled toward the sound of my voice, ready to launch a sizeable chunk of rose quartz in my direction. "Strega Girl? You're in on this too?"

"Calm down," I said to the Grigori. "You are safe, I promise. We are only trying to help you."

I didn't see Marcus get back to his feet, but he must have. All I saw was Azra pitch forward because Marcus tackled him from behind. Unwittingly I'd served as the distraction Marcus needed to get the upper hand. His advantage didn't last long; Azra reached behind him and grabbed his assailant by the hair. In a single, fluid movement, he bent forward even as he yanked on Marcus' hair. This served to fling Marcus over Azra's head and onto the ground before him.

Azra winced in pain, but still summoned his Celestial Blade, holding it to Marcus' face. When he spoke it was at me, "You conniving little spell slinger. You're the one responsible for this, aren't you? As soon as I am weak, you attacked."

"That is enough!" Nona bellowed from the sidelines.

Marcus froze at the command. Azra didn't; when he heard Nona's voice, he took the opportunity to make a break for it. He thrust his way to the edge of the grove only to be blocked by an unseen force. When he hit the boundaries of the circle, he was flung back far enough to land roughly on the table he started out on. The force snapped the table legs and it collapsed with a thud.

Dazed, he staggered to his feet, one hand holding his now bleeding wound and the other splayed out for balance.

Marcus rushed forward intending to attack again. If he did, I was sure Azra would kill him on the spot. I couldn't let that happen.

I grabbed the obsidian knife that Roderigo had dropped and leapt over the broken table. I was just in time to put myself between Marcus and Azra.

"Get out of the way, Stella!" Marcus shouted, outraged.

"Leave him alone," I replied as I crouched, ready to take my own cousin on if need be.

"I said, that is enough!" Nona shouted again. The anger in her voice made me cringe. I didn't relax my stance; I was ready to defend Azra, no matter who it was that attacked.

My grandmother stepped between me and my cousin. "Marcus, go check on Roderigo."

"Sylvia, this thing is dangerous. It isn't wise to let him be free," he said between gritted teeth.

Nona didn't back down. "That is not your choice. Go. I will handle the Grigori."

Reluctantly, and with a lot of glaring, Marcus headed to where his father lay on the grass. Lisbeth was already at Roderigo's side, trying to revive him.

"Stella, get up. No one is going to hurt either of you."

I stood, keeping the obsidian knife in my hand. Nona regarded terrified and confused angel who had taken one of the broken table legs and brandished it like a club.

"Mister Azra, please, put that down. We are only trying to help you."

"Stay back!" Azra shouted, waving the table leg wildly.

Nona gave me a look as if to say 'calm him down so I can talk some sense to him'. With the dagger still in my hand, I faced my traveling companion.

"Azra, it's alright. You are safe here. We both are."

"You betrayed me, Strega Girl," he shouted, enraged. "The minute I was vulnerable, you captured me and tried to do all sorts of horrible spells on me! If I hadn't woken up, you would have turned me into a toad. After everything we've been through, you still do me wrong? You are despicable."

"That's not what happened!" I fired back. "You're injured! We couldn't teleport out of the safe house. I worked my ass off to get you back here."

"Lies! I've never NOT been able to teleport. Besides, I'm perfectly capable of healing myself."

"Not from that injury! Do you even remember the

masked angel? You were on the brink of death for days!" I screamed back. He was so infuriating. "You should be thanking us. Not even three hours ago you were on death's doorstep."

"I'm not going to thank you witches for anything! You sabotaged me! You were about to offer me up as a sacrifice! I'm onto your tricky ways!"

"Do you not remember anything that happened in St. Petersburg? You don't remember burning down your safe house? You don't remember getting stabbed in the stomach?"

By the uncomfortable silence that followed, I knew that Azra did know what I was talking about. He was too embarrassed to admit he had been wrong.

"It doesn't matter," he said finally. "I didn't ask any of you to start doing voodoo on me. There is such a thing as consent."

"You were unconscious! It was a miracle we made it out in one piece! Sorry for trying to make sure you survived!" I'd had enough of his stupidity. If he didn't have the good graces to at least be thankful for the help we tried to give him, then I was done.

He must have reached the same conclusion because he aimed the table leg at me and demanded, "Let me go, Strega Girl. Give me my clothes and let me out of this witches trap."

I opened my arms wide, "I'm not stopping you!"

He eyed the knife in my hand dubiously. "I don't trust you."

I turned my back to him. "Fine. Don't."

Something crashed through the foliage around the grove. Before I knew what was happening, whatever it was broke through the protective circle and jumped over me. All I saw was a tan and white blur arching through the sky. When I turned to see where it landed, Azra was on the ground, clutching his groin. I blinked at Beth standing over him, baaing.

Nona ran over, fear written all over her face. "Are you alright?" she asked.

"I'm fine," I answered, watching as Beth took a stance between me and the Grigori. Had the goat just saved me?

"Beth? How on earth did you get here?" Azra got to his feet, his face full of anger. "What, did these witches find you in New Zealand? Did they goat-nap you again?" He took a step toward Nona and me, his anger returned. "How did you even know what pasture to look in? It's not like New Zealand isn't covered in them!"

I didn't think goats could growl, but Beth did, her ears flat against her lowered head. It brought Azra up short.

"You're the one that taught her to teleport, idiot," I told him scathingly. I didn't let the confusion on his face keep me from getting my point across. In a softer, calmer tone, I said, "Azra, I'm sorry we scared you. We thought you were dying. We were only trying to help."

"You shut your mouth, you deceitful wretch!"

Him shouting at me again annoyed me even further. "I saved your life, you arrogant jerk! If it wasn't for me, you'd still be somewhere in Russia and Ascher's thugs would have caught you by now. They would have finished the job too."

That point must have hit home because the face the Grigori made was sour.

I tried again. "Look, after that night, I don't trust Ryan any farther than I could throw him. I don't know what kind of game he's playing. The only thing I do know is that they don't have the mirror."

Azra rolled his eyes. "Really? Did Ryan tell you that? Did he say 'gee, we don't have the ultimate object of destruction on hand, but if you see one at the store, let us know?' Is that what you two talked about that night?"

It was hard to resist the urge to slap the hell out of him. I exhaled to allow the impulse to leave before I said in slow, measured tones, "If Ascher had the mirror, they wouldn't have attacked us the way they did. They wouldn't have hunted us down on the trains demanding it. There wouldn't have been any reason for any of that."

Azra frowned at the logic trying to find holes in it. "It could all just be a ruse. Ascher is crazy and so is Ryan. They could have done it to make us think they don't have the mirror; to throw us off."

"I doubt it."

"So what you are saying is that the mirror is still out there," Nona spoke up.

Uncle Roderigo had come to and he blinked as Marcus and Lisbeth helped him to his feet.

"Yes, it is still out there. Azra and I can find it."

"*No!*" Both Azra and my grandmother shouted at once.

The vehemence with which they said it took me aback. "What do you mean?"

Azra was the first to answer, cutting off Nona. "I'm done with this circus. As far as I'm concerned, I've fulfilled my part of the deal. I got you to Ryan. I can't help it if he doesn't want anything except maybe to kill us. Beth and I are finished with you. I'm not sure how you witches got her here, but don't plan on ever doing it again. We have a surfing competition to prepare for."

He grabbed Beth's collar. Together, they stomped to the edge of the clearing. The goat went with him, whatever anger she had with him long gone.

My family gave Azra and Beth a wide berth. When they reached the edge of the circle, Azra hesitated. Beth, however, sauntered through the protection spell and took Azra along with her. They passed through and kept on walking until they were out of sight.

"How did the goat get through the circle?" Roderigo asked, bewildered in the stunned silence left in the angel's wake.

No one had an answer for him.

Just like that, the only angel that was on my side was gone.

As Marcus and Lisbeth helped Roderigo back to the house, I rounded on my grandmother. "Nona, we have to keep looking for the mirror. If we don't get to it first, they will have it before long."

She closed her eyes as though asking for patience. "Stella, enough. The mirror is lost. If you were unable to get it with this last venture with Azra, I don't believe we will ever recover it."

A pit grew in my stomach and I couldn't believe what she was saying. "Nona, I have to find it!"

She shook her head and began to gather the tools that had been scattered around the grove.

I wanted to rage, I wanted to argue. I needed her to understand the danger of the object just being out in the world with someone like Ascher looking for it.

Aunt Bianca spoke up for me. "The girl is right, Sylvia. It is dangerous to have it out there where someone like this Ascher person can find it."

"I am tired of arguing about this," Nona sighed. "Stella has tried and look what happened. Azra refuses to help anymore. Are we to send her out into the world on her own to search for something that cannot be traced? It was one thing when she had an angel to help her."

"I didn't say she should go," Bianca responded. "I am saying that someone should go. We have many who would be able to travel. The mirror isn't just one person's responsibility. It was given to our whole family. Let the Stregheria help find it."

I could tell Nona was weighing the decision. After a long, silent moment, she agreed. "Alright. We will send five others out. In six months, they will come back and we will see what progress has been made."

My heart sank. Five of the coven members? Six months? That wasn't even close to enough manpower or time. With the rate that Ascher and Ryan could travel, they would have covered the globe five times over in six months.

"It's not enough," I said. "We have to find another way."

"We will try this for now," Nona said. "In the meantime, you and I will head back to California and see if we can find an alternative."

I opened my mouth to argue the point, but the look my grandmother gave made me close it again. A horrible chasm opened in my heart. After everything that had happened over the last six weeks, I was back to square one.

Chapter Seventeen

Ryan sat bound in a cell. The only light source came from a halogen lamp mounted on a brick wall on the other side of the metal bars. The angle of the light was set at just the right height to blind him. He was alone at first, listening to the steady drip of a leak somewhere. A door opened and two men came into the prison. They stood in front of the light so shadows hid their faces.

"You say he lied about the girl being alive?" one of the figures asked.

The taller figure answered, "Yes. It makes one wonder what else he's lied about. For instance, the whereabouts of the mirror?" The voice and the demeanor identified the tall stranger as Ascher.

"I didn't lie. When I left, she was dead. How was I supposed to know she would show up?"

The stranger ignored Ryan as he folded his arms across his chest and tilted his head as though trying to make a hard decision. "It could be that the girl still has the mirror," he said at last. "He could have been trying to protect her."

"Why would I protect her? She's just a stupid human. She doesn't matter."

Ascher kicked the bars of the cell. The noise of the metal boomed around the small space. "How dare you presume to speak out of turn?"

The stranger held up a hand signaling Ascher to stop. "Hold on. I want to hear what he has to say." He knelt down and grasped a hold of one of the metal bars of the cell. The shadows no longer shrouded his face and Ryan found himself staring into warm, dark eyes. The stranger smiled. He had the kind of face you would immediately trust with your deepest, darkest secrets. "Why doesn't Stella have the mirror, Ryan?" he inquired.

"She sent the mirror away. I don't know where."

A disappointed sigh escaped from the stranger's lips. "I had such high hopes for you, Orion." With a wave of his fingers, the ropes around Ryan tightened until he was gasping for breath. The stranger stood and said, "Well, there's only one way to find out for sure, isn't there?"

"You won't be able to get near her. She's protected by her coven," Ascher answered.

That didn't deter the stranger in the least. He looked down and caressed Ryan's face. "Well then, if we cannot go to her, then she will have to come to us. We just have to think of the right incentive."

The vision vanished. The cursor on the email I'd been writing blinked at me, bringing me back to myself and my bedroom.

Since returning to California a week ago, the visions of Ryan hadn't stopped. They came even without the charm or my focus. According to Nona, they wouldn't until the binding spell either faded or the connection was severed. Severing the spell meant that either Ryan or myself had to die. Once two things are bound by blood, the connection was for life. Despite the lapse of time, all indications showed the spell was growing stronger.

This last vision gave me a grim satisfaction. In a savage way, I was glad Ryan was imprisoned. He deserved everything he got and more.

Doing my best to put Ryan out of my mind, I turned my attention back to the email.

Dear Thomas,

Well, I'm back in California. Azra left me in Italy after a disastrous night in Russia. There was a big misunderstanding and he thought we were trying to kill him when we were really trying to heal him.

Nona thinks it is for the best. She believes that we need to rethink our strategy. By rethink our strategy, she means keep me home and find some other way to track the mirror. She wants me to go back to school tomorrow. Can you believe it? What on earth makes her think that going back to high school is even remotely important compared to stopping the end of the known world?

I suppose I shouldn't complain. She and Aunt Bianca did send out some of the Stregheria to look. That's at least something. Plus, between you and me, I'm coming up with my own plan to find the mirror. I can't just sit around and do nothing.

It's strange being back home. Things have changed. Donatella and Aurelia have joined a church. Weird, right? I was sure Nona would have blown a gasket. They're supposed to be witches and now they are embracing this savior based religion? Nona says they're free to believe what they wish and it isn't for the Stregheria to dictate personal beliefs. She also reminded me that many members of the family were still Catholic. Maybe all the strange fanatics Azra and I encountered on our journeys have made me suspicious of Auri and Donatella's sudden faith.

Oh, Auri has a boyfriend too. His name is Peter. I haven't met him yet. From what Auri says, he goes to the church that she and Donatella now belong to. I guess he's the one that got them into it. He's supposed to come to dinner tonight to meet Nona. Auri won't stop talking about it. You'd think the sun shone from his ass or something.

So what is going on with you? I was expecting some sort of email from you when I got back. You better write me soon or I'll just have to go over there and smack you. Better yet, when can we do a video chat again? I miss your face.

You better stay safe out there. Write me soon!
Love, Stella

I pressed the send button and closed the laptop wishing Thomas was home. If he'd been there, I wouldn't have resented being back so much.

What I told him was true; despite my frustration at being back, I was working on my own plan to find the mirror. Ryan didn't have it, of that I was sure. That meant he had to have gotten rid of it between the hospital and meeting up with Ascher. There was a good chance the mirror was close by. Nona scrutinized me too much to go out on my own, but I could search Southern California until she relaxed her vigilance.

"Hey Stella," Aurelia asked as she came into our bedroom, "who is Bethesda Gregory?" She peered down at a rather beaten up brown package, squinting at the lettering.

"Bethesda's the goat. You know, the one that I was watching for a while?" I frowned and took the package from her to verify the name myself.

She choked back a peal of laughter. "Why is someone sending the goat a package? Don't they know she's not here anymore?"

I accepted the box with a sigh. "I have no idea."

Auri chuckled as she left to finish getting dinner ready. "I swear, Stella. The people you hang out with." My cousin was in a much better mood these days. Since dating this Peter guy, she seemed more confident, more assertive. The change was subtle but still noticeable. I was happy for her. As long as I could remember, Auri was this shy, quiet girl that had the habit of fading into the background as best as she could. As long as her relationship with this boy continued, I doubted we would see a return of the timid Aurelia.

I straightened up and considered the box. The postmark said London and the dates were from over a month ago. Azra must have sent it before we'd gone on our adventure. I cut through the tape with a nail file.

Instead of reaching in, I upended the box onto my bed. Small packets of Weetabix tumbled out along with a folded length of bright red wool and a handful of postcards from all over the world. There was also a crumpled napkin with messy writing scrawled on it.

Dear Bethesda,
I'd forgotten how friendly Manchester folk are. The pubs here are as rowdy as ever. And look! I got you a scarf! I hope you are doing well and that the Strega Girl is taking proper care of you. Kick her if she isn't. Oh! Look! Another beer! Off to watch the game. Write you again soon.
Azra
P.S. No sheep were harmed in the making of the scarf.

Ridiculous. The Grigori was ridiculous. Picking up the next postcard, I merely glanced at the stunning picture of glaciers in front of a setting sun and turned it over to read the message.

Dear Bethesda,
Greetings from Greenland! It's boring here. It's no wonder that the Vikings were the only ones who were able to inhabit this place. They had a certain talent for dealing with excessive white landscapes. That's a polite way of saying they were dumb. There's nothing new to report, but I will keep you posted.
Azra
P.S. When I get back, remind me to show you the snow angel I built. I took a picture of it with my phone.

The next had a picture of a beautiful mountain landscape. A dark-skinned girl with long black braids and bright colored clothes stood next to a particularly hairy llama.

Dear Bethesda,

Guess where I am. WRONG! I'm in Chile. There are so many llamas walking around here. Tell the stupid Strega Girl that this is starting to look hopeless. I'm running out of places to look for him. I'll write you soon.
Azra
P.S. Don't be mad. I had to ride a llama . . .

The next postcard meant for the goat had a stunning view of the Sydney Opera House overlooking a bright blue ocean.

Dear Bethesda,
I wish you were here with me in Sydney! The waves are amazing. There is this surf tournament over in Bells Beach. We should enter. We would completely rock that. Talk to you soon!
Azra
P.S. Get to practicing! I'm signing us up.

There was one more postcard, this one scratched out in pencil. The photograph on the front was that of an extreme close up of a moose against a plain blue background. When I read the message, I could see where he had originally written "Dear Stupid Strega Girl". Instead, he put down over the badly erased marks, Dear Stella. Shaking my head, I read the message.

Dear Stella,
Hope I spelled your name right. I'm in Toronto. I thought of you because you remind me of Canadians. No sign of Ryan yet.
Azra
P.S. Thanks for taking care of Beth again.

"You remind me of Canadians?" I muttered out loud. What did that even mean? I wasn't sure if it was a compliment or an insult.

"Knock, knock," Justin said as he came through the bedroom door. "Hey, you better get out here. Peter is here and dinner is ready."

I groaned before sliding off my bed. "I don't feel up to having dinner with this guy. Do you think if I said I was sick I could get out of it?"

Justin laughed. "I doubt it. Auri's been planning this for weeks. She's bound and determined for us to meet this guy. Believe me, if Nathan and I can't get out of it, neither can you."

"Fine. Let's get it over with." Together, Justin and I made our way to the small dining room just off the kitchen. Everyone was already seated; Nona was in her customary seat at the head of the table with Donatella on her left and Nathan on her right. Aurelia sat beside her mother. In my usual seat at the other end of the table was a blond boy with his back to me.

Justin took his usual spot next to his twin leaving me with the folding chair next to him.

"Stella!" Aurelia gushed. Her grin was wide and infectious. "I want you to meet my boyfriend, Peter. Peter, this is my cousin Stella."

As I approached the table, the stranger stood to greet me. When I finally saw his face, time seemed to slow down to a crawl. Those piercing blue eyes were familiar; I knew the slope of that forehead and the odd angle of his nose. Peter was the same person that attacked Azra and me on the train. He was the same boy that spoke Ascher's damning words at the house in St. Petersburg. He had jumped off the train after he tried to kill me.

It felt surreal having someone who was so determined to kill me now standing in my house. My breath caught in my throat. How could this be? I saw him jump. How was he here at my dining room table?

"Hello, Stella," he said, a quirk of a smile on his thin face.

It was the voice that convinced me I wasn't dreaming. As soon as the realization that he was real came, I launched into action.

The spell that left my lips was hasty but effective. Instead of shaking his hand, I shoved the boy hard in the chest. With the extra energy I packed into that shove, he flew backward ending up against the wall next to the china hutch. Words of power constricted his movements. His arms and legs flattened as though pinned by a giant magnet. I wasn't going to let him get away this time.

I shouted at the top of my lungs, "How the hell did you get here? Is Ascher close by? You think you can to kill me now? You think you can to hurt my family?"

As I advanced, Aurelia stepped in my way and blasted me with a decent amount of her own power. While it wasn't enough to do any real damage, Auri's attack did break my concentration on Peter's bindings. He sagged away from the wall and gasped for air.

"What is wrong with you?" she shrieked even as she hit me with another surge of power. It zapped my skin in little pinpricks of annoyance.

"Get out of my way," I warned through clenched teeth. My eyes never left Peter's face. "I won't allow him to hurt anyone here."

Aurelia threw the full weight of her body into mine. Together, we tumbled to the floor.

While Aurelia and I were about the same size, I had the advantage of fighting alongside Azra for the last two months. She wasn't a match for me physically. After I shoved her, she righted herself and her lips moved without sound. The small piano bench near the entrance way started to levitate.

"Girls, that is quite enough!" Nona's voice pierced through the commotion. The piano bench wobbled and fell a couple of inches from where it started with a loud thump.

As I got to my feet, I shouted at Peter, "What are you

doing here? Is Ascher in that head of yours, controlling you?"

His blue eyes were wide with fear and something else. Was it satisfaction? An odd expression on his face and I fought the urge to smack it right off.

"Stella! I said that's enough." Nona demanded.

Donatella didn't waste any time in jumping in. "How dare you treat Aurelia's boyfriend this way!"

The twins edged closer on either side of Peter. Justin gave me a slight nod, signaling they were ready and with me. I wondered why they had so much confidence in me, but the thought was fleeting.

Glaring at our guest, I closed the gap between us. "He's not Auri's boyfriend! He's one of Ascher's minions. Ascher might even be in his head controlling him right now."

"Shut up!" Aurelia screamed. She was on her feet and coming at me with more rage than I had ever seen in her. She smacked me hard across the face with her eyes full of tears.

"What the hell is your problem? Why do you need to make everything about you? Tonight's supposed to be about Peter and I. Do you just not like the fact that I have a boyfriend? Or is it the fact that Peter is a good guy when Ryan dropped you like a bad habit that you can't stand? Why you are being such a selfish bitch?"

"This is not about me! That boy is a liar and a willing host for an angel that wants to kill us all! I don't even know how he is still alive. The last time I saw this boy, he jumped out of a moving train!" As proud as I was about Auri being more independent and confident, this was just plain asinine.

"*STOP!*" She screamed the word at the top of her lungs. "Do you even hear how crazy you sound?"

My angry retort dried up in my mouth. Yes, I did sound crazy and there was nothing more I could say that would convince her that I wasn't. I had to show her.

I lunged for Peter. The twins, unprepared for my sudden action, attempted to grab ahold of him to keep him in place. Peter was just too fast. He dodged their efforts and twisted out of my way. He ran to Auri's side. The two of them faced off against the family defiantly.

Donatella protested to our grandmother. "Stella is completely deranged! Peter has done nothing to deserve this."

Nona turned to the boy in question. "Peter, that is your name, isn't it?"

He glanced at Auri for reassurance. "Yes, ma'am. Peter Rudkovski."

Nona sighed. "I'm afraid I must ask you to leave."

"What? No, Nona, you can't!" Auri cried.

With a subtle wave of her fingers, Nona enchanted Auri so she couldn't speak. Her mouth gaped open and closed several times as she tried to argue. All that came out were ragged squeaks.

Nona eyed Peter before saying, "My granddaughter seems to believe you are a threat to us. Why would she think that?"

"She's obviously delusional," Peter responded.

His answer steeled Nona's decision. "No, she is not delusional. I am sorry, but you are not welcome here any longer. Boys, please see Mr. Rudovski out."

Peter's expression turned dark at the sudden change of atmosphere. Coldly, he addressed Aurelia, "What's going on, Auri? You invite me to dinner and this is how your family treats me? I knew they were heathens, but I didn't think they would be so rude and intolerant."

Though Aurelia couldn't say anything, her eyes conveyed sheer mortification.

"Yeah, it's almost as rude as trying to kill your girlfriend's cousin," I said.

Peter's mouth curled into a snarl. Without warning, grabbed my mute cousin by the waist and swung her around so that she was in front of him like a human shield. From out of nowhere he produced a large hunting knife and pressed it against her throat.

"Nobody fucking move," he barked, his voice becoming heavy with a Russian accent. "I will slit her throat right here and now."

Frozen in place, Donatella let out a helpless cry. The twins stopped mid-stride, just out of reach of their sister.

"I wouldn't do that if I were you," Nona said, her face set in a formidable expression.

"Shut up you old hag! If you want your granddaughter to live, you're going to do what I say. I want the mirror."

"We don't have it. Peter, please, just let her go!" Donatella found her voice, though it wavered.

"I'll let her go when I get the mirror and I'm out of here safely." He held his ground, the knife scraping against Auri's throat.

My muscles tensed, waiting to catch him off guard. Nona must have felt me shift because she grabbed onto my arm, holding me back.

"Whoever informed you that we have the mirror is mistaken."

He backed out of the dining room, heading for the front door. "You're lying. If it's not here, then you know where it is." Despite the confidence of the words, his voice faltered, leaving doubt hanging in the air.

Nona pressed, "I do not lie. Please, let Aurelia go. We don't want to hurt you."

"Like hell we don't," Justin said. He and Nathan inched toward Peter.

Seeing them advance, Peter wrenched Auri into place, causing her expression to fill with pain. "Keep coming and this knife may just slip."

"Don't be stupid." Nona drew his attention back to her. "You aren't going to get anything from us. We do not have it to give. You can still leave here in one piece though."

"You're right. I will leave in one piece because I'm bringing Aurelia with me. You'll get her back once I get that mirror."

"That is not acceptable," Nona replied, steel in her voice.

"Don't even think of trying any of that magic stuff. I can promise that she will be dead before you even finish your spell."

There was nothing we could do; he was too far away for any of us to overtake and keep Auri safe. We stood helplessly as he backed out of the house. Auri cried in his arms and the knife biting into her neck. When the jangle of bells on the front screen door signaled his exit, Nona and I rushed to the front yard followed by Donatella and the boys.

We opened the door just in time to see Peter heave Auri into his car and then jump in himself. Before we get out into the yard, the gray Audi roared to life and peeled out of the driveway.

"Donatella, call the police," Nona ordered.

"There's no time! We've gotta catch him," Nathan said. "Come on." The twins raced to the driveway.

"Wait, I'm coming with you!" I yelled and ran after them. The three of us crammed into the old white pickup the twins shared.

Nathan was behind the wheel. As he revved the engine to life, Justin said, "He headed toward Gonzales."

We followed Peter's car, tires squealing and engine roaring. We kept up with his sudden, tight turns designed to lose us.

"Look out!" I shouted as Peter flipped a U-turn at a busy intersection.

Justin skidded the truck around. We slid to the left, crashing into each other. The wheels on the right came off the ground. The moment those tires touched back onto the asphalt, we accelerated after the blue Audi.

"Aradia keep us!" I exhaled a prayer when we slid back into the seats.

"Don't worry," Nathan assured me over the roar of traffic. "Justin is the best at GTA. We'll be ok."

Panic and adrenaline made my voice shrill. "This is not a video game!"

"Yeah, well, tell that to Peter," Justin said and gestured in front of us.

I looked up to see Peter's car launch into the steep hill of bushes and that lined the looped entrance to the freeway. Speeding up, the Audi plowed through the plants and cut off a couple of cars as it jumped in front of the traffic. There was a horrendous screech of tires and a sickening crunch of metal and fiberglass. Stunned, Justin pulled to the side of the road. We piled out of the truck to peer over the edge of the broken guard rail.

Peter's car landed hard and the oncoming traffic swerved to miss him and slammed into other cars instead. Somehow, the car Peter drove squealed to life and took off down the freeway.

"Come on!" Justin shouted and we climbed back into the truck. It wasn't any use though. We lost sight of the Audi after that. We spent hours combing the streets, hunting for them.

It was nearing midnight by the time Nathan called a stop to the search. We had made it all the way to Bakersfield, but the trail had gone cold. It had been hours since we last saw Peter and Auri. With heavy hearts, we returned home empty handed.

Chapter Eighteen

Two muscled demons escorted Ryan down a flight of stairs. Ascher waited for them at the bottom. There was a palpable dankness in the air.

Ascher raised his hand. "The young prodigy graces us with his presence." He allowed his hand to fall and said, "If it were up to me, you'd be dead by now for that little stunt in St. Petersburg. Don't think you have me fooled in the slightest."

"What is this about, Ash?" Ryan asked wearily. He stood between the goons with his arms crossed. It was hard to tell if they were there to protect him or to restrain him.

"This," Ascher gestured behind him. There was a man, tied to a chair looking frantic at the predicament he found himself in. He was a soldier—American by the looks of the uniform. His piercing gray eyes were angry and confused all at once.

"Who is that?" Ryan didn't seem upset or outraged. His tone held all the emotion of asking about the weather.

Ascher flashed a wicked smile. "Does it matter who it is? Or what he has done? Who he's related to? Would that change what you must do?"

"It might," Ryan allowed, "it depends on what it is that I have to do."

Ascher's grin deepened. "His name is Thomas Evangeline. I believe you know his sister, Stella? We picked him up outside his base in Afghanistan."

The news didn't affect Ryan in the least. "Why is he here?"

"Think of this as the aptitude test that will shape the course of your continued education with me. It is a

testament to your loyalty to our Lord."

Ryan nodded once, accepting the challenge. His voice was steady as he asked, "What do you need?"

The older Grigori stepped aside, allowing the bound man to have the spotlight. "That depends on what information you can get. He may well know the whereabouts of the mirror. If he doesn't, then he will be used to entice Stella to give it to us. You have three days to get whatever information we can use and decide which one it will be."

Looking grim, Ryan stepped forward. With sharp, jerky motions, he removed the duct tape gag from the man's mouth. Immediately the soldier began muttering something too low to be comprehensible. To shut him up, Ryan backhanded him so hard that the sound echoed off of the damp concrete walls. The bright red gleam of blood stained the soldier's lips.

Ryan didn't miss a beat. He grabbed the man's ear and jerked his head up and to the side. He hissed, deadly, "You will tell me everything I want to know. You will leave nothing out. Do you understand?"

***

Ascher sat at a desk. Open windows allowed sunlight to stream into the room. He busied himself with paperwork, jotting down notes here and there. As one of the double doors to his office opened, he didn't even glance up.

"What have you found out?"

Ryan remained standing, his clothes streaked with blood. Some spots were a dark red-brown, looking more like mud than anything else. In other areas, the liquid shone vibrantly red. Fresh.

"He says he doesn't know who has the mirror. The last he heard of it, his sister said it was safe somewhere, but didn't give a location." The statement was flat and without emotion.

Ascher set his pen aside and shuffled the papers into a

neat stack. "No matter. We have our orders. Our Lord has decreed that the girl must die. We will use her brother to bring both her and the mirror to us."

Keeping his hands in his pockets, Ryan strolled closer to the desk. Sounding only politely interested, he asked, "What makes you think she will do this?"

"From the reports I've received from my agent, she will do anything to protect her brother. She would go to Hell and back if it meant he would be safe." An evil grin stretched his lips across his face. "In fact, that is what the Lord will have us do."

"I don't understand," Ryan frowned. "Why are we going into Hell?"

"Think about it, Orion. There's no better place to start the end of the world than in Hell, is there?"

"Stella! Hey! Snap out of it!" Justin shook me roughly. "We're home."

Blinking, I brought myself back to reality. I hadn't gone to sleep so much as the vision had overtaken me. My heart raced as a sick, anxious feeling formed in the pit of my stomach.

Thomas. He was in trouble.

Climbing out of the car, I ran into the house, completely awake and in full panic mode. The clock in the kitchen read two forty-five in the morning. Both Nona and Donatella were up waiting for us.

"Did you find her?" Donatella demanded as soon as we got through the door.

"No, Mom. We didn't," Justin admitted, his eyes fixed on the ground.

"What did the cops say?" Nathan chimed in.

Donatella looked horrible; her usually perfect red hair stuck up at odd angles and was bushier than normal. Dark circles had materialized under her eyes. Somehow deep wrinkles appeared in her usually smooth face. She had aged at least twenty years in the space of a few hours.

"They said we need to wait for Peter to call for a ransom demand. They have their people looking out looking for her," Nona explained. I could hear the worry in her voice.

"Nona, I had another vision," I said, unable to keep the images to myself any longer.

"Who cares?" Donatella spat at me. "My baby was taken right from this house and it is your fault. Your visions don't mean shit."

I tamped down my initial reaction to yell back at her. Her daughter had been kidnapped at knifepoint right in front of her. She was upset and had every right to be. Fighting with Donatella wasn't going to accomplish anything except getting everyone upset. There were other things to think about.

"Thomas was kidnapped by Ryan and Ascher. They were torturing him!" I struggled to keep my panic at bay. My brother meant the world to me. If he was hurt . . .

"When did you have this vision?"

Justin coughed. "She fell asleep on the way back. She was talking, but I couldn't make out the words. Are you sure it was a vision and not just a nightmare?"

That suggestion made me pause. There wasn't much of a difference between vision and nightmare. Was it possible to differentiate them?

Nona rose from her seat and came to embrace me. She assured me, "It's all right, Stella. If there was a problem with Thomas, the military would have contacted us. I think perhaps this time the stress of what happened to Aurelia has gotten to you a bit."

I clung to that knowledge as though it were a life raft. Nona was right. Of course, she was right; it had just been a nightmare, nothing more. Thomas was safe. Then why was there still a lingering moment of doubt that made me sick?

"Go get yourselves cleaned up. We are going to do a

protection for Aurelia. Donatella and I waited until you three got back."

"Us too?" Justin asked, surprised. He and Nathan didn't do magical work. If Nona was asking for them to participate, it showed a level of desperation rarely seen.

"Yes. Blood calls to blood. You're needed if we are to bring her home," Nona explained. "Now, everyone into the backyard. The sooner we do this, the better."

The twins started a fire in the backyard pit at Nona's request. When it was crackling against the night sky, the five of us gathered around it.

Nona walked the circle, handing out large stalks of green with purple flowers at the tips. "Each of you get a sprig of betony. As you hold it, think on Aurelia. Imagine her at home with us. Picture her safe and healthy in your mind."

Nona pricked our fingers with the point of her bone handled knife.

"Repeat after me, *chiamate di sangue al sangue che vi guida indietro per la sicurezza della famiglia. Canta il sangue al sangue, la nostra connessione ininterrotta.*"

The Italian spell rolled off my tongue easily. We repeated the chant nine times, our blood mingling with the leaves of the betony. At Nona's signal, we tossed our stalks into the fire. The flames flared bright red as the spell wrapped around the plants ignited and dispersed into the air around us. A breeze swept the magic off into the night.

"What do we do now?" Donatella asked. There was a tremor in her voice that made her sound afraid and weak. I felt bad for her.

"We wait," Nona said and settled down in a chair near the fire. "You heard the police; they are doing everything they can. Now, so have we. She will come back to us safely, Donatella. Have faith."

For once, my cousin didn't have anything to say. She wrapped her shawl tighter around her shoulders and went inside.

"Nona, do you need us for anything else?" Justin asked as he cast nervous glances toward the house. Worry etched over his face.

Our grandmother shook her head. "Go comfort your mother. She needs you. Stella and I will stay by the fire for a while."

Nathan gave me a pat on my shoulder before following his brother into the house. I took a seat across from Nona. The flames illuminated her wraith-like figure.

"This isn't your fault," Nona said at last.

I blinked. "What?"

"It's not your fault that Aurelia was taken."

"Nona, it's not—"

She interrupted me. "Stella, I owe you an apology. I expected life to go right back to the way it was before you met Ryan. I hoped you would forget about that angel and to move on with your life. That was not fair." She fed some more twigs to the fire, lost in its crackling light. "I need you to tell me everything you know about Peter."

I shrugged. "There's not much to tell. The first time I saw him was in St. Petersburg. Ascher was controlling him both at the safe house and I think on the train too. Peter's more of a puppet for Ascher than his own person."

"Did you know that Aurelia has been dating him for the two months? She met him at school."

"I knew she was dating someone. I didn't know it was him and I didn't realize it had been for that long." I frowned at this information.

"What I mean to say is that if it wasn't for you, we wouldn't have known how dangerous he is. He could have done a lot more damage."

"Yeah, but Auri still was taken. Waiting around isn't doing anything. We've got to find her."

My grandmother shook her head. "We don't know

what we are dealing with here. There's no way to know where she is. I spoke with the police and they assure me the best thing to do is wait, even though it seems counterproductive. Peter will contact us with his demands; we already know he wants the mirror. We will get her back, one way or another."

I didn't like it, but she had a point. We had to wait.

It was the doorbell that broke us out of the tense silence born of many hours of waiting. My eyes flew open at the sound. The twins cast surprised glances at me as their mother leapt to her feet and ran to the door. We followed her. Nona, who had been in her room, beat us there.

As we piled into the front hall, Nona opened the door. Soft words were spoken. Nona's hands flew to her mouth.

"Nona?" Donatella asked. "Who's at the door?"

In answer, she allowed two uniformed officers into the house. I stared at them as they removed their hats and waited for Nona to lead them further inside. As they shuffled into the living room, we all followed. A chill overtook me.

"Won't you please sit?" Nona gestured to the couch. The men did as she asked. When they were both seated, she inquired courteously, "Would you like something to drink?"

One answered for them both, "No thank you, ma'am."

Donatella, Justin, Nathan, and I eased into the room and took stock of the two gentlemen before us. They perched on the edge of the couch and gripped their caps in front of their bodies as though they were shields. One was older than the other; I could see the peppering of gray in his closely cut black hair. The younger one looked to be around Thomas' age and all tan and blond.

Nona lowered herself into her recliner—the only

one of us to sit—and folded her hands in her lap. To the two strangers, she must have seemed calm and stoic, however I could see the fear course through her that manifested in the slight tremble in her clasped hands.

We waited for the officers to speak, the silence sharpening to rigid and painful points.

It was the older one who spoke first. "Ma'am, we are here about your grandson, Thomas Evangeline."

"Yes?" The question was asked with seeming disinterest. There was a subtle, yet jarring thread of desperation tinging the edges of the word.

"I am sorry to inform you that Staff Sargent Evangeline has gone missing in action. His last known whereabouts were outside of Camp Qargha."

"What? What do you mean?" I didn't know I spoke until I heard the questions come out of my mouth. The panicked note in my outburst made it shriller than it should have been. "How can my brother be missing?" My questions made the officers wince.

"Stella," Nona admonished. "I apologize for my granddaughter. Please, can you explain what you mean?"

The older officer shifted in his seat and answered, "It means, ma'am, that we have not been able to locate Staff Sargent Evangeline since his last mission, three days ago. His unit was doing a routine patrol. They came under enemy attack. When the fire ceased, Staff Sargent Evangeline was the only one not accounted for. I assure you, we are doing everything we can to locate him."

I stared at the officers, not wanting to believe what they were saying. Unbidden, the vision of Ryan torturing my brother came to mind. Had that been real after all? I fought not to be sick.

Nathan put his hand on my shoulder, consolingly. More words were said, but I didn't hear any of it. At last, the older officer ended the conversation by handing Nona a card and imploring her to call if she heard from her grandson.

Nona assured him that she would. Donatella escorted the officer's out. My mind raced with what to do. There was no more doubt that my dreams had been real.

Nona and I stared at each other in shock.

I whispered, "They did take him. They are going to take him down into Hell."

"Hell? Like, *Hell* Hell? Are you sure?" Justin asked.

My grandmother shook her head as if she could keep the reality of what was happening at bay if she continued to deny it.

Donatella ran into the living room, taking shuddering breaths even as fresh tears poured down her cheeks. "Peter sent me this." She handed her phone to Nona.

Frowning, my grandmother squinted at the device. "Stella, hand me my glasses, please."

I grabbed the frames from the lampstand next to her armchair. As I handed them over, I peered down at the screen. An image of Aurelia, blindfolded and bound, floated above a menacing text that read *If you want to see her alive again, surrender the mirror. Stella knows where to bring it. Do not call the authorities or she will die.*

My blood ran cold at the words. Both my brother and my cousin were now in the hands of Ascher and Ryan.

"Nona, we can't let them hurt my Auri. Stella needs to give up the mirror." She turned to me. "I don't understand why you aren't going to deliver it right now."

"It's not that simple," I said.

"Of course it is. Give them what they want and we get Auri and Thomas back."

Nona spoke up then. "What Stella means is that the mirror is still missing. We don't know where it is, so there's no way we can give it to Peter for ransom."

The sick expression on Donatella's face mirrored how my stomach felt. "So you're telling me that my baby is going to die, all because she lost some stupid antique compact mirror?" She waved her finger at my face.

"No one is going to die," Nona said, her voice rising. "Both of you calm down! We need to call a meeting with the coven. When we are all together, we can come up with a plan."

Both Donatella and I made loud sounds of protest. "We don't have time for that! Nona, we have to act now!"

I blinked, realizing that Donatella and I had just agreed on something.

Nona quieted us with a level stare. "Listen to me very carefully. Lives are at stake. We need a plan. We need the support of the whole coven behind us."

"By the time we have all that, both Auri and Thomas could be dead!" I shot back. "Nona, remember how you told me I'm supposed to be the one to change the world and bring about a religious revolution? You either believe those things or you don't. Well, I am telling you right now that I believe! I can get them back. I'm going to save Auri and Thomas."

My grandmother appeared stricken; the sadness in her eyes was vivid, but she didn't argue. Instead, she drew in a sharp breath and gave me a nod. "Alright. Do what you must. If you need help, send word and the whole family will be behind you."

I squeezed her frail frame before heading to my room to grab the bag that I kept at the ready (some habits from traveling with Azra were hard to break).

Donatella followed me into the bedroom. "Stella, wait."

I halted, closing my eyes against what she was about to say. For all I knew she was going to keep slinging blame.

"Listen, I know we haven't really been close. I know we've been at odds in the past, but I need you to know that what you are doing means a lot. It takes a lot of courage to go save someone who's been your rival for your entire lives."

"Auri was never my rival," I told my cousin. "I've never once thought of her like that. She's family. You know as much as I that the Stregheria takes care of their own." Picking up the bag and slinging it over my shoulder, I offered, "Do you want to come with?"

Making a grateful, yet sad face, Donatella said, "I would just get in your way. I'm not as powerful as you are. You have the best chance of finding my daughter. I don't want to hinder that." She hesitated before reaching out for an embrace.

The hug was uncomfortable, but we made it through. I was grateful we got to clear the air some. Maybe this marked the start of a better relationship between my cousins and I. At least I hoped so.

Donatella left the room without saying anything more and I made sure I had what I needed.

The one thing I did take aside from my travel bag was the picture of me and Thomas. I picked up the blue plastic frame and gazed at the photo, steeling myself for what I was about to do.

We were both smiling in the picture, our faces mashed together, cheek to cheek. I remembered that day. We'd just moved back to the states and decided to go to the Santa Monica Pier. The picture was taken after the roller coaster ride, so we both had that windswept look and the flush of adrenaline in our cheeks.

A surge of determination coursed through me. Thomas would not have given up; he would have done whatever it took to save me if I were in his shoes.

I would bring him and Auri home, no matter what. The fresh resolve spurred me into action. With the picture and my car keys in hand, I made for the front door.

I was bound for Hell and nothing could stop me.

Chapter Nineteen

All the way to Malibu, I formulated a plan. There was only one person in the world that I could think of that would help me get into Hell. While Azra wasn't going to like it I had to figure out a way for him to help me. He had made it clear that I wouldn't be able to strong arm him with threats of magic.

I gunned the engine with renewed anxiety. I was doing the right thing; I had to keep that in mind at all times. Fear and doubt had no part of my plan and would be just as dangerous, if not more, than whatever Ascher and Ryan could dish out.

I pulled off to the side of the road near Leo Carrillo beach. Without bothering to lock my door, I raced down the sand riddled wooden steps.

The beach held dim memories of that fateful first battle between us and Ascher. The images overlapped with the sunny afternoon, making the whole thing surreal. Few people were out along the water and I couldn't imagine why not. Still, the lack of a crowd worked to my advantage. When we were traveling together, Azra taught me that if we ever got separated, to find someplace with water and signal him. He'd given me an old party favor—the kind that when you blow into it a tube and some paper uncurls along with a deep kazoo-like sound. Blow into it seven times, he'd told me with the utmost serious expression on his face. Though I still thought the whole process was ludicrous, I was desperate. I had to try.

As I approached the shoreline, I raised the party favor to my mouth and blew into it as instructed.

Nothing happened. At least not right away. With the

next swell, two figures that appeared bobbing in the waves were coming ashore. An outline of a goat stood precariously upon a yellow surfboard.

"Holy shit, it worked," I muttered to myself as the figures became clearer. Sure enough, Beth and Azra were sailing toward the beach.

Despite my restlessness, it was amusing to see Beth holding her own on the water. The wave brought her all the way to shore and she leapt onto the sand, bleating excitedly. She trotted forward to greet me.

"Hey, girl," I murmured. "It's good to see you too."

"Beth! Get away from her. She might cast a spell on you and then let her crazy Italian family dissect you." Azra picked up both boards and lugged them to the dry sand, glaring at me the entire time.

Shifting my attention away from the goat, I stood tall and addressed the Grigori. "I need your help. Your nephew kidnapped my brother and my cousin."

He stuck the surfboards into the sand and pulled up one of the beach chairs. From a small blue cooler, he withdrew a can of beer and cracked it open. After taking a long pull, he asked, "What do you want me to do about it?" He didn't give me the chance to respond before he said, "I'll tell you exactly what I'll do—not a damn thing."

"They're demanding that I take the mirror to Hell to get them back."

He winced at the word Hell but otherwise kept his aloofness. "I don't have any ties to H-E-double-hockey-sticks. Even if I did, what makes you think I would help after your witchy family tried to take me apart like some biology frog?"

"We were healing you, you moron!"

He folded his arms and lifted his chin stubbornly. "See? You can't even admit to what you were doing. Look, even if I wanted to help, I can't. There's no way to get a living human into the Devil's domain. It's kinda off limits."

"Then how can Ascher and Ryan take my brother and my cousin there?"

"Are you sure you heard them correctly? Maybe they're taking them to some sort of theme park? Or a circus? I've heard those places can be like Hell."

"This isn't an idle threat. Ascher and Ryan are taking Auri and Thomas down to the underworld." I glared at the Grigori as he sat there, unmoving, holding his beer.

"I don't care how many times you repeat it, Strega Girl. It's not my problem," he said and took another pull from his bottle.

He was being stubborn. Fine. I had one more trick up my sleeve.

Plopping into the sand, I stared out into the ocean. The tears came easy enough at the thought of my brother. When my sight was blurry with unshed tears, I gave a little whimper. Putting every ounce of desolation I could into my voice, I said, "Azra, I have to get my family back. Ascher and Ryan will kill my brother and my cousin if I don't give them what they want. Please. Help me save them."

Just as I thought, at the sight of my tears, Azra began to panic.

"Why are you leaking? That's just not sanitary! Stop it, okay?"

I let out a quiet sob and bowed my head.

The angel let out an aggravated huff. "Fine. I'll help you as much as I can. Just stop crying already."

I dared raised my head, tears still in my eyes. "Really?"

Azra asked with resignation, "Yes, really. Now, what do they want in return for your family?"

Instantly, I regained my composure. I answered in my normal tone of voice. "What else? They want the mirror."

"You sneaky little witch!" He shook his head in

disgust at my quick recovery. "Well, last I checked, you don't have the mirror, so this whole conversation is moot."

"I'll create a decoy mirror. I'll enchant it and fool them into thinking it's the real deal."

"Can you do that? Make a fake mirror?"

"I can make something that will pass long enough to get Thomas and Auri out of there."

At this, Azra stood and started pacing in what I liked to call his thinking circle. I'd seen him do this many times during our travels. If you watched him long enough, it would make you dizzy.

"Okay, if you can do that, I think I know someone that can help us get into the great pizza oven of the damned." He dove for the beach bag hanging on the back of his chair. From within its depths, he pulled out a crumpled piece of paper and a stub of a pencil. He scribbled excitedly.

When he finished, he pressed the paper into my hand and said, "I need you to get everything on this list and bring it back here by dusk. We're going to need these things to entice them to come."

"Them?" I was almost afraid to ask.

"The demons of course!" He put his hand over mine, crushing a wad of cash into the supply list and stared at me with the utmost seriousness. The golden flecks in his bright blue eyes gleamed and it reminded me that despite his bumbling appearance, he was still an angel. His words resonated in the air as though they had special significance. "Until I call for you, prepare yourself for the worst and pray with all your might for the best." He pulled out a leash from his back pocket and put it on Beth. Within seconds, they were gone.

"What does that even mean?" I asked the empty air. Still, Azra's excitement gave me a certain measure of hope. For the first time since I got the news about my brother, I felt like I was in control. Breathing in a deep lungful of ocean air, I looked at the piece of paper in my hand and read the list.

"What kind of ceremony is he planning?" I asked the wind. The only answer were the cries of seagulls overhead. There wasn't a lot of time to linger on the list. Taking one last look at the waves, I crammed the paper into my pocket and trekked back up the beach to where I had parked.

***

The streetlights were lit along the freeway by the time I gathered the items on Azra's list as well as the fake mirror and brought them back to the beach. It took two trips to get it all to the ritual area Azra made on the sand. He'd set up a circle of stones and had built a bonfire in the center before I arrived. The Grigori was sitting next to the fire with Beth next to him. The blue cooler rested on the other side of the chair. Azra munched on Chex Mix as he surveyed my pile of bags imperiously over the flames.

"Did you get everything?" he asked as he stood. It gave me a good look at his chosen outfit; a dark robe with little red horned demons dancing along the hemline. It cinched at the waist with what looked like a belt from a Santa costume. In the fading light, with his face illuminated by the fire, there was a sinister cast to his features.

I set my backpack next to the pile of grocery bags and answered, "I think so." I handed him the piece of paper and he read aloud from it.

"Four saint candles: Mother Mary, the patron saint of impossible causes; Anthony of Padua, the patron saint of lost items; Christopher, the saint of travelers; and, of course, the patron Saint of Canada, Joseph."

I pawed through one of the bags and removed the paper-wrapped glass pillar candles, lining them up for inspection.

He nodded in approval. "Three pounds of white and powdered sugar sifted together in the light of a pool of rainwater."

I hefted the sugar out of the bag and sat it next to the candles. "It didn't rain, so I hope a swimming pool will work."

"It'll do. Next are the Mardi Gras beads with the lobster attached to them, the day-old doughnuts, and the sparkling apple cider instead of wine because you are under age."

"Got them."

He grinned his approval. "Good! How about the portable CD player and the thirteen-inch length of papyrus with the quill made from a raven feather?"

"Will a ballpoint pen and notebook paper work?" I asked as I presented the CD player.

Azra shrugged, "Eh, sure. Okay, I think we are ready to start." He picked up the bag of sugar and began walking backward in a circle around Beth and me, letting the sugar spill onto the ground just outside of the rocks that he set up earlier. The powder left an uneven line and puffs of white in his wake. He sneezed a couple of times and muttered something about the sensitivity of corporeal olfactory senses. Once the circle was completed, he tossed the bag to the ground.

The sun had completely set by this time and the bonfire was the only light on the beach. Beth wandered over and started chewing on the discarded sugar bag.

I opened my mouth to tell Azra what Beth was doing. He shushed me before I even uttered a word.

Holding his arms above his head, he announced to the deserted beach and the rocking ocean, "I will now put in the sacred music." From within his robe, he withdrew a thin CD case. With an air of reverence, he put it into the player and turned it on. Enya blared from the cheap speakers.

"You've got to be kidding me," I groaned as he pirouetted over to get the candles.

"There will be silence in the sacred circle!" he bellowed. Then, after a thoughtful pause, he asked, "Did you remember matches?"

I raised my eyebrow at him and pointed to the bonfire crackling next to us. Comprehension dawned on his face. Without another word, he picked up two of the candles, upended them, and went to stick his hands directly over the flames.

As soon as I realized what he was about to do, I moved to stop him.

"Why don't I do that?" I intercepted the candles and managed to bat his arms away from the flames. "I can do it without getting hurt."

He squinted at me. "Is it a witch thing? If I recall correctly, didn't they burn your kind? Shouldn't that make you sort of flammable?"

I didn't even dignify that with a response. Instead, I simply grabbed a small piece of kindling and held it to the edge of the fire. Once the end was lit, I touched the unlit candles wicks with it, setting them aglow.

"That was not as entertaining as I imagined it would be," Azra commented as I tossed the stick into the fire. He surveyed the uneven circle. "Now, where were we? Oh yes. Set the candles along the perimeter."

"Do you want them at the cardinal points?" I asked as I picked up the candles. The flames gave the saints on the outside of the glass a warm glow.

"Don't be stupid, Strega Girl. There are no points in a circle."

I was having doubts about Azra's summoning abilities. He couldn't even set a proper circle. Then again, maybe angel summoning spells were different. Quelling my misgivings, I continued to set the candles along the sugar in the sand.

He gestured for the bottle of sparkling cider and the

box of doughnuts. Beth was still licking at the sugar bag, completely ignoring what was going on. I opened the bottle and flipped the top of the doughnuts. Swiping the glass bottle from my hands, he plucked a glazed jelly pastry from the box.

"I am now initiating the sacred consumption!" he shouted at the top of his lungs.

"Why are you shouting?" I asked. "I'm right here."

He glared at me through a mouthful of fried dough, raspberry jelly smudging the corners of his mouth. He swallowed thickly and took a quick swig from the bottle. "I am addressing the powers that be. How else do you think we will get them here? You need to shut up lest you scare them away!"

I bit my tongue and kept quiet.

Azra threw his hands skyward. "Oh great powers, I beseech thee! Grant me the presence of those demons that can guide me through the caverns of Hades to the presence of the Dark Betrayer of all creation! Give me the guides required to confront the most cursed of all angelic beings, the purveyor of sin and lies!" He scampered over to the blue cooler and eased the lid open.

"I offer unto you the following sacrifices." He pulled the first item out of the cooler and tossed it into the bonfire. It was a tin foil wrapped package that oozed out of the side. An unholy stench wafted out of the tin foil. I almost threw up right then and there. Azra wasn't affected.

"First, I offer unto you the baked potato that has been living in my fridge for the last decade as well as the left-over goulash from last week. I'm sure you would also enjoy the brick hard chicken with a sour mustard demi-glaze." He leaned over and whispered to me, "I made that myself."

As he chanted out the names of the sacrifices, he tossed them into the fire. Each time they met the flames, a spark of color would erupt. I wondered what kind of chemicals he used when cooking to cause that sort of reaction. Mentally, I vowed not to eat anything he gave me from here on out.

After dumping the remaining cider onto the sand, he was out of sacrifices. He looked at me and commanded, "Write what I say word for word. It has to be perfect."

I scrambled to grab hold of the notebook and pen. When they were in hand, I settled into a cross-legged position. With the pen poised against the notebook page as I waited for Azra.

He shook his head with impatience and began his dictation. "Dear minions of Hell. Stop. How are you doing today? Stop. Sheranacth eran thakkor illium. Stop."

"What was that last part? What language are you speaking?" I paused my writing.

Azra hissed at me, his eyes wide in reaction to my interruption. "Just shut up and write! We can't afford to stop now!"

"I can't spell any of that," I protested.

"Use Ebonics! Just sound it out."

"I think you mean phonetics," I corrected him.

He scowled and resumed his position with his arms outstretched. "Whatever. Just keep up." He cleared his throat and continued his dictation. "Asheller nomeralda kaffer fish tacos. Stop. Ilicker ojarap xatern coronas hafner. Stop. All my best to the kid. Stop. Love Azra. Stop."

I finished with a flourish, hoping I had it right. One thing about Azra I'd almost forgotten was how random he was. He seldom did what anyone expected. Still, he was my only link to getting Thomas and Auri back in one piece. I offered the paper to him for review.

Azra didn't even read it over. He handed me the empty sparkling cider bottle and simply told me, "Roll it up nice and small and put it into the bottle."

I did as he asked, then, at his gesture to follow, we exited the circle. He led me to the water. Together, we set the glass container adrift in the ocean.

Something flashed out in the water and a chill went down my spine. Someone was watching us. Possibly two someone's because the bonfire reflected in what appeared to be two sets of eyes.

The water drew back out of the natural rhythm and much farther than it should have. A loud crashing sound erupted as the ocean balled itself up into a massive wave. My mouth dropped. Had the stupid ritual worked?

The wave came rushing back and I edged backwards leaving Azra standing at the shoreline. I could hear laughter as the wave crashed. I grabbed Beth, who was still gnawing on the sugar bag and pulled her to the other side of the fire, away from the water.

"Oh good," Azra said over the din. "They're here."

Chapter Twenty

The firelight illuminated two figures on surfboards coasting on the wave crest. They landed in the sand, just in front of the bonfire, still sitting on their boards.

"Ha!" the male figure crowed triumphantly, "I beat you!"

The woman shook her head and muttered under her breath.

Azra approached the two things. They weren't quite human; there was something off about them, something that screamed danger. Plus, their auras were strange. Stranger even than Azra's. They had the same feel of Fallen Ones, but somehow, they were more than that.

"Levi, Betty! Thanks for coming!"

The man turned to Azra and grinned. "Hey, Az, my man! Got your text about the party." He glanced around. "Are we early or something? Why isn't anyone else here?"

"Text?" I glared at the Grigori. That stupid ritual was for nothing? Who knew how much longer Thomas could hold out, and Azra was having me write love notes in Demonese! My hands balled up into fists and I stood.

The female thing— Betty, I assumed, cocked her head at me. Unlike her companion, her expression was disdainful. Of the two, she gave off the air of being the more dangerous. "You shouldn't take it personally you know," she said to me as she ran a hand through her short-cropped black hair. Her voice was dark and husky. "He's a Grigori. It's in their job description to be obtuse, I think. If it will make you feel better, we can blame Orion for giving him a cell phone."

I was taken aback. Had she read my thoughts?

"Now, listen here, little miss," the male demon— Levi wasn't it?—addressed me sternly, "Do you know how much harm littering causes? I expect you to clean this entire place up before we leave. Here," he tossed the bottle I'd set adrift with the note back at me. The cap had been lost, but the paper was still in it, soggy from the sea. "Recycle that."

I caught it and blinked. Did a demon just tell me to recycle?

"How was your trip?" Azra interjected before I could react. "Did you catch some nice waves?"

Levi held his hands up, halting Azra. "Where are your manners? Corona me, Grom. Then we talk business."

Azra's eyes widened. "Grom? Look, I know our shared affinity for surfing is what keeps us civil with each other, but let's be real. Who beat you in the last three competitions?"

Levi grinned, "Betty. There is a reason why I love that demon." He cast a sly wink at Betty and she smiled in response.

"I still beat you," Azra said, undeterred. "Get your own beer. They're in the cooler."

Levi stuck his board upright in the sand and casually sauntered over to the cooler. He stopped short when Beth looked up from her bag of sugar and baaed in warning. She lowered her head, ready to ram him in the knees.

Levi spread his hands open at his sides to show he didn't mean any harm. In his most placating surfer tone, he said, "I really need to get into that cooler, little goat."

Beth stomped her right hoof and stood her ground over the sugar, not at all impressed with the creature in front of her.

Levi endeavored to explain, "See, that cooler has a Corona in there for me. It is something that I need to maintain the balance of the universe. Or at least my personal universe."

Beth lowered her head and grunted, nudging her bag to the side protectively.

Heaving a sigh, Levi turned to Azra, "Would you call off the attack goat already?"

Azra pretended not to hear him and instead struck up a conversation with Betty. "To business. The reason why we summoned you—"

Movement out of the corner of my eye made me glance over in time to see Beth nip at Levi's outstretched hand hovering over the cooler. He withdrew it with a muted curse and continued to plead his case.

"You don't understand, little goat. There are starving children in Asia that I could help if I had a beer. Think of the children."

Beth rushed forward and head butted Levi in the stomach, sending him sprawling backwards onto the sand. He scrambled back to the water. "Azra! What did you teach this thing?"

The goat launched herself after him in a sugar induced vehemence. She managed to get hold of Levi's flame patterned swim trunks with her teeth. Beth slid to a halt, but Levi kept going and there was a loud rip as the material split.

Levi let out a scream that reverberated against the beachside cliffs and dove straight for the water. It was only a moment after the splash that I realized Beth managed to disrobe the demon completely.

Had I just seen my first streaking demon?

Beth stalked up and down the beach, just out of the water's reach, chewing on what was left of Levi's swim trunks. If it hadn't been so comical, the sight would have been menacing.

I chanced a fleeting look at Azra and Betty to see if they had witnessed what had happened.

Apparently, they had not because Azra was busy trying to explain to Betty what we needed. "What I'm trying to say was that we—this Strega Girl," he waved in my general direction to indicate who I was, "and I need to get into Hell. To do that, we need a pass. How can we get in contact with the Eminence of Darkness, the big Devilled Egg, Head Honcho, or whatever he is calling himself these days?"

Betty laughed, snorting a little bit. "I gotta tell him that one. I don't think he's been called a Devilled Egg before."

Azra looked annoyed. "Can you help me or not?"

Betty quieted her chuckling and asked her partner, "What do you think Levi?" When he didn't immediately answer, she whirled her head up and around, looking for him. "Levi? Where are you?"

A splash sounded out in the water, "Over here." Levi waved, he then pointed to the goat, not wanting to explain any further.

"Call off your goat," Betty sighed. "Then we'll talk."

Azra nodded and called out to his companion, "Beth! Come here, girl. Let the nice demon out of the water."

Beth remained at her post, glaring and chewing at the now thin strips of fabric. She ignored Azra, keeping her eyes on Levi, almost daring him to try.

"Beth!" Azra barked. "Stop that this instant young lady!"

I groaned and headed over to the cooler. I had a suspicion why she was acting like she was. "Beth!" I called out. "Come here and get your sugar."

At the "S" word, the goat whirled around and pranced over to me. She head butted my hand until I dropped the bag onto the sand.

Betty called out to Levi, "Will you get out of the water? You're embarrassing me."

The sullen reprimanded tone floated from the direction of the waves, "Yes, dear."

We all settled down near the bonfire to talk. I was surprised to note that Levi had somehow conjured up another pair of swim trunks. The demon delicately positioned himself away from Beth, keeping Betty and myself between him and the goat. Beth happily licked the inside of the bag and didn't pay the slightest attention to him anymore.

Betty popped open her bottle of beer and asked, "Why do you need to talk to Luce? I know you said, but say it again for my partner here."

Before Azra could respond, Levi snapped to attention, "You want to chat with the Big Kahuna?"

Azra sighed and for the first time ever, I could see that he was trying to think of the best way to phrase our situation. At last he spoke, "We are on a top secret rescue mission. Bad fish headed down to the Big Barbeque Pit for some less than kosher activities. We've gotta go down there and make sure that doesn't happen."

As I tried to sort out what exactly he said, both of the demons blinked at Azra. Betty asked in a skeptical voice, "Az, have you been to Hell? Ever?"

Ryan's uncle appeared affronted. "Of course not, thank you very much! This will be my first trip if we can talk to your Evil Emperor and get a weekend pass."

"Weekend pass?" Levi cocked his head to the side.

"Unless you have a park hopper pass so we can do Heaven on the return trip, yeah, we need to get passes into Mordor's Mount Doom."

"Dude, what's with the euphemisms? Can't you just say Hell already?"

Azra sniffed. "I was under the impression that Tolkien was universal, much like Star Wars. If he can't get what I'm saying, then the morally depraved hate mongering satyr that you call a master is an idiot."

He was rewarded with angry glares. It was obvious that all joking aside, Azra had just crossed a line with the two demons.

"Look, I'm sorry for Azra's . . . well, let's just say I'm sorry for Azra. We need your help. We need to know how to get into Hell so I can save my brother and my cousin. Ascher and Ryan are going down there for a reason. I don't know what exactly, but it's big and my family is caught up in it. Please, let us talk to Lucifer, or Hades, or Pluto, or whatever he's called. I just want my family back safely."

Betty rolled her eyes and glanced at Levi in askance. He was fighting back tears and sniffling. "I bet he was a good brother too, huh?"

My voice caught in my throat, "The best big brother I could ever hope for."

Without warning, Levi got up and scooped me into a tight embrace. "I wish I had a good big brother. All mine are bastards." He squeezed me and I fought to keep my panic at bay. It was the first time I'd been hugged by a demon.

At last, he let me go and patted me affectionately on the head. "Don't you worry little witch, we will talk to the Big Kahuna for you."

Betty sighed and pulled out her cell phone. Taking into consideration her bikini, I didn't want to contemplate where it had been stashed. She hit a button and held the bright red contraption to her ear. "You are such a softie," she admonished Levi as she waited for the line to pick up.

Levi snatched the phone from her hands and hit speaker just as it connected. The voice that issued out of the small device sent shivers up my spine. "Talk," a deep, masculine voice demanded.

"Big Kahuna!"

"Levi? What do you want this time?" I couldn't be sure, but there was a slight inflection to the voice's cadence and pacing. Almost like an accent I couldn't place.

Was this supposed to be the Devil? He sounded like a menacing, yet beleaguered and overworked security guard.

Betty took the phone from Levi. "There's a situation here with a Grigori and a Strega."

"And?"

"They claim they need to go into Hell to rescue two humans." She covered the phone with her hand and hissed at me, "They're not dead, are they? Because if they are, there's not much we can do about that."

"No, they should be alive," I said, hoping I was right. I didn't want to believe that Thomas was dead.

The demon removed her hand from the phone and resumed talking. "Both humans are still alive. A rogue group of Grigori took them down by force."

The Devil growled in an exasperated tone, "Betty, you know if living humans enter Hell, they're dead, soon to be dead, or better off dead if they do manage to get out. Either way, rescue is the last priority. My sincere apologies to the family, but that's how it is."

Betty's emerald green eyes flicked up to me and she bit her lower lip before saying, "Sire, I think we need to try on this one. They're saying something's about to go down. This little witch thinks she can stop whatever apocalypse is about to be unleashed if she can get into Hell." The demoness smiled lightening her offsetting demeanor. "She just might have it in her to pull it off too."

The compliment took me off guard. Was she endorsing me to get into Hell?

I heard the person on the other line heave a sigh, "The world is always ending, Betty. Wait—I'm on speaker, aren't I?"

Levi shouted, "How's it hanging, Big Kahuna?"

"Take me off of speaker, Betty. Now."

The female demon looked at the phone with panic like she had no idea how to take the speaker function off. She settled for shushing us before she responded, "Okay. Sorry about that, Levi stole the phone from me."

"Where are you?"

"Currently we are at 34 degrees—"

"Give me the city, not latitude and longitude. You've been in the water too long."

I could see Betty bristle at the comment, but she bit her lip to keep quiet. Levi smothered a chuckle with his hands. I glanced over at Azra, surprised he hadn't spoken up yet.

He sat next to the fire, holding his mouth shut and rocking back and forth. He was trying not say anything though he desperately wanted to. From his attitude, I jumped to the conclusion that he and this Luce fellow didn't get along. What had I asked him to do for me and what was it costing him?

"Malibu," was Betty's terse reply.

"Then tell them that we will meet at Saints and Sinners in Los Angeles. It's neutral enough territory."

"Saints and Sinners. Got it. When?"

Betty looked to me, the question unasked.

"I need to get Thomas out of Hell now," I whisper-yelled to her, hoping the cell phone didn't pick up my voice. "We will meet him in one hour."

Nodding, Betty conveyed my request.

There was a growl from the other end of the line. "Fine. But fifteen minutes is all she gets."

"Bye Big Kahuna!" Levi shouted, waving enthusiastically at the phone.

Betty snapped at him to shut up.

There was an angry exhalation from the other end of the line before she disconnected the call.

Azra stood, shaking his head as he grabbed a beer from the cooler. He popped the top off and downed it in a matter of seconds. As soon as it was gone, he reached for another.

"Alright, we'd better go," Betty sighed, getting to her feet. "Don't be late and whatever you do, be respectful. He agreed to meet with you, he's willing to help. You have no idea what a gift that is." After a thoughtful pause she said, "He's nothing like you've heard. So don't treat him like he is."

Before I could respond, Betty disappeared into thin air, taking her surf board with her.

"Well, Az buddy. It's been real," Levi said as he juggled the remaining Corona bottles in his arm. "See you at the next World Surf League tournament. Oh, you should bring the Big Kahuna some devil's food cake. He loves that stuff." The demon paused and turned to give me a meaningful look. I thought I saw the glimmering of more tears at the edge of his pale blue eyes. "I hope you find your family. Good luck. You'll need it in Hell," he told me before he too vanished.

Chapter Twenty-one

I tried not to get my hopes up about the meeting. There was no guarantee that Lucifer would help me. There was even a decent chance he'd kill me on the spot for even asking for his help. All I knew for certain was that I had to try.

When I returned with the devil's food cake, Azra was waiting for me in the parking lot decked out in oven mitts, aviator goggles, a surgical mask, and holding a beekeeper helmet. A little red wagon was hitched to Beth via a leather harness. The goat was also equipped with her own set of goggles. An oversized wooden rosary hung from her neck. A thick white canvas covered the contents of the wagon. I didn't even want to think about what was under it.

I balanced the neon pink frosted cupcakes encased in plastic on one hand and walked over to the waiting Grigori.

"You're late." He tapped his foot and shifted the bee keeper's helmet to his other hand to look pointedly at his bare wrist.

"It's going to take us 10 seconds to teleport." I protested.

"Exactly. We needed to be there at least 20 seconds ago to stake out the premises." He eyed my box of cupcakes. "Are those devils food?"

"Yes."

"Good. We must feed the beast. He's probably hypoglycemic. Before we go, I must prepare you. Don't be alarmed if you notice a lot of Fallen Ones hanging around. They flock to him like cockroaches in a nuclear winter."

Azra cut off the sarcastic reply about to leave my mouth.

"This evil, pitchfork wielding, poor excuse of a messenger may not recognize you as a sentient being. That means I do all the talking. Prepare for the worst. There's no way to tell if he's had time to turn this establishment into a den of sin already. Beth will wait for us outside. We only have one shot at this, so don't go messing it up by doing something stupid. Oh! I almost forgot." He reached into his pocket and proffered to me a surgical mask similar to his. "Put this on."

"Why?"

Azra made a face that meant I was being particularly dense. "Because he is the Master of Sin! The stuff radiates off of him like bad body odor. We need to take every precaution so we don't get infected with it and wind up as one of his minions. Here are your oven mitts."

In disbelief I refused to take the mask nor oven mitts he shoved at me. "I'm not wearing these. Come on. Time is wasting."

Azra shrugged as if to say 'your eternity' and then grabbed my hand. "Alright let's go." The familiar sensation of teleporting gripped my stomach. Except there was something wrong; we lurched about and hit a lot of turbulence. I shook so much it felt like my teeth were coming loose.

At last, we landed. Letting go of Azra's hand, I fought off the urge to be sick.

When I was certain I wouldn't vomit all over the place, I glanced around. The city bustling around us wasn't at all familiar. It definitely wasn't L.A.

"Azra, where are we?"

He peered at the lights and the people over the top of my head. "New Orleans, it looks like."

"What? Why are we here?"

"I don't know," he said shrugged through the

beekeeper helmet. "Something was off. You didn't try to do any witchy stuff did you?"

"Of course I didn't!" I consulted my phone and let out a frustrated sigh. "Come on. Let's go before we are late."

We held hands once again and before we even left New Orleans, the tilt-a-whirl sensation started up again. So intent was I on not being sick that I didn't even notice when we stopped.

"Okay, something's seriously wrong here," Azra huffed as he removed his mesh encased helmet.

Still feeling ill, I chanced a look upwards and was met with the abrupt vision of a dense rainforest. Monkeys scurried through the tree branches and the humidity was chokingly thick.

"Come on, Azra. Stop messing around. I know you don't want to go see the Devil, but I have to. This is getting ridiculous." After scolding the Grigori, I grasped his hand once again, screwed my eyes shut, and hoped for the best.

This time when we landed, I couldn't stop myself from throwing up. There was no time to even open my eyes before it all came out. Beyond the sound of my retching, I heard Azra's gasp and felt him drop my hand.

When I opened my eyes, I was confronted with the sight of black leather boots covered with my vomit. Spitting the rest of the bile off to the side, I lifted my gaze.

The person belonging to the boots was tall—taller even than Azra. He was dressed in jeans and a black t-shirt covered by a worn looking leather bomber jacket. I couldn't place his age. He could have been in his mid-twenties or early thirties.

He had shoulder length, black hair that shone under the streetlights. It was his eyes that drew my attention; they were a hue of blue I'd never seen before. They held me transfixed. That is until they shifted color and deepened to an angry red.

It was about then that his aura hit me like a wave. It took all my focus not to be swept away by it. With trepidation, I stood to my full height and wiped my mouth.

Tall, dark, and handsome wasn't alone. Flanking him were Betty and Levi as well as a third demon. The third had red hair and dressed in an expensive looking pinstripe suit.

Azra pressed against my back, almost falling over me. He brandished an aerosol can menacingly at the collection of demons. "Stay back, Beth! I'll keep you safe. Just don't look at it straight in the eyes."

Despite my embarrassment, I wondered how Azra could work the spray mechanism with his oven mitts on.

Levi must have felt the need to break the pervading tension because he made introductions in a forced upbeat tone. "Goat Boy, Strega Girl, you already know Betty and I. This is Lucifer, aka the Big Kahuna. That one over there is Death Dude. You'd know him as the angel of death, but you can call him Azrael. Boss, this is Goat Boy and Strega Girl."

There was no reaction from Lucifer at the introductions; he simply stood there, glaring at Azra.

It was time for some damage control. I pushed Azra's hand down.

"It's nice to meet you. I'm so sorry about your shoes. Azra's driving made me motion sick. Anyway, my name is Stella." I extended my hand to Lucifer, all the while trying to reconcile the vision before me versus how he was supposed to look according to myth; no cloven hooves, no horns, and no red skin. As far as I could see there was no tail, either. I honestly wasn't expecting the Devil to be so . . . pretty.

Lucifer responded in a terse voice, "You're late."

I winced at the sharpness of his tone. I was not making the best of impressions. "Yeah, I'm sorry about that too."

"I am going to clean my shoes. When I am done, you will have five minutes to plead your case."

"You promised me fifteen, though!"

"That was before you kept me waiting and then threw up me. You're lucky I'm going to listen to you at all." He turned his back on us and made his way to a drab looking building that must have been the Saints and Sinner's bar. The red haired demon, who Levi introduced as Azrael, followed along with Betty.

Levi stage whispered, "Bummer. That was a gnarly first impression, man." He trotted to catch up with the rest of his group.

Azra looked at me, impressed. "Good job, Strega Girl. I never thought to vomit on the Devil."

"Oh, shut up," I groaned.

"Beth, stay here. I don't want that Seducer of Souls to get the idea he wants goat tonight."

In response, Beth wandered over to an errant patch of grass in the vacant parking lot, her wagon squeaking behind her.

Together, Azra and I followed Satan up to the building, stopping short of the front door. An intricate spell had been woven on the outside of it; one that had been crafted by a talented Fallen One. I could see the threads of the spell like tiny sparks of light.

This barrier was it: the point of no return.

Taking a steadying breath, I hooked my arm around Azra's. "Come on. Let's do this."

It took a bit of pulling to get the Grigori moving. Finally, he shuffled after me. We passed through the barrier and the door. Power washed over me in a strange tingling sensation.

The place was abandoned. A layer of dust covered the white sheets over some of the furniture. The bar itself was dull and grimy. Some distant lights were on in the back, but it wasn't enough to illuminate the whole area. The Devil and the redhead sat in a booth near the back of the bar. Otherwise, the place was vacant. Betty and Levi must have left. Warning bells rang in my head as the full weight of what I was doing crashed onto me. I was about to make a deal with the Devil.

Azra, as if sensing my sudden panic, regained his composure and drew himself up to his full height. "Remember, let me do the talking," he muttered.

We approached the booth and stood awkwardly in front of it. The demons waited for us to start.

The Devil's black hair hung loosely to his shoulders and he never once lowered his still glowing red eyes from us. It felt like he could see right through me.

Azra glared across the table at them from under his beekeeper's helmet. Despite wanting to do the talking, he didn't say a word.

After a long moment of tense silence, I decided I should get things going. "I'm sure Betty and Levi told you why we are here," I said.

"Five minutes," the Devil replied. His tone was dark and it sent goosebumps down my arms.

"Alright, the short version. I need to get into Hell. My brother and my cousin were kidnapped and taken there. I need to pay the ransom and get them out. I was told you're the person to talk to for safe passage."

Azrael cleared his throat and folded his well-manicured hands on the table. "Who kidnapped your family and took them into Hell?"

"Four minutes, fifteen seconds," Lucifer reminded me.

"It was a Grigori named Ascher and Azra's nephew, Ryan. They want the mirror that will bring on the end of the world. I think they want to start the destruction from Hell."

"Why should we care who was kidnapped? As for the mirror, there are about five of them that could destroy the world right now." Azrael appeared bored, brushing non-existent specks from his suit. I got the overwhelming impression that I was wasting his time.

Azra flared at the demon's nonchalance, finally breaking his rigid silence. "Orion happens to be the one in the prophecy; the one destined to bring the war between Heaven and Hell to an end. The only angel born on earth and not created. Have more respect, you ignorant—"

"Azra, stop it!" I turned to face the demons and ignored the fact they were snickering at Azra's outburst. "Ryan is beside the point. The mirror is not actually a mirror. It's a tool that was used in the creation of the earth. Legend has it that it was given to my family generations ago by the goddess Ariadne. We disguised this tool as a mirror. If it gets into the wrong hands, it has the power to unmake existence."

"So, let me get this straight: you want to take the equivalent of a nuke into Hell?" The Devil scoffed. "I don't think so."

"I don't have the mirror. What I have is a fake."

"Let's see it."

Immediately, I took my backpack off and unzipped it. Pulling out the plastic shopping bag, I showed him the contents. "See? I still have some spell work to do so they're fooled."

Lucifer reached in and extracted the small, metal compact mirror I'd bought. He held it up to the lights overhead and examined it. When he was satisfied, he placed it in the palm of his hand and at once, flames engulfed the little compact.

"Wait!" I cried, dismayed at the destruction.

Within seconds, the mirror turned to ash. Lucifer wiped his hands on one of the paper napkins on the table. "That's for throwing up on me."

Azra put his oven mitt on my shoulder, signaling for me to keep calm.

Ignoring Azra's warning, I slammed my fists on the

table. "I told you I was sorry. You didn't have to be an asshole about it."

To my astonishment, the Devil smiled at me. "There it is," he said, a smidge of satisfaction edging his voice.

"There what is?"

"The fire in your soul. You're going to need it to get into Hell."

With that, the mask of the arrogant jackass slipped away. His eyes faded back into their haunting blue as he asked in a somber voice, "Do you understand what it is you are asking? You'll be risking not only your life but your soul. And for what? Some half-baked scheme to fool kidnappers into giving your family back? What happens when your enemies figure out your ruse? What are you going to do if this mission claims your life, yet your enemies still live? How will you protect your precious family then?"

Azrael sighed and leaned back in his seat, shaking his head at me. "You're a child playing a deadly game with creatures who helped create the game boards. Can you honestly stand there and tell us it's worth it?"

There was no hesitation in my answer. "My brother means the world to me. I don't think I could live with myself knowing I didn't even try to save him. Not after I've gotten this far."

The two demons exchanged a long glance with each other. Something was decided between them in those uncomfortable minutes; I just hoped it was in my favor.

Finally, Lucifer and Azrael looked at me. It was Lucifer who spoke though. "You shall have your pass into Hell, but only if you can get yourself to a Hellmouth in twenty-four hours. After that, your pass will be revoked."

Hope fluttered in my chest like a caged bird. "Okay, twenty-four hours to get to a Hellmouth. Seems simple enough."

"What about getting out of Hell?" Azra asked.

The Devil regarded the Grigori. Something flashed

in his blue eyes that I couldn't name. Seconds later, his face was a neutral mask as he answered. "If you're clever enough to get yourselves in, then you better be clever enough to get yourselves out again. That's my last warning to you both."

Fear, true fear, found its way into my heart. I stifled it as best as I could, but I couldn't erase it completely.

"Now," the Devil went on, back to business, "I want something from you in return."

Azra poked me in the stomach to get my attention. "Evils-day ood-fay," he whispered.

"Oh! Right. Here," I pulled the package of prepared cupcakes out of my bag and slid them across the table. "Payment."

A disgusted look passed over Lucifer's face as he considered my gift. "I should be more offended," he said more to himself than to me. He slid the package back. "No, what I want in return for your passage into Hell is your first born child."

Next to him, Azrael turned wide-eyed to his boss.

I froze in place, stunned. This sort of thing happened in fairy tales, not in real life, right? No, the Devil was serious. He waited patiently for me to react.

My stunned silence caused Azra to stand in outrage and sputter, "You want what? Why? Who in their right mind would give you their children?"

"I'm kidding, of course," the Devil chuckled darkly at his own joke. He gave Azra a sidelong glance and said, "Aside from an exception or two, kids aren't my thing. No, what I really want is a favor."

With my heart thudding in my chest, I couldn't decide if a favor was better or worse than my first born child. I hazarded the question. "What kind of favor?"

"One equal to the one you are asking of me now. No more and no less." He smirked and tacked on, "You'll be indebted to me." He looked between Azra and me. "Both of you."

I considered his proposal. It was a small price to save Thomas and Aurelia. Besides, it wasn't like I had anything he didn't.

"Deal," I agreed.

Lucifer nodded once and extended his hand to me. His hand was cool and his grip firm. I wondered what exactly I'd agreed to.

"You should know the path into Hell is easy, it's getting out that's the—" A sudden burst of music interrupted him. AC/DC's Highway to Hell blared from someone's pocket. Lucifer grit his teeth and answered his cell phone. "Talk," he growled.

"Talk? You did not just answer my call with a command, did you Satan-butt?" A high pitched arrogant girl's voice issued from the device. The call wasn't on speaker, but she was still clearly heard. "You got this phone for Aria and I to get ahold of you because we're not all telepathic monstrosities like you, remember?"

"Syn," Lucifer growled as he slid out of the booth, "I need to put you on hold for—"

"Put me on hold and I will put sugar in your motorcycle's gas tank!" The girl screamed. "The world is about to end, for your information and I need—"

Lucifer put his hand over the speaker and looked at Azrael, "Finish up here? I have to take this." With his hand still over the phone, the Devil walked away from the table.

Azrael nodded and turned back to us. His brisk manner didn't invite idle chit chat. "Alright. As Lucifer said, you have twenty-four hours to get into Hell. Choose whichever Hellmouth you desire and a guide will meet you there. Follow that guide and you get in unharmed."

"There's more than one Hellmouth?" I asked.

He tsked and regarded the Grigori next to me, "You should've prepared her more, Watcher."

Azra stiffened at the reproving tone. "I do not hang about your main gates, Fallen One," he sputtered. "I am no expert on your vile ways."

The red-haired demon ignored the outburst and withdrew a slim pad of paper and an expensive looking pen. He scribbled on the pad for a few moments. When he finished, he tore the piece of paper off of the pad. He reached into his coat shirt pocket and withdrew a coin slightly larger than a silver dollar. He handed it and the sheet of paper to me. "There are several entrances. Humans have been able to successfully travel through only two of them, even if it was in *antiquity*," he said, pausing and adding an almost unnatural stress on the last word. "Good luck finding them. Here is your pass. When you get to the Hellmouth, show it to the guardian stationed there. They will let you through."

I accepted the piece of paper with a trembling hand. I had my key. Now I had to find the door.

Levi poked his head in. "Yo, Death Dude, Big Kahuna says mundo badness is going down in San Fran. We gotta go. Oh Goat Boy, Strega Girl, he says your twenty-four hours starts now." He started to exit the building again but stopped. "Uh, and BTW, stay out of San Francisco for the next—" He paused as he did some mental calculation. "—forty-eight hours or so."

Azrael gave both Azra and I a brisk nod as he stood. With a quick tug that straightened his suit jacket, he disappeared.

It was just Azra and me in the vacant bar now. We stared at each other in shock.

"We just made a deal with the Devil," Azra whispered, mollified.

I examined the piece of paper, trying to read through the harsh, archaic script of the Fallen One. It was no help; I couldn't even make out the letters. "Can you read this?" I asked Azra and shoved the paper at him.

He squinted at the page for a long time until finally he gave it back. "Not one word. Must be whatever language they use in Hell."

I inspected the coin; it was the same strange spidery script that was on the note. A complicated design embossed the ancient looking metal. "Well, at least he gave us one clue." I sighed as I tucked the note and the coin securely into my pocket.

Azra snorted. "What clue?"

"Azrael said only two humans made it in and out of Hell and I know about one of them. We have to get to Lake Avernus in Naples. There's a cave there that is said to be an entrance to the underworld."

Azra eyed me with suspicion. "How on earth do you know that?"

I shrugged as I hitched my backpack onto my shoulders. "I'm an Italian witch. We know our *antiquities*."

Chapter Twenty-two

Azra had a safe house not far from Saints and Sinners. As he went to find a cheap compact mirror to replace the one the Devil had incinerated, Beth and I made our way to the address he gave us. It took only about ten minutes for the goat and I to walk to the house. The time and the walk gave me some much-needed privacy to come to grips with everything that had happened. Beth, as always, proved to be the best listener.

"I was ready to write Ryan off as a bad experience and move on. Then he had to go and kidnap my brother. He knows that I don't have the mirror so I don't understand why he keeps messing with my head. That night he convinced me that he was on my side. Now, on top of completely double-crossing me, he goes and does this?"

Beth chewed on a mouthful of weeds.

The safe house was a single story ranch house in a rundown neighborhood. It boasted two giant orange trees in the front yard. The paint was peeling and some boards in the fence looked to be loose.

We went to the front door and I put the key Azra had given me into the lock. Before I could turn it, the door flew open and Azra screamed out, "Boo!"

Out of sheer reaction, I yelled and immediately drew back my fist and belted him in the eye.

He stumbled back and cried out, "For the love of everything sacred! What was that for?"

"I could ask the same for you, jerk face!" I was so mad that I wasn't even sorry for punching him. Beth and I came through the door and I shoved Azra once more on principle.

The inside of the house was as though it hadn't been touched since 1953. A brown sofa and a couple of matching arm chairs sat around a large television that doubled as a small table. Heavy orange curtains hung over all the windows, leaving the only source of light to come from the lead crystal lamps sporting cylindrical lampshades that dotted the available surfaces.

"What do you need for this spell of yours?" Azra asked.

I could tell the prospect of me doing any sort of magic around him made the Grigori more than a little nervous.

"Don't worry. I don't need you to do anything at all. Just point me to somewhere that I can concentrate."

Azra led me down a short hall and pointed to the room on the right. "Use Ryan's room. Make it quick, okay? We've only got so much time to get to the realm of the damned." With that final reminder, he went back to the living room and clicked on the giant TV.

"Great," I sighed as I opened the door to the room. "No pressure at all."

Based on the classic rock posters and excessive tie-dye, I was willing to bet Ryan was last here sometime between the late sixties to mid-seventies.

I took a moment to look around the room. Ryan's imprint on it was faint; it had been a while since he had been here. There was a sense of innocence about it. The emotion that bubbled up inside of me was mostly anger with a generous dose of sadness. I sat on his bed, remembering the feel of his arms around me and the softness of his voice in my ear as he promised to be there when I woke up.

Those memories weren't going to help me get this spell done. Quelling those feelings, I renewed my focus on getting Auri and Thomas back and got to work.

There wasn't a whole lot of maneuvering space in the room; I had to shift some things around to give me at least a wide enough area to cast a circle. With that done, I took out my magic supplies. There was a small container of moon water, sea salt, a couple of tea light candles, a book of matches, some oils, and a rather large amethyst.

The replacement mirror Azra got was cheap, bright pink, and plastic—the exact opposite of the ornately carved silver and blue inlay of the original. A crumpled receipt at the bottom of the plastic bag proclaimed that his total was ninety-nine cents.

I exhaled as my nerves became more and more unsettled. How was I going to make this mirror look like the original? Fighting to center myself, I arranged my tools in front of me; oils, water, and salt on the left and the candles and matches on the right. In front of me were the amethyst and the pink, plastic mirror. I just noticed the name "Barbie" scrawled across the top of it in white.

"Seriously?" I muttered, my concentration completely breaking. Sitting back, I contemplated my tools. I picked up the bottle of rosemary oil and rolled it between my fingers as I summoned what information I had on the plant.

Rosemary was a protective herb used for purification. Not really something I could use in an illusion spell. I set the bottle down and reached for another. Anise; another purification oil, but this one had a bit more potential. It could stimulate the mind and leave it open enough for certain influences. Influences such as an illusion spell infused into the oil itself and covering a toy mirror.

Yes! That was it! I took in a deep breath, centered myself, and cast my circle. The protective barrier gave an iridescent green shimmer to the air. Candles were lit with the strike of a match and a softly murmured prayer.

"Sweet Aradia, let this spell work. May your power flow through me, may your wisdom guide me, and may your blessings be upon me and mine."

While the prayer wasn't necessary, I didn't think it would hurt to ask for a little divine assistance.

I selected one more oil from my stash; cedar wood. It would help balance out the spell work and make it more stable.

There was only a small amount of moon water in the glass container, so I poured it over the mirror and sprinkled sea salt over it as a cleansing. Promptly, I dumped the contents of both oil bottles into the moon water container. The sudden, intense smell of cedar and black licorice made me blink and lean back a bit. Breathing through my mouth, I put a few pinches of salt into the mix.

I took the amethyst into my left hand and the oil mixture into my right. The stone would amplify the power before projecting it into the oil along with the illusion spell. The goal was to use the oil as a conduit. That way, when the oil was painted on the plastic, it would give the illusion of the real mirror.

That's what I intended to happen, at least. Usually, there's a fair amount of effort in getting my energy focused enough to do any sort of spell work. This time, it was as if the floodgates opened. It was all I could do to control the flow of energy. Even with me trying to hold back, it was way too much to handle. It poured out of my fingertips, causing the air to crackle with green tinted energy.

The oil blend bathed in the light to the point that it and the bottle turned green. This was not at all normal. My focus wavered and the green energy started spreading beyond where I wanted it. Beads of sweat dotted my brow as I fought to regain control.

Clenching the amethyst in my hand, I gently shook the oil blend, mixing it even as I projected my intent into the liquid. The humming started in the back of my throat, almost as an afterthought. It was only a few notes at first, but it grew into a haunting melody. It was with mild surprise that I realized it was, in fact, one of the lullabies Nona used to sing to us when we were little.

With great effort, I projected the image of the original mirror through the amethyst and into the oil. I brought forth every detail I could remember: the weight of it in my hands, the feel of the cool silver against my fingertips, the intricate design around the pale blue stones that seemed to reflect the sky.

Along with the physical appearance, I layered in my own memories and the legends passed down through the generations.

I set the oil blend down and held the amethyst with both hands over the container. The sheer amount of power building up around me was staggering. Channeling the information was exhausting, but I refused to stop.

Peering into the liquid, I could just see the reflection of the mirror—the true mirror. Suddenly, the surface of the oil blend rippled. It was time.

I released my grip on the amethyst, placing it on the ground. I picked up the plastic mirror as I dipped the fingers of my right hand into the oil; it was warm to the touch. The humming began again. I was barely aware of the sound coming from my own throat, so focused and deliberate were my actions.

The oil dripped from my fingertips. It was thick and the sheer amount of energy in it made my skin prickle. With slow, measured movements, I anointed the pink mirror, covering every inch of it. Slowly, ever so slowly, the plastic began to melt and morph, fading and re-emerging as polished silver and sky-blue stones.

"Yes!" I whispered, dropping the melody completely. At the sound of my excited whisper, the illusion faltered. The silver faded back to the sickeningly bright pink. With my momentary elation gone, I redoubled my concentration and began my humming once again. Within seconds, the illusion was back. I just needed to bind it all together now and make it stick.

In my mind, I visualized a string of green energy. I wrapped that string of energy around the mirror, seeking to keep the enchantment in place. When it was as tight as it could be, I set the mirror onto the ground in front of me and peered at it.

It looked exactly like my mirror, except for the telltale signs of my energy stamp. I was confident though; the visual parts of the spell would fade, but the magic would remain.

I just hoped it would fool Ryan and Ascher.

Time was wasting. I re-wrapped the amethyst in the black bandana and capped the empty oil bottles. They, along with the salt and the other unused items went back into my bag. The mirror went into the blue velvet bag that once held the real mirror. The bag wound up in my hoodie pocket. With the mirror went the rest of the oil blend, ready for another application if it was needed. When everything was finally put away, I took down the circle, allowing the excess energy to disperse. As soon as the circle was down, I grew tired. All I wanted to do was curl up and sleep for days. There wasn't any time for that, though. As my favorite poet once wrote, 'and miles to go before I sleep'.

I took a last glance around Ryan's room, searching for a possible life where our paths hadn't been so convoluted. Maybe things would have been different. Maybe in that alternate timeline, he wouldn't have betrayed me and we could have been together. Closing the bedroom door on those wishful hopes, I went to find Azra.

He sat on the living room couch, staring off into space and not paying the slightest attention to what was on the television. His thoughts must have had him far away because he didn't notice when I walked up behind him. It was only when I touched his shoulder that he whipped his head around.

"What the—?"

"Come on," I said, trying not to smile about making him jump. "We've got to get going."

He hoisted himself off the couch. "Alright. I am leaving Beth here. She's not feeling well since meeting Satan." The words were accusatory.

"What's wrong with her?" I glanced at the goat. She looked fine to me.

"Can't you see? She's pale and not speaking. She needs to rest."

Beth baaed at me and I knew Azra was full of it. "Whatever you say. Let's just go. I don't want to be late and miss our entrance window." I took his hand and the familiar, fluttery sensation in my stomach began. Before long, the dizziness came on which made my exhaustion even more pronounced.

Through the wind and the blur of everything passing us by, I heard a voice. One that was sickeningly intimate and somehow familiar.

"What makes you think you can win, little witch?" the voice sneered. It seemed to ricochet around me. It was a hissing sort of voice, wispy and sharp. "You should know when you are out of your league. You are not ready for this."

"Come out!" I demanded with more confidence than I felt. "Let me see your face."

Laughter echoed through the leaves of the giant tree before me. "I have many faces. Many do my bidding. I suppose I will show the face you think you can defeat."

Ascher stood before me as I had last seen him; expensively dressed and sinister looking. "You won't win, you know," he said. "There's no way you will ever be able to fulfill your destiny. I've turned the one that was to join you to my side. Without him, you will never do what you're supposed to." The would-be Ascher paced around me.

I adjusted myself so that I was always facing him.

With every step he took, my stomach lurched and the sickness intensified.

"Why are you doing this? What do you want? " The questions sounded desperate and pleading, but there was no help for it.

He laughed a strong and forceful exultation. "I want many things, little witch. For right now, your death would do nicely." Faster than thought, he rushed me. I held out my hands and forced what little power I had left into my fingers. There was nothing.

The would-be Ascher reached out to grab hold of my neck. Abruptly, a strange energy snapped and enclosed me in a protective shield. It reminded me of the protective shield Ryan and I created on the beach except this was a wilder, more primal energy. I was at a loss as to where it came from.

The vision of Ascher stopped short of the barrier, a surprised snarl forming on his pointed features. "How is this possible?"

Even though I was wondering the exact same thing, I lifted my chin in defiance. "Guess you don't know everything, do you?"

A sense of calm filled me even as Ascher raged. A little girl's voice, quiet and soft, whispered into my ear, "He's just trying to scare you. Everything is going to be alright."

I don't know why, but the voice relaxed me; whoever it was, they were on my side and it meant I wasn't alone.

The would-be Ascher realized it about the same time I did. He backed away and hissed. "This isn't over, little witch. You can do nothing to save them." He evaporated into a cloud of black smoke. A breeze wafted the tendrils away from a giant tree that appeared out of the mist.

Once it was all gone, the barrier disappeared along with the strength that kept me standing straight. Falling to the ground, I tried to catch my breath.

"I was hoping I would find you here," the child's voice said off to my right.

A little girl stared at me and I wondered if this was another one of the would-be Ascher's guises. She had to be about eight or nine. Her features, her build were so similar to mine that we could've been related. Her pale blue dress was covered with a white pinafore and there was even a black ribbon holding the hair away from her round face. Her hair was what caught my attention. It was extraordinary, shifting colors going from the darkest black to the palest white and every imaginable shade in the rainbow between. The changes in it captivated me. An eager smile belied her excitement.

"Who are you?" I asked, warily. Just because she was a cute kid didn't mean that I could let my guard down.

She stepped forward. "You're exactly how I imagined you would be."

I considered the girl. She was different and yet somehow familiar. Curious, I peeked at her aura, just to see if I could tell what her intent was. Her aura was blinding—a vibrant fire of rainbow colors that made me avert my eyes from its brightness. "What do you want?"

The girl cocked her head to the side as though the answer to my question should have been obvious. "I wanted to meet you. This was the only way I could." She regarded me in turn, a puzzled expression on her face. Sudden comprehension made her eyes widen. "Oh! You think I'm an illusion, don't you? Well, you shouldn't worry so much. He can't get to you here. He can only try to scare you. You aren't scared, are you?"

I shook my head, intending to put on a braver face than I felt. Soon, though, the stubbornness faltered and I bowed my head under the weight of my worries. "Yes, I am scared. I just want everything to turn out right."

The girl's grin faded as she stepped closer. She put a small hand on my arm and watched me with violet eyes. Ryan's eyes. "It will all turn out, but it may not be the way you intend."

Confusion swept over me. "What do you mean?"

A wolf howled in the distance and the wind kicked up as if in answer to the plaintive call. It whipped my hair about chaotically and I had to work to keep it out of my face. The girl wasn't affected by the sudden gust; her hair stayed perfectly still as did her dress. She said something, but I couldn't make it out over the howling of the wind. The gusts became so strong I was almost blown off my feet. I leaned against it, trying to understand what the peculiar girl was telling me.

The wind was too strong and it swept me back against the tree. Despite its comforting presence, the long, leaf covered branches were not a safe haven. I gripped the black bark, desperately trying to hold on. The girl looked on, a sad frown on her face before she turned and walked out into the windstorm.

Chapter Twenty-three

I still heard the wolf howling in the distance when I woke from my dream. An icy breeze chilled me to the bone and made me want to go back to sleep, but the hard ground wasn't comfortable enough. Wait. Hard ground? Icy wind? My dream came back in a rush and my eyes flew open, searching my surroundings with panic. Where was I?

"Good, you're awake," Azra said. I barely detected the sound of relief in his tone. "I won't have to pin this to you after all." He waved a folded piece of paper in front of me.

"Where are we?" I sat up. He'd covered me in an oversized green trench coat. Snow drifted down from the overcast sky.

"Berlin," came the terse reply. "I can't carry you anymore, Strega Girl."

"What? Why not?" I stood up and brushed the cold, white flakes off of my face.

"Your coven did something to me. My teleporting isn't working like it once did. You witches must have crossed some wires when you were doing your evil experiments. I tried getting us to Naples, and we ended up everywhere else instead."

"The coven healed you. We didn't hurt you. If it wasn't for us, then you would have died."

Azra's expression was dubious. "It was either your coven messing with me or your snoring that's causing this problem. I don't know how you can sleep through that ruckus."

"I do not snore!"

Azra raised an eyebrow and pinned the note to the

lapel of the coat anyway. "Whatever you say, princess. Fact of the matter is that we've made pit stops in Moscow, the Amazon, Cairo, Poughkeepsie, and now Berlin."

My mind couldn't wrap itself around that statement. "Berlin? How did we end up here?"

"Ask your witchy family, Strega Girl."

"If you can't get me to Naples, then how am I going to get to the cave?"

The Grigori shoved an envelope at me. "You're going on a plane. Here is a ticket to Rome and enough money to get you a taxi to Naples. I even threw in some food money for you because I'm not sure when you ate last. Don't your kind need to eat every two to four hours to keep you from turning all warty and green?"

"Ha ha, very funny." I scowled even as I opened the envelope to find a large stack of Euros and a plane ticket. I was to be at terminal C no later than four p.m. "What time is it? How much time do we have left to get to the Hellmouth?" I demanded.

"Calm down," Azra told me. "It's only two in the afternoon. You have two hours to make your flight. Plenty of time to get yourself something to eat. I recommend the Sauerbraten."

"Two in the afternoon? It took you that long to get us here? That means we only have five hours to get to the entrance of Hell!"

"Hey, it's not my fault you've got a deviated septum. Besides, it's two p.m. local-time. In California it's five in the morning. We'll make the deadline, okay?"

I groaned as I thought of the traveling I had ahead of me. "Customs is going to be excruciating. Oh no!" I snatched my bag from where it was resting and started pawing through the stuff inside. "My passport! How am I going to explain how I got here?"

"Ahem," Azra coughed to get my attention. When I glanced up, he offered me a small blue book. "I took the liberty of going back and getting it stamped for you."

I accepted the passport with disbelief. "Why did you do that?" The question slipped out before I could bite it back. Who was I to look a gift horse in the mouth? I flipped through the pages and found not only the stamp for entering Germany, but also leaving Poughkeepsie. "Thank you," I told him with heartfelt sincerity. He just made my life a million times easier when it came to customs.

He coughed again and fixed his eyes on the ground proving that even an angel could appear sheepish. "Well, you slept through it all and I felt bad about not at least getting you a souvenir. I thought this would be better than a postcard."

I smiled up at him and he fidgeted uncomfortably.

"Now, if you will excuse me, I have more preparations to make before we go traipsing into Hell." He was about to disappear when I grabbed a hold of his arm. He rewarded me with a glare and a reproving admonition. "What? We just went over this, Strega Girl. You're taking the plane."

"I know that. Can you at least tell me where we are, exactly? Or at least give me a hint where the airport is?"

Azra removed my hand while rolling his eyes. "Strega Girl, you need to look behind you." He took my shoulders and spun me around so the entrance of the airport was in plain view.

"Oh," I turned back to thank him, but Azra was already gone, leaving me in what I now realized was the parking lot for the airport. "Fabulous," I muttered and slung my bag over my shoulder.

As I made my way through the parking lot and to the airport itself, I felt like I was being watched. No matter how many times or how carefully I checked out the surrounding trees, there was nothing to see. The feeling persisted and by the time I made it to the airport doors, I felt nothing but relief.

Getting through security wasn't as difficult as I thought it would be. Customs was even faster and before I knew it, I was waiting outside of terminal C. Taking Azra's advice, I stopped to get something to eat from one of the fast food places outside of the gate. I never liked German food; it always seemed so bland in comparison to the vibrant flavors of Italian cuisine. Still, I ate as much as I could, keeping in mind that my next meal was uncertain.

Once I'd eaten, there were still a good thirty minutes to kill until boarding. I sat and watched the planes come and go along the tarmac. The purpose of my journey weighed on me, but I couldn't falter.

My thoughts turned to my dream. It had been so vivid, so real. The strange little girl told me that I needed to prepare myself to pay a price. I wondered what exactly that price would be.

Something moved just beyond the concrete of the runway outside and caught my attention. The largest wolf I'd ever seen stood just outside of the sanctuary of the woods. The odd part was that it stared right at me.

Yes, the creature was out in the snow and I was in a giant building, three floors off the ground. Still, I was certain it was watching me. The feeling caused the hairs on the back of my neck to stand on end. Completely unnerved, I got up and moved away from one window to the other on the opposite side of the terminal's gate. I watched the workers move carts full of suitcases and other baggage onto different planes. It didn't reduce the sensation of being scrutinized. Just as a train of carts left the tarmac, the wolf appeared, closer this time, still gazing intently up at me.

Relief flooded through me when my flight number was called for boarding over the intercom. It sounded first in German, then English. Glancing at the paperwork, I realized Azra sprang for a first class ticket. That meant I could relax and concentrate on my mission instead of crammed between two large men from Bulgaria.

Boarding the plane was uneventful. My first class seat was large and comfortable and I settled into it gratefully.

As I waited for takeoff, I opened Nona's Book of Mysteries. Maybe I'd find something that might help me on my mission into Hell; some sort of protective spell or quick defense move that I could use.

I was so engrossed in reading that I didn't pay attention to the other passengers as they filed past. I didn't notice the tall man who claimed the seat across the aisle until I realized he wouldn't stop studying me. He didn't hide the fact when I met his gaze pointedly.

His skin was so dark it seemed to glow. There was no hair atop of his head, but a carefully groomed goatee covered his chin and upper lip. His dark, chocolatey eyes glinted. The most unnerving part was how seldom he blinked.

He looked like any other business person, dressed in a nice suit and carrying a briefcase. Out of caution, I checked his aura. Muted gold and yellows surrounded him in a tight radius. He wasn't human. Warning bells went off in my mind. My instincts had my energy already pooling, readying itself for use. The doors to the plane closed and we were already headed for the runway. There was no way off the plane. Warily, I returned my gaze to the page in front of me, but my attention remained on the stranger.

By the time the flight attendants buckled themselves in for takeoff, I was a tense ball of anxiety waiting for the creature across from me to make a move.

At last, he leaned toward me and said, "Some boys just put you through Hell, don't they?" His voice was deep and he had a thick accent. It sounded vaguely British, though, I wasn't entirely sure that was right. Perhaps South African?

I struggled to act calm. I wasn't going to give

anything away. This flight was too important to risk in a fight. I responded, "Excuse me?"

He adjusted himself so that he was even closer and repeated in a thick accent, "You know he isn't worth it. No one is worth all that trouble."

This was too weird. "Who are you talking about?"

"A boy is the whole reason why you're going to Hell, isn't it Stella?"

The alarm bells that were already sounding in my head went ballistic when he said my name and my real destination. My eyes narrowed. "How do you know my name?"

He smiled at my suspicion. "I know many things about you. I know your past, I know your future, and I know you're on your way to the pit because you think you can save your brother and your cousin."

I met his stare to show I wasn't scared. With the power already in my hand, I summoned forth a barrier of between him and I. The energy crackled green, inches away from his face. It was a warning and by his sudden jerk backward, he knew it.

"What are you and what do you want?"

He nodded, looking impressed, but not afraid. "Very good, Stella. It seems your grandmother has taught you well."

My temper flared even as my wariness skyrocketed. He was trying to trick me. "Leave me alone."

The smile dropped from the man's face and something flashed in his eyes. Within seconds, the disguise he was maintaining stripped away and I saw exactly what he was.

Large wings protruded behind him. They shimmered with an otherworldly glow that reminded me of sunlight glittering on a pool of water. His aura, no longer muted, was blindingly gold. The human form he wore to cover it was like a shadow against the sun.

Almost as soon as it was revealed, the true form of

the stranger disappeared. I gasped as the cabin of the airplane came back into focus. He was an angel! Not a Grigori like Azra, or even like the demons I had just met, but a different class altogether. He must have been one of the other choirs.

I made a concentrated effort to stop my heart from pounding and I regarded the angel as levelly as I could. "What do you want?" I was proud that my voice didn't shake.

Facing one of the Heavenly Host was much different than dealing with a Grigori. For one, there was a certain level of comfort with the exiled choir. They'd made their home on earth and lived among humans for untold centuries. In a way, they were familiar because they worked so hard to blend in.

Now that I saw the stranger for what he was, I understood this angel was nothing like a Grigori. He wasn't trying to blend in or be familiar. He wore his human disguise formally. The power radiating off of him was staggering. Despite how terrifying it was to be confronted with something so otherworldly, Nona taught me never to bow in the face of such displays of strength.

I couldn't tell if my lack of reaction to his presence impressed or aggravated him. Either way, the angel's face was sculpted into an expression of calm indifference. "My name is Padiel. I am here to make you reconsider your current course of action."

I crossed my arms over my chest. "Divine intervention, huh?"

The amused quirk of his mouth lasted briefly as he replied, "Something like that."

The intercom dinged and a voice came over the loudspeaker to inform passengers that it was safe to move about the cabin. In one fluid motion that seemed to be just a blur, Padiel undid his safety belt and moved to slide into the seat next to me. My barrier of power stopped him.

"Do you mind?" he asked politely.

"I do," I answered.

"I'm not going to harm you, you silly girl."

My lips pursed at being called a silly girl. "Stay over there." My words caused the barrier to flare, driving him backward.

Scowling, the angel settled back into his seat. "You aren't going to make this easy on me, are you?"

"Why would I?"

"Do you understand what you are going to do?"

"I'm going to arrive in Italy, just like every other person on this plane," I answered, keeping my sarcasm in place like armor.

The angel let out an exasperated sigh. "I meant, do you know your fate?"

I kept my lips shut and the confused look on my face.

Another sigh emitted from the angel. "You mean to tell me that you don't have any inkling at all to what your future holds?"

My head moved back and forth and I told him, "It's not possible to read your own future." It was a lie and I think he knew it.

"You have been chosen, Stella Evangeline."

"Chosen for what, the lottery?" I swear I hadn't meant for that to come out. It earned me a stern glare from the angel.

"You have been chosen," the angel continued, "to be the mother of the divine Daughter."

This information was new to me. "What are you talking about?"

He tried again, "You are destined to be the mother of the girl who will either save the world or end it. Your daughter will be the dawn of a new era."

The laughter that came out of me wasn't intentional. It was a sort of knee-jerk reaction. "You're kidding, right? Me, a mom?"

Padiel's expression remained grave. "This isn't a joke. Stella, you will be the One of Legend's mother. It has always been written in your stars."

My giggles gave way to denial. "No. You're mistaken."

"There is no mistake," he said this with absolute conviction and sincerity.

A certain truth rang through the proclamation that I couldn't ignore. Despite how ridiculous it all sounded, Padiel believed what he was saying wholeheartedly.

My mind raced with the implications of his claim. I'd be the mother of a goddess. The idea was absurd. "Oh sweet Goddess," I breathed, frustrated that I even considered believing what he said. "I'm not going to be the mother of a deity."

"Yes, you are."

"No. It's impossible."

A flight attendant paused next to us with a gray cart full of beverages. "Would you like something to drink?" She flashed an overly white smile at me.

My answer was more clipped than I intended, because Padiel's announcement had rattled me. "No thanks."

The flight attendant went on to the next passenger, completely skipping over the angel as though he weren't there.

If Padiel noticed the snub, he didn't seem to care. He continued as though we hadn't been interrupted. "What I've told you is true. Now, with that in mind, let's discuss what you are about to do."

"Why?" I challenged. "Going to Italy has nothing to do with anything."

"I'm not talking about going to Rome. I'm talking about your plan to descend into the underworld for some high-minded purpose that has to do with an outlaw Grigori."

The pause lengthened into an awkward silence as I

stared at the seat in front of me. It bought me time to adjust to the fact that he knew exactly what was going on.

"Think about it, Stella. You, the future mother of the most important child in the history of existence—you are going to sacrifice not only your own life but the future of this world if you go into Hell. It just isn't safe."

It took me a moment to realize that the angel was pleading with me.

"Not to mention the company you're keeping on this excursion. A Grigori who is completely irreverent to anything except surfing and a goat. How did you even fall in with that idiot?"

I clamped my lips tight against the biting retort I wanted to deliver. None of this was Padiel's business. "Enough."

The angel blinked. "What?"

"I think you have the wrong witch. I am not going to be anyone's mom, much less the girl you are talking about. I know what I have to do. If Heaven wants to stop me, then they're going to have to send more than just you."

Padiel continued, either oblivious or indifferent to my anger. "I know you love your brother, but you have to understand there's no guarantee he'll come back whole or even at all. After everything Ascher put him through on top of being in the underworld, he could be damaged beyond all repair. He could have died and is now stuck. You are risking too much for someone already too far gone to save."

"Stop right there," I advised him, my voice pitched low. "Who do you think you are?"

Padiel looked bewildered. "I told you. I'm—"

"Shut up. I've listened to what you had to say and I don't like it. Allow me to set a few things straight: first, my brother is not dead. You may think he's not worth saving, but to me, he is. There's nothing you can say or do that will stop me from getting to him. Do you understand?"

Padiel blinked, stunned that I was arguing.

Emboldened and a more than a little pissed off, I went on. "Second, who I associate with is none of your damn business. You have no say in my life or decisions. I've only just met you so what makes you think you can dictate my choices? Third, while I appreciate your concern, it isn't warranted or wanted. I know what I am doing and I can take care of myself. I don't need you or anyone else protecting me."

"You don't understand. There are powerful forces who do not want your daughter to be born. These forces will do anything to stop the Age of the Daughter from happening. What better way to do that than to kill you before you can give birth? This whole situation is a trap designed to eliminate His competition."

"Whose competition?" I demanded. "Who is after me?"

"I cannot say."

"That's some bullshit," I said and crossed my arms.

There was sadness in Padiel's eyes. He warned, "Stella, there's a high probability that you won't survive if you go down there."

The words struck hard at the fear dwelling inside of me. Squashing it down deep, I lifted my chin rebelliously and said, "I'm still going. You aren't going to change my mind."

He nodded. "I can't force you. I wish I could, but this is one of those things that I cannot influence. Good luck, Stella Evangeline. You will need it." He shimmered, fading from sight. The fear Padiel roused didn't fade as easily.

With a heavy, anxious heart, I pulled the fake mirror out of my pocket and gripped it tightly.

Chapter Twenty-four

Luckily, the ticket Azra purchased was to Naples International Airport. If he'd gotten a ticket to Rome, it would have meant an additional two hours to my trip. The downside was I wasn't familiar with this airport at all. Couple that with the conversation Padiel and I had on the plane replaying in my head, it's a recipe for getting lost. I left terminal three and, after a few detours, found where a fleet of taxis waited to whisk people away to their chosen destinations.

After hopping into the back of one, I informed the driver that I wanted to go to Lake Avernus. This earned me a surprised glance through the rearview mirror. With concern coloring his words, he asked, "Why would you want to go there?"

"Someone is meeting me there. Please hurry." As added incentive, I shoved a few bills at him.

"You're not from around here."

"Nope," I agreed and pointedly stared out the window hoping he would get the hint that I didn't want to talk. What I wouldn't give for my headphones right about then.

As the taxi sped through the night, with every kilometer we traveled, my anxiety rose. For the first time, I had second thoughts about my choices. I should have just let Ryan go. I shouldn't have coerced Azra to find him. If I hadn't chased after him and that stupid mirror, Thomas and Auri would be safe. Because of me, they were involved in something that had nothing to do with them. I was the one that put them in danger. I alone would be responsible for their deaths.

With those thoughts plaguing me, I spent most of

the car ride staring out at the dark, passing countryside. Every so often, the cabbie would try to strike up a conversation about random things. I gave the minimal responses. Finally, he ceased his friendly interrogation.

I was sick with the realization that I had bitten off more than I could chew. I wished I could talk to Nona, but I couldn't; my phone was dead.

It took only thirty minutes to get to the cave. I paid the taxi driver and assured him that my friends would be there shortly and he could go. There was a fair amount of convincing before he drove off into the night, leaving me at the bottom of a trail. Trees lined the path and a large mountain loomed against the night sky and the lights of the nearby town were far off in the distance.

There was no sign of Azra anywhere. He was probably already at the mouth of the cave, waiting for me. By moonlight, I made my way up the road to Hell.

A rustling in the bushes next to the pathway came unexpectedly. I froze.

"Azra?" I called out.

A low growl emanated from the darkness. Immediately, I thought of the wolf from the airport. It couldn't be . . . could it? Barely breathing, I stood still, waiting for the creature to emerge. Silence overtook the night, punctuated only by distant crickets.

There was no sign of the creature in the bushes, but something was there, something that followed with each step I took. Suppressing a shudder, I adjusted my bag and started up the trail, keeping an ear out for whatever followed.

I was close to the cave when something small and hard hit me in the arm. Muffling my curse, I whipped my head around to see what had hit me. Scanning the darkness proved useless. I couldn't see anything beyond the shadowy tree branches swaying in the breeze.

A moment later, a rock came whizzing past my face. It landed to my left and this time there was a loud

"Pssttt" that accompanied the little missile.

"Strega Girl! Get out of the open! They'll see you! Get over here! Hurry!"

I whirled to find Azra's face poking out of a tangle of bushes. He'd smeared his cheeks with dark green and blue greasepaint. Around the lines, his skin was coated with dirt and grime. It looked like he was fresh out of a war film. A helmet covered in leaves sat atop his head. His pale blue eyes glowed in the dim light as he waved for me to join him.

I didn't move. "What are you doing?" I shouted.

"Shhh! We don't want to be seen until we are ready," he yelled. "Hurry up and get over here before you blow our cover!"

I rolled my eyes and walked into the foliage with him. It was with mild shock that I realized he wasn't in his signature outfit of swim trunks and flip-flops. Instead, he garbed himself in dark green and brown khakis and a matching tank top. His usually visible feet were encased in large steel-toed boots that laced halfway up his calf.

Beth knelt in the dirt just behind Azra, artfully covered in camouflage netting and her own helmet. I patted her flank.

"It took you long enough to get here," Azra reproved. He was on his stomach and had put on a pair of night vision goggles to peer intently at the trail.

"I can't help traffic," I snapped back.

Azra demanded silence by holding up his hand in my face. "Something's coming!"

I held my breath, wondering if it was the creature that had been following me. There was only the sound of tree branches in the wind.

After a few minutes, Azra removed the night vision goggles and muttered, "Damn squirrels." He adjusted so that he could see me and the road at the same time. "From what I've observed, there's one human guard. He makes his rounds every thirty minutes or so in a golf cart. Our point of entry is over there," he said as he pointed to a dark clearing. Beyond the trees was a trapezoidal sort of opening in the pale cliff face.

"Let's go then," I said as I started to edge my way from the hiding spot. "The coast is clear now."

Azra's hand clamped down on my arm, preventing me from going any farther. "No, we don't know what traps they have out there. We can't just go walking up to the front entrance. They'll be expecting us to do that."

"Azra, the Devil himself gave us a pass into the underworld. Why can't we just go in already?"

He closed his bright blue eyes and sighed as though he shouldn't have to answer such a ridiculous question. When he spoke, his voice was low and restrained and his words were slow as though to make sure I understood. "Just because the Devil says you can go into Hell doesn't mean he is going to roll out the welcome mat. We aren't going to get in without a fight."

"Why? He gave us permission to go in. That doesn't make any sense."

Azra threw his hands up in the air, causing his helmet of leaves to slide a bit. "He's Satan! How should I know what his thought process is?"

"What do you suggest then?" I asked shortly. Time was running out and arguing wasn't getting us any closer to the cave.

"Do you see those trees over there?" he indicated to a cluster of tall spruces.

I nodded.

"That will be our first staging point. If we can get over there, we'll be able to distract them away from the entrance long enough for us to get through."

I eyed the distance. "How are we going to distract them?"

"Trust me," Azra said as his gaze flicked up to the treetops above us, "they are out there." Shaking himself a bit, he returned his attention to me. "We'll use Beth. She'll lead the Fallen Ones away. Meanwhile, you and I will make a run for the cave. Don't worry; I have this, just in case." He hefted a large super soaker up so that I wouldn't miss its neon-bright presence.

"A squirt gun? How is that going to stop them from attacking us?"

A grin spread across his grimy face as he patted the plastic. "Holy water. Here, take this," he shoved a large duffel bag at me. "It is for later. I made you an underworld safety kit."

The bag was heavy and I wondered if I would be able to carry it all the way into Hell.

"What about Beth? Will she know what to do?" I turned to look back at the goat. She was trying, unsuccessfully, to bite the leaves hanging down from her helmet. Doubt filled me. This was our grand distraction? How was a goat going to distract the minions of Hell long enough for Azra and I to get in?

As if she knew that I was questioning her, Beth stopped her pursuit of the leafy headdress and bleated her scorn as she turned her attention to the ground.

Azra assured me, "She can take care of herself. Now, let's do this!" He pumped the super soaker, ready to drench anything that got in our way. "One, two, three. Go!"

He was out of the bush quicker than I could blink. Beth ambled after him. She soon got distracted by a patch of grass and stopped squarely in the middle of the trail.

Azra made it to the stand of trees undetected. He pressed against the bark.

"This is stupid," I muttered under my breath. Azra motioned for me to follow. Ignoring him, I walked confidently toward the entrance of the cave, leaving the Grigori behind. Rambo Azra was not the most cautious nor the most rational creature. Right then, I needed caution, I needed rational.

As he chased after me, Azra let out a low staccato whistle, Beth's signal to start a distraction.

Out of nowhere, an explosion sounded into the night. There was just enough time to see a blaze of fire before Azra slammed me to the ground.

After that initial blast, the night air filled with the sharp rapport of gunfire, punctuating the darkness with short bursts of light. Azra shouted, but I couldn't make out the words. There was no way to know where the shots were coming from or even why there were shots at all.

"Beth," Azra bellowed during a short lull of sound. Without further ado, he tore down the road, abandoning me in the maelstrom of explosions and flashing lights.

As far as a distraction went, whatever was happening was doing the job. In the distance fireworks went off, peppering the sky with colored sparks.

With my eyes wide and locked onto the shadows around me, I got to my feet while trying to keep my head down at the same time.

Something large and furry nudged the back of my knee. When I glanced down, my eyes met with those of a massive wolf glaring up at me. It was double the size of a normal wolf and all I could see was teeth and claws.

"Nice puppy," I whispered. Terrified, I held out my hand. "Good puppy."

A tail wagged and an urgent whine escaped passed the sharp teeth. Gently, it prodded the side of my leg and I stumbled forward. It wanted me to go to the cave.

I shuffled in the direction the animal wanted me to go, keeping a close watch on it. The wolf seemed satisfied to walk next to me with its tail wagging and tongue hanging out.

The closer we got to the cliff face, the more I realized there was a creeping fog covering the ground. With the cave in plain view, I noticed an orangey-red glow coming from within. The fog became denser and warmer.

Soft yipping sounds filled the night. Something moving under the fog stirred its surface. The wolf snuffled the ground for whatever was making the noises. About half a dozen wolf pups jumped at the sight of their mother. They were no bigger than my hand and they had the same orange and black foxlike coloring as the larger wolf.

One brave puppy made his way over to my foot. He sniffed my shoe and then raised his head to let out a squeaky howl into the night. His brothers and sisters took up the call as well. Soon, there was a chorus of puppies competing with the noise of the fireworks.

Worried they would draw the wrong sort of attention, I picked up the small wolf pup and held him to my chest. "Shhh. It's alright little one."

The mother wolf let out a soft growl when she noticed that her pup was in my hands. Immediately I set the puppy on the ground and backed away. It was persistent though, and stumbled after me, yipping the whole way.

Azra lurched into the clearing, screaming at the top of his lungs. "They got her! The bastards got her!" Out of sheer surprise, I dropped my bag, narrowly missing the puppy.

"Azra? What's going on?" Horrified, I stared at the blood dripping from his forehead.

"Go! Go on without me! I'll cover you!" Giving me no time to argue, he plunged back into the war zone, shouting with a chilling determination.

"You know there's no one else out there, right? He's putting on a show." A voice commented behind me.

I whirled to face a rather tall creature covered in an oversized black cloak with a hood. From inside the hood glowed a set of red eyes. Scaled hands grasped a spear made of volcanic glass.

Startled by the creature's sudden appearance, all I could do was stutter. "W-what?"

The spear raised and motioned to where Azra had run off. "That whooping and hollering; it's all him. No one is out there trying to get him. He's putting on a show."

"How do you know that?"

The creature shrugged. "I heard him talking to the goat."

I wasn't quite buying it. "Who are you?"

"Oh, I'm sorry. How rude of me." He let out a chuckle and lowered his hood.

I wasn't prepared for the handsome young face or the odd ink-black, yet iridescent scales marring half of his perfect features. It looked as though he were wearing a mask or some sort of special effect makeup. Patches of his pale skin faded to a sickly gray.

"My name's Ted. I'm the guardian of this gate. You must be Stella." He stuck out his right hand, which was also covered in black scales. Some of the fingers had shortened and curled into vicious-looking claws.

Still unsure what was happening, I shook his hand. "Ted? The demon, Ted? Are you serious?"

The shoulders of his black cloak rose and fell in a shrug. "It's easier to pronounce than my real name. Is your friend done making a scene?"

"I don't know. Honestly, I'm not sure what's going on."

"Watchers have always been a superstitious lot. Beyond that, well, he's your friend. You'll have more of an idea about why he does things than I would."

The large mother wolf let out a short howl and a series of growls that made me jump. She stalked closer to me and gave me another nudge with her massive head.

"This is Daisy. She's been following you for quite some time. She is your escort. No one knows the ins and outs of Hell like the hellhounds."

"Hellhound?" I gazed at the wolf with even more trepidation.

"I reacted the same way. But the boss says you get a hellhound escort, so that's what happens."

"You mean you aren't my guide?"

"No. I don't leave my gate. Daisy will be guide enough for what you are going in to do. She will lead you to the farthest bank of the river Styx. That's where your party is waiting."

"Okay. Well, when my business is done, how do I get back here? Will Daisy guide me back here?"

"You don't come back here. There are many ways into the underworld, but there is only one way back out for the living. You go to the Gate of Ivory, on the other side of the Elysian Fields."

A thrill of panic made me shiver. "Are you sure you can't guide me?"

Ted's humorless laugh sounded like dry leaves in a brisk wind. "It is not my journey to make. This task is for you and you alone. And I told you, no one knows Hell like the hellhounds."

Fear made my throat dry. I coughed a little, wishing for some water.

"I am permitted to give you some advice."

I waited, my eyes never leaving his sparkling gray ones.

"Hell is amorphous. The only shape is the one you give it, so it's imperative that you keep a firm idea of your surroundings in mind. If your concentration slips, even for a moment, you'll be exposed to other perceptions of the underworld. Being subjected to another's version of Hell will make you go mad. Do you understand?"

"Yes."

Daisy nudged me again, letting out a soft woof.

"It's time for you to go. There's still a long journey

ahead of you."

At his words, the inside of the cave glowed even brighter in its terrifying orangey-red hue. Daisy ran past me, pausing for only a moment to look back before disappearing into the now glowing cave.

"Follow Daisy. She'll take you where you need to be. And be cautious of the Sybil. Don't let her distract you." With that, Ted disappeared, leaving me standing in front of the cave alone.

A wave of nervousness washed over me. This was it. This what I had come for. Was it still the right decision? Was I so sure Padiel was wrong?

Steeling myself, I forced the conversation with Padiel out of my mind. I knew what I had to do and it was time to focus on that. Some strange angel on a plane wasn't going to decide my fate.

Picking up my bag, I looked for Azra, hoping Ted was wrong about him chickening out on me. All I could see was a fresh batch of fireworks booming just above the horizon. Azra wasn't coming and I couldn't wait around to convince him. I was on my own for this.

I followed the hellhound into the trapezoidal opening. The orange-red glow came from strange writing on the walls. The carvings pulsed with an inner fire, first black, then orange, and finally red before receding back into darkness.

Fog covered the sloping ground. My shoes inched forward as the path was uncertain. It was oddly quiet; the only immediate sound was that of my breath, gasping from exertion and fear.

As I inched along the cave, I half expected something to grab ahold of me. When that didn't happen, my tiptoes lengthened into confident strides. Every so often, Daisy popped her head up and waited for me to catch up before running ahead again. I did my best to keep a steady pace.

We must have walked for hours. My leg muscles

ached and my shoulders bowed under the weight of the bag.

Finally, when it felt like taking even one more step would kill me, we arrived at a dead end. Outcroppings of rocks formed benches and shelves. Little hollows in the walls held stubs of candles and the remains of flowers. The glowing script that illuminated my journey seemed thicker and there was more of it. Daisy sat in the middle of the room, glaring at what looked like a carved archway over a solid rock wall. She growled at the slab of rock and scratched at the base of it.

With nowhere else to go, I sat on one of the ledges and allowed the bag to slide off of my shoulder. Digging into it, I found a bottle of water and drank half of it in one gulp. Rubbing my sore legs, I looked around the small chamber. It was definitely the end of the cave.

"Well now what?" I asked the hellhound. My voice echoed in the chamber. When the echo died, I rested my back against the stone wall and shut my eyes. Daisy whined.

"You've finally come," a raspy voice said in a thick accented Italian dialect.

My eyes flew open. Nobody else was in the cave except for the hellhound.

"Who said that?" I demanded. Getting to my feet, I summoned a trickle of energy into my hands, shaping it into a sphere.

A gust of wind rushed past me out of nowhere as the voice responded, "Stella Seraphina Evangeline. I have been waiting for you." The wind stirred a pile of dust from the ground. The dust swirled up until it formed into a person.

Shivers danced down my spine. "What are you?" I asked, switching to Italian.

The dust spun faster, animating the body it created. "See me as I once was. You will understand then what you will soon be."

With the echo of that ghostly spell, the entire grotto transformed. The once bare stone ground was now covered in thick woven carpets of green. The natural benches held cushions of silk and intricate tapestries covered sections of the wall. Between the hangings were murals of the ocean and the slopes of Vesuvius. Flowers of every description overflowed from the nooks and crannies, spilling errant petals to the ground.

The sudden scenery change should have had me on edge. Instead, a strange sort of lassitude washed over me. Without knowing why, I relaxed my stance and dissipated the energy I had summoned for defense.

A young woman stood where the dust figure had been. She couldn't have been more than twenty. Her thick black hair coiled around her head in the Grecian way and her pale robes clasped at the shoulders with large bronze broaches.

She smiled at me. "Welcome, Stella Seraphina Evangeline. I am the Cumaean Sybil. I've been waiting for you."

Through the sensation of calm acceptance, I struggled to remember what I knew about the Cumaean Sybil. Hazy memories of the stories with Aeneas and the golden bough surfaced, but nothing too concrete. The only thing I was sure of was that the Sybil let him into the underworld.

Then Ted's warning came to mind. *Be careful of the Sybil. Don't let her distract you.*

The Sybil gestured to the ledge behind me. "Please, sit. Let's talk."

"I'd better not. I don't have much time." Even though the protests came out of my mouth, I found myself sitting back down. All of a sudden, I wanted nothing more than to talk with this woman.

"Nonsense. There is plenty of time."

As the words left her mouth, my body relaxed. She was right; there was all the time in the world.

Daisy growled, snapping me back to my mission. I struggled to break out of the stupor.

The Sybil hissed at the hellhound and waved her hand. The slab of rock under the archway shimmered and melted away to reveal a swirling vortex of orange-red light. If I didn't know better, I'd have said the passage was full of fire.

With another, harsh gesture, she managed to send Daisy through the archway and materialized the rock back in place.

"Stay and listen," the Sybil ordered, her dark eyes glowing with power.

Against my will, I did as she said. As my muscles followed orders, my mind grew more placid. I knew I should be fighting back, but the overwhelming sensation that there was no need won out. Obeying the Sybil was the only thing I wanted to do.

Chapter Twenty-five

"I've waited a long time for someone with your power to come," the Sybil said. "It is high time someone took my place."

"Took your place," I repeated, staring into her eyes.

She came to sit next to me, her thin arm draping over my shoulders. "You will be a powerful Sybil. It is a much better fate than what is awaiting you out there."

"I'm not . . ." I struggled with my response. The words were difficult to spit out.

The woman laughed, a harsh, rasping laugh that reminded me of the rustle of dead leaves. "Of course you are, my dear. You're the one who will allow me to rest. There must always be a Sybil here. She is the daughter of fate. She guards the passage into the underworld. You will take my place and spend the rest of eternity here safe. You will not suffer. You will never experience pain again." She began whispering in a strange, guttural language similar to Italian, yet completely foreign.

Her words made me sleepy. I wanted nothing more than to rest there. Everything else I had been fighting for seemed so distant, so unimportant. It would be so much easier to just give up.

I decided to stay. The world could fall down around me all it wanted. I was tired and would have nothing more to do with it.

A sharp, piercing pain in my ankle caused me to yelp and jump to my feet. The movement was enough to disrupt the spell the Cumaean Sybil had woven. Glancing down, I saw what had bit me; the hellhound puppy growled to keep my attention. It must have hidden in my bag when Ted had warned me about getting distracted.

In a sudden rush of clarity, I shoved the Sybil backward and picked up my bag from the ground. There had to be a way out of here.

"You will not leave!" the Sybil screeched. When I squinted back at her, the beautiful young Roman woman had vanished. In her place was a shriveled mummy-like figure that dripped with dust and dirt.

Panicked, I summoned up some energy and blasted the Sybil into the cave wall. The glowing sigils flared as the creature slammed into them. With the sheer force of impact, her body disintegrated before my eyes. As she broke apart, the archway glowed orange-red and the slab of stone melted away. Daisy was on the other side, waiting for me.

Scooping the puppy back into my bag, I bolted for the archway. An invisible barrier threw me backward.

"You will not leave!" The voice of the Sybil echoed around me. "Nothing but death and madness await you out there, Strega."

"I'll take that over being stuck here with a shriveled old hag any day," I shouted. Coiling my power around my body, I ran straight for the archway. As soon as I collided with the invisible barrier, there was a sharp crack and a stinging sensation exploded all over my skin. The Sybil's power and mine warred in violent sparks and loud crackles. Her power was ancient, but the energy that fed into it had been outside the living world for far too long. At last, my power won out.

I fell through the archway of orange and red light, propelled by my own momentum.

As I passed through, the Sybil's raspy voice filled my head. "Never forget I gave you the chance to live, Strega. Remember I warned you of your fate and you did not listen."

Then there was silence.

Sometime later when I could open my eyes again, there was no sign of the grotto or the dusty hag. I sprawled next to a low, crumbling stone wall that gave way to black rubble. The fog was thick and all-encompassing, which made it difficult to see beyond the gray to the bleak landscape. I barely made out the dark smudges of charcoal colored trees set against a dismal sky.

Focusing my energy into the palm of my hand, I ignited a flame of green witch light. The ball of energy was bright enough to dispel the thick fog at least five feet in front of me.

My immediate surroundings reminded me of the stories I'd heard as a child about the underworld; all dark and quiet as the grave. Ted told me Hell was amorphous, so my ideas about the place were going to be the reality. I pause to thank the stars that I never believed the fire and brimstone version.

Just as the thought passed my mind, the dreary landscape transformed into lava, sulfur, smoke, and unbearable heat. The sudden switch was disorienting. I fought to bring back the underworld I grew up with, its serene fields and distant trees. When the image was back and the oppressive heat and brimstone had vanished, I let out a sigh of relief. Now I understood what Ted had meant.

Daisy let out a long, sustained howl before starting out beyond the gap in the wall.

I stepped past the wall to begin my search.

The emotional atmosphere of the underworld was vibrant in degrees of anguish, sorrow, and pain. Pain was the one thing that underscored everything; I felt it in the air as I walked further.

Though I tried to keep my fear parceled in the back of my mind, tremors slid down my spine. My steps faltered as a hot wind picked up. Screams echoed in the breeze, conveying terror from somewhere around me. It was a battle to keep back the despair.

My progress slowed after a while. Looking back, I

could no longer see the crumbling brick wall where I started. The tree line in the distance hadn't gotten any closer either.

There was no way to tell how long I had been following the hellhound.

Just when I resigned myself to roaming these fields forever, everything changed. The drab scenery withered right before my eyes and shifted into a parched desert. A stooped figure emerged from behind a boulder. Confusion swept over me with the next scorching wind. I squinted, trying to understand what was happening. It was a woman. Her skin blistered and blackened, giving her the appearance of being roasted alive.

"Water," she begged the air.

Horrified, I scrambled to dig out a water bottle from the bag Azra had given me. Fumbling, I unscrewed the cap and ran to the woman. She didn't notice me at all. Instead, she shuffled past, crying out for relief.

My lips cracked from the intensity of the heat radiating off of her and my skin flushed with warmth. As I brought the container to my own lips, I discovered that instead of cool, refreshing water there was just dry, gritty sand. Sputtering, I coughed it out and wiped my pain filled lips with the back of my hand.

As quickly as the desert appeared, the world changed again. It grew bitterly cold. The once hot winds now chilled me to the bone. The ground, seconds ago cracked dirt, turned to ice. Another soul drifted past, naked and blue, his discolored hands clasped together for warmth.

I didn't go near the soul this time; I was too busy shaking.

In a blink of an eye, the landscape changed to a dark tunnel. Sewage sloshed under my feet. The stink was horrendous. I backpedaled and managed to trip over something large which caused me to fall into the muck. To my disgust, the thing I'd fallen over was a man covered in filth. He regarded me with deadened, bloody eyes.

Something licked my hand and the skin on my arm met with cool scales. It was some sort of dragon-like monster nestled at my side.

Fighting back a scream, I backed away from the creature. It followed with its yellow eyes intelligent and piercing. It grabbed hold of my pant leg with its sharp teeth. Giving a small shake of its head, the creature made a noise somewhere between a growl and a hiss. Its scales grew into fur and, after a minute, I recognized Daisy in her full hellhound glory. Her eyes seemed to say 'it's me, you moron'.

As Daisy let go of my pant leg, her thick fur receded back into the iridescent black scales that reminded me of Ted's.

I was more than a little freaked out.

Remembering Ted's advice, I realized what happened; I'd gotten sucked into someone else's version of Hell.

With the horror of what I'd just witnessed fresh in my mind, it took longer than it should have to bring back the grey landscape. After what seemed like forever, the familiar backdrop was back with renewed force. I had to be more careful.

Rising to my feet, I tried to get my bearings. While it was still the vision of my peaceful valley, I was in a different location than before. The mountains were closer and clusters of trees dotted the field.

"Let's keep going, I guess," I said to Daisy. Forcing my revulsion to her scaled skin down, I rested my hand on her shoulder and we continued walking. One of the trees stood out in the distance as different from the rest. This one was taller with fuller branches and there was something hauntingly familiar about it. Unbidden, the memory of a little girl talking to me came to the forefront of my mind.

The branches dipped down to the ground and, on the other side, they fell into a wide, slow-moving river of the blackest water I'd ever seen. The river Styx.

As Daisy and I got closer to the giant, looming tree, a figure appeared near the base, waiting in its shade. I couldn't see who it was, so I wrapped my thoughts around me like a blanket to keep the meadow in place. I would not get sucked into someone else's version of Hell again if I could help it.

"Stella," a familiar voice shouted. The figure waved.

Hesitantly, I squinted to see who it was that called out to me. When I got a good enough view, my eyes widened and my mouth dropped open. "Auri? Is that you?" I sprinted forward, hoping my eyes hadn't deceived me.

They hadn't. Aurelia was there; her clothes were dirty and torn as though something had ripped them. Her long golden hair was tangled and sticking up in places like it had been through a wind storm. She rushed forward, relief etched on her tear streaked face.

"Stella! I'm so glad! This place is horrible! Peter attacked me. He knocked me out and then I was here. I'm so scared! Everything keeps changing. I've seen terrible, awful things. I don't know what's real and what's not anymore." A horrified expression halted her ramblings. She pulled away, but still clutched at my arms. "You're really here, aren't you? This isn't some trick?"

"I'm really here," I assured her. "How did you get away from Peter?"

She cringed at the name. "There was a point where I wasn't tied up. I managed to slip away when he and Ryan were arguing; they weren't paying much attention to me at that point."

"Ryan's here? What about my brother? Auri, is Thomas here?"

Upset confusion colored her words. "Yes, I saw him tied up. Stella, I don't understand what's happening.

Where are we?"

"I'll explain later. Can you take me back to where they were keeping you?"

Panic widened her eyes. "Wh-what? No. I can't go back there. I can't."

"We have to get Thomas. Then we will all get out of here, I promise."

She hesitated more than I liked, but she pointed into the distance. "That way. Along the river."

"Great," I said and adjusted my bag over my other shoulder. "Come on, Daisy."

The hellhound wasn't there anymore. She was nowhere in sight. A wave of foreboding washed over me. We were on our own now.

"Who's Daisy?" Auri asked as we began following the river.

"Someone who got me this far."

"Tell me you have a plan to get us all out of here," my cousin moaned. Her steps were halting and slow. The fact she didn't want to go back was plain with every movement she made.

I considered how much to tell her. Less was more, I figured. There wouldn't be as much a chance of her blowing the secret when the time came. If all went well, I'd let her in on it once we got back to the land of the living.

"I'm going to give them what they want."

"You brought the mirror? I thought it was lost."

I didn't answer, instead focusing on the terrain. The path grew steeper and narrower, to the point that we were climbing more than walking. The river was far below us now. Soon, we reached the top of a plateau overlooking a sloping depression that broke off to a sheer cliff face. The drop ended in a sluggish winding river. Sharp outcroppings of rocks punctuated the flat ground. Figures prowled around those boulders. My gut feeling told me the figures were Ryan and Ascher.

I pointed down and Aurelia peered in that direction. As we concentrated on the distant figures, a rustling noise came from behind us. I swiveled around to see what had made the noise only to come face to face with four Fallen Ones.

They towered over us and in their hands were dangerous looking blades dripping with energy. I had no doubt that if they struck us with those swords, our souls would be completely obliterated.

Aurelia turned a moment after I did and a grim smirk spread over one of the Fallen One's mouth. "Come with us," he growled. "Ascher has been waiting for you." At his command, the other three Fallen Ones strode forward and grabbed hold of us. Auri cried but didn't make any attempt to escape. I didn't fight back either; it was the quickest way to get to my brother.

The Fallen One's grip on my arm was tight, as though he expected me to resist. Aurelia struggled against them. Her voice high-pitched and panicked as she tried to bargain with them to let her go.

"Don't," I told her. "Stop fighting. They'll take us to Thomas."

The lead guard pulled out a length of thick rope. Wrenching my hands behind my back, he bound them together. "Don't even think about trying anything, witch. If you do, your brother will die."

With my head held high, I nodded once to show I understood.

The Fallen Ones hauled us roughly over the rocky terrain and all the while, I strengthened the vision of the landscape in my mind. Perhaps the stronger I made the connection the longer it would last without my direct focus.

At last, we arrived at the group of rocks on the plateau. I braced myself for the coming confrontation.

I saw Ryan first. He sat on a boulder, looking somehow bored and annoyed at the same time. My heart wavered as he glanced over me without so much as an acknowledgment. I must have made a move toward him because the grip on my arm tightened and I jerked backward.

"Ah, so you did get my message," a low-pitched voice greeted us. From behind another boulder, an angel appeared. I recognized him at once. The oily black hair, the tall, confident figure, Ascher grinned down at me with an air of smug approval. "You're a clever one, aren't you?"

I kept still. He didn't appear armed, but there was no telling what was under his suit jacket.

Ascher admonished the guards holding us, "I don't think restraining them is necessary. These are our guests. We do not manhandle guests."

Immediately, the hand that clasped my arm withdrew and the knots that bound my hands were removed. Aurelia moved to my side as soon as she was free.

Ascher smiled and opened his arms wide in salutation. "Welcome to Hell, Stella. Shall we get down to business?"

"Where's Thomas?" I demanded, my gaze never wavering from Ascher's eyes.

"Where's the mirror?" he countered.

My hand started for my pocket, but I forced it to stay still. "I have it. I want to see my brother first."

My enemy pursed his lips even as he gave a flick of his wrist. Ryan hopped off the rock he was lounging on and shoved it to the side as though it was no more than Styrofoam.

The question of his sudden strength vanished as I caught sight of my brother. Thomas was bound and gagged, lying on the hard ground. I could hardly see the rise and fall of his chest. His aura was weak; no more than a faint glimmer of color, still it was there. Peter knelt above him, knife in hand and ready to strike.

I didn't think; I ran for Thomas, heedless of the goons surrounding me or Ascher's surprised chuckle. Fear shot through me as I realized my brother might already be dead.

I was just about to shove Peter away from Thomas' still form when Ryan stepped in my way and gripped me by my wrists. I heaved with all my might against his hold on me. My fighting did little good; Ryan was just too strong. Furious, I lifted my chin and glared at him.

He gazed back at me, his scornful expression cracked, giving a glimpse of the worry and raw emotion behind his eyes.

My heart threatened to break. "Ryan," I pleaded, "Please, let me go to him."

"Shut up." He whirled me around so that I faced Ascher again.

My version of the underworld, the drab gray landscape with its relative light and soft edges, flickered into a more sinister interpretation. Instead of rounded boulders dotting the gray grass, sharp columns of obsidian stabbed the pitch black sky. From within the semitransparent stones shone a deep orange, like an ember in a dying fire.

Whose version of Hell was this? Shaking myself, I re-constructed my non-threatening landscape, reminding myself not to lose control again.

"Come now," Ascher admonished, "you've seen your brother. I assure you he is quite alive. Now it's your turn. Where is the mirror?"

Casting a sad glance at Ryan, I said to Ascher, "I want a guarantee that once I give it to you, this whole thing is over. You will leave my family and me alone."

"Is that all you want?" Ascher and the other Fallen Ones present began laughing.

"Yes." I tried not to let it show how much their laughter bothered me.

Ascher recovered and studied me. As the chuckling

of the guards died down, he gave a curt nod. "So be it. You have my promise I will not stop you and your family from leaving once I have the mirror."

I hesitated, weighing his words, trying to find some loophole that he could slip through. "Just one more question, why are you doing this? Why do you even want the mirror?"

"You're wasting precious time," Ascher said, his own voice rising in anger. "Or do you need an incentive to make you comply?" He made another quick gesture and a Fallen One grabbed Thomas, lifting him forcefully. My brother moaned, though he didn't open his eyes.

"Okay," I said, terrified at what the demon would do. "Please, just don't hurt him anymore." I fished the compact out of my pocket and held it up so Ascher could see it. Allowing myself a breathy whisper, I prayed that the disguise held up to scrutiny. A pale glow surrounded the mirror making it appear just like the original.

When he saw the mirror, Ascher's eyes widened and a maniacal sort of glint shone in them. "Finally," he said to himself. He didn't so much walk as slide closer to my outstretched hands still just out of reach. His fingers twitched at the thought of holding it. His whole demeanor screamed *want*. I realized then just how hard and how long he'd been searching for it. A reaction like his only came from years of pursuit. He rearranged his features back into a non-pulsed façade.

"Aurelia, my precious, would you be so kind as to bring my prize to me?"

I didn't understand. Why would he call Auri his precious?

"Of course, my Lord," Aurelia answered. She snatched the mirror from my hand with a strange satisfied and vicious smile on her face.

Out of reflex, I grasped for it back. Ryan's hold on my shoulders tightened, keeping me in place.

"Just let her have it," he whispered. "This is what

you came down here to do. Don't give them a reason to kill you."

The words Ryan said didn't even register, I was so outraged. "You bitch," I exclaimed. "You've been working with them this whole time? You faked your own kidnapping?"

The malice in her radiated in waves as she brandished her prize and said, "I'm taking my rightful place, Stella. You don't know how long I've waited for you to fall. I'm the one who will bring the Age of the Daughter, not you. It was never you."

I couldn't believe what I was hearing.

"Fine," I replied, exasperated, "You're the One of the Legend. Whatever. You can have it—tell Nona and she'll train you. I want nothing to do with it."

The sneer that came to her face made her normally pleasant features ugly. "As if I'd want that old hag to train me. Soon she will just be a bad memory and then nothing will stand in my way."

Nona. An icy lump formed in the pit of my stomach. "What do you mean? Auri, what did you do?"

She gave me a withering, contemptuous glare and went to Ascher's side, handing him the mirror. "Nona is getting what she deserves for choosing you over me. She will suffer for that decision and the rest of the family will have no choice but to embrace me as the One of Legend."

The intense realization that she hated me so much that she betrayed the entire family took me aback. Still, the question remained; what had she done to Nona?

Peter called from his position next to Thomas, "Careful, Princess. Don't give too much away."

Aurelia's eyes flashed and she regarded Peter with annoyance. "We have the mirror. What does it matter what I tell her?"

Ascher interjected, "This is no time for family drama. Don't forget we are here for a reason." He motioned for Ryan to step forward. "It's time to activate the weapon. Ryan? Come do your job."

Instead of going toward the other Grigori, Ryan said, "Ash, release Stella and let's get out of here. There will be plenty of time to unlock the weapon once they're gone."

I couldn't believe what I was hearing. Ryan wanted to release me? That didn't fit with the Ryan who'd set me up to be ambushed in St. Petersburg.

Ascher sighed. "Yes, I suppose it won't do to leave so many loose ends." He pocketed the mirror.

"You're not going to kill her?" Aurelia demanded incredulously. "You promised she wouldn't make it out of Hell alive!"

Her viciousness astounded me. Never had I seen my cousin act this way. This couldn't be the girl I grew up with saying these horrible things.

Ryan kept a firm hold on me, though I could feel the anger in him building. It radiated off of him in powerful waves. The struggle to keep himself in check, so obvious to me, was also not lost on Ascher.

He watched the younger Grigori and mused, "Orion, you have an objection?"

Ryan addressed Ascher emotionless, his words slow and measured. "We don't have time for this. Our way out isn't going to be available for much longer. It would be wise to just leave with the mirror and let the realm swallow her and her brother."

I held my breath, waiting for Ascher to respond. My eyes drifted to Thomas' prone form. How was I going to get him out of here?

Ascher mused, "You know, I didn't want to bring you on this mission. If I had my way, you'd still be rotting in some abandoned cell in Siberia after that stunt you pulled in St. Petersburg. The Son, however, insisted. He believes you are going to be a great help in the war to come." He gave Ryan a once over, a curl of disgust on his thin lips. "He may think you're useful, but I don't. If you don't come back with us, there's nothing he can do about it. After all, Hell is a dangerous place, especially for someone that shouldn't exist." Ascher glanced at his guards. "Kill them."

There was no time to think. In a sudden whirl of motion, Ryan released my arms and pushed me aside. In that split second, his whole body changed. Out of his back sprouted massive wings unlike anything I'd ever seen before. They were bright with energy, yet transparent in their web-like design. Ryan himself grew bigger; his human face and limbs elongating and morphing into something alien. He wasn't recognizable as the angel I thought I knew.

The most striking thing was the rage emanating from him. As the Fallen One guards approached him, all it took was a few hand gestures for them to suspend motionless in the air. One or two beats of his mighty wings had two of the guards disintegrate into dust.

"You're not playing fair, Orion," Ascher challenged. "Fine. Neither will I." He stood still and closed his eyes, whispering something under his breath. Around his feet, a strange sigil appeared.

My surroundings wavered and my vision began to shift in and out of darkness. My head pounded with the sudden onslaught of a migraine. I felt nauseous.

"Stella! Don't let him in! Fight him off!" Ryan's voice sounded far away.

At once I felt something else in my body, a foreign entity trying to control my mind. It reminded me of the nightmares about the fight on the beach only a few short months ago.

Ascher was trying to take over my body again! The moment that realization came, my head began to throb and my arms moved on their own accord. The sinking sensation of helplessness encompassed me. Ascher was going to destroy me from the inside out.

Chapter Twenty-six

I couldn't allow my growing panic to overrun me; that was the quickest way to lose. I ran through my options. Ascher hadn't completely taken me over yet, so I still had a chance. What had it been like the first time this happened? I struggled to remember. Then it dawned on me. There was one crucial difference his time around: I had all my power at my disposal.

Latching onto that knowledge, I tried coiling some of my energy around my left foot. The relief of feeling that familiar tingle of power under my skin was short-lived. Pain exploded in my head as Ascher pushed further in. Like a marionette on strings, my body lurched forward under his direction.

The one thing that didn't move was my left foot.

It gave me hope. Fighting through the pain, I ran as much energy as I could through and around my body. With my energy pulsing over every inch of me, Ascher's tendrils of power were easily recognizable. It felt like needles, sharp and stinging against the fire of my own power. The longer I saturated those points with my energy, the more the discomfort faded.

It was time to turn this trick around on Ascher. I focused on one of the throbbing points. Though Ascher's grip on me had loosened, it would hold just long enough.

I willed my energy to latch on and travel along the link back to Ascher, intending on severing the connection at the source.

I wasn't prepared for the sudden onslaught of images. There was a whirlwind of memories and thoughts, of strong emotions and physical reaction; I felt his body as though it were my own. Underscoring all this information was the stunned shock of the Grigori.

He backpedaled, trying to prevent me from gaining control over him. He couldn't. Like wildfire, my energy consumed everything that he was. I reveled in the control of an angelic being. This much power was like a drug. I could do anything. I laughed. The sound of Ascher's voice cackling into the air echoed all around us.

An upheaval in his energy severed my control over the being. Abruptly, I was back in my own body, alone and aching. When I opened my eyes, I realized I'd fallen onto the ground.

I only saw him coming out of the corner of my eye. Peter leapt from the top of a nearby boulder. It was the flash of a blade arching above Peter's head instilled a terror that wouldn't leave my chest. There was no time for me to react.

Ryan snatched my attacker out of the air before Peter even got close. I heard Peter's frightened yell before Ryan tossed him away. The human collapsed against the hard, rocky ground, unconscious. Ryan continued toward Ascher, intent on taking him down.

Still dazed from the sudden ejection from Ascher's mind, I didn't see Aurelia casting the spell to attack. It hit me in the leg, her curse spreading over my skin and paralyzing me in place. As I lost my ability to move, my vision became dimmer until there was nothing but inky blackness all around me.

My eyes were wide open, but all I could see was blackness. All my attempts to move failed. When had she learned this? It wasn't the sort of spell that Nona would have taught us.

"What's wrong, Stella? I bet you didn't think I could do anything like this, did you? Well, there are many ways to learn tricks like this when you understand who is really in charge."

Aurelia's voice heralded an icy wind so cold that it burned my skin. I strained against the confines of the spell, forcing my own power upward into my hands. It moved lethargically through me.

Something sharp sliced its way across my face. The sting lingered, giving a sharp contrast to the biting cold. The cutting continued in measured bursts down my cheeks. Every cut shook my concentration and caused my energy to slow down even more.

"I always hated you. Ever since we were kids, everyone always compared us. Nothing I could do was ever good enough. Everyone always told me how I should try to be like you. But now things are different. Now I have the upper hand. I'm the one with all the power."

I wanted so much to scream at her to shut up. With the pain of the cuts, my concentration wavered more and more. The energy I desperately tried to summon slowed and finally stopped. That's when the real worry kicked in. If I couldn't summon the energy to break free, Aurelia would kill me.

Redoubling my efforts, the energy moved just a little faster than a snail's pace. It took monumental effort to ignore everything else and focus my attention on building that energy, to make it flow.

The power pooled into my belly where it warmed my core. With the energy flowing more freely, I could finally sense the web of Aurelia's spell. It was woven in thick strands, but the pattern was erratic and uneven. Some of the threads were weak. On the whole, her spell had the appearance of a tangled mess of a knitting project gone wrong. For all of her sudden power, it was still unrefined.

When there was enough of my energy gathered, I concentrated on shaping it into a blanket of sharp spikes. The spikes grew and, with a sharp crack and loud sizzle, they snapped the uneven knots of Auri's spell. In a matter of moments, the tatters fell away and I was able to see.

The landscape of Hell had changed yet again; bitter, freezing wind swept over a wasteland of ice and snow. It was so cold that even moving was enough to cause burns on my skin.

Auri, realizing I had broken out of her snare, muttered something under her breath. She lobbed another spell, misshapen and much weaker than her last one.

In defense, I drew up my own energy into a shield of blazing green electricity. The impact of Auri's spell against my shield was loud and painful. As soon as the spell dispersed, I struggled to my feet. Another impact of energy made me stagger. While Auri worked to shape another blast, I rushed her. She was unprepared for a physical attack. My shoulder connected with her stomach and I used my weight to take her to the frozen ground.

We landed hard. I was on top of her and had the advantage. Drawing back, I punched her in the face as hard as I could. Blood poured out of her nose and she cried out in pain and rage.

I issued out a spell that bound her hands and feet, anchoring her to the ground. As I did, Auri still had the sense to speak in a language I didn't recognize. Too late, I realized my mistake in not ensuring she couldn't talk. The spell that came from those words knocked me off of her and into the ice.

As soon as I fell, a grumbling came from below. The ground rippled and shuddered. Loud cracks accompanied by the hiss of escaping gas announced the formation of deep chasms. The smell of the gas was atrocious. I gagged against the noxious odors, opting instead to breathe through my mouth.

When I got to my feet, I ran straight for Thomas. The terrain was treacherous because every few moments the ground would shake and split. More geysers of foul smelling gas spewed into the air.

My brother was still, but alive. I fell to my knees next to him and put my hand on his shoulder.

"Thomas, Thomas, wake up."

Peter appeared, towering above us. There was only enough time for me to whisper a hasty protection over my brother before the kick to my stomach sucked the breath out of me. Gravel scraped my skin raw as I slid along the ground.

He didn't say anything; the sneer on his face showed his loathing well enough. He pulled a knife from his boot. I struggled to my feet, my mind racing. I didn't know how to defend against a knife attack.

All of a sudden, Peter collapsed, twitched a couple of times and fell still. I stared in horror at the convulsing body. It didn't take long for his eyes to lose that certain spark that signified life. His demise made the danger all around us intensify.

"Peter!" Auri shrieked. Somehow she'd wriggled out of my binding spell and rushed to Peter, blood and tears pouring all over her face.

I cast a wary glance around. Ryan, still in his transformed state, had his hand wrapped around Ascher's throat. Ascher must have been controlling Peter when Ryan got ahold of him.

The older Grigori fought against the vice-grip. Despite his struggling, Ryan grabbed hold of Ascher's left arm and pulled. There was a sickening pop and a meaty gush as the whole arm came off.

Ascher's pain-filled scream reverberated around us.

I was so transfixed with the horror before me that I didn't notice Auri leave Peter's side. An intense wave of power slammed me from behind. There was so much of it and it was so uncontrolled that it made me dizzy and sick to my stomach.

It was hard to tell if this attack was erratic on purpose or if it was an impulsive emotional outburst.

Either way, I had to use my own energy to

counterbalance the onslaught. I fought hard not to be sick. That onslaught must have been everything Auri had left magically. She tackled me to the ground, shrieking as she slapped and scratched at my face.

It was almost impossible to defend myself against her unrestrained fury. With her arms flailing, it was difficult to get a clear hit. Finally, I batted both of her hands to the side. I balled up my fist and swung for her nose with all my might.

There was a loud crunch. My hand throbbed with the impact. Auri screamed and both of her hands flew to her bloody face. This time, I did break her nose.

I used the moment to fling her off and scrambled back to Thomas. He was still safe behind the barrier I had put up around him.

The hellhound pup was there with him, licking his face and whining.

"Thomas?" His skin was clammy and he moaned as though he were having a nightmare. My hands moved around him, seeking the best way to hoist him up. He was just too heavy.

"You know you never belonged in this world, Orion!" Ascher roared. "You're meant for one purpose and one purpose alone—to bring an end to the human infestation that is a plague on this earth! We angels will be elevated to our rightful place when the Son rules everything! The Grigori exile will end once all three realms are combined. You cannot turn your back on your destiny!"

Ascher's words brought everything to a standstill. Ryan stood with Ascher's dismembered arm still in his hand and the older Grigori a few feet away, panting between his words. With every syllable Ascher uttered, Ryan's body tensed. His fury built up and the tension in the air was palpable.

Any sane person wouldn't push Ryan any further. Not Ascher. The next words out of his mouth served as proof he was nowhere near sane. "Your mother knew what your purpose was. How dare you betray her memory! For what? A human girl? Indira would be ashamed of you."

"NO!"

That one syllable carried with it a blast of energy that was akin to a nuclear explosion. I had scant seconds to reinforce the protection shield around Thomas and I. Screams of agony resounded as the wave passed over what was left of Ascher's guard. Their skin blistered and burned as they roasted alive.

I stared in a sort of frightened fascination at the devastation Ryan caused with just one word. Everything was in shambles. The boulders that dotted the landscape crumbled into rubble.

The only ones left more or less intact were Ascher and Aurelia, who was clinging to Ascher's side. How that was even possible was a mystery to me. The energy Ryan unleashed didn't leave them completely unscathed though; burns marred their skin and there was a sudden frailty to how they moved. Auri gripped Ascher's remaining arm as though her life depended on it.

Ascher didn't respond as he removed my cousin's grasp. She whimpered before he shoved her out of his way. Out of nowhere, a large sword materialized in Ascher's hand. It glowed crimson in the dim light. He announced his attack with an earsplitting roar as he bolted forward.

Bracing himself, Ryan drew up his sword. He met the older Grigori's attack with a shockwave of energy that crashed against my protective barrier like the surf against the sand.

It deterred Ascher by making him falter and slow enough for Ryan to catch him off guard. The clash of the two swords was nothing compared to the thunderous clap of their energies colliding. Sparks flew from the edges of their blades, igniting the air. Ryan was on the offense, backing Ascher away from Thomas and me.

The landscape didn't change. Instead, the bits that disintegrated left nothing but an aching emptiness where there was once substance. The void, the darkness, scared me more than anything else. While Ascher and Ryan took their fight into the air, my brother and I were still stuck on the rapidly disappearing ground.

I had to get Thomas out of here before we couldn't leave at all. With the landscape crumbling around us, I realized the only way was to carry my brother out on my own.

Another massive blast of energy from Ryan rolled over the protective barrier. This shockwave was bigger than the last one. The sheer force of it made me cling to Thomas for fear we'd be blown away.

My spell flared and burned until it parts of it collapsed into itself. I couldn't keep it intact like this. Without a second thought, I removed the barrier around us and re-cast the protection spell just around Thomas. With a securely placed energy tether, I tied him to me so we wouldn't be separated.

Aurelia huddled alone against the aftershocks of Ryan and Ascher's fight. I watched as she scrambled away, avoiding the crumbling landscape. I wanted to stop her, to keep fighting, but my own strength waned. My focus needed to be getting out of there.

At last, Ryan struck a serious hit. Dripping with his power, his sword sliced through Ascher's defenses and severed one of the Grigori's wings.

The shrill scream of pain resounded through the realm as Ascher tumbled from the air. Ryan dove after him.

More of the terrain fell and disintegrated into ashes. There wasn't much left of the changing landscape; the black void had taken over most of it.

There was no more time; we had to move.

I pulled my brother up and leaned him over my

shoulder as best as I could. Half carrying, half dragging him, we navigated around the sinkholes of nothingness.

One more blast of Ryan's power ripped through the air. Along with it was a loud, sustained wail of pain and then sudden silence.

The silence scared me more than anything else. I couldn't tell what had happened, or who had won and that made me more than anxious to get out.

The ground shook violently. Terrified, I had to let Thomas down to readjust my grip. He was still out cold and a lot heavier than I could handle. Determined to make it out, I grabbed him from under his arms. I dragged him along in what I hoped was the right direction to get us out of Hell.

"Stella!"

The sound of my name froze me in place. Still gripping Thomas, I lifted my head to find Ryan limping toward me.

He looked like he had when I first met him, if not a bit more banged up. There were no giant wings protruding out of his back. He no longer had that otherworldly quality about him. He was close enough for me to see the still bleeding scrapes and cuts all over his dirt smeared skin.

"I was so worried," he said right before he gasped and fell to his knees. He clutched his side, hissing in pain. When he withdrew his hand, it was coated in blood.

"Dammit!" I cursed under my breath. Ripping off my hoodie, I ran over to him.

"I'm okay," he said.

"Shut up and let me look." When I moved his shirt away from his stomach, a fresh gush of blood oozed out. "Here. Put pressure on it. Maybe that will help stop the bleeding." I opened up the hoodie and did my best to cover the wound as I tied the arms around his waist.

"I'll be okay. We've got to get out of here. Right now."

"Fine. Can you walk?"

A grimace and a single nod was the only response.

"Good, because I can't carry both you and Thomas out of here at the same time."

"You know a way out?" The question held more of a surprised tone than I expected.

I pointed to the Hell hound pup who remained loyally next to my unconscious brother. It wagged its serpentine tail and its tongue lolled out the side of its mouth.

"That little guy is going to lead us out."

Ryan struggled to his feet. He gingerly followed me as I returned to Thomas. My arms ached just thinking about dragging him out of Hell. Maybe there was something I could do about it.

Closing my eyes, I brought forth more of my energy. Concentrating, I shaped it into a sort of sled around my brother. His body rose up off the ground until he rested inside my construct. I didn't even know how I'd done it. This sort of magic was completely out of my league. I chalked it up to desperation and the fact I was in another realm. Instinctively, I advanced the sled with my brother forward with a wave of my hand.

"How'd you do that?" Ryan asked, amazed.

I couldn't answer him since I didn't understand it myself.

"Alright, puppy," I said to the little hellhound. "Show us the way out of this hell hole."

Chapter Twenty-seven

We didn't talk much as we followed the hellhound. I mean, what could I say? The first thing we had to do was get out of Hell, not fight each other and that's exactly what would happen if we talked. Instead, I put my focus on the energy sled that held my unconscious brother.

Ryan broke the silence first. "He'll be alright, you know. As long as we get him out of here, he's going to be fine. We didn't hurt him when we picked him up."

"Then why is he unconscious?" I snapped, making a point not to look at him. Yes he defended me, yes he was on my side, but there was still the fact that none of this would've happened if it wasn't for him.

The fact I still felt drawn to him despite all of it infuriated me.

"We put him under with a ward. He fought against us so much that there was no way to get him down here without knocking him out, magically speaking."

"How did you get down here? Did you use one of the Hellmouths?"

"Hellmouth? No. We teleported here. The Son brought us in."

"The Son?"

My question went unanswered as just then, the puppy erupted into a fury of growls and barks. Or what I assume would have been barks if they hadn't been so screechy.

Ahead of us appeared a Japanese Buddhist temple. Noxious green fumes rose from pitch black waters of a river that curled around the temple entrance. Two large and terrifying looking demons stood at the base of the steps, just on the other side of the water. They were massive, scaled beings. One was taller with three arms protruding from its dull rust colored torso. The second had strange, yellow wing-like appendages coming out of its back. They weren't actual wings, rather mismatched stumps with odd horns. Each of the demons held a long halberd tipped in what appeared to be razor-sharp volcanic glass.

"Is this where you came in?" Ryan asked, watching the two demons.

"Not even close. I think it is still a way out though." Digging into my jeans pocket, I pulled out the coin that Azrael had given me. "Come on."

Propelling the sled forward, I strode confidently toward the temple. Ryan trailed behind.

When the guards noticed us coming, they shifted their stances and lowered their weapons so they were pointing at us.

"Stop where you are. Don't come any closer," the one with three arms grumbled. Its voice was an odd combination of low and high end back notes.

I paused at the edge of the black river. Things swarmed under the surface, making the water ripple. Wrenching my gaze away from the splashing, I held out the coin. "I have a pass. Let us through."

The demons squinted at the coin.

"No one leaves Hell," the demon with the mismatched wings shouted.

"I'm not no one," I shouted back as I stepped into the river of unknown to show that I wasn't scared. My foot never touched the water. Instead, it landed solidly a good three inches above the surface. As freaked out as I was, I acted as though this was the most natural thing in the world. I continued to walk above the water until I reached the crumbling stone steps of the temple.

The demons were agape at my progress before they aimed their halberds at me and charged down the steps to cut me off. I stopped just short of the blades pointed at my chest.

"The Devil himself gave me safe passage. Let us out." I flipped the coin at the demons, one of which caught it in its claw. The mustard colored creature wrestled the token away from its cohort with the third arm.

Together they peered at the object with awe.

"We are leaving now," I said with as much force as I could. With a wave of my hand, I propelled the sled holding Thomas over the river and to my side. Ryan shuffled forward, stopping short of the river. His brow pinched in pain. He'd have to get medical attention soon, no matter how much he denied it.

"Hold on," mismatched wing snarled. "You two can go. That one stays." A twisted claw gestured to Ryan.

I glanced back at him in time to see the alarm settle onto his face.

"No, we are all going together. The three of us."

A dark rumbling issued from the throats of the demons. It took me a moment to understand that it was laughter.

"This token is good for two souls, not three. So make your choice on who you will take with you because the other we will drag back to where they belong."

"Hang on a moment," the other said, staring at Ryan. "The coin is good for two *human* souls. This one isn't human." The creature with the third arm brushed past me, intent on getting ahold of Ryan.

"No!" I shouted, dodging between the Grigori and the demon. "All three of us are getting out."

I was flung aside. The stone steps of the temple made a hard landing.

That was the final straw. I'd had enough of being shoved around. Without thinking, I lashed out at the creatures advancing on Ryan with my power.

I don't know where it came from. By all accounts, there was no way I had enough power left after Thomas' sled and the fight I had just been through. Still, there it was; a thick green rope of energy snaked down around the demon's legs. Wrenching the energy rope backward, the creature fell face first into the black river. Whatever was just beneath the surface immediately began thrashing. The demon cried out in burbled screams and fought to get out of the water.

Ryan had drawn his sword, but he didn't have the strength to do more than to lean against the hilt with the tip in the ground. He looked as though he would collapse at any moment.

Hoping I had enough power to do what I envisioned, I whispered my intent. The green energy rope that tripped the three-armed demon splintered into a fine net all over its body. The spell sank the creature further into the river, weighing down so that no matter how hard it pushed, the spell would only become stronger. The thrashing of the water became more violent.

I got to my feet, feeling exhilarated. There was no more exhaustion, no more ache in my body.

The other demon with the mismatched wings ran to help its friend out of the river. As soon as the guard tried to help, the net of energy expanded to include him as well. When both guards were contained, I raised my hands, levitating the bundle of demons. The one that had was in the river had giant leeches stuck all over his face and body.

Controlling the net wasn't easy. Still, I managed to hang it off the edge of the temple that marked the gateway out of Hell. The two demon guards were suspended a good twenty feet in the air.

"Come on," I called to Ryan.

He stumbled, and fell on the bank of the river inches away from the water. The leech-like things sensed a body close by and began thrashing, breaking the surface to get to his flesh.

Out of reflex, I extended my arm as if to catch him. At my gesture, Ryan flew into the air as though something launched him violently off the ground. He flipped once before landing onto the steps next to me.

He groaned but didn't move to get up.

"Ryan!" I ran to see how much damage the landing did. "I'm sorry. I didn't mean to throw you in the air like that." *HOW?* The question flashed in my mind again. *How did I do that?*

He didn't respond. I checked to see if he was still breathing. He was.

"Dammit!" I cursed. Now I had to carry Ryan out of here too.

"Don't even think about taking him with you!" One of the demons bellowed from above.

I scoffed at them. "You can't exactly stop me." Mentally, I gave the net a spin and watched with satisfaction as the demons cried out with dizziness.

It took time to get Ryan into the sled next to Thomas. In the back of my mind, logic told me I shouldn't have been able to accomplish any of this. By all rights, my power should have been gone long ago. Still, the influx of energy was a strange and welcome change.

Finally, Thomas and Ryan were tucked into the energy sled. I faced the temple doorway. It was time to go home.

Propelling the sled with both of them in it was more difficult than when it had just been Thomas. Maybe it had something to do with the extra weight. Remembering my disorienting entrance into Hell, I paused. What if my focus on the sled broke? What if I lost both Thomas and Ryan on the way?

I stopped the doubts swirling in my mind and took a deep breath. A tether of energy connected me to the sled, I just had to trust that it would keep us together. There was no other way. I ascended the remaining steps. A large green door nestled between elaborately sculpted pillars.

Without so much as a glance backwards, I pushed

open the door and stepped through it into a dense fog.

Past the door, the floor was rocky and uneven. Through the fog, shadowy outlines of trees became visible. The deeper I went into the fog, the more surreal I felt. There was a shift and suddenly . . .

I was a little girl again, marveling at the way my skirt swirled around my legs with every move I made. The fog receded and gave way to an untamed forest punctuated by a smattering of old ruins.

Nona was there with me, but she was different. Younger. Her strawberry blonde hair flowed loosely to her waist and her skin was smooth.

Time seemed to speed up all around us. The clouds raced overhead and the sun traveled its predestined course at supersonic speeds. It was as though someone hit the fast forward button.

Our movements, however, remained humanly slow.

"There are things you need to understand," Nona said. "Things that I didn't have time to tell you when I was alive."

The words should have jolted me; I should have reacted more. Instead, there was only a mild curiosity and the dulled emotions of a dream state. "What things?"

"There is a choice in front of you. This choice will shape the future of the world. To make this decision, you need to be aware of the consequences."

"Consequences?"

Nona gripped my hand. "I'll show you."

The thick, vibrant woods faded into a dilapidated neighborhood. Gray concrete buildings crumbled against a smoke filled sky. Rubble of all sorts littered the streets. There was no one in sight, even though it was the middle of the day. The city was oddly quiet. The stink of fear and death permeated the air, making me gag at its cloyingness.

"Where are we?" I choked.

"This is the world of the future should you decide to

not embrace your destiny," my grandmother explained. "This is how every city, every town, and every village in the world will look."

I eyed the ominous graffiti that provided the only color in the drab scenery. Everywhere I looked, on all of the buildings, was a thickly spray painted red double-cross sprouting out of flames.

Chimes sounded in the distance and reminded me of church bells from some of the old European cathedrals. Something moved out of the corner of my eye. A girl in tattered clothing sprinted from the busted doors of what looked like a warehouse. Why was she running?

A second later, a pair of battle ready soldiers in what appeared to be black Kevlar suits followed her in pursuit. On the chest of their thick vests was the same symbol graffitied on the walls. Automatic weapons rose, ready to emit a spray of bullets at their target.

Shouting filled the silence. Harsh orders to stop and desist echoed against the buildings. Soon, the sharp rapport of gunfire deafened us where we stood. The girl collapsed bleeding in the street under the expulsion of metal. The soldiers approached the girl, guns still at the ready. To ensure she was dead, they kicked her still body and then let loose another burst of gunfire.

When they were satisfied she wouldn't get up, they left her there and moved on to other business.

Horror filled me. "What? Why is this allowed?"

Nona answered, "In this timeline, the world needed a leader to stop the growing tyranny overtaking them. A new crusade happened, intending to glorify the Son and ensure that his reign would last forever. There was no one to contest this, no one to stand up against the Son. The Daughter never came." She spread her hands to encompass the gruesome scene. "This is how they keep their power—militarized witch hunts against anyone that disagrees with the reigning power."

"Why doesn't someone stand up? Why doesn't

someone stop this idiocy?"

Nona looked pointedly at me. "There were some in the beginning. They did what they could but failed. Only a god can defeat another god, Stella."

I chewed my lip as I considered what she said.

"Now, we will see the other future—the one where you decided to accept your destiny." Again, she gripped my hand and the terrifying city faded out of focus.

Within seconds, we stood in a park. The rushing sounds of a fountain lulled me as did the soft chirping of birds. Houses stood at the edges of the grass like sentinels standing guard. One look beyond those cheerful facades gave me the impression that the city was in the midst of an epic celebration. Banners stretched taut between lamp posts. Bright ribbons flapped about like thousands of flags. There was the constant thrum of cheering and laughter from the people gathered. Upon closer inspection, it wasn't just people. All manner of creatures that came straight from the pages of mythology roamed the streets. Centaurs galloped in wide stretches of grass. Griffins landed on rooftops, screeching. There were many more that I couldn't immediately identify.

I glanced at Nona. "Where are we?"

"The same place we were before, except this is the timeline in which you embraced your future."

We began walking toward the crowd and Nona explained further. "Because the Daughter was here, she and her allies were able to win the War. This the Age of the Daughter."

We passed into the swell of people lining the streets.

Raucous cheers erupted as what appeared to be a parade turned the corner. A mounted guard of nine uniformed men preceded a horse drawn carriage. Sitting in the open topped affair was the most striking women I had ever seen. Her multicolored hair was pinned up and her smile was open and welcoming. The aura that surrounded her was vibrant—almost blinding. Her head swung toward us and I was caught in the most intense gaze I'd ever beheld. It was somehow familiar. She waved enthusiastically as though genuinely pleased to see us.

"I've met her," I said, struggling to remember where I'd seen those arresting eyes before.

"That is the Lady," Nona smiled. "She is your daughter—your future."

My mind flashed to the vision I had before descending into Hell. The tree and the impossible wind tossed up with images of a little girl in a blue dress. She had the same aura; the same hair; the same piercing eyes.

Nona voiced the words that I was unable to grasp. "Stella, my dear, you are destined to be the One of Legend's mother. Even now she grows within you."

My hands flew to my abdomen and I looked at Nona, panic stricken. "I-I'm pregnant?"

Before Nona could answer, an angel appeared at the side of the woman, my daughter. With his majestic wings spread out, they blocked out the sun. He walked with another, younger man with black hair toward the waiting carriage. Standing on either side, they held out their hands to help the Lady down. Together, the three walked into a large building.

I couldn't believe what I saw. "Is that . . . Ryan?"

"Yes," Nona affirmed. "The Watcher is always with the Lady. He is her protector."

I stared in amazement. Ryan looked only a few years older than when I first met him.

I was impressed, but that only distracted me from the growing alarm inside. "Where am I? If I am her mother, why aren't I here?"

"Come now. Our time grows short." Nona's fingers once again clasped my own. The scene disappeared and we were back in the woods sitting among the rubble of some ancient temple.

"Nona, you didn't answer. Where am I in that timeline?"

Her heavy sigh made me tense.

"This action of yours—this descent into the underworld—it was not part of the plan. A price must be paid to get you out in one piece."

Doing my best to not let dread overtake me with that comment, I asked, "What price?"

The sadness in her eyes almost broke my heart. "Usually the price for going into the underworld before your time is your life or your sanity. Yours is a special case though. The rules are bent because of who your child will be. Once you've fulfilled your destiny, you will have to pay for this venture. You must be prepared."

"You're telling me after I give birth to this child, I'm going to die?"

My grandmother bowed her head.

"What about Thomas? Is he going to die?"

"No. His price will not be death." She stood next to me then and pointed her finger at the flickering distance. "Look! A star fell."

I peered into the woods and thought I caught just the faintest of glittering.

"Come with me to see it." I tugged on her hand.

With a sad smile, she ran her fingers through my hair. Unshed tears made her eyes bright. "No, my dear. This is something you must do on your own." Her embrace was warm and loving before she turned me away to where the star landed. "Go on now, before it's lost."

So I went, following the elusive shine of the fallen star into the woods. I looked back only once.

Nona was gone.

An owl hooted nearby, cutting off my intention of calling out for my grandmother. The snowy white bird flapped its wings, drawing my attention to the tree branch it rested on.

Keep going, *it seemed to say.*

I pressed on, moving toward the glimmering star ahead.

Chapter Twenty-eight

I don't know when or how I passed from Hell to the realm of the living. The darkness that surrounded me was complete. Only bits of images broke through and I couldn't be sure that any of it wasn't just a dream.

More than the visions, I heard voices. Sometimes the words would come in great clusters and sometimes it was a single name whispered as soft as velvet.

Time passed, but I couldn't be sure how much. Sensations returned to me; the cool breeze hitting my skin and the smell of a campfire. The darkness receded and I found myself on the ground staring at the sky as the dawn broke through the canopy of trees.

My body ached more than I thought possible. It took a couple of tries to sit up. Thomas and Ryan were on the ground a few feet away. Both were motionless.

Since my legs weren't quite ready to work, I crawled over to check my brother first. There were a few scratches on his face and some bruising on his arms, otherwise, he seemed alright.

Ryan was a bit worse for wear. I peeled away his shirt to inspect the slash on his stomach. There was a lot of blood, but it wasn't new. That was something at least.

Now, I just had to figure out where I was. Nothing looked familiar. There was no lake, there was no cave. I'd returned from Hell in a completely different location than where I went in.

With much effort, I got to my feet, grabbing hold of a nearby tree trunk in order not to fall back down. Leaning against the tree, I called for Azra. The party favor was crumpled and didn't hum properly. All I could do was hope he heard it. Whatever extra power I had in Hell was long gone.

Sliding down to sit against the tree, I waited, fading in and out of consciousness.

Azra came, though I couldn't say how long we had waited for him. He peered down at me with concern in his bright blue eyes.

"Strega Girl! What are you doing here? What happened?"

It took too much energy to smile, but I tried anyway. "Hell didn't want me. Please, Az. Get Thomas back where he belongs. Then Ryan . . ."

"Ryan?" The Grigori glanced over to where his wayward nephew lay on the ground. "You mean you brought him back too? Why would you do that?" Despite his words, Azra was at his nephew's side, checking over his wounds.

"He helped us," I replied. "He fought against Ascher. I couldn't leave him."

"After everything he's done, you damn well could have!" Ryan's head cradled in his arms and there were tears of relief glinting in his eyes.

"Azra!" I gasped, fighting to stay conscious. "Please. He saved my life down there."

"Fine, but it's only because I don't want to be in this forest for longer than I have to. It's not because I've been worried sick about him during this whole ordeal." Gingerly, Azra laid Ryan's head down. "Beth will stay with you while I get Thomas to a safe place. I'll be back."

As though summoned by her name, the goat came and settled next to me, laying her head on my lap. Feeling the weight of Beth against me, gave me a sense of calm and security. I watched as Azra picked up my brother from the ground. Within moments, they disappeared.

I ran my hand over Beth's head and closed my eyes. Thomas was safe and whatever else happened, at least there was that.

***

A series of banging pots and pans served as an alarm. My eyes eased open and I was greeted by the sight of a familiar ceiling. I was back in my room in Italy. Flowers gave the room a sort of sweet wild scent that competed with the aroma of sizzling sausage and eggs. The smell of it all made me nauseous. Something small and furry moved on the bed and nuzzled my arm.

My limbs refused to move and I fought the terror of being paralyzed. Then, my leg shifted and my head rolled to the left. I could move. The groan of relief emitted from my throat was loud enough to bring whoever was standing in the corner of the room forward.

"Stella?" Ryan was next to the bed at once. His expression was worried as he peered into my face. "Are you awake?"

The sight of him brought the memories of Hell forward in a rush. My anger got the better of me and while I'm not proud of what happened next, it was a sheer reaction.

My right arm snaked over to the vase of flowers on the nightstand. With as much force as I could muster, I launched the bouquet, glass vase and all, at Ryan's head. It was to my utter disappointment that he ducked out of the way. The glass crashed against the wall and water and flowers exploded around the room.

I was determined. Ignoring the stiffness in my body, I grabbed for more ammunition. So intense was my rage, that I didn't speak, I didn't scream, I just aimed. The bedside lamp flew across the room next, followed by my alarm clock and a couple of picture frames. I found my voice as the last item left my grasp. "How *dare* you come here! How could you show your face after everything you've done? Because of you, my brother almost died! *I* almost died! My family has been torn to pieces and you have the audacity to show up here?"

He managed to dodge all the objects thrown at him and grabbed hold of my wrists. "Stella, I know you're angry. I deserve your hate, but please, calm down. I'm here because I needed to know you were alright. I needed to know you were safe and sane."

The small furry creature on my bed growled and nipped at Ryan until he let me go. It was the hellhound pup, somehow still with me. Outside of Hell, the pup looked more like the wolf I met in front of the Sybil's cave than the scaled dragon-like creature in the underworld.

Tears of rage seeped out of the corners of my eyes. Though the fight left me, I wouldn't cry in front of him. I refused to.

Ryan moved to sit at the end of the bed. I couldn't bear to look at him. After everything that happened, after all the deception and pain, what was left?

"How did I get here?" My voice was hoarse so the question came out no louder than a whisper.

"I woke up in the forest. You were out and your brother was gone. Not long after that, Azra showed up. He brought us both here. Azra left. He said he didn't want to hang around a witches den."

I forced the next sentence through my lips. "And Thomas? Where is he?"

Hesitation on his part made me wonder what he was keeping from me. "He's safe. Azra placed him outside one of the U.S. military bases in the Middle East. They take care of their own."

I was going to ask what he was leaving out when the door to the bedroom opened. Ryan retreated to the corner where the shadows were the thickest. The brightness of the morning seemed concentrated in the doorway. I winced at the light, completely unprepared for it. Aunt Bianca and her tray of food were no more than a shadowy outline.

"You're awake!" My aunt exclaimed. She set the tray of food down on the side table and glanced at the mess. "What happened here?"

"Nightmares. I got pretty violent without meaning to," I said. Out of the corner of my eye, I watched Ryan's reaction to my lie. Relief made the circles under his eyes into even darker smudges. His skin looked ghostly in the sudden flood of light.

I wondered about the price he had to pay to get out of Hell. Did those rules even apply to him?

Aunt Bianca examined me. "How are you feeling?"

"My head hurts," I told her. "I don't know what happened."

I caught the flash of pity in her eyes and wondered at it. "You don't need to worry about that right now. Here. Try to eat something and we will see if that helps your head."

The thought of food made my stomach roll. "No thanks. Where's Nona?"

I knew the answer by my aunt's reaction. She shifted her gaze downward and bowed her head. It confirmed the hazy memories of my dream and the odd sense of loss that settled into my chest.

"Oh, Stella, my dear sweet girl." Bianca set the tray of food on the nightstand. Sitting on the edge of my bed, she took my hand. Now that she was closer, I could see the telltale marks of grief on her rounded face. As she squeezed my hand in hers, tears brimmed her dark eyes. In a wavering voice, she said, "There's been an accident. A fire broke out. Sylvia . . . Donatella . . . they died. I'm so sorry." Those few sentences were all it took to reduce my aunt to heart-wrenching sobs.

The hollowness in my chest threatened to overtake me. My mind refused to move past those syllables. I remembered Aurelia's threats in the underworld. I croaked out, "The twins? Did they . . .?"

"No," Bianca sniffled. "No, thank the stars. They're

safe." As if she were afraid to ask, she whispered, "Thomas and Aurelia?"

I didn't know what to say. "She and Thomas are alive. I didn't see Aurelia make it out, but I have a feeling she did." I'd wait to tell her about Auri's betrayal. Right now there was too much grief and I didn't want to add to it just yet.

Bianca blew out a sigh of relief. "The twins will want to know their sister is alright. Now that you are back and awake, we need to go to California. There are arrangements that need to be made."

Ryan emerged from the shadows to protest. "I don't think that's—"

My aunt whirled around, completely taken aback at his presence. "You!" she shouted. I'd never heard her so shrill before. "I told you to leave her alone! She needs to rest!"

The grieving woman was gone, replaced by an angry Italian. She grabbed Ryan by the ear and dragged him out of the room. It was satisfying to see Aunt Bianca get the best of him. I didn't miss the longing in Ryan's eyes before the door shut. My aunt's voice echoed through the walls of the house. "When she is ready to see you, she will send for you. Until then, let the poor girl have some peace!"

With fresh grief weighing me down, I slid out of the warmth of the bed. My bare feet touched the plush carpet. They'd dressed me in baggy flannel pants and an ill-fitting shirt. My muscles ached with every movement. I shuffled to the window and, with as much strength as I could muster, parted the curtains to allow the light of day into the room.

The puppy made a noise from the bed and laid there, watching me with dark eyes.

Satisfied that I could see the outside world, I edged my way to the bathroom. The fluorescent lights were harsher than the sunlight and the mirror wasn't too kind either. The exhaustion evident on Ryan's face was nothing compared to my own. Bruises mottled my once tanned skin. The discolored circles made my eyes seem sunken and hollow. Shallow cuts ran down my cheeks in uneven lines. My hair was a tangled mess around my head.

Horrified with myself, I considered the shower. Twisting the knob caused a spray of water to come shooting through the nozzle. I stripped out of the borrowed clothes and stepped into the hot spray.

I don't know what it is about a hot shower after a bad experience that makes you feel alive again. It makes you feel human again. The process of cleansing was more than just the outside. The soap also washed away the filth that seemed to coat my soul, like a residue from the realm of the dead that still lingered. My headache abated to the point of being bearable. It was still there, but no longer the intense constant throb.

Hours seemed to pass in that steamy cocoon of warmth and cleanliness. I savored every second, every drop of water. It made me feel more human. All too soon, the warmth began to fade and I had to turn the water off. I took the large, plush towel, wrapped my hair and basked in the steam. The sooner I left this place, the sooner I would have to face what happened. I wasn't sure I could do it.

I needed to confront them if I wanted any answers.

With trepidation, I left the bathroom and returned to my room to get dressed. I took my time combing through the tangles in my hair, stopping often to rest my weary arms. The hellhound puppy was awake and chewing on the quilt he was laying on. I picked him up and held him close.

"What am I going to do with you, then? I suppose you need a name, don't you?"

The puppy wagged its tail.

"Virgil. After all, you were my guide through Hell.

What do you think, Virgil? Is that a good name?"

The puppy gave yips of approval even as he tried to lick my face.

Finally, I couldn't put it off any longer. Steeling myself, and with the pup in my hands, I left my room and descended the stairs.

The movement hurt. A lot. I winced and inched my way down the steps.

"Stella, we need to talk." Ryan's voice came from behind me and almost made me fall.

"What are you still doing here? I thought Aunt Bianca kicked you out!" I hissed, clutching at the banister just to keep my balance. I had to be careful with my anger at Ryan. How I handled him from here on out was part of my destiny, I just wasn't how I wanted to deal with it yet.

"Please, I want to talk with you. I need to explain."

"Explain what? How you betrayed me and you kidnapped my brother and took him into Hell? How you took advantage of me in St. Petersburg? How you let Ascher and his religious nutjobs find us?"

"That's not how it happened."

I sighed. "Fine." I descended the stairs and made my way to the sofa in the parlor. Ryan trailed after me, keeping a keen eye out for Bianca. After settling myself as comfortably as I could, I gestured for Ryan to take a seat himself. He chose the arm chair across from me.

"My aunt will be in here in a few moments," I told him. "You better talk fast." I kept Virgil in my lap. The hellhound settled in, happy I was petting him.

Ryan took a deep breath, leaned his elbows on his knees and clasped his hands. "First, I am so sorry about your grandmother and Donatella."

"Don't." My voice turned the air to ice. I wasn't ready to talk about that, much less with him.

Understanding, Ryan gave a single nod in acknowledgement before continuing. "I know you think I betrayed you in St. Petersburg. Ascher had some of his goons follow me when I went to see you. I didn't know until after it was too late.

"Ascher thinks I lied to him about you being dead. He figured that you still had the mirror and he decided to use your family to get it from you. It didn't take much to find out where your brother was stationed. Ascher has lots of connections in the Middle East. He makes it a point to stay close to the conflicts there. It was a simple enough matter for him to snatch Thomas and leave enough clues to blame it on the enemy."

I studied Ryan as he talked. The angel was careful not to make eye contact and he kept one ear toward the kitchen where Bianca was still puttering around. He acted like the Ryan I knew before the battle on the beach. Here was the angel that showed up in my room in St. Petersburg and begged me to leave for my own safety. It was difficult trying to reconcile this Ryan with the more sinister and destructive one I'd seen in my visions. Which one was the real Ryan? Which one could I trust?

Aware of my scrutiny, Ryan pressed on, sitting back in the chair. "I had no choice but to go along with this. I went down there with Ascher, I was hoping to protect Thomas from the worst. I wasn't expecting you to show up in Hell."

I laughed at that. "You threaten my family and you didn't think I'd show up to get them back? What kind of witch do you think I am?"

Ryan hung his head and murmured, "Listen, I was trying to protect you. After the battle on the beach, I never wanted to see you that hurt again. Please understand I'm sorry."

"You should be sorry," I shot back. "For wanting to protect me, you've got a damn funny way of showing it. All you've done over these past few months has caused so much damage. To think I believed that you cared for me, even for a second."

"Stella, I do care for you. I love you!"

The force behind those words, the emotion made me pause. Nona's voice echoed in my mind. *There is a choice in front of you. This choice will shape the future of the world.*

When I didn't respond, Ryan continued, his voice strained. "Ascher would have killed you months ago. Don't you understand that if I hadn't left you in the hospital and gone over to him, he would have tortured you to get that damned mirror?"

I raised my head to look him in the eyes. "What do you think you have done? I've been living with the fact that you lied and abandoned me for months now! Months of believing that I made a mistake trusting you. Months of seeing you do all those awful things to people one minute and the next you are sketching my face! You convinced me you were just after the mirror! Then, when we finally do talk in St. Petersburg, you tricked me into trusting you and all those horrible things were for my protection. Ryan, I slept with you because I believed what you told me and you promised to come back. All that toying with my mind and my heart. Wouldn't you consider that torture?"

"It was better than seeing you dead." He sounded miserable, defeated. If I wasn't so angry, it would have broken my heart.

"Better for who? Because it sure wasn't for me. Explain to me what part of protecting me meant tricking me into going into Hell?"

Ryan clinched his hands together, forcing himself to remain seated. There was a vicious sense of satisfaction that this conversation was just as difficult for him as it was for me.

"Ascher chose the underworld to be the battleground. It was his plan to activate the weapon in Hell to kick-start the apocalypse. He was ready to go out with the blast. The bonus for him was that even if you did get out, you'd be too insane to pose much of a threat to his employer. Unless a human has some sort of divine assistance, they don't come out of Hell whole or at all." He pointed at Virgil. "Looks like you had some help."

I thought about my final conversation with Nona and the price I had yet to pay for my escape from Hell. "What price did you have to pay?"

He shrugged. "I'm not exactly mortal. Besides being exhausted, I'm fine."

"And my brother?" The question hung in the air between us long enough to make me scared. "You said he was ok, that the military found him and they are taking care of him."

He shifted his eyes downward, away from me, but didn't say anything.

"Tell me, Ryan."

"Physically he is alright."

With a catch in my throat, I asked, "What is wrong with my brother?"

"He's not one hundred percent himself. He is safe, though. The Army will put him in a good facility. They'll take care of him."

I realized what he meant; Thomas had paid for his exit out of Hell with his sanity.

None of it was fair, or just. My brother had always been smart and independent. Now, he would most likely have to be taken care of for the rest of his life. He may not even recognize me, depending on how severe his condition was. There was no way to know until I saw him.

"I know where the mirror is, though. The real one. I didn't lie about that," Ryan confessed quietly.

I lifted my head. "You do?" All this chaos, all this tragedy and he still had the mirror? I held out my hand. "Give it to me."

"I can't. Not yet."

"Why not? Ascher's dead. There's no reason for you

not to give it to me now."

Ryan bit his lip before confessing, "Ascher's not dead. He was hurt badly, but he managed to get away. He's probably reporting to the Son as we speak. You have to understand, they won't stop until they have it. You and your family aren't safe yet."

My head began to throb from the expectations laid upon me in the last few hours. The door to the kitchen opened and my aunt came out in a sudden onslaught of delicious smells of baked goods. Her floral print apron wrapped around her. She spotted me in the parlor. "Oh, Stella. I wasn't expecting you to have come down already. Why are you sitting in here by yourself?"

I looked to where Ryan had been sitting. He was gone.

Surprised, I answered my aunt, "I—I just got tired after going down the stairs. I'm alright now." I struggled to get out of the couch, setting Virgil to the side. When I was on my feet again, the puppy leapt into my arms with a happy yip.

"I am not sure how I feel about that animal in my home," Bianca said.

I hugged Virgil to me. "Virgil saved my life. I'm keeping him."

Bianca shook her head and I had to look away from the pity and sadness showing on her face.

"Can we talk about—" My breath hitched. "Can we talk about what happened?" Tears welled in my eyes and I had a moment of doubt. I wasn't ready for this. I thought I was, but I didn't think I could handle her making it real.

At once her face grew somber and she motioned for me to come with her.

"Come on into the kitchen with me. I will make you some tea and we can talk. There are things I need to ask you as well."

With Virgil in my arms, I followed my aunt.

Chapter Twenty-nine

I sat at the kitchen table while Bianca prepared the tea and placed a plate of fresh baked biscotti in front of me. "What do you know?" she asked. The question was a simple one yet it was the most difficult to answer.

"I know Nona's dead. I don't know how it happened." My blunt answer sounded harsh, even to me. I clutched Virgil close to my chest and he struggled to get to the food on the table.

A pregnant silence followed my quiet statement. I waited for my aunt to answer. She placed the cup of tea in front of me and took the seat across the table.

My aunt took a breath before beginning. "Sylvia called me and said we needed to get everyone together. Aurelia and Thomas had been taken into the underworld. To get them back, we needed to be at our full strength.

"Then she called again and said things had changed. You'd gone off on your own and she was worried. There was no time to fly out. My sister decided to stay in America and work her magic to keep you, your brother, and Aurelia safe all on her own."

The guilt built up in me, competing against the anger and the sorrow. That was so unlike my grandmother. She relied so much on the family just as they relied on her. "What happened?"

"There was a fire. No one knows how it happened, though there's some talk about a gas leak of some sort. The authorities said the blaze started in the kitchen. Neither Sylvia nor Donatella made it out of the house."

Every word was like a punch in the stomach. The cup of tea shattered in my hands. The hellhound pup whined and licked at my face. I didn't even move as the hot liquid spilled over my skin. Instead, stunned tears sprang to my eyes as I processed what Bianca told me.

My mind fumbled with the information, trying to get it to make sense. The thought I kept returning to was that Nona was dead.

"The twins are staying with friends. They will be returning with us after we take care of the arrangements to bring Sylvia and Donatella's remains home."

"How long have I been asleep?" I asked.

"That crazy angel friend of yours brought you home yesterday. It seems he had a difficult time getting you to safety. He and his goat left quick enough. The other one refused to leave your side. I had to banish him just so you'd rest without him hovering over you. I didn't think the spell would have worn off so fast. I still don't know how he got into your room." She picked up the shards of porcelain and mopped up the spilled tea. The smell of chamomile and honey brought a sad smile to my lips. It had been Nona's favorite.

"Have you heard from Thomas? Is he alright?"

Bianca rinsed the tea-soaked towel in the sink. "Yes. The military sent word that he is being sent back to America for treatment."

"Treatment? What for?"

"The twins didn't say. I don't know what the officers told them. They have an address for where he will be admitted later on this afternoon."

I stood and the chair I was in fell backwards with the force of my movement. "I have to see him. I have to make sure he is alright."

At once, my aunt was there, making sure I didn't topple over myself. "We will. Our flight leaves in the morning. Right now there are other things that we need to discuss." Bianca righted the chair and made me sit once again. "My sister was our family's matriarch. She was the hub of this family."

"I know," I said, trying not to let the tears flow again.

"No, you don't quite understand. You see, Sylvia named you as her heir. With her passing, you are now the high priestess of the coven and the matriarch. You are now the leader of this family."

It took a moment for the words to sink in and another moment for their meaning to be clear to me. "You mean I'm responsible for the whole family?"

Aunt Bianca nodded solemnly.

Panic gripped me. "I can't. I mean, I can't even protect myself let alone the whole family. I don't know anything about being a high priestess. I don't know how to be a matriarch. I just can't." I broke down then, sobbing at the kitchen table. It was all just too much to handle.

Aunt Bianca must have realized it too because she put a hand on my shoulders in an attempt to comfort me as I cried.

"I'm sorry, my dear," she said. "I shouldn't have brought it up. You need time to heal before you worry about these things."

Regaining some of my composure, I sniffled. "I'm not Nona. There's no way I can fill her shoes."

"I understand. This is too much for right now." Aunt Bianca's hands rubbed my back in an attempt at comfort. "We can discuss it later."

I laid my head against my arms allowed my grief to swallow me whole.

***

The twins met us at LAX, each looking more rough and somber than I'd ever seen. We hugged each other and I could feel the sorrow emanating from them. Aunt Bianca rented a car and went to take the luggage to the hotel. She wanted to rest, and I didn't blame her. The flight had been long and there was much to do while we were in California. The hospital Thomas was in wouldn't allow visitors until the next day. The funeral home where Donatella and Nona's ashes were waiting agreed to meet the day after. Then we could begin the process of shipping their remains to Italy for burial. Instead of going to the hotel with Aunt Bianca, I opted to stay with the twins.

From the airport, my cousins and I went to the house. Listening to them explain what happened in halting, hesitant words was one of the hardest things I ever had to do. An accident, they said. A horrible accident that made us homeless and alone. They didn't know what happened or why. There were just more questions than there ever would be answers. They had arrived home just as their mother dove back into the fire engulfed house to save Nona. Neither of them came out.

Nathan was the first to ask the question I dreaded the most. "Did you find Auri?"

I stared at the ground in what used to be our front yard trying to figure out what to say. "Guys, I'm sorry to tell you this. Auri manufactured her kidnapping. She was behind it the whole time."

"What the hell are you talking about?" Justin demanded. There was anger in his voice. I understood it all too well.

"Auri faked her kidnapping. She and Peter were in on it together."

Nathan crossed his arms over his chest. "Why would she do that? It doesn't make any sense."

"From what I understand, she and Peter were working for the angel that wanted the mirror in the first place. This was all a big trick to get it. I saw her down there. She wasn't herself." I paused, recalling the hate my cousin had in her eyes. "She wasn't the Auri that we knew."

"Was she controlled? You said these angels can control people."

I shrugged. "It's possible, but I don't think that's what happened."

"Did she get out?"

I glanced between them, noting the hope in their eyes. I had to tell them the truth, which was a lot harder than telling them that she died. "I don't know. She and Ascher left the area. I don't know what happened to them after that. Thomas and I barely got out. If she did manage to survive, I don't know what state she'd be in. I doubt she'd come home."

The twins were silent for a long time, sorting through what I'd said and coming to their own conclusions. Soundlessly, they both came up to embrace me at once. I started crying, I couldn't help it.

"I'm so sorry, Justin, Nathan. I wish I could have gotten through to her. I'm so sorry."

They accepted my apology and squeezed me tighter.

When there were no more words and no more tears for the tragedy that had befallen us, we gazed at the half burnt up shell of a house and feeling lost.

"What are we going to do?" I asked them, staring at the charred wood and the soot stained bricks. Only the front part of the house had succumbed to the fire. The back of the house where the bedrooms were was still standing.

Justin shrugged. "We go back to Italy. The family is there. We can get back on our feet. You're the matriarch now. It's kinda up to you."

I wished everyone would stop reminding me about that part. It made me feel even more helpless and alone. "You can do whatever you want. I'm not going to be in charge of your lives."

"Hey, isn't that Ryan?" Nate asked. "What's he doing with Spike?"

I turned to see Ryan watching us from across the street, leaning against the side of my car.

"I'm going inside. Maybe some stuff survived the

fire," I said, looking away from the angel.

"I'll go with you," Nathan said. He waited for his brother to join us.

"No, I can't go in there. I'll wait for you here."

Nathan nodded in understanding and followed me.

It took more than a little mental preparation and courage to make my way through the front door. The smell of wet smoke was overpowering. Under my feet, the carpet squished. Scorched pieces of my life littered the ground. A heavy layer of soot-blackened the walls. I regarded the singed furniture in the living room with sadness. Echoes of memories assaulted me with every step.

The kitchen was the part that brought the most horror. It wasn't recognizable with its blistered walls, shattered windows, and charred cabinets. The magic battle that waged there left a residue that I could almost see. Remnants of Nona's energy clung in the air along with faint traces of Donatella's. It was enough to make me weep. Both Nona and Donatella had died fighting. But why?

"What happened?" I whispered more to myself than Nathan. "Who were you fighting?"

"Stella?" Ryan's voice startled me into wiping away the dampness on my cheeks.

After recovering myself a bit, I faced him with fresh anger. "I don't want to talk to you right now." I shouldered past him and Nathan, pushing into the wreckage of the hallway leading to the bedrooms. Here damage was in the form of fallen pictures and bits of the ceiling; otherwise, the back of the house was intact. I went into the room I shared with Aurelia. The fact we lived in the same room and yet she could deceive me so thoroughly, filled me with disgust.

Opening the closet, I started pulling out clothes. The stench of smoke permeated the fabric, but I was confident a good washing would remedy that. The suitcases I found offered more than enough space for my wardrobe. My poetry, scribbled in spiral bound notebooks and journals, also found their way into the bags.

"Do you want us to help?" Nathan offered. He and Ryan filled up the doorway of my room.

"No." My answer was clipped as I took a final glance around. Nothing else in the room was practical to take, but there were a few things of Nona's that I wanted to keep.

"Actually yes. Here," I offered the bag of clothes over to Ryan. "Take this out to the car."

He didn't reply as he accepted the bag and trundled off. The familiar bells on the screen door sounded soon after he turned the corner out of sight.

"He's just trying to help," Nathan said. "Give him a break."

The admonition made my cheeks burn. "He's also the reason why I had to go down to Hell in the first place. I'm getting some of Nona's stuff."

Nathan held his hands up as if in surrender. He looked tired and not in the mood to fight. "Fine. I'm going to see what there is to salvage from the living room."

Fresh tears welled up in my eyes as I pushed the door open to Nona's bedroom. It was exactly as it was the last time I was there, with the exception, of course, of the ever pervading burnt smell and a fine coating of soot. I went to the bookcase and took into my hands the two photo albums from the middle shelf. I didn't open them right then; I just placed them in the extra duffel bag. Lower on the shelf was a carved box that contained her tarot cards. With only a moment's hesitation, I put it in the bag next to the photo albums. I did the same with my grandmother's craft items; her boline, athame, scrying mirror, pendulum, and more. I knew she'd want me to have these things.

At last, I couldn't be in the room any longer. I shut

the door and returned to the kitchen.

The leftover energy was still intense and raw. There was so much damage, so much pain in what remained of the walls, it was nearly impossible to know what happened. If only someone had survived.

Then it hit me. "Max!" I called out to the soot filled walls. "Max I need you!"

There was no answer and the hollow pit in my stomach expanded. Did something happen to Max? Maybe he couldn't come. Maybe he was held up somewhere. The worry and the feeling of utter helplessness were too much. In the wake of silence, I took stock of what remained of my life.

Both Nona and Donatella were dead after fighting who knew what. Aurelia was missing and presumably out to get me. Thomas was safe, for now. Max was gone, though there was still a chance he would turn up. The twins were moving back to Italy. Aunt Bianca expected me to do the same and to take Nona's place as matriarch of the family. I just wasn't sure I could do that.

The vision of Nona as I left Hell came to the surface of my thoughts. The two timelines she showed me loomed, almost suffocating. I couldn't make the wrong decision.

My hand made its way to my abdomen.

"My child will be the One of Legend. She will begin the Age of the Daughter. My child." I spoke the words out loud to make them more substantial, more real. I mulled them over in my mind. The truth of them shone like a polished golden cage surrounding me.

If Nona was right, then the child I carried was the only reason why I was alive right now. Otherwise, I'd have died in Hell. Or I'd have lost my sanity.

If Nona was right.

I hugged my arms around me and left the house. There was one thing I needed confirmed before I made any decisions about my future. Hopefully a drug store pregnancy test could confirm the presence of an angelic baby.

Ryan and the twins put a few bags into Justin's truck. When Ryan saw me lugging the extra duffel, he rushed forward to take it from me. He nodded and loaded the bag in the back seat of Spike. "What now?" he asked as he slammed the car door.

"I know I said we would talk, but I need to do a couple of things first. Can we meet up tomorrow afternoon? After I see Thomas?"

Ryan looked a little disappointed, but he nodded in agreement. He handed my keys over.

"Thank you," I told him.

He gave a slight smile and waved to the twins before walking away.

Chapter Thirty

The seconds ticked by with maddening slowness. My eyes shifted between the cell phone in my hand and the pregnancy test perched on the bathroom counter. I hunched over the knot of worry in my stomach on the edge of the bathtub. The tension in the small, hotel bathroom ratcheted up a few notches as the seconds ambled by. At last, the most excruciating minute of my life passed and I jumped up to peer at the test.

Two lines. What the hell did that mean?

I fumbled for the instructions I'd thrown into the garbage. Once the pages were smoothed open, I read what the two seemingly innocuous pink lines meant.

Pregnant.

I willed the spinning room to remain steady as my fingers crumpled the instructions into a tight ball. My arms wrapped themselves around my own stomach as though to give myself a reassuring hug. No. I would not freak out about this, I refused to.

"Stella," Aunt Bianca called from the other side of the closed door. I jumped at the sound, knocking the pregnancy test onto the floor. "Are you alright in there?"

"Fine," I croaked as I scrambled to hide the evidence.

"We better get going. The doctor wants to speak with us before we see Thomas."

"I'll be right out." The test and its packaging went in the plastic bag the clerk gave me when I purchased the thing. After tying it, I buried it in the bathroom trash.

I gave myself a final once over, adjusting my dark blonde ponytail and smoothing out my shirt. My hand lingered over my belly, trying to feel if there was a living thing inside of me. Could it be possible? I sighed at my reflection and allowed my hand to fall. I couldn't focus on this. Not now. I took a deep breath and opened the door.

Aunt Bianca stopped and her brown eyes narrowed as she frowned at me. "What's wrong?"

"Nothing. I just miss Nona," I lied as I fought the panic and the urge to cry. The last thing I needed was to burst into tears at the drop of a hat. I forced my face into a somewhat calm if not focused expression. "I just need to grab my purse and we can go." I maneuvered around my aunt. She waited with a pensive expression as I snatched the purse from the chair near the window.

"Are you sure you are alright?" Bianca asked. "You don't seem like yourself."

I flashed her what I hoped would be a convincing smile. I didn't need her brand of pressure when I had enough of my own. "I'm just nervous about seeing Thomas."

She still wore a concerned frown though she didn't argue. Together, we left the hotel. The pale blue rental car was waiting for us in the parking lot.

The drive to the mental health facility was short but silent.

When we arrived, Bianca assured me, "Stella, everything will be alright."

I couldn't speak; I just sniffled back tears and swallowed the stress. She squeezed my hand and together we got out of the car and headed up to the front door of the large building.

Thomas' ward was on the fourth floor. Outside of the elevator lobby was a check in desk with a plump receptionist behind it.

"Hi," I greeted the receptionist. "I'm here to see my brother, Thomas Evangeline, please."

"Alright. Go ahead and sign in here and I will call Dr. Sevag to let her know you're here."

"Thanks." I scribbled my name and then settled

myself down in a chair next to Aunt Bianca and grabbed an errant magazine. I'd only flipped through a couple of pages before the receptionist called my name. "Stella? Come on back."

Aunt Bianca and I followed the receptionist to the hall and through a large door.

The doctor on the other side of the door was in her thirties and had a pleasant smile. "Hi, I am Naomi Sevag, Thomas' doctor. You are his sister, yes?"

I shook her hand. "Yes, and this is our aunt."

"Bianca," she extended her own hand to the doctor.

"It is nice to meet you. Let's sit and talk," she gestured to a small conference room off to the left.

"What about Thomas? Will we get to see him?" I asked as I perched in one of the plastic chairs.

"Of course. He's been asking for you. First, I want to explain about his condition."

I gave her a hopeful smile. "That's a good sign, right? Him asking about me?"

She nodded, "It is. Tell me, when was the last time you saw your brother?"

"I . . . I don't know. A while ago?" I shrugged the lie off. "Why?"

Dr. Sevag folded her hands on the table. "Your brother experienced some pretty serious trauma. We don't know exactly what happened to him, but he's displaying dementia symptoms stemming from traumatic brain injury. More tests are needed to be conclusive. In the meantime, we have started him on some medication to treat anxiety, insomnia, and to improve his memory."

I nodded. "Is he going to get better?"

"Perhaps with treatment, but there is no telling with these kinds of symptoms. The best we can do is to keep him calm and reassure him that he is safe. Once more tests are done and we know more about what is causing this, we can try some therapy in addition to the medications."

My heart thudded in my chest and sorrow caused a pit in my stomach. The guilt was more than I could stand. Swallowing, I said, "Can I see him now?"

"Of course. Just one at a time. We don't want him to get too overwhelmed. This way." We left Aunt Bianca in the conference room and she guided me down a wide hallway. Numbers were next to the closed doors. We stopped at room 413. Dr. Sevag opened the door and gestured for me to go in first.

Taking my cue, I went into the room. It was a sparse area with only a bed and a chair. The walls were beige to keep the overwhelming hospital whiteness at bay. On the bed was a bright patchwork quilt that Nona had made for him years ago. He must have had it with him when he was in Afghanistan. Besides being an object of familiarity, it lent more color to the room. Next to it was a small bedside table that supported a single picture frame. Much younger versions of me and Thomas peered out from it, laughing.

The bathroom was more of a closet large enough for a shower, a toilet and a sink. Light came through a single double-paned window next to the bed. Thomas stood at the window, gazing outside.

"Hey, big brother," I said, forcing a cheerful tone. I didn't know what to expect.

At the sound of my voice, he turned to look at me. The welts and bruises accentuated the fragile look about him. Something had completely broken inside of my brother. It left him looking much older than his twenty-five years. When he saw me, the tiredness left his eyes. A giant smile lit up his face.

The sight of my brother so damaged and yet so jubilant both broke my heart and gave me hope.

Without a word he rushed over and scooped me up into a big bear hug. My brother wasn't huge, but he wasn't scrawny either. The Army had made his rather tall and svelte figure strong.

"Little sister," he greeted. His voice was rough with a grainy quality that was both familiar and endearing. His close cut brown hair was growing out into a shaggy mop of curls.

Intending to keep everything light, I ruffled his hair and told him, "We need to get you a haircut. It's getting too long."

He released me and touched his hair anxiously as he echoed, "Too long."

Dr. Sevag went to leave. Before closing the door behind her, she said, "Stella, I'll be back in a few minutes to check on you. If you need anything, I'll be down the hall."

"Thanks, Doctor."

Thomas waved to her and repeated, "Thanks, Doctor." He looked at me and smiled again. "Little sister came to visit. Still hiding from the monsters on the outside?"

The way he talked took me aback. It was so unlike him. Fumbling, I answered the best way I could. "Don't worry. The monsters won't get me. How about you? How are you doing?"

Thomas shrugged and looked out the window. "I want to go home. When can I go home?"

A lump formed in the back of my throat. "I don't know. We want you to get better first."

He made a face. "Doctor doesn't believe me. She thinks I'm lying about the monsters." A worried look clouded his face. "I'm not lying, am I?"

"No," I assured him. "You're not lying."

He sat on his bed, his fingers running over the stitching of the quilt. "I miss the family, little sister. Will Nona come visit me?"

I sucked in a sharp breath. I had to tell him. I owed him the truth.

Just not yet.

We stared at each other for a long time. His eyes peered deep into my own as though searching for the words I wouldn't say.

"Something is different," he said after a while. "Little sister is different." He reached for me, his hands going straight for my stomach and his eyes grew wide. "Little sister has a secret," he whispered, laughing. He let go of me and danced around in a circle, chanting. "She has a secret!"

My hands flew to my stomach. "What?"

"A secret," Thomas pressed. He jumped on the bed in excitement before bouncing off. He landed next to me and dropped to his knees and pressed his ear against my belly, listening. "She has a baby. A secret baby. That's the secret. I know the secret." He got to his feet and spun around to face the wall. "*Shhh!* Don't tell the secret. It is little sister's secret to share."

I backed away from my brother, not sure how to react. He turned and watched me, frowning at my stunned behavior. "What is wrong? The walls are nosey, but they won't tell if you ask them not to."

"Thomas, there isn't any secret," I said, though my voice wavered. In my head, I was rationalizing. Thomas didn't know what he was saying.

"Yes, there is. You can't lie to me. You have a secret baby." A smile broke upon his lips. "She is going to be beautiful. She is going to rescue the world."

Okay, this was freaking me out.

Thomas' face changed from grinning to a sort of sad anger. "After the secret baby comes, little sister will not come back." He rushed forward and gripped me. His hands clenched around my arms and he put his face against mine. "She will have a choice. She will choose to die." He wrapped his arms around me and cried into my hair. "I love my little sister. I don't want her to die. She should stay. Her and the secret baby. Let the angels fight their wars, but leave my little sister alone."

His body shook with silent sobs and I rubbed his back trying to comfort him. He was so convinced of what he was saying. How could I get through to him? "It's okay Thomas. I promise I'm not going anywhere. Everything will be alright."

A knock sounded at the door and Dr. Sevag poked her head in. "Everything okay?" she asked.

At the sound of her voice, Thomas whirled around and shoved me behind him. He crouched defensively and yelled the doctor, "No, you won't take her away. Leave my little sister alone!"

Dr. Sevag shouted something into the hallway and then came into the room. Speaking as soothingly as possible, she tried to get my brother to calm down. "Thomas, it is me, Naomi. It's okay. No one is going to take Stella away. You're in a hospital. You're both safe." Her hands extended to show she was harmless. A couple of brawny orderlies filed into the room, each flanking Thomas.

Thomas maintained his defensive stance in front of me. By the movement of his head, he was protecting me from more than just the threat of the hospital staff. His hands moved like he carried a gun and his head cocked to the side as though listening to something just out of range.

A sheen of sweat formed on his skin and the flush of fever colored the back of his neck. I reached out to touch his shoulder. "Thomas, everything is al—"

In a blur of motion and without any warning, Thomas lashed out at the visions. He fought to keep whatever imaginary monsters in his head away from me. In the process, he hit one of the orderlies and came close to hitting the doctor too. The orderlies shifted, each moving in tandem to restrain him. Dr. Sevag rushed out of the room and returned moments later with a needle. Right before my eyes, she injected my subdued brother with the drugs.

I hated seeing it happen; it made me sick to my stomach.

When he stopped thrashing, the orderlies moved Thomas to his bed and covered him with the blanket. Dr. Sevag glanced at me, wisps of her dark hair escaping out of the tight bun. "You alright?"

I nodded, not able to take my eyes off of my brother. "What happened?"

I struggled to find my voice and when I did, it came out hoarse. "I don't know. He didn't think I was going to come back."

She nodded in understanding. "I think that's enough excitement for today. Why don't we let him get some rest?"

Before she could usher me back to the waiting room, I removed myself from her grip and went to Thomas' bedside. My brother blinked up at me, his eyes out of focus. I caressed his cheek and his hand fumbled to find mine.

"Be careful, little sister. Keep the secret safe. I love you."

With tears in my eyes, I brought his hand up to my lips. A whispered spell, a final protection for him while I was away, was the last thing I could give him. Dizziness came with the last word and I had to pause a moment before I could get up. With the power still throbbing on my lips, I told him, "I love you, big brother. I promise I will be back as soon as I can."

Letting go of his hand, I dispelled the energy I'd gathered, smoothing out the ripples in the air around me and walked out of the room. As I went through the door to the waiting room, Thomas called out in a sleepy, sing-song voice, "Secret, secret. Little sister has a secret."

I was returned to the small conference room where Aunt Bianca was waiting. When I appeared in the doorway, she dropped the magazine she had been perusing and stood up. She came immediately to my side, staring into my face. "Oh, Stella, was it that bad? Is Thomas alright?" she asked.

"He's not ready for more visitors," I said, choking on the words. Aunt Bianca immediately enveloped me in a strong embrace. My heart broke. The image of Thomas fighting against the imaginary monsters wouldn't go away. Is that what my brother was reduced to?

The scariest part was that there was a chance they could get at him again. Auri and Ascher had gotten out somehow. Not to mention Ascher's employer, the Son.

"He will be alright," Bianca assured me. "The family will protect him. We'll see about making arrangements to have him transferred once he's discharged. According to the doctor, that may happen once the tests come back."

"I put a protection spell on him," I told her, though the words sounded hollow. I wanted to believe that Thomas was going to be safe. A persistent doubt nagged at me. What if all the protection the family could give wasn't enough?

Chapter Thirty-one

We'd returned from the hospital only a few hours before when I decided to call Ryan. Seeing Thomas had shaken me, but it made me realize what I had to do. It wasn't right to keep Ryan hanging.

"I'm surprised you called," Ryan said when I appeared in the hotel lobby. He stood, waiting for me.

"You still have my mirror," I reminded him. "I want it back."

Ryan blinked, taken aback at my defensive response. "What happens after that?"

"We'll see once I get it back."

"How was your visit with your brother?" he asked.

I pursed my lips. The fact he brought up Thomas made me angry. As we walked through the doors and into the parking lot, I finally managed to say, "I don't want to talk about Thomas right now."

Noting the restrained emotion in my voice, Ryan responded just as distantly. "No problem." He offered his hand.

I raised an eyebrow at him.

"I can't teleport you if you're not at least holding my hand. I promise you'll be safe."

I grit my teeth. "Alright. Let's get this over with." The second our hands touched, the familiar tingle danced along my skin. It was an electrical current that I never quite got used to. By the expression on Ryan's face, I could tell he felt it too.

I closed my eyes and waited.

Teleporting with Ryan was nothing like teleporting with Azra. With Azra, things swirled and passed by in a dizzy blur. With Ryan, it was more of a blink and we were there. Not expecting to have arrived so swiftly, I clung to Ryan for a moment longer than I should have.

I took in our surroundings with incredulity. We were in the familiar sprawling entrance to . . . "The Getty? You hid my mirror at the Getty Art Museum?"

He smiled. "It's safe. It always has been. I've told you that over and over again."

Torn between relief and fury, I followed through the lingering crowd and up the steps into the lobby. I struggled to keep up with his pace as he breezed to one of the buildings beyond the center courtyard.

I hadn't been to the Getty since before the mirror had been stolen. Though it was only a few months ago, it seemed like years. The memories held a sense of innocence; I'd been a silly kid with no real concept of what I was about to do. It seemed as though I'd aged decades since then. We walked past the fountains and the room where we first kissed. There was a poignancy in the air and a kind of poetic justice that the mirror had remained amid happy memories.

I followed him through doors, up flights of stairs, and around the rooms of paintings, until he finally came to a halt in front of one particular piece.

Standing next to him, my eyes fixed on *The Farewell of Telemachus and Eucharis*. The image of the sketch Ryan left in my bag came to mind. It was of this painting, but with mine and his face instead of Eucharis and Telemachus. He'd given me the location of the mirror from the start. Why didn't I get it all those weeks ago? How much misery could have been avoided?

Ryan cast me a mischievous smile. "Watch this." Faster than any human should be able to move, he darted forward and lifted the oversized gilt frame of the painting. Something from behind it fell into his waiting hand. He set the frame back and returned to my side. The docent at the corner of the room didn't even twitch.

"As promised," he said and deposited a carved silver

compact mirror into my hands. The blue inlay sparkled against the silver. The weight of it brought a rush of relief coursing through me.

I turned the object over in my hands, amazed and relieved. "It was here, the entire time?"

He shrugged, not daring to smile, "It was the only place I could think of."

I shook my head, unbelieving that it had always been this simple. "Why here? Why this painting?"

"Because it was the last place I saw you truly happy before I fouled everything up. It was where I wish I could've done things differently."

I clutched the mirror to my chest. The feel of it in my fingers was the best thing I'd felt in a long time. I opened my eyes, to find Ryan studying me. "Thank you," I whispered.

"You're welcome," he said. "Listen. I'm not innocent. There's a lot I need to atone for. What I've done . . . I've no right to expect anything. Still, I've gotta ask. Where does that leave us?"

I hesitated, taking the time to gather my thoughts. How could I even begin?

Ryan misunderstood the prolonged silence. When I didn't answer right away, he gave me a brisk nod and stuffed his hands into his pockets. His expression was forcedly neutral, but I sensed the pain hiding behind it.

"Alright. I understand. I'll leave you alone from now on." He turned his back and walked away.

I panicked. This wasn't how it was supposed to go. Without knowing how else to phrase it, but needing him to stay, I called out, "Ryan, I'm pregnant."

He froze in his tracks. I held my breath until he faced me.

His eyes were wide and his jaw was slack. In shock, he asked, "You're—what?"